Elections Have Consequences

A Cautionary Tale

by

David Shephard

THE OAKLEA PRESS

RICHMOND, VIRGINIA

Cheri, For the love of Virginia politics. Dave [illegible]

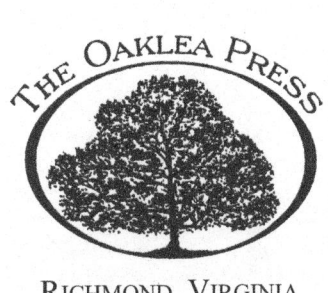

Elections Have Consequences: A Cautionary Tale © 2022 by David Shephard. All rights reserved. No part of this book may be used or reproduced in any manner whatsoever without written permission except in the case of brief quotations embodied in critical articles and reviews. For information visit:

www.OakleaPress.com

"For twenty years, the soldiers of the South remained behind the counter or plow, until Johnston led them out to lay the cornerstone of what the South designed to be: a fit memorial to the matchless Lee. A few years more, and when the figure stood upon the pedestal, the word went out that every man who wore the gray should muster in the ranks again and pass before the chieftain on old Traveler. A day that was when love became the meat of life!"

Douglas Southall Freeman
"The Last Parade"

For Mrs. Kowalski

Foreword

I feel a need to confess upfront that before this undertaking I had never written—or attempted to write—a book, or a short story or even an essay. My writing was limited to status updates on social media and blog posts on my site *The Virginia Gentleman*. I have always been somewhat terrified by writing assignments. In school there was nothing I dreaded more than a 10-12 page writing assignment. So, I am a complete amateur writer. I am a reader, not so much a writer.

What inspired me to write a novel?

Well, years ago I read a novel by Garrett Epps, *The Shad Treatment*. It is one of my all-time favorite books. As a man interested in (well, obsessed is perhaps the better word) Virginia politics and history, I was naturally drawn to the book. For anyone interested in those subjects, *The Shad Treatment* is a must read. It tells the story of a Virginia gubernatorial election. It is fiction, of course, but It seems eerily similar to the 1973 election between Mills Godwin and Henry Howell. By reading the book, I learned a new literary term, *roman a clef*. That is, fiction which takes real events and makes up characters.

Since then, I thought I should write a political thriller based on Virginia politics. But like so many brilliant ideas, this simply lingered in the back of my mind. Well, fast forward fifteen years and I decided to start my own novel, my own *roman a clef*. And this is what came out: *Elections Have Consequences: A Cautionary Tale*.

So, this is my attempt to follow in the Garrett Epps tradition.

The reader may wonder who the characters are supposed to be in real life. This is a mistake for a few reasons. First, the characters Ronnie Norton, Angela Parrish, Steve Cohen, and Jack

Elections Have Consequences

Villiers are purely figments of my fertile imagination. Secondly, the characters really represent whole groups of people. There are lots of Ronnie Nortons in the Virginia Democratic Party, and the Virginia media is full of Steve Cohens. My favorite character in the novel, and I bet she will become your favorite as well, is Angela Parrish. She represents, to me at any rate, normal Virginia. There are lots of Angela Parrishes still left in Virginia. At least I am optimistic enough to still believe that, and perhaps Glenn Youngkin's election proves that there is still hope for Virginia.

The third point is that there are parts of the novel that are pure coincidence. For example, in my novel the Republican gubernatorial candidate, Angela Parrish, played basketball at Stonewall Jackson High School, and her campaign ran an ad of her shooting a basket. I wrote this before I discovered Glenn Youngkin played basketball and cut an ad of himself shooting a basket.

However, I did borrow one line, perhaps the most famous line of the 2021 gubernatorial campaign. I had a character say, "Parents have no business telling schools what to teach." This line was too good not to use. I wrote this and a couple of other familiar lines after the 2021 election.

Also, the reader will notice I write the "Democrat Party," rather than the "Democratic Party." I got into this habit years ago when I heard that Ronald Reagan also referred to them as the "Democrat Party." So in honor of the 40th President, I have adopted the same name.

I would point out that this book should not be used as a primer on the workings of the Virginia government. For the sake of simplicity, I enhanced the powers of a Virginia governor. A governor can indirectly appoint a university president or a state judge; however, for the purpose of this fictitious novel I streamlined the process a bit.

Finally, I wrote this mostly in the evenings after work. And when I wrote I maintained the habit of listening to music. The room I wrote this in was never quiet. I listened to songs by Joan Baez, Bob Dylan, Joni Mitchell, Crystal Gayle, and Tom Petty.

If you read this and take away one idea, or learn some bit of Virginia trivia, or get a good laugh, or even a chuckle. I will be happy.

David Shephard

Author's Note

To my fellow Virginians, I wish to clarify a few things before you read this book. I mention a few places and Virginia traditions which are purely a figment of my fertile imagination, and I wish to point them out. I made up the following: there is no hotel in Richmond called the Jefferson Davis Hotel, there is no school in Richmond named Virginia Commonwealth College. There is no Almond High School. Also, there was not an airport in Richmond named after Harry Byrd. I made up the debate about which school, Mary Baldwin or Hollins College, has the prettier women, although it is true the Hollywood legend Tallulah Bankhead did go to Mary Baldwin. Also, I made up the tradition of Tuesday being meatloaf night in Virginia. The historical figures such as Harry Byrd and Jerry Baliles are real, but Hank Parrish is fictitious.

And of course Ronnie Norton and Angela Parrish are fictitious.

Indeed, the story, all names, characters and incidents portrayed in this book are fictitious. No identification with actual persons (living or deceased), places, buildings and products is intended or inferred

Prologue

I spent a career covering politics, both national and local, and I am asked from time to time to tell a memorable story or two from my career. This one is my favorite. I was writing for the famed *Winchester Star*; it was my first job with a big paper. The office was located in downtown Winchester, in an ornate historic building on Kent Street. The newspaper was once owned by the Byrd family. Harry Byrd inherited it from his father, whose main job was the Speaker of the House of Delegates. The story goes that Byrd saved the paper from financial ruin. He ran the paper and he ran a political machine that controlled Virginia for several decades. At the time of my employment his picture was proudly displayed in the lobby. They say a picture is worth a thousand words, and when I first looked at the picture I realized the truth of that saying. The picture seemed to capture an earlier time in Virginia, a bygone era. The picture on the wall was of Harry Byrd and his son; his son later took his father's seat in the Senate. They were wearing white linen suits, the kind old southern senators used to wear. They were standing by an old black Ford circa 1935, or that is what it looked like to me. In the background was an old country road. I would see that picture every day I worked there.

Well, one day early in employment there I got a break.

"Your assignment, if you choose to accept it, is to do an investigative story on a Virginia State Senator from Fairfax, a man named Ronald Milsap Norton, known predominantly by his friends and constituents as Ronnie. Don't feel bad if you have never heard of him. Few outside of Fairfax have." So said my editor at the time, Larry Bixby.

Since I was still young, my experience was limited. I had worked for the school paper when I was at the University of

Elections Have Consequences

Richmond, but this was my first big job, and my first big assignment

Bixby went on, "Gary, I'm not sure how familiar you are with Virginia politics, but Norton was just elected last Tuesday to the State Senate. He came over from the House of Delegates; our sources are convinced that he is eventually going to run for governor. So, we want to compile information on him, a file on him, and be fully ready for his candidacy. Are you interested in doing some research on him?"

My response was quick. "Of course. Absolutely."

Bixby proceeded to spell out what he was looking for. "Gary, we want a really deep dive. We don't need biographical info, or voting records; we can find that. We want you to find out what type of man Norton is, what he believes, what makes him tick. Who he is beneath the veneer of a politician."

He offered a suggestion. "Perhaps start in Richmond on the campus of VCC–Virginia Commonwealth College–interview former teachers, look up some of his friends, girlfriends, fraternity brothers. Also, yearbooks can be a great source of information. Even visit some of Norton's hangouts in Richmond. People there may remember him."

I started right away. I booked a hotel in Richmond, and worked as hard as I had ever worked. I tracked down as many people who knew him as I could. I must say he had a lot of friends. But two things struck me early on in my investigation. First, one name kept popping up. People kept referring me to a man, John Edward Villiers, predominantly known as Jack although a few called him Jacky. I was told at VCC that he was the closest to Ronnie. One guy told me, "With the exception of

Elections Have Consequences

Mrs. Norton, no one is as close to Ronnie as Jack." He went on, "To understand Ronnie, to really get to know him, you should talk to Jack."

Well, I found out that after he graduated from VCC, Jack went on to medical school and became Dr. Jack Villiers. He eventually set up practice in Henrico County and based on my research he built up quite a practice. He was routinely named as one of the top doctors in Virginia. I found out that he spent a lot of time at the MCV hospital in Richmond, and based on my persistence I acquired his cell number. I admit I acquired this in a rather underhanded fashion. A lady I was interviewing, a friend of Norton and Villiers, went off to the restroom, and I reached into her purse and found her cell phone. From the address book I got his cell number.

So I called, expecting I would leave a message. But he picked up. My guess is that he was expecting a call, and simply picked up.

I said, "Dr. Villiers?"

"Speaking," he responded.

I began my spiel. "My name is Gary Frank. I'm with *The Winchester Star* newspaper, and we're doing a background story on State Senator Ronnie Norton. I understand you went to school with him, and I was wondering if you would like to do an interview about him, what he was like when you went to school with him, that sort of thing."

There was this pause, an eerie pause. For several seconds he didn't say anything. He was probably at this moment thinking, *"Should I hang up on this nosy reporter?"*

Then to my great relief, I heard him reply, "I know Ronnie."

I interjected, "Well, I could meet you at your convenience. I understand you work a good deal out of MCV. I could accompany you on your rounds and ask questions, or meet you at the hospital during a break. It shouldn't take long. I just want to get a sense of the man, Ronnie Norton."

Villers then tersely responded, "Well, call my office. Perhaps we can find an arrangement." With that he hung up.

I called his office. He never responded.

The other thing that stood out: Norton had a nickname. They called him "Huggy Bear." The thing is, I found this out by accident. A couple of times in talking about him, a friend might let it slip; they would say, "Huggy Bear was a funny guy," or "That was Huggy Bear." I would ask how he got the name, but then they would claim not to remember, or play it off, as if they hardly ever called him that.

Well, it all ended, that is, the assignment, very abruptly. It was a Tuesday night; I was having dinner with my girlfriend. She came to my hotel room in Richmond to visit me. We were watching a movie on TV after dinner, and the phone rang. It was my editor, Bixby. He simply said, "Change of plans. We are reassigning you." Seems Bixby was ordered by his boss to cancel the background report on Norton. I got the sense Bixby was not happy about it, but had no choice.

I told him I had a notebook full of information. I asked what I should do with it. I will never forget what happened next. He said, "Let's be on the safe side and shred it. And do it quickly." Then he hung up.

I have no proof, but I am convinced that one of Norton's many friends got the background research project quashed.

Eight Years Later

1) Virginia Inaugurates A Governor

It all started on a cold and sunny Saturday afternoon in January, in the city of Richmond. Virginia State Supreme Court Chief Justice Robert Lee Carrico asked Ronnie Norton, "Mr. Norton, are you ready to take the oath?"

Norton replied, "I am." In between them stood Dr. Paula Norton, Ronnie's long-suffering wife, whose sacrifice made this day possible for Norton and Virginia Democrats.

Carrico gave the instruction, "Please place your left hand on the Bible and repeat after me," Carrico began. "I, Ronald Milsap Norton, do solemnly swear..." and with that began the most controversial governorship in Virginia history. At the moment he was sworn in, the crowd's attention turned to the heavens, as they watched three F-16 Flying Falcons soar over the Capitol Building, courtesy of the US Air Force.

The Inaugural Committee suggested, and Norton agreed with, the Orwellian-sounding "Through our diversity comes our strength" as the inaugural theme. This banal theme, which eventually would become Virginia's new state motto, was printed on all the programs, and the TV networks included the slogan while covering the event. In addition, this theme was inscribed on Norton's governor's pin, which is given out to staff members and supporters.

Those present on that January day will never forget how cold it was. By the time of the swearing in, the noontime sun raised the temperature to a frigid 12 degrees. The effects of the cold were probably made less harsh by the volume of the crowd packed into Capitol Square. All those people packed in like sardines may

Elections Have Consequences

have raised the temperature by a few degrees. Still, it was cold.

Virginia political columnist for the *Richmond Daily Dispatch*, Stephen Cohen, said that it was the coldest inaugural that he remembered since the Allen inaugural in the early 1990's. Unlike the cold, the speech left little impression on the crowd, Norton spoke in glittering generalities. You see, he was never good at uplifting rhetoric, but on a really cold day most people shivering on Capitol Square probably preferred a short speech so they could come inside and warm their hands and feet. Norton, being a good politician, kept it to just over 15 minutes

Stephen Cohen, predominantly known as Steve, a native of Petersburg, loved to tell the story of how his dad took him to his first inauguration as a kid. He watched a tall, distinguished looking man named Mills Godwin take the oath of office, on the very steps where Norton took the same oath decades, even a century, later. Cohen confessed a George Mason University student, and reporter on the school paper, the Broadside, "I love being here for this, I wouldn't miss this for the world. I don't care if you are a Democrat or a Republican, the inauguration of a Virginia Governor is a majestic event. After all, Virginia is the world's oldest democracy. It all goes back to Jamestown."

Cohen invited a college journalism student, Billy Smith, to come to Richmond and stay with him for the weekend and hang out, or "shadow," him for inauguration day. Cohen had met Billy when he spoke to Smith's class at George Mason University. In addition to the inauguration, the two went to the governor's mansion together for a reception afterwards. Cohen gave a bit of advice to the budding reporter. "Billy, I have known and covered nearly a dozen governors, and I was tough but fair in my coverage.

Elections Have Consequences

But I will say that I became as successful as I have because I built a relationship with them. Each and every one of them, Democrat and Republican. I showed some discretion. That is, I didn't report every foible, or rumor, or gaffe. I even offered to give them a mulligan on a small matter or two. And you know what? That helped them trust me, take me into their confidence, and that led to bigger scoops. No, seizing on every little mistake is short sighted. A reporter has to realize that the governor is going to be there"–Cohen pointed to the Governor's mansion–"for four years. It's good to build a relationship with the governor and his administration. I am not saying to give soft coverage, but we in the press must not be adversarial either."

To reflect the changing demographics of the state, and in the words of the inaugural committee, "to provide a more inclusive inauguration experience," the religious officiants included an Imam from Northern Virginia, and a woman minister and friend of Norton's, confidant Reverend Ann Lee Brand. The minister belonged to the United Church of Christ, a church which could claim about 0.004 percent of Virginians as adherents, but no one was going to point that out. In effect her brief remarks were well received. They included a passage from a poem by Maya Angelou.

In the Virginia inaugural tradition, Norton dressed in a dark blue morning coat, with gray pinstripe suit pants, a winged collar, and a gray ascot. Despite the low temperature he did not look too cold. That might be explained by the fact that there was a heater under the podium. After he concluded his speech, he turned to his wife Paula and said, "Short, sweet, and to the point."

Norton did one thing which extended the inauguration: he insisted they play the song, "Oh, Shenandoah." He and Paula both loved the song. Virginia does not have a state song, so many have adopted "Oh, Shenandoah," even though it is not actually referring to the Shenandoah Valley in Virginia.

The Grammy award winning singer Emmylou Harris, a native of Woodbridge, Virginia, flew in from warm and sunny Miami to sing it. The Nortons appeared to know the words. The camera caught them singing along:

> Oh, Shenandoah, I long to hear you
> Look away, you rollin' river.
> Oh, Shenandoah, I long to hear you
> Look away, we're bound away
> Across the wide Missouri.

The band also played the Star-Spangled Banner, which is always played at an inauguration. The Inaugural Committee recommended that the band, a high school band from Fairfax County's Edison High School, play the Black National Anthem for the purpose of inclusivity, but Norton vetoed the idea, telling the committee's chairperson, "We only have one national anthem. No other anthems can be played."

Norton's inauguration was the capstone of the career of the veteran Fairfax Democrat, who had seen so much change in his three decades in politics. Virginia was a state that had changed almost beyond recognition from his first for public office in 2001. The divisions in the state included political differences, racial differences, and a divide between rich and poor, urban and suburban. When Norton started in politics, the tobacco and coal industries were still powerful. Now they were almost nonexistent. Rural legislators had once dominated the assembly, and now it

Elections Have Consequences

was controlled by urban and suburban legislators. When Norton started in Fairfax politics, support from police organizations and business groups were vital.

Norton became governor in the era of the social justice warrior, something he wouldn't fully realize until a couple years into his term. Norton's political guru, Steve Beaman, used to say that in politics you must "adapt or die." He would say, "When your voters go woke, don't stay asleep."

Norton's victory solidified not just Northern Virginia's dominance of Virginia politics, but Fairfax County's. The Governor, the Speaker of the House of Delegates, the Senate Majority leader were all from Fairfax. Even the senior senator called Fairfax home.

Never in Virginia history did one county have so much power. Norton could not be described as a leader of any real political movement; rather, he had the fortune and skill to be on good terms with every part of his party's coalition. It seemed he never offended anyone in his party. He even had a few friends on the other side of the aisle.

The Republican Lt. Governor, Jim Morrison, and Norton became friends when they both entered the House of Delegates years earlier. They were part of the same freshman class. Once, after a committee meeting, Norton and Morrison were walking back to the General Assembly building together. It was a bright, sunny, and unseasonably warm February day. Behind them was the Governor's mansion. Morrison stopped, looked back, and asked Norton, "Ronnie, which one of us will make it there first?"

Norton laughed, looked back, and said, "One term for you and one for me."

Elections Have Consequences

Morrison said, "Ronnie, politics is all about timing. You have years where a conservative like George Allen wins and years when a liberal like Tim Kaine can win. The secret in politics is to know when to run." Morrison opined, "Ronnie, I would say that there are two ironclad laws in Virginia politics. One, if your party controls the White House it is not a good time to run for Governor." Norton agreed.

Morrison then said, "The second law of Virginia politics is that governors only get one term. I don't just mean that they can't succeed themselves constitutionally, I mean even after waiting another term, the people of Virginia don't want anyone to get two terms, so a Virginia Governor has got to make that one term count." Morrison then made a prediction, "These are two laws both of us will have to consider in the coming years."

Norton smiled and said, "Sure." They both took one last glance at the Governor's Mansion.

***

The incoming administration sought to end what Norton called "destructive competition" between neighboring states. Previous Virginia governors would aggressively pursue businesses from Maryland and Washington, DC by pointing out that Virginia had lower tax rates, a right to work law, and more business-friendly policies. An easy sell, Virginia was much more business friendly.

Rather than trying to "poach" businesses away from Virginia's neighbors, Norton introduced a new policy of "constructive cooperation" between Virginia, the District of Columbia, and Maryland.

Elections Have Consequences

Norton and his party's base mainly consisted of a coalition of federal workers, academics, nonprofit employees, public employees, and pensioners. It was a base which did not really have many small and mid-sized employees and business owners, so higher taxes and anti-business regulations were not really an issue with his base.

Norton and his policy of ending "destructive competition" and moving to "constructive partnership" was really political in nature. He, and the Democrat run legislature, abolished a fund used to attract businesses to the Commonwealth. In exchange, the District and Maryland promised not to try to lure Virginia businesses away from Virginia. It was a silly promise, since they really had little to offer businesses relative to the pro-business Virginia. Norton privately promised the leaders of the neighboring jurisdictions that he would not cut taxes, to maximize an "unfair advantage" for Virginia.

George Mason University president and economics professor Leonard Milstein attacked the policy as Maryland, the District, and Virginia were "colluding to keep taxes high." He claimed, "It's unilateral disarmament. Governor Norton doesn't want more private businesses in Virginia, because they would be more likely to have employees that would vote Republican. Sure, we can move to keep our taxes at DC and Maryland levels, and that would protect their residents and businesses, but what do we get out of it? Nothing but Norton colluding with the leaders of Maryland and DC to keep the government growing."

During this period, the state was doing well economically in large part because of the economic policies of Republican President Marvin Pierce Bush, but that was the only thing people could agree on.

Elections Have Consequences

President Bush had never held an elective office before becoming president. His background was in education, first as a professor, and then as the president of Hillsdale College, a conservative liberal arts college in Michigan. Bush bore a physical resemblance to the conservative icon, Whitaker Chambers. He wasn't quite as heavy as Chambers, but like Chambers he would occasionally smoke a pipe.

Bush believed that Western civilization was under attack from the left. The left was trying to undermine the founding of the United States and to destroy the Constitution. To further the cause, the left took control of the schools and the media and, according to Bush, this greatly furthered their cause.

As president of Hillsdale College, he became famous in conservative media. He would broadcast regular commentaries on the US Constitution and American history which were aired nationwide. Most conservative and Christian radio stations would carry them. Bush quickly became the most prominent conservative voice in the country and, for millions, his were the only lectures they would ever hear on the Constitution. Bush served in the federal government as the Secretary of Education, and later ran for president.

***

One of Ronald Reagan's earliest political advisors, Michael Deaver, once said of Reagan, "All you wanted to do was put the camera on him and let him speak." Deaver had the benefit of advising the candidate who was known as "the Great Communicator." This was not the case for Ronnie Norton, who was remarkable neither in appearance nor intelligence.

Elections Have Consequences

However, no one outworked him as a politician. He had a great skill in reading the political winds. Perhaps his greatest accomplishment as a politician was the fact that while thought of as a moderate, centrist Democrat, he never did or said anything that would offend his progressive base. Sure, he opposed gay marriage in the early 2000's, but he had the same positon as Obama at the time. He was excused for his opposition to gay marriage then, as long as he "evolved on the issue," that is, dropped his view that marriage is exclusively the union of one man and one woman, which Norton did.

Norton earned a lifetime rating of a "C plus" from the Virginia Chamber of Commerce, something he would tout, and with such a relatively high rating for a Democrat, he was thought of as a pro-business and a centrist Democrat. He was willing to give in to the left on everything, except business or economic policy.

The Washington Press Democrat and the *Richmond Daily Dispatch* always referred to him as a "moderate" or "centrist" Democrat. By comparison, his Republican opponent, Angela Parrish, was usually referred to as a "right wing" or "ultra conservative" Republican.

For Norton, who was predominantly known as Ronnie, his Mike Deaver was Steve Beaman. A portly, balding, mid sixty year-old and former television executive, Steve was an advisor and guru to many Virginia Democrats.

Norton, a member of the Fairfax County Board of Supervisors, first met Beaman in the late 1980's. For several years, Beaman ran the local ABC television affiliate in Washington, but he always kept a hand in partisan politics. His advice was considered golden. He was reliably astute and totally ruthless. His maxim was "Always have dirt on someone. You never know when you might need it." He said that with a smile, but he was not joking.

You would never know by listening to Ronnie's slight twang of an accent that he was from Fairfax County. One explanation is that Ronnie grew up in the Pimmit Hills section of Fairfax, which in the 60's and 70's was full of transplants from West Virginia, Pennsylvania and North Carolina. The area is still referred to as the slums of McLean, Virginia. Every one of Ronnie's friends, from grade school through high school, was born in another state. Ronnie used to joke, "Well, I grew up in occupied territory," and other times he would describe it as "Yankee territory."

Ronnie Norton's family came from western Pennsylvania. Ronnie's dad was in the construction business. Tysons's Corner development was booming, and more construction workers were needed. The family stayed in the area because Tysons Corner kept growing, so work was plentiful. His parents were by tradition Democrats, but not very political.

In the late 1980's, Virginia was trending Republican, and Ronnie started in politics calling himself a moderate Democrat, running first for the Board of Supervisors. He also would occasionally refer to himself as a "Chuck Robb Democrat" or a "Radical Centrist."

There were even a series of palm cards that described him as a "Byrd Democrat." The campaign stopped at one printing but they failed to collect all the cards. The opposition brought up this incident during Ronnie's first run for the House of Delegates.

In fairness to Ronnie, it was not Byrd's racial views or mass resistance for which he was expressing support; rather he was embracing Byrd's fiscal conservatism and political independence, and he may have been referring to Byrd Jr, who served as an Independent in the US Senate.

However, as Ronnie learned the hard way, never ever offer praise of Harry Byrd, Sr. He may have built roads, built schools, and built Virginia's reputation as a business-friendly state, but by praising him you will automatically be deemed a racist.

A lawyer by profession, Norton's specialty was corporate law. He used to joke that "he put more people to sleep talking about corporate law than he did as a politician." He also described his work as a lawyer as his "day job," and said, "politics is just a hobby for me." In truth, politics was his passion and ambition; it was in his blood. In politics, they say a successful candidate must have fire in the belly. Norton had that fire.

The other thing he had going for him was a wife who supported his political ambitions. Paula Norton raised their three children while Ronnie spent most of his time politicking. He once remarked that if he had married any other woman, he would never have become governor. No doubt it was true.

His wife Paula was a typical upper class, white, well-educated limousine liberal, what people used to call a yuppie. The kids, of course, were privately educated, and they lived in an exclusive part of McLean.

Paula met Ronnie at a church singles event; both were members of the Episcopal Church. She was not a native Virginian. She grew up in Massachusetts, but came to Virginia to attend Hollins College in Roanoke.

Her father was in the foreign service so she traveled and lived in a few different countries. She even put on an air of sophistication. For example, she would never say there was a line, rather she would describe it as a queue. She would be at the grocery store and might say to Ronnie, "Get in the queue, and I will get a couple more items." She would sometimes refer to her years spent "on the continent." She would call a tomaAto a tomAHto, using the same pronunciation for a potato. Her pretentiousness may have originated in her childhood, as her parents instructed her to call her grandmother, "Grand Ma Ma."

Her values really came from politically correct clichés, and while claiming to be a feminist, she had the role of a traditional wife. She worked part time while she raised their children. For Ronnie, his work came first.

Paula longed to be a social justice warrior. She felt bad because she had never really had a Hispanic friend, an African American friend, a Jewish friend, a Muslim friend, a gay friend, or a transgendered friend. While she was good at all the virtue signaling, deep down she felt that she was just a phony, wealthy, white McLean liberal.

On the campaign trail, her husband always praised her, expressed his love for her, and in a funny line, which only those who are familiar with Virginia political history would understand, he would declare, "John Warner had Elizabeth Taylor campaigning for him, but I got Paula Norton."

Fairly unimpressive looking, Norton always had a disheveled look about him. The former Fairfax County Democrat Chair Ginger Williams once said he looked like an unmade bed. She claimed it was the oddest thing. "He could go to the dry cleaners, get his fully pressed suit back, put it on, and then somehow it would become wrinkled again."

Elections Have Consequences

At just under 6 feet tall, Norton was of medium build. He had black hair, short, only slightly longer than a crew cut, and many suspected that he dyed it to keep the gray away.

Norton once estimated that in campaigning for different offices in Fairfax County, he had been to every Fairfax County Fair for 20 straight years. It is a must for every candidate in Fairfax. Even in a non-election year an incumbent must have a presence. Over those years the location changed a couple of times, but it was predominantly held at George Mason University.

Every year Ronnie would be there, in a politician's summer uniform— khaki pants and blue polo shirt. He would walk around the fairgrounds with his palm cards and his campaign sticker on his chest. He had his lines down. "I'm Ronnie Norton, and I'm running for the House of Delegates." Some of the time he would stand at the fair's front entrance to greet people as they walked in; at other times he would walk the grounds with a staffer at hand with balloons and campaign literature. He would approach people at picnic tables and people waiting in lines for the rides. He always had a staffer with him to take notes. The staffer also carried Norton's sunblock and hand sanitizer, which Norton would reapply twice an hour, reminding the aide, "You can never be too careful. Franklin Roosevelt acquired polio as a young politician by shaking hands."

When Norton would approach a parent, he would also be sure to acknowledge the child. He would pay the child a compliment; he noticed parents seemed to like that. He might say of the child, "Looks just like you," or to a mother he'd say, "The baby gets her beauty from you." He would always reach his hand up in front of the child and say "Give me a high five."

Elections Have Consequences

If he noticed the child didn't have a Vote for Ronnie balloon, he'd ask one of his volunteers to go get him one. If the child was near the age of one of his children, he would point that out.

The campaign usually had a moon bounce for the kids, with the sign above it proclaiming, "Norton for State Senate." And every year they would have Norton campaign balloons, given out by teams of Young Democrat volunteers. Ronnie loved to look out at the fair and see a sea of his balloons, but if he saw his opponent had as many balloons in circulation, Norton would get nervous.

One veteran of a Norton campaign described Norton as a candidate, "Ronnie always worked hard, and he genuinely seemed to enjoy meeting and talking to voters. He seemed to be energized by talking to people. Ronnie told me the best way to get to know the district is to talk to the people, he said it was like a businessman talking to his customers." He went on, "Ronnie, like all candidates, wants to get all the votes he can, every hand you shake is hopefully a vote, but sometimes someone may come up to you and say something you disagree with, well, Ronnie still didn't want to lose the vote. So, he might look for a way to agree. Also Ronnie used the phrase, "I hear ya" when he heard something he probably didn't agree with but still wanted to keep his disagreement unknown to the voter."

The most common issues Ronnie would hear whether he was running for the Board of Supervisors, the House of Delegates, or the State Senate were the same. They were mostly issues involving education, transportation, crime and taxes. Norton upset his fellow Democrats on a few issues, namely his opposition to a meals tax in Fairfax county.

Elections Have Consequences

One person gave Ronnie an earful on the issue of crime and the gang problem in Fairfax county. "Ronnie, I live in Providence and have voted for you in the past."

Norton interjected, "Well, I appreciate that."

The voter continued, "But I am concerned about crime, specifically the gang problem. In Merrifield, near my house, last weekend, we had a stabbing at the movie theater, it was gang related. The gang is based in central America. We all know why we have a gang problem. Its because of illegal immigration. The feds won't protect our border and they won't deport gang members. So we have to deal with it."

Norton seemed to sympathize, "Well, look I agree with you that the Federal government has failed to control our southern border, but there is not much I can do about it on the Fairfax county board of supervisors."

Ronnie then pivoted to all the things he is doing on the board to fight crime,and even mentioned programs to help give young people things to do, "Because of my efforts the Wakefield recreation center is open longer hours. That gives kids a safe place to play." Presumably a place out of the reach of gang influence.

***

After two terms in the state senate, Ronnie decided that it was time to run for governor of Virginia. Norton's legislative record was mediocre, with no significant legislative accomplishments, but he compiled a moderate voting record, with nothing controversial that Republicans could seize on to be able to paint him as a left-wing kook. Considered pro-business and socially liberal, he was probably a good fit for Northern

Virginia and the Richmond suburbs.

Norton made the rounds like no other politician. Every Little League opening day, every charity drive, every big school event, every community ribbon cutting, most high school football games, you'd see Ronnie.

Based on his voting record, one might think he would have a tough time getting the Democratic party's nomination. After all, the party of Harry Byrd, A.L. Philpot, and even Chuck Robb, was no longer recognizable. That Democrat party moved into the party of Bernie Sanders.

His kitchen cabinet, as Cohen would describe it, would be led by Steve Beaman and Mark Thompson, both old friends from Fairfax. After the inauguration Norton appointed Thompson to be Secretary of Public Safety for the Commonwealth. No one could have imagined at the time how important that position would become.

The two other members of Norton's transition team included a progressive Democrat from Alexandria, Reverend Ann Lee Brand, and a young Democrat party activist and lawyer, Mike Jackson. Both would have prominent roles in the Norton administration. Cohen would tell friends that it was no surprise Brand would be in the cabinet claiming "Norton owes Brand big time." He would never explain exactly why Norton owed her so much.

Cohen knew a secret; he knew why Norton owed Brand so much, and it was a secret that he would never put in his column.

***

Elections Have Consequences

Despite their differences, Brand, Norton, and Beaman could agree on one thing, but for different reasons: they all wanted to get rid of George Mason University president Leonard Milstein.

They shared that objective, though they differed, however, on the timing and the method of how to throw him overboard. Unlike virtually all Virginia university presidents, Milstein, who was Jewish and from New York, was a Republican, indeed fairly conservative. Norton and Beaman could not forgive him for backing Parrish, Norton's Republican opponent, and saying, "Having met Angela Parrish on several occasions, and discussed economic policy with her, I am confident that if elected she will be the best governor Virginia has had in decades."

Brand had different reasons, that is, more than party politics. She rightfully concluded that Milstein would stand in the way of implementing a social justice agenda on campus. In addition, Milstein would also stand in the way of a school name change. Brand wanted to change the names of George Mason University, James Madison University, and Randolph Macon College, since they were all named after slave-holding white males.

The presidents of James Madison and Randolph Macon told Brand that they would, "seriously consider" supporting a university name change. However, Milstein summarily dismissed the idea, telling Brand, "If you had any understanding of academic freedom, you would realize what a repugnant campaign you are engaging in." He told others, "The fact that Governor Norton appointed Brand Secretary of Education is to his great discredit."

Beaman and Norton wanted to appoint a fellow Democrat, but even more than that they wanted to "get something" for the appointment. Norton told Beaman, "Being president of GMU is worth an awful lot. We can put our person in that position, but we also need to get something for it. A real payoff." In other words, they wanted to wait for an opportune moment to appoint someone in exchange for a political favor.

Before becoming the president of George Mason University, Leonard "Lenny" Milstein taught economics. He started right out of college and quickly became an adjunct professor, received tenure, and became nationally known. He also brought great credit to the university when he was awarded the Nobel prize in economics.

Born in Brooklyn to Jewish immigrant parents, Milstein was a red diaper baby; his parents were politically far left. However, in school he became transformed by the writings of Irving Kristol, Frank Meyer, and Milton Friedman and he joined the conservative movement.

Milstein received the prestigious award based on his paper on the effect of insurance on the cost of a service. In his thesis, Milstein concluded that for much of the 20th century people paid for dental care out of pocket. However, in the last couple decades of the 20th century, dental insurance became more available, and a high percentage of people took out policies

What Milstein found is that during that period, despite the availability of insurance programs, most customers still paid the dentist out of pocket, perhaps out of habit. The official price that a dentist charged, to the insurance company that is, outpaced inflation. However, the customers who paid out of pocket overwhelmingly paid a lower cost than the official price. In fact, he found that the out-of-pocket cost, unlike the official cost, actually underpaced inflation.

Elections Have Consequences

Not too long after he received the Nobel prize, the George Mason University Board of Directors selected Milstein to be the university president. Now, in his selection, the board seemed to dismiss an old charge of sexual harassment made against Milstein by a co-ed while Milstein was an adjunct professor.

The board dismissed it because it was mostly a "he said, she said" case and because it had happened so long ago. There was nothing to validate the charge. It took place decades before he became the president, so it would be impossible to find reliable witnesses. But Norton and Beaman thought they could resurrect the old scandal to force Milstein out at an opportunistic time.

Beaman told Norton, "It's perfect. We tell Milstein that if he doesn't want this to get out he should resign. If he tries to fight it we go to the board and tell them they should have looked at these charges before he was approved. The board won't want to defend their negligence in making the decision, especially in the Me Too era, so they will pressure Milstein to step down."

Norton nodded and again insisted, "Look, being president of GMU is a plum appointment. It is very valuable. Steve, we got to get something for it. There needs to be a big political payoff for it."

Beaman concurred. "When we find a good opportunity for an exchange, we will initiate Operation Venona." Beaman gave the project to oust Milstein the code name "Venona," probably an homage to one of his heroes Kim Philby.

Norton said, "Excellent, just let me know when we should make our move."

Norton smiled and with sincerity in his voice said, "Honestly, Steve, I don't know where I'd be without you." The words were music to Beaman's ears.

A governor cannot fire a university president, only the Board of Visitors can, but the board members are appointed by the governor. In time, Norton would have the votes to get rid of him. Milstein would be removed in a few years.

2) The Daughter Also Rises

Angela Parrish was a strikingly beautiful woman. One might say unnecessarily beautiful, so beautiful that she looked out of place for such a dirty business as politics. There is an old expression that politics is Hollywood for ugly people. That was not the case for Parrish. Steve Cohen remarked that if Hollywood were to make a movie about her, they would fail to find any actress as beautiful. Cohen said, "Perhaps in its Golden Age Hollywood could have come up with an actress to play her, maybe Tallulah Bankhead or Julie Adams or Audrey Hepburn." Cohen then paused, visibly seemed to reflect, and with his voice rising added, "Maybe Marlo Thomas, circa 'That Girl', but today's stars like Jessica Alba or Jessica Biel just can't measure up. Sure, they may be almost as beautiful, but they wouldn't have the command of the English language or the intellect to credibly play her."

A former state legislator and 5th District Republican Party Chairman, Tucker Wilkins, said of Angela, "In Virginia politics, you will hear the names of different legislators and activists around the state, and you may forget which ones you have actually met at different events and conventions, but that is not the case with Angela Parrish. If you ever met her, you would remember." Wilkins said with a chuckle, "No one has ever said, 'I am not sure if I have met Angela Parrish.'"

Just 32 when she ran for an open state senate seat in Prince William County, beating the odds, she defeated a longtime Democrat delegate to capture the seat for the GOP. Parrish may have been young, but as the daughter of a politician, she was very familiar with campaigning; she became familiar with Virginia politics in childhood.

A lawyer by training, Parrish, a natural debater and speaker, could quickly spot the weakness in any argument. The other thing she had going for her was her last name, the Parrish name still meant something in Manassas. Her father was Hank Parrish, a delegate and former Speaker of the House of Delegates. Her mother was a Dogan. The Dogans came to Prince William County in the 18th century and the Parrishs came in the 19th century. The Dogans were for the most part Methodists and the Parrishs were Catholics.

Her first campaign manager told her, "Your campaign signs can't just say "Angela"; this is Manassas, it has to include the name Parrish." Henry "Hank" Parrish, a former Speaker of the House of Delegates, served in the House for several decades, representing Manassas and parts of Prince William County.

Generations knew and loved Hank throughout the county. He died within a few years of leaving office, and as a former Speaker of the House of Delegates, his casket lay in state in the capitol rotunda. For a day, it sat in front of the George Washington statue. People from all over Virginia came to pay their respects.

Hank had always wanted a son to follow him in politics, but he instead had two daughters. Hank proudly said that when he first looked at his baby girl, he saw the face of an angel, so he named her Angela. Actually, Angela was probably named after his mother-in-law, Angela Dogan, who was the first woman to be elected to the Manassas City Council.

His wife assured him, "Hank, a girl can grow up to be governor of Virginia."

Hank thought about it, picked up his baby girl, and said,

Elections Have Consequences

"That's right, baby, will you be gov'ner of Virginia one day? Hmm?" His baby's eyes sparkled with wonder and she smiled, showing her dimples. Hank said, "Are you going to invite your mom and dad to visit you in the Governor's Mansion?"

As she grew up, Hank found that Angela took to politics "like a duck to water" he used to say. His other daughter would eventually take over the family's construction firm, Angela would follow him on to politics. Hank used to joke that Angela "inherited her love of politics from me and her good looks from her mother."

When Hank Parrish was elected to the House of Delegates in the 1970's, there were only 15 Republicans out of the 100 delegates. The majority Democrats paid Republican members no attention. Hank laughed, "We Republicans didn't even get offices. My office was a phone booth on 9th Street." Hank learned all the legislative tricks. He described filing, or so he thought, his first bill. The House Majority leader, Mitchell Wiley, told him, "Hey freshman, give me your first bill; I will review it. Make sure it is good and then send it to the proper committee." Hank said he remembered thinking, "How nice of him to help me, a freshman, and from the other party to boot."

Parrish described the experience, "So I gave him my bill. He put it in his suit pocket and said, 'I will take care of it.' Well, I heard nothing for two weeks, so one day I caught up with him on capitol square and I asked, 'What's the status of my bill?'"

He told me he sent it to the Subcommittee on Safety and Security." I asked him, "When do they meet? I would like to testify."

He said, 'No, they won't need you to testify.' Well, I said that I would like to go to a hearing in case they have any questions.

He responded, 'No, the bill is plain enough, they don't need you to answer any questions.' Well, he kept coming up with all kinds of excuses. So naturally I got suspicious and did some digging and found out that there was no such thing as the Subcommittee on Safety and Security. He just made it up to kill the bill." Parrish laughed and said, "That is when I learned why they called it a pocket veto."

Many times, Angela would come down to Richmond to visit her father during the session. Her childhood memories included seeing her father running the House floor, holding a big gavel, hearing him speaking to the assembly, saying things like the chair "recognizes the gentleman from Fairfax," and "The ayes are 52, the nays are 48, the motion carries." Then, she would hear the loud "thud" of her dad slamming down the gavel. She once asked him on the House floor, "Daddy, why do you have to hit the gavel so hard?"

He responded by pointing to the back of the chamber. "Darling, they need to hear it all the way in the back row."

As a little girl she witnessed her father's power. When they walked across capitol square, she remembered, "Everyone wanted to talk to my father. All these men in suits would line up to chat with him. They would form a circle and wait for a turn to speak; they would practically follow us all the way to the Jeff Davis Hotel where Daddy always stayed during the session."

Considered to be the premier hotel in Richmond, the Jefferson Davis, built in the early 1900's, became a landmark for the wealthy and powerful. It quickly gained a reputation throughout the rest of the 20th century.

Speaker Parrish had a suite there during the session. The hotel was built on the foundation of a building where Jefferson Davis, as the President of the Confederacy, had an office. So when they built the hotel they named it after him.

The hotel was known for its lobby and grand staircase; indeed, the staircase is recognized worldwide today. It became famous because of one man and one event that took place in April 1912. The man was an English businessman with a company named the White Star Line, which ran passenger ships across the Atlantic. He marveled at the hotel's staircase and staterooms.

A few years later, he had the task of designing the line's newest ship, named the Titanic. He copied the hotel's staircase almost exactly to scale; he also borrowed the design of the hotel's main dining room and the presidential suite. As a girl, Angela did not remember the staircase or staterooms, rather the hotel had another feature that struck her. "It was that the hotel had a barbershop, the Jefferson Davis Barber Shop. I thought it was interesting that a hotel would have a barber shop off its lobby."

The hotel became one of Virginia's leading tourist destinations. Tens of thousands of couples would visit the hotel to get a picture on the staircase. Even weddings were performed on the staircase.

One year, the same year as the Oscar winning film about the Titanic came out, the staircase was declared the number one tourist destination in the state, according to *Travelers Magazine*. Lovers would come and get a picture on the staircase.

By the late 1970's, the pressure to change the name became too great for the owners to resist. A major hotel acquired the property. By early 2000 it had a new owner and had become the Trump Richmond hotel.

Despite her family's wealth and her dad's prominence, Angela grew up as a middle-class kid. She attended Seton Catholic school in Manassas; the whole family attended All Saints Church. An "A" student and the valedictorian at Stonewall Jackson High School, she went on to graduate from Hillsdale College in Michigan, and then from the University of Virginia Law School, and entered the workforce.

As the apple of her father's eye, she almost always made him proud. He thought she was perfect in every way. Despite being a very busy and powerful man, he tried to be there for her childhood. He attended as many sporting events, school plays, and other events as possible. When she was accepted to the university, the proud Hank put a "Cavalier Dad" bumper sticker on his car. He used to push her to succeed in everything she tried. He used to tell her, "Never waste a minute, never waste a minute," and "Don't dally in the pleasant valleys of amusement." He taught her the Kipling poem, "If." She memorized it.

Angela read *Atlas Shrugged*, and for a period flirted with becoming an Objectivist. The nuns at Seton didn't approve. Her Rand phase didn't last long, though, Angela moved on to the writings of Edith Stein and Flannery O'Connor and grew into a strong Catholic.

After law school, she went to work for the Prince William Commonwealth Attorney, and prosecuted cases, mostly small criminal cases. After several years in the office, she got a big break– a big case that would make her famous in the Washington Metro area, and even nationally.

For several weeks the region was terrorized by a sniper, two snipers. They traveled to the Washington area to reenact the sniper shootings of the early 2000s. They say there is always disinformation in war, a phenomenon known as the fog of war. A

Elections Have Consequences

similar thing happened in response to the terror of the shooters, which at the time was believed to be just one shooter.

At one of the early shootings, a witness claimed that he saw a white van, with a "Make America Great Again" bumper sticker flee the scene. So, the media, not so much the police, believed that a white nationalist was behind the shootings. One DC area television network came up with a composite sketch of what their profiling experts concocted. It was a sketch of a white man, blonde, with a light beard, about 5-11, 180 pounds. They were way off. It was not one shooter. It was two recent converts to Islam. They were young people, radicalized in Falls Church, Virginia. They decided to engage in a two-man religious war. The media decided to downplay their motivations, simply saying that the shooters failed to understand the meaning of their religion, but rarely did the media mention their religion or race.

The two shooters traveled together, randomly shooting people from the back of their car. They were finally caught, and since their first couple of victims were killed in Prince William County, they were tried there first. Angela led the prosecution.

The first pictures of her that the public saw were not actually pictures but courtroom sketches, since cameras are not allowed in the court. They depicted Angela questioning a witness, or Angela in front of a judge, or speaking to the jury. The sketches showed a woman with long black hair and sharp features.

Nightly news viewers might see footage of her going into the courtroom, but mostly people in the area recognized her name more than her face. As the trial went on, she became a local hero.

It didn't take long for the DC area media to fall in love with her, portraying her as a great lawyer and an accomplished professional. After the defendants were convicted on all counts, Angela became a local hero, a young woman whose future potential was limitless; no glass ceiling, no matter how thick, could stop her rise.

The Press Democrat did a puff piece, the type reserved for Democrat women. It didn't take long for people to speculate that she would run for office. One national television executive and progressive Democrat told Angela, "If you ran and won as a Democrat, we'd make you a national star." He also told her bluntly that if she ran as a Republican, she would be, "constantly attacked, and if you run for a higher office, you will be dragged through the mud."

She responded, "Perhaps you are right, but if I ran as a Democrat I wouldn't be me."

Her successful prosecution of the case made her well known in the area and provided a springboard, indeed a perfect springboard, for her to run for a senate seat, which opened up with a retirement from a long-time member. The district included Manassas and parts of Prince William County.

The fawning coverage would change when she became a Republican candidate for the State Senate.

Cohen, when pressed by a Republican friend as to why Parrish got soft coverage before she decided to run as a Republican, responded, "Well, being a prosecutor and being a political candidate are two very different things. But, I admit some bias. We didn't know she was Ultra MAGA." Cohen chuckled.

***

When the Democrat incumbent decided to retire, the party nominated a long-time member of the House of Delegates. Once

Parrish announced herself as a Republican, the media and Democrats tried to portray her as an inexperienced rich girl who was trying to make it on her family name. *The Washington Press Democrat* wrote a profile piece titled "The Daughter Also Rises." Other Virginia pundits described her as a "Daddy's girl." One Democrat legislator claimed, "She is not known as Angela Parrish down here. She is known as 'Hanks's girl.'"

Hank Parrish passed away a few years before she had entered politics and decided to run for the state senate. She felt his presence on the campaign trail. Every day, people would come up to her and tell her all the great things that Hank had done for them in Richmond. They assumed she would be just as effective a legislator. One constituent said, "Hank always fought hard for us folks in Manassas and I know Angela will as well." Angela also felt Hank's presence at the capital. This was not hard, because on the wall of the House chamber was a giant painting of him as the speaker. In the painting he looked like an older version of Cary Grant—the salt and pepper hair, the big glasses, wearing a sports coat... One might even have thought Cary Grant had posed for the painting.

Cohen talked about the differences between Angela and Hank's first runs at public office. "Well, unlike Angela's, Hank's parents weren't rich and well known in Prince William County, and Hank didn't prosecute a high-profile case. Hank went to school at UVA and came back home to work in his dad's construction business. He married his sweetheart, Nicole Dogan, a woman also in politics, and with her blessing decided to run for the House of Delegates. He was a nobody, a guy fresh out of college."

He smiled at a memory. "Hank used to tell a funny story about his first race. He would go to any meeting in the county where he could speak. Didn't matter what it was, as long as he could get up and introduce himself. So, he discovered that the local Rotary Club had a Saturday meeting and they allowed anyone to speak. They just had to sign the registry and in that order people could speak for up to five minutes. Well, Hank went, sat in the front row, and waited for his turn. Well, one by one all these people got up to speak. It seemed to take forever. Finally, Hank got his turn. He got up to the podium, and he looked out and saw just one person in the audience! A dispirited Hank started to thank the guy for coming and listening to him speak, but then the guy suddenly stopped him and said, 'No need to thank me, I am the next speaker.'"

Cohen started laughing. "Hank loved to tell that story. But that is a big difference between him and Angela. She never has, or will, have to worry about drawing a crowd."

Despite being a slight underdog, Parrish won the race by a decent margin. The senate seat was the top target for both parties, and the most expensive state senate race in Virginia history. On election night, Republicans gathered at the Hampton Inn in Manassas, the traditional election night hotel for the Prince William County Republican Party. A Parrish volunteer described the night: "I arrived at 7 p.m. I knew I was at the right hotel by all the Parrish bumper stickers in the parking lot. The crowd continued to file in, people I recognized from the campaign trail, people I saw at events, rallies, people I saw at the Saturday lit drops, people that I recognized as friends of Angela. Everyone wants to think of themselves as friends of Angela's.

Elections Have Consequences

"Well, as the returns were coming in, the crowd kept growing. The ballroom, which seemed too big when I first arrived, became quite crowded. I could hear people talking about their day working the polls, what they thought of turnout, what they thought of Angela's and our chances. And throughout the night a swarm of people also continued to grow. They gathered by what I thought was a TV but was actually a projection of the State Board of Elections website on a monitor. From there you could see the returns and it showed the percentage of precincts in. For those that don't follow politics it's hard to explain the excitement. Watching the returns is like a rollercoaster. I guess in baseball the excitement grows with each inning, but nothing like this."

Well, Angela maintained the lead most of the evening, which kept people excited and happy. but at 65 percent of precincts reporting she lost the lead. You could literally hear a groan go through the crowd. The noise level dropped tremendously; it was like a punch in the gut. Many people, who were smiling from ear to ear a second earlier, now looked gloomy. But at 70 percent she was back up. The place went wild! And at 80 percent she was still up! At 90 percent, the crowd's excitement grew, then 95 percent we were still up! It got a little tighter, but still up. Still holding on! We might win!

"Everybody was glued to the monitor, and we were speculating where the five percent outstanding was? In our precincts or the Dems'? So much depended on where the outstanding vote was. Could the outstanding precincts be in Brentsville or Gainesville? It makes a world of difference.

"The tension was high. Any second 'our Angela' could be declared the winner. The crowd was packed in. Then, everybody's attention turned to a big TV screen. The announcer said, 'We are told that the decision desk is ready to make a call', and then there was a scene I will never forget for as long as I live. The graphic, which was a map of Virginia, zeroed in to Northern Virginia, focusing on our state senate district. I could make out the outline of Prince William County, and then a big picture of Angela appeared on the TV screen, a picture the networks had prepared for this night, no doubt, a picture of her in a business suit, with the Virginia flag in the background. It showed her beautiful face, with a flawless smile and a look of serenity and confidence. The screen said 'Projected Winner', but the thing that really drove the crowd wild was a big check mark next to her name. The cheering and yelling were amazing. This level of excitement could surpass the Super Bowl and World Series combined. In anticipation of victory the DJ played an upbeat song, which I will always associate with that victory night– the Avicii song, *Wake Me Up When It's All Over*."

Shortly after the network declared her to be the winner Angela received a concession call from her opponent. She then came down to the ballroom to address the crowd, telling them, "It's on to Richmond."

Her election sent shockwaves of fear through progressive Richmond. The media and Democrats knew they would have trouble with her. She was beautiful, wealthy, smart, came from a Virginia political dynasty, was conservative and fearless. She couldn't be intimidated, silenced or canceled.

***

Steve Cohen's strategy seemed to be to acknowledge that Hank Parrish was a "moderate Republican," but "his oldest daughter (Angela) is no moderate." Cohen joked at a Rotary Club speech in Staunton that "Angela is so far to the right of Hank that one might wonder if Hank and Phyllis Schlafly had an affair and produced a love child." The group laughed, but several days later a tape of Cohen's speech hit the media and for that joke, Cohen was forced to apologize and received a one-week suspension.

In the speech Cohen explained why he thought Hank Parrish, unlike Angela, was a moderate. "Speaker Parrish got through a major tax increase, which was designed to raise funds for transportation. Now it's true Parrish was a Northern Virginian and he knew the state needed more money for roads in his district, but Hank was the embodiment of moderation and compromise. That is the Virginia way. Today he would be described as a 'RINO', or what we used to call a 'Gypsy Moth.' His daughter, on the other hand, promises to vote against any and all tax increases."

Angela Parrish would cite the libertarian Thomas Jefferson, founder of the University of Virginia, as her political hero, even having his bust on her desk. And just like her hero, Jefferson, she believed, "A wise and frugal government which shall refrain men from injuring one another, shall otherwise leave them free to regulate their own pursuits of industry and improvement, and shall not take from the mouth of labor the bread it has earned."

Virginia Republicans believed that Parrish was a breath of fresh air, a purveyor of sunny populist conservatism. Cohen called her a "female George Allen." However, Parrish, like Allen, also had a penchant for loose talk. She claimed that northern Virginia was "occupied territory," and implied that the Russians might have colluded to elect a former Democrat president. She once claimed that gun control was "using both hands."

Once, in a heated argument, a state senator corrected her by pointing out that he once took a class with the great professor, Lawrence Seavers. Angela put her finger in the air, made circular motions, and said, "Whoopty doo." Cohen joked that it was probably the only time the phrase, "whoopty doo," was ever used on the Senate floor.

Parrish may have preferred to remain in the background, but that was not to be. Instant attention went to her, both from within the party, which needed leadership, and from the media, which hated her and knew they had to defeat her. As the dean of Virginia media, it was up to Cohen to take her down a peg or two.

Now Cohen was not actually a reporter. After about 20 years as a reporter he transitioned away from reporting and instead wrote "news analysis" columns, which really are just thinly disguised editorials. It is possible that his sources and quotes for many of his columns were pure fiction. He had tenure and a certain credibility, so he could get away with it, and it was probably easier for him to just make up the sources and quotes. In addition, the new publisher of the paper was politically pretty far to the left so Cohen was given free rein.

He had an unmistakable style. Probably in an effort to show off his knowledge of Virginia history, his formula was to take a contemporary political event and create a parallel with a past Virginia political event. But inevitably, in trying to make such a comparison, he would get all tied up in knots. The point would get so convoluted in the process that by the end of the column a reasonably intelligent person with a knowledge of Virginia history would conclude that it didn't make any sense. Fortunately for Cohen, reasonably intelligent people with a decent understanding of Virginia history don't read the *Richmond Daily Dispatch*.

Cohen and the paper's editors wanted to try to link Parrish, the rising Republican star, with Democrat segregationist Harry F. Byrd, Sr. Cohen found an idea for a possible hook for such a column. Harry Byrd's father Richard E. Byrd served as Speaker of the House of Delegates, and Angela Parrish's father Hank Parrish served as Speaker of the House of Delegates. With that fact, the one and only thing the two had in common, Cohen wrote a column titled "Birds of a Feather." He ignored the fact that Parrish was a different gender, a different political party, and that she didn't represent a rural part of the state. Parrish was a lawyer by profession, and Byrd was an apple farmer. But somehow they were "birds of a feather."

Cohen claimed that they both "appealed to an alienated white electorate." Cohen knew that was false. Byrd represented the Democrat elite; in Virginia that is the establishment. His supporters were not alienated. But the whole point of the article was the claim that Parrish and Byrd both harbored animosity towards black people. His evidence: Byrd wanted to shut down the schools to keep black kids out, and Parrish was opposed to Critical Race Theory being taught in schools. Byrd wanted to administer literacy tests for voting, and Parrish wanted a photo ID. Parrish was opposed to mail-in voting, and Cohen speculated that Byrd would also have opposed mail-in voting.

There were really no objective similarities, but the editors were happy and the flawed column appealed to the left-leaning readers of the *Daily Dispatch*.

Parrish chirped a response, "The strongest comparison between me and Byrd is that he once owned an apple farm, and I once went apple picking." She went on, "I used to respect the *Richmond Daily Dispatch*. It was a good paper when the Kilpatrick family published it. The new owners are to the publishing industry what Dan Snider is to NFL football."

3) Norton's Secret Crush

For one term, Norton and Parrish served in the state senate together, and upon meeting, Norton developed a crush on Parrish—a schoolboy-like crush. It did not go unnoticed by some members of the state senate. Fortunately for Norton, the press never caught on. Norton naturally found her to be attractive, which most men did, but he made the mistake of fawning and doting on her.

Democrats controlled the state Senate. The House, however, was in Republican hands. So while Norton was the Chairman of the Judiciary Committee, Parrish served on the committee as a freshman Republican member. Norton would always be doting on her, asking her if she needed anything, if the heater was on too high, if she needed any testimony repeated, was she able to see the screen, etc. "Senator Parrish, do you have a follow up question for this witness?" He even offered to give some of his time for questioning to her. Offering a member of the other party extra time is something that is never done.

The Democratic female senators got furious when he started doting on her, giving him icy stares. One day Norton politely asked, "Angela, I am headed to Chickens,"—the cafeteria in the basement of the Capitol—"can I get you anything?" She responded rhetorically, "Sure, a cup of coffee. I take it with just a bit of milk, and a cherry filled doughnut." She had no idea he would actually get it, but he did!

The committee met on Mondays, Wednesdays, and Fridays at 8 a.m. Norton would stop by Chickens and buy Parrish coffee and

Elections Have Consequences

a doughnut before every meeting. It became a ritual. Norton had a puppy dog crush, just as a schoolboy waits for a girl and the opportunity to offer to carry her books to her next class.

All this didn't go unnoticed by the other members of the committee. Even senate staff were starting to notice his schoolboy-like attention. Fortunately, Maddy Clack (Channel 4) and Steve Cohen did not notice.

It all came to head on a particular Wednesday in February. Norton made it to Chickens at five minutes until eight, so he figured he would have enough time to get Parrish's coffee and doughnut. However, the barista ran out of milk, so she would have to go back to the kitchen to get some. Norton had a split second to say "Forget it, I'll just get the coffee black" but he didn't, because he couldn't disappoint Angela, so he said he'd wait.

It took about four minutes, Norton nervously watched the second hand of the clock sweep around the oversized industrial clock above the cash register. After what seemed like an eternity the kitchen door swung open and the barista announced, "Got it." He finished making the coffee perfectly with a "little bit of milk."

Meanwhile in the committee room about 15 legislators sat around a horseshoe shaped table, with staffers sitting behind them, all waiting. The only chair empty was Norton's, the chairman of the committee, and they couldn't start without him.

Everyone was awkwardly looking around, some tapping their pens on the table looking bored. Then, suddenly the door opened, in walked Chairman Norton at 8:07, with a sheepish look on his face he scanned the room and walked over to Parrish's desk. Parrish reached her hand up to take the coffee but Norton awkwardly set the coffee and doughnut down on her desk. As he

Elections Have Consequences

extended his arm the napkins fell to the ground. Norton looked up, scanned the room and explained to the committee, "Sorry, the lady ran out of milk, so I waited for her to get more."

As he spoke everyone in the room just stared silently at him. He then realized that he needed to go to his seat and start the meeting. Stepping on the fallen napkins, he walked to his chair. The Democrat female members of the committee just glared at him, and then they exchanged looks with each other.

After the meeting they discussed the situation and determined that Norton needed to knock it off. They decided to ask Paula to speak to him, and she agreed. Paula realized that Parrish could be her husband's opponent in the race for governor and she couldn't afford to have him develop a soft spot for her. In virtually every race Norton ran in he threw mud at his opponent, and this would be the toughest race he'd ever have.

Paula was not in a good mood and decided to open the liquor cabinet early. Norton would not be in for a pleasant evening. Her usual routine was a drink with dinner, and a nightcap. But once she started drinking early, she could turn nasty pretty quick.

After dinner Paula brought up the subject, "I heard about your performance in the Judiciary committee meeting this morning."

"What are you talking about?"

"Holding up the meeting to get coffee for that Parrish girl."

"What's the big deal? I was going that way anyway, and so I waited a couple extra minutes to get a bit of milk for the coffee. I'm chairman of the committee, so the meeting doesn't start without me."

Paula snapped, "She can get her own fucking coffee! How is this going to look to all the other women in the room? You are engaging in lookism. If she were ugly, you would not get her a cup of coffee! Would you get a doughnut for State Senator Janice Lambert?"

Norton responded, "About the last thing Janice Lambert needs is a doughnut."

State Senator Janice Lambert represented Norfolk; she was in her early 60's and fairly heavy set. Some might say rotund. Lambert had served in the state Senate for about 30 years.

Norton conceded, "Okay, no more coffee trips for Parrish."

"Think of how dangerous this is. What if those three stooges"–she was probably referring to Maddy Clack, Steve Cohen and *Press Democrat* reporter Bhavna Agarwal–"noticed you making goo-goo eyes at Parrish, like a love struck Romeo? She may be your opponent for Governor! What if Reverend Brand noticed and publicly accused you of engaging in lookism? Do you want Brand to make an official announcement? To stand up in the pulpit of a church and say 'Ronnie Norton engaged in lookism!' Just think how devastating that would be to you and me, and our chances at making it to the Governor's mansion!"

Norton responded, "Fine, no more coffee, or any other attention to her. I will save all my sweetness for you and the ugly Democrat female legislators."

Paula smiled sarcastically, and said, "Excellent. Look, Democrats want someone tough to run against Parrish. They need to know you are tough enough to go for the jugular. They need to know that if it gets tough you have the stomach to drag her through the mud like she was in one of those Tough Mudder contestants, that contest that people used to enter in the 2000s. They don't need you at the Bar Association debate at the

Elections Have Consequences

Homestead Resort telling Parrish, 'Oh boy, Angela, don't you look pretty tonight,' or 'that's a pretty dress, is it blue or purple?'"

"I get your point. Why do you have to beat everything to death? I will do whatever it takes to win, the party knows that."

Paula calmed down, she reached her hand across the table to touch him and said, "Look, I may seem tough on you, but her election would allow the racists to retake control of the state. State Senator Parrish graduated from that right-wing college in Michigan, Hillsdale; she was there when Bush ran the school. He has said publicly that she is the greatest student he ever had. Hell, he probably wants her to replace him as president. If she is elected governor then that's possible. Actually, the day she's elected governor of Virginia is the day she becomes the frontrunner for the Republican nomination for president."

Norton sighed, "I know, I know."

"And she would empower zealots who want to destroy our public schools. Parrish was one of those right-wing nuts who pushed the lie that the Russians helped get former President Frost elected, and she claimed there was no insurrection on January 6th. A Capitol Hill police officer gave his life defending our democracy, and Parrish denies it."

"Yes, I know all that, but the social media companies have mostly erased those lies from the cloud. But okay, the only thing from now on I will do regarding her coffee is to spit in it if she's not looking."

"Hardy har har, you are so funny, really you are. A regular Lawrence O'Connell." She hadn't watched that late night comedian in years. "I'm going to bed. Perhaps you can show me what a true Virginia gentleman you are and do the dishes."

Elections Have Consequences

She took the last sip of her beer, dangling the can above her open mouth to get the last drop. Then she crumbled the can and slammed it on the table.

Norton loved Paula and was thankful she was his wife. He knew he would never be where he was now and be ultimately governor if it weren't for her. A very small percentage of women would be willing to be so supportive of a politician's life.

No one knew it, but there was a reason he seemed to notice and fuss over State Senator Angela Parrish. She reminded him of his first love, Mary Patricia, "Mary Pat." Ronnie first saw Mary Pat at Virginia Commonwealth College in Richmond, in a line to sign up for classes. He looked over her shoulder, and signed up for a couple of the classes she picked–neither of which he had to take–solely so he could see her again. He never told her that story. He just pretended he needed to take an art history class.

That summer session Mary Pat transferred from Mary Baldwin University. For Norton it would be a summer session he would never forget. There has always been a running debate in Virginia–it is literally known as "the great debate"–about which school has the prettier women, Mary Baldwin or Hollins. For generations Virginia men have been conducting this debate, arguing in bars and restaurants, school gyms, civic meetings and homes since the Civil War. For Norton, Mary Pat was ironclad proof that Mary Baldwin had the prettier girls.

Angela Parrish bore a striking resemblance to Mary Pat–her hair, her smile, her expressions, the same gleam in her brown eyes, her build, the way she laughed, the way she argued. Norton had no romantic interest in her and was happily married, but Angela struck a chord in him. She inadvertently brought back a flood of memories that Norton had long ago buried.

Ah, to be young and experience your first love, Norton thought. He realized that in all those years since his college days with Mary Pat, nothing has ever quite compared with the feeling. Little things he remembered from his youth. With youth comes a feeling of invincibility and energy, a feeling that all is possible. The senses are stronger, the desires stronger.

To be with Mary Pat was the greatest feeling of his young life; it would never be forgotten. They'd ride down Broad Street in his new Chrysler LeBaron convertible. Mary Pat wore big sunglasses, almost oversized–she claimed they were the same ones Carly Simon wore. She loved the wind blowing through her long brown hair, and she had a habit of putting her bare feet up on the dashboard. He never forgot the pink polish on her toenails.

Ronnie, like a lot of people, had a bad habit of speeding down Broad Street, so to get him to slow down Mary Pat promised him that every time they made a stop light, he would be allowed to lean over and kiss her. He'd stop at the light and say, "Okay, pay the toll." They'd kiss until the light turned green. Norton once bragged that he had earned a kiss at every light on Broad Street. Ah, to be young, Norton thought. To be young, with a pretty girl in your car. And not just any girl–a Mary Baldwin girl.

The game only applied to Broad Street, however, so Norton tried to take Broad Street as much as possible, even if there was a quicker way. Sometimes Norton would slow up and try to catch the red light, much to the chagrin of the people behind him. Mary Pat would laugh and say in her southern drawl, "I know what you're up to, Ronnie." She responded by tickling him because he thought the harder she tickled him the faster he'd go.

One day he got more daring. He stopped at a green light. No cars were behind them; it was a couple of blocks down from the famed Richmond department store Miller and Rhodes, or as the Richmonders pronounced it, "Millin Rhoads."

Looking in the rear-view mirror, Ronnie said, "No one's coming. Give me an extra kiss."

Mary Pat smiled. "Of course," and they kissed, while both keeping an eye on the rear-view mirror. Then cars crossed over two blocks behind them. Mary Pat broke the embrace. "Okay, let's go."

Ronnie, with his foot still on the brake, said, "Look, Mary Pat, we have enough time for one more kiss."

Mary Pat looked in the rear-view mirror. "No, Ronnie, we better go,"

Cars were getting closer. Ronnie explained an idea, "Look, Mary Pat, if I turn on the hazard lights, we can make love for hours. They'll just go around us. Oh, just think, Mary Pat, we can make love right here, on Broad Street! What a great story that'd be!"

Mary Pat became adamant. "Ronald Milsap Norton, go! Cars are coming!"

Norton sighed, thought for several seconds, and looked into the rear-view mirror. Cars were really starting to get close. Norton took another look and thought to himself, Wow they are really coming up fast. Ronnie broke the tension by ending the joke. He took his foot off the brake, accelerated, and crossed the intersection. Years later Norton commented that if he had waited another second longer they would have heard a "chorus of horns."

"Yikes, you could have gotten us killed! Are you out of your cotton-picking mind?" said Mary Pat.

In defense Ronnie claimed, "Babe, the hazard lights were on. People would have just gone around."

"I'm pretty sure they didn't put hazard lights on a car so you can stop in the middle of traffic and make out on a busy street. Ronnie Norton, I declare you have a habit of taking jokes too far."

Not to be denied the final word, Norton again responded mockingly, "Babe? Babe? The hazard lights were on. Okay? I'm telling you the cars would have just gone around us." He flashed a goofy "case closed" grin.

He drove her to her dorm, ten minutes away. There was nothing said between them, just silence. He pulled up to her dorm and turned to give her a goodbye kiss, but he only saw the back of her head. She hopped out of the car, slammed the door behind her, and walked briskly into her building.

Whenever Mary Pat chastised Ronnie, she would use both names: "Ronnie Norton." If she was really mad it was "Ronald Milsap Norton." She could be blunt with him sometimes. If she wasn't having fun on a date, she would tell him, "Ronnie, I'm bored," or "Ronnie, this is so lame. Take me back to my dorm." He did all he could to impress her.

When she flirted with him, her southern accent grew stronger; when she was mad at him her southern accent disappeared. They even had their own song, Jackson Browne's 1982 hit "Somebody's Baby." He heard it and he thought of her—he still does.

He could still remember the time they were cruising down Broad Street with the convertible top down, and the song came on. He turned it up. The wind was blowing through Mary Pat's long brown hair, the late afternoon sun was coming down. He looked at her and thought that Jackson Browne must have written the song with her in mind:

"Cause when the cars and the signs and the street lights light up the town,

She's got to be somebody's baby;

She must be somebody's baby, she's so fine."

Many years had passed since those summer days, but all those memories would come back to him whenever he saw Angela Parrish. The very sight of her would become a distraction even in a committee meeting or on the senate floor. Angela had the face of Mary Pat; the sight of her would take him back. He thought of all those times he had met Mary Pat after class. They had a routine; after her 10 o'clock class, they would rendezvous near a bench on the quad. It would be the first time that he would see her during the day, so it was a most special moment for him, something he always looked forward to. In fact, it was the very first thing he thought of when he woke up each and every morning.

Norton could never forget that feeling of waiting by the bench, too nervous to sit down, so he would stand and watch as classes emptied at the top of the hour. The quad would rapidly fill up with students going off to their next class. Norton would keep his eyes peeled in anticipation of the sight of Mary Pat: how her hair would be done, what she'd be wearing. Sometimes she wore dresses, other times skirts. Sometimes she'd be in a casual mood and wear jeans. He concluded that once a man starts to notice what a woman is wearing, he is falling in love.

Elections Have Consequences

No matter how many times he'd wait for her he'd still get that feeling—the first love, butterflies in the stomach feeling of youth. As she spotted him and got close her face would light up with a smile. She would usually indicate how her day was going while walking towards him. She would smile sometimes, or she would pout, or make a face if it was a really rough morning.

He fell in love with Mary Pat that semester. He still remembered everything about her, every odd quirk. How she would get hot even on a mild summer day, how she liked pizza with banana peppers on it, how she'd chew Big Red cinnamon flavored gum. He never forgot that scent when he kissed her, and he remembered how at the end of the summer she left him for another guy.

Angela Parrish brought back all of his memories of Mary Pat, and of those youthful, carefree days. When he looked into Angela's brown eyes, he saw his youth, a youth that was spent and irretrievably lost. Norton concluded that a human heartbeat might last many, many, many decades, but youth won't last much more than a couple, and all the wisdom and experience acquired in life can never bring back the happiness of youth.

4) Norton vs. Parrish: the Battle of the Century

The Norton-Parrish battle became the most expensive gubernatorial election in Virginia history. Money poured in from all across the country. One main reason for the national attention: it was an off year. There were only two governor's races, in New Jersey and Virginia, that November. The national media focused an enormous amount of coverage on this race, and with Bush in the White House, they were determined to help get a Democrat elected in the Old Dominion.

The two major news organizations covering Virginia politics are the *Richmond Daily Dispatch* and *The Washington Press Democrat*. The Daily Dispatch's unofficial motto is "There aren't always two sides to every story" and the Press Democrat's is "Democracy dies from lies." Both papers believe that false or misleading information must be kept out of circulation, lest people believe false information, and adopt erroneous views.

They both provided heavy coverage of Angela's state Senate race. The owner of the Press Democrat, Jeff Amondoza, summed up the view of his paper and that of most in the mainstream media: "We do believe in freedom of speech, but we also believe that the information shared by the public needs to be correct. And to the extent that false information gets out it weakens our democracy."

Traditionally the *Richmond Daily Dispatch* had been a conservative newspaper, but when the Kilpatrick family sold it, the paper lost its conservative edge. The paper drifted to the left editorially. Accelerating the leftward drift was the fact that many of the reporters were young, woke millennials.

Another reason for the paper's leftward move deals was marketing. As circulation numbers declined the paper had to appeal to a younger demographic to survive. Younger meant more progressive, more woke. At first the paper's leftward tilt was limited to the editorial pages, but then it extended to the reporting. The editors told Cohen to move to the left, "The further the better." Being the tool that he was, he said, "Will do!"

The other main newspaper, *The Washington Press Democrat*, didn't have to worry about finances. Amondoza accepted the paper as a loss leader. The paper provided him a platform.

The two giant social media companies were Chirp and Bolshebook. Tom Andrews, a billionaire and a prominent Democrat donor, created Chirp, and Bolshebook was founded by a Russian immigrant. He and his friends started the company while they were in college. The title was aspirational. Bolshe comes from the Russian word for majority. They hoped one day to get a majority of the people on their site. The company was run by a board known as the Politburo. This board also decided what content would be allowed and what must be throttled.

***

In her one term in the State Senate Parrish proved to be a solid conservative, voting for tax cuts, against increases in regulations. The conservative Family Foundation gave her their highest rating. The progressive Moms United to Save Virginia gave her an F. The most high-profile vote dealt with the question of amending the constitution with the equal rights amendment (ERA). Parrish led the opposition. One of her arguments was that the amendment was unnecessary since the constitution already guaranteed equal rights in the 14th amendment.

In their time together in the Senate Norton and Parrish did see eye to eye on a few issues. In fact, Norton co-sponsored two of her proposals. Parrish had an idea for a rule change to the Virginia state Senate. She wanted to adopt a filibuster, similar to the filibuster rule used by the United States Senate, enabling a minority of Virginia State Senators to be able to hold up and shape major legislation. Parrish told the Washington Press Democrat that she believed a filibuster at the state level would make it harder for bad legislation to get through. In addition, she believed that it would force the majority to get some input from the minority, and such cooperation would lead to better, more bipartisan legislation and help prevent tyranny.

The media denounced her for wanting to bring back a "relic of Jim Crow, and place it in the Virginia State Senate." They claimed that her underlying motive was to employ the filibuster to stop future state civil rights legislation.

However, Norton also backed the idea, but for political reasons. He knew it would not be adopted, but the business community liked the idea of a filibuster. The Main Street business community believed that a filibuster would guarantee that Virginia's right to work law would always be protected. Norton wanted to please the business community and keep his pro-business reputation; his lifetime chamber of commerce rating was a "C plus," higher than any other Democrat in either House of the Virginia General Assembly. So he came out in favor of it.

But the media did not accuse him of wanting to "bring back a relic of Jim Crow." In fact, they seemed to ignore his cosponsorship of the proposal. The filibuster issue would come up later in the gubernatorial campaign.

Norton also supported Parrish's proposal to limit future governors' emergency powers. Norton hated his predecessor's decision to shut down the state over a flu virus for several weeks. Norton agreed that the legislative branch would need to have a say in future emergency cases.

***

In his regular column, Cohen outlined the candidates' backgrounds and pointed to some similarities, one being they were both northern Virginians and had some common regional interests. He also had one column, "Parrish vs. Norton: All Roads Run Through Tysons Corner." Cohen pointed out, "If it weren't for that little hamlet of Tysons Corner, these two would probably not be on the ballot." Cohen reminded readers, "Norton's parents moved to Virginia from Western Pennsylvania to work in construction, which was plentiful because of Tysons Corner's ongoing developments. The work was there. Without Tysons Corner, the Nortons probably wouldn't have moved to Virginia. Hank Parrish owned a construction company which made millions on building projects in Tysons Corner. As a member of the House of Delegates Hank Parrish helped facilitate Tysons Corner's growth." Cohen went on, "For good or ill, and I think many conservatives would say ill, Tysons Corner will have changed the state forever, no matter who wins this election."

Most political consultants and pundits expected the Norton campaign would spend lots of time and money trying to tie Parrish to the unpopular, at least in Virginia, president and fellow Republican Bush. Surprisingly, they didn't. A few reasons: first, the

Elections Have Consequences

Norton campaign was concerned that trying to link Parrish, a woman, with President Bush, a man many Virginians viewed as a misogynist, might turn off independent women voters. Secondly, it seemed awkward when Norton brought up Bush. His line, "If you like Bush you will love Parrish," just didn't seem quite right.

But primarily, they didn't need to bring Bush up because Parrish had a record in the state Senate, a record that they believed offered plenty of lines of attack. She also had plenty of her own statements that they felt they could use.

Parrish had Virginia's most prominent Republican campaign strategist, Mark S. Boyd, running her campaign, and Norton had his trusted Steve Beaman at the helm of his. For Beaman this was a dream come true, a chance to go up against the Republican Party's top campaign strategist. Beaman thought defeating Mark S. Boyd would be the perfect capstone to a political consulting career. Beaman told Norton, "Me going up against Boyd, why is it like Patton going up against Rommel?" In addition to Beaman, Norton gave Reverend Brand the position of campaign co-chair.

In his mid-60's, Boyd had acquired a record of statewide wins unmatched at least in recent Virginia history. Cohen claimed "Boyd elected more candidates in Virginia than anyone in history, with the exception of Harry Byrd. If we had a hall of fame of political strategists he'd be inducted on the first ballot."

Boyd possessed an amazing knowledge of Virginia politics. He could cite figures from past races, turnout numbers in key precincts and counties, demographic information, turnout rates for different age groups, and more.

Boyd, a former UVA offensive lineman, stood a lanky 6'2," with big blond hair. For a short period, he tried to grow a beard, but it was blond and scraggly. The story behind the beard was that Boyd, a workaholic, was so busy that he didn't have the ten minutes available to shave.

Fortunately, his wife talked him into shaving it. In the 1980's, while working on a congressional campaign another staffer nicknamed Boyd "Chewbacca," after the Star Wars character. No one ever called him "Chewbacca" or "Chewy" to his face, but it seems no one ever used his first name either. Everyone, with the exception of his wife and kids, called him Boyd.

Cohen, a longtime friend, said, "It's as if he doesn't have a first name. It's no disrespect. We all call him Boyd and he never corrects us."

Boyd, a whiz with numbers and very analytical, could be rather shy. Sometimes he'd seem to mumble and didn't always look people right in the eye when he answered a question, but he knew everything about Virginia politics. Cohen described him as possessing "an encyclopedic knowledge of state politics."

He had never run a statewide campaign for someone as young as Parrish; in fact, he had a daughter who was about the same age. Ironically, Boyd started his career as an aide to Delegate Hank Parrish. Hank liked and trusted Boyd. He even left his old office desk to Boyd when he retired.

Cohen said, "I never met anyone who loved Virginia politics more than Boyd." Cohen laughed. "Some people say there is more to life than Virginia politics, but I doubt Boyd would agree. I was at a Gilmore Christmas party several years ago, and I saw Lawrence Seavers and Boyd standing by a punch bowl discussing the reasons why Wyatt Durette lost the gubernatorial election in 1985! They were probably the only two people in the world who would think about that." Cohen laughed again. "I joked with Boyd that when he dies, he'd want his ashes spread on that hill in Wakefield so for an eternity he'd make every shad planking." Cohen went on, "Boyd said that was okay with him, but he'd want some of his ashes to be left for Chancellorsville, the scene of Lee's greatest victory."

Conventional political wisdom, and Vegas, considered Norton to be the overwhelming favorite, especially with the unpopular Republican Bush in the White House. Traditionally the party out of the White House won the governor's race in Virginia the following year, and with a Republican in the White House threatening to drain the swamp, a swamp which included much of northern Virginia, odds favored the Democrats even more.

One Virginia political pundit described the nomination of Parrish as "a major league team calling up a top prospect to pitch in the World Series." He continued, "She has the potential to be a political star, but she is only 36! Only been in the state Senate for one term."

Steve Cohen said he believed that she was the youngest major party candidate for governor in Virginia history. "Marshall Coleman, if memory serves me correctly, was 39 when he got the Republican nomination in the 1980's. So, she broke Coleman's record for youth. Frankly, I never thought that would be broken."

Lt. Governor Morrison, perhaps sensing this would be a Democrat year, decided to pass on the nomination for governor and deferred to Parrish. Many in the Virginia Republican Party, after her successful DC sniper prosecution, thought Parrish would be a great candidate to run for attorney general, but she deferred to conservative Fairfax lawyer John Q. Adams. Four years earlier he had almost won. It was close enough that there was a recount, so naturally the party felt he was owed a second shot.

Parrish and Morrison were the two biggest stars in the Virginia Republican party. Morrison, however, had already been elected once statewide, and for Parrish this was her first statewide race. Many in the party urged Parrish to adopt the slogan "Making History, Making Sense." This slogan was used by Democrat women for years, and since Parrish could be the first woman governor in history it would be appropriate. Instead, Parrish went with the Henry Howell slogan "I'll Keep the Big Boys Honest." The "Making History, Making Sense" slogan ended up being used by Democrat Attorney General candidate Deb Foster.

Angela and Deb Foster were the two history making candidates. Angela, if elected, would be the first woman Virginia governor, and Deb Foster, if elected, would be the first transgendered attorney general. Deb grew up as Dan. He went to UVA and played on the LaCross team, even being elected team captain. He became a successful attorney and started a family, but then transformed into Deb. In addition to changing her gender Deb also changed political affiliation, becoming a Democrat. But, as a qualification, Deb claimed to be a "Joe Manchin style Democrat."

Cohen remarked of Foster, "She went from being a man to a woman, and a Republican to a self-described 'Joe Manchin Democrat.' Deb has got to be the most confused person on earth."

Well, for this comment Cohen got hauled into his editor's office and told to issue an apology. It is politically incorrect to call a transgendered person confused. Cohen's editor explained the politically correct rule. "It is like papal infallibility. The Pope can't be confused regarding matters of doctrine, and a transgendered individual can't be confused when it comes to their gender choice. If you allow the possibility that trans men and women are confused, then you undermine the whole movement. We can't do that!" His editor then got emotional, raised his voice and said, "And as long as I am editor, we will not do that at this paper."

Cohen took to Chirp:

"I wish to express my profound regret for my comment that Deb Foster was confused. I didn't mean to undermine her personal choice to transition to a woman. I simply meant her transfer from the Republican Party to the Democrat Party was confusing. That was simply my opinion on her political choice, not her choice of a gender selection."

***

Traditionally, on the Friday before the major party nominates their candidates, *The Washington Press Democrat* runs a profile piece on each candidate. At about 2000 words, the lengthy piece starts on the front page and jumps into the center of the A section and covers two full pages, complete with a few old pictures. The paper gave the assignment to their chief Virginia political correspondent, Bhavna Agarwal.

Since Norton was the first to be nominated, he got the first spread in early June. It focused on his law career and his life growing up in Fairfax County with middle class parents. It talked a lot about Norton's mom and her determination that he make something of his life. His mother, Janice Norton, grew up poor in southwestern Pennsylvania. She was determined that her son would go to college and become a success.

The piece also focused on Norton's time as a member of the

Board of Supervisors and his time in the House of Delegates and in the State Senate. For the most part they skipped over his time at VCC, but did talk about his work as a missionary in Guatemala, which he took a semester at VCC off to do, and his days in law school.

On the eve of the Republican convention the Press Democrat ran a profile piece on Parrish with the title "The Daughter Also Rises." It covered Parrish's career, from her work in the Prince William County Commonwealth Attorney's office, to her successful prosecution of the DC snipers, to her upset win for the state Senate.

Argarwal's piece also touched on Parrish's childhood, and growing up in a political family. She interviewed friends and family and even tracked down a man named Clark Jones. He claimed, and Argarwal verified through numerous sources, that he was Angela's high school sweetheart. In addition, a photo in the class yearbook confirmed their relationship. The senior class voted Clark and Angela—the caption lists her as Angie—as the cutest couple. The picture from the yearbook of the two of them ran in the article. She still looked about the same, except in the picture her hair seemed a little poofier, and she didn't have her confident politician's smile. That was yet to emerge. Rather, in the picture she had a hesitant smile. It was perhaps the smile of a young woman who had just had her braces removed.

Jones said, "I met Angela at Stonewall Jackson, specifically I met her in our 4th period math class. We hit it off and started hanging out. Well, one Saturday, we were at an event during the afternoon and I needed to take her back to her house so she could change her clothes before we had to go to a dinner party. I remember driving to her house; it wasn't far from downtown Manassas. To get there I went through a nice subdivision and as I got closer to her house I noticed that the houses got further apart. I drove up this hill and at the top was the Parrish house. It looked to be on two lots, a good bit of distance from their neighbors. They had a flag pole out front with a big American flag. I drove up the driveway.

"Well, she asked if I wanted to come in and meet her father. Her mother was not home, but she said 'Daddy is', so I said sure. Their house was nice. Once you walked in the door you could tell they were well off, yet the furnishings were still modest. They had lots of trinkets, things you might find in gift shops at historical sites, and historical photos on the walls. I remember a painting of Washington at Valley Forge. They had a crucifix on the wall, and a collection of busts of famous Americans. It seems her father collected busts.

"Angie went to change and I sat in the kitchen talking with Speaker Parrish. It was not just light banter; he asked some probing questions, and while I responded he seemed to look me over. It was eerie. He just looked at me with a blank expression on his face when I spoke." Jones laughed, "I was getting rather nervous, and as we kept talking I kept thinking come on Angie, come back and save me. I kept thinking, my God, how long does it take to change an outfit?

"Well, after about ten minutes, maybe the longest ten minutes of my young life, I could hear someone coming down the steps, and I thought, thank God. Angie came into the kitchen. I jumped up and said, 'Shall we go?' and as we were walking out the door, Speaker Parrish and Angie embraced. He kissed her on the cheek, and we left. But I knew he hugged her in front of me as a way of saying 'She is still mine; you better watch yourself, buddy.'" Jones laughed.

The two went their separate ways for college, but got back together when they both went to UVA for law school. Jones said they started dating again, but it didn't last long. It seemed that they were different people four years removed from high school. Jones ended up getting married and having three kids. At the time of the election he lived in Ashburn.

A few years after the election campaign, Bhavna Argarwal's profile articles would come under fire with charges of her lack of thoroughness, especially in her article on Ronnie Norton.

***

Parrish was nominated in June at the Richmond Coliseum, the first female Virginia Republican gubernatorial nominee ever, and the first of either party since Mary Sue Terry. Boyd managed the convention perfectly. He produced a great video montage of Parrish, showing her in action as a state senator, pictures of her at UVA, and a touching picture of her as a girl holding the family Bible as her father was being sworn in as Speaker of the House, with the familiar Houdon statue of George Washington in the background. Parrish was to accept the nomination and give her speech at 2 p.m.

Boyd was nervous, more like an expectant father than a campaign manager. He went to her room at the Richmond Marriott to give her final instructions, and as he got in the elevator on the way to her suite suddenly his mind reeled back to the moment he first met her. The vision became as clear as if it happened yesterday, but it was decades ago, when he was an aide to Speaker Parrish. Angela came down to visit her father. At that time she was a student at Stonewall Jackson High School, just a kid. That's where he first saw her, sitting in her father's office. Hank said to Boyd, "I'd like to introduce you to my daughter Angela. Now take good care of her when she is here in Richmond."

Boyd thought, *I doubt Hank could have dreamed this. I'm taking care of her all right; I'm running her campaign for Governor.* Boyd felt a thrill go right up his spine. He saw that he had goosebumps. He muttered, "Yes, Hank, I will do the best I can to take care of her."

He got to her room and was surprised to see her wearing a red dress. "I thought we agreed you were going to wear the purple dress?"

"I think red is appropriate." She joked, "Boyd, I was thinking—there will be about 20,000 people there, virtually all Republicans, so I can't go wrong with red."

He smiled and said, "I guess that makes sense." He added, "This is the largest state convention since Obenshain's in '78. I was there for that convention. I will never forget hearing that crowd, and that chant, 'Obenshain! Obenshain!' The loudest crowd I ever heard. And like '78, the Coliseum is packed today!"

"This will be the biggest crowd I ever addressed." She quipped, "Bigger than the Manassas Rotary Club meeting last Thursday." She then recited a line from Kipling, "If you can talk to crowds and keep your virtue, or walk with kings nor lose a common touch, if all men count with you, but none too much."

"Well, do it just like we practiced, and remember to smile. You have some tough lines in the speech, but you mustn't come across as angry or harsh. Also, keep a good tempo, and don't step on the punch line. Tell the joke and pause for the crowd to react before moving on with the next sentence."

As Boyd headed towards the door, he joked, "Angela, I really think you should take out the line 'Extremism in the defense of liberty is no vice and moderation in the pursuit of justice is no virtue.' It didn't really work for Goldwater."

She laughed and responded in kind, " I've taken that line out and replaced it with 'Ask not what your country can do for you, ask what you can do for your country.'" They both laughed.

Boyd embraced her; the laughter stopped. He looked at her and tried to come up with some pithy, profound final words, but simply said, "Good luck, Angela," and then walked out the door.

Her motorcade of about seven cars drove to the Coliseum. However, she had one stop to make before she entered. There was a group of well-wishers from the Chesapeake Republican Party waiting. Angela had agreed to greet them before she gave her nomination speech. So, an area was roped off for them to wait outside. Her motorcade was scheduled to stop for her to get out and thank the volunteers and take some pictures before heading into the coliseum. A GOP activist and mother of three from Chesapeake brought her kids up to see Angela—most activists simply called her Angela.

The mother described the scene later: "The motorcade suddenly stopped. Angela just seemed to bounce out of the backseat and came over to talk to us. She shook hands all around and thanked us for coming, then she told us about her last trip to Chesapeake and how much she appreciated our help. She saw my six year old son Billy with his Angela sticker, and asked him how old he was, where he went to school, and things like that. Well, Billy just stared at her, and you know kids can ask the oddest questions, well, he looked at her and said, 'What color are your eyes?' Well, everyone who was gathered around just laughed. My God, I was so embarrassed, but Angela took it great. She laughed and shrugged her shoulders and said, 'I really don't know.' Then she bent down, got right in front of Billy, and she opened her eyes really wide, and said, 'What color do they look like?' Billy laughed and said they looked brown. Angela stood up and said, 'Well, then they must be brown.' Everyone laughed.

"We all wished her luck; people were telling her to keep fighting, don't let the lying media get you down, more people were yelling 'We love you Angela, we love you,' and she responded, 'I love you too.' Another guy said, 'Give 'em hell, Angela!' Angela laughed and said, 'I will!' Then she got in her limo and the cars headed into the coliseum."

She continued, "You mark my words: one day she will be president!" The others around her cheered. "After she serves as governor, look out, she can be president, she will be president, the first woman president!" She added, "Virginia is the mother of presidents, and Virginia will produce the first woman president."

***

Boyd went to a skybox practically in the rafters of the old Coliseum to watch the speech alone. It had become a ritual he developed years ago. He had watched five Republican nominations from there, always alone. There was nothing in the box but a table and a folding chair. Like a gymnastics coach watching his star protégé in the Olympics, he was almost too nervous to watch.

Delegate Christopher Killian of Hannover, a law school classmate of Angela's, officially nominated her, and she then walked on to stage promptly at 2 p.m. The crowd went wild, with nearly 20,000 people standing. Boyd's adrenaline was running high. Angela walked around the stage waving while cameras were going off in the darkened Coliseum with thousands of bursts of light. Angela seemed genuinely touched when she spotted the Prince William County delegation on the floor holding up big banners that read, "Prince William County: Home of Angela Parrish," and "Stonewall Jackson Raiders for Parrish."

At 2:10 she stepped up to the podium. The crowd would still not quiet down. Boyd nervously muttered, "Just start speaking, Angela, just start speaking and they will quiet down." Angela finally began. A few minutes into the speech Boyd finally relaxed. He thought, *She is doing great. My God, she is beautiful; she was right to go with the red dress.* He thought for a second *She is almost the same age as my daughter. I must be old.*

He muttered as she was speaking, "Watch the tempo, watch the tempo," and whispered almost as a prayer, "Just like we practiced, Angela, just like we practiced." Boyd paced throughout the speech, never once sitting down. He knew the speech almost by heart, so he knew one of her best lines was coming up. He said out loud, "Don't step on the punchline, don't step on the punchline." Pleased with her delivery, he yelled, "Yes, yes, you got it, perfect!"

Parrish accepted her nomination and acknowledged that the Democrats also had a nominee, declaring, "Now the battle is joined." She promised a tireless statewide campaign from "The marshes of Tidewater, to the rugged deer-infested terrain of the Cumberland Gap, to the tobacco fields of Southside, to the bustling suburbs of Northern Virginia, to Bristol and that lonely street, where one state ends and Virginia begins."

Angela talked about her career as a prosecutor, how under Democrats the state was getting soft on crime, claiming that Democrat commonwealth attorneys were refusing to charge illegal aliens with felonies so they couldn't be deported. She claimed that families had to work longer to pay their state taxes than ever before. She predicted that Democrat and Norton's economic policies would lead to higher unemployment and reduced economic opportunities. She joked, "Businesses will be leaving our state at a faster rate than kids will be able to move out of their parents' basements."

The crowd loved the line. She stated that Norton's woke social justice policies would destroy public education in Virginia. "As governor, I will keep political indoctrination out of our classroom. To the social justice warriors currently running our schools I say— Hands off our kids. Your days of indoctrination will soon be over."

She continued, "For many, the public school system is a jobs program. A boondoggle, where in most school systems 12 percent of the employees are not teaching children. This boondoggle grows as new positions are created. The latest innovation is the school equity office. Their job is to advance the ideological conformity of the school system. We must do all we can to eliminate such offices. I promise, as governor, I will."

Angela went on, "Public schools must compete. As it stands, schools get the students and the money that comes with them, whether the school is good or not. We must turn it around; the money follows the student to the best schools. Now, I believe in local control of schools, and what's one step to achieve that? As governor, I will fight to abolish the State Board of Education. They have too much power. Local schools, principals, and teachers don't need orders from bureaucrats in Richmond.

"As far as privileges go, we are all privileged to live in the greatest state in the union, where anyone—black, white, yellow or brown, male or female—can go as far as our drive, discipline, imagination and skills will carry us."

Parrish raised her arm high above her head and thundered, "I am a proud daughter of Virginia. I will make no apologies. I will oppose every name change of every school, every school nickname, every street. I will oppose every effort to remove our statues, monuments, historical markers and plaques." She dropped her arm on the last syllable, just as the crowd rose to their feet.

She continued, with everyone standing in the coliseum, "To the kids who try to attack our monuments and destroy public property, I say your parents may not believe in spankings, but I do." The crowd laughed. "And I will prosecute you. If you try to desecrate our monuments, you will be grounded, and forced to take your time out in a jail cell."

The crowd chanted, "Ang L Ah! Ang L Ah!" The crowd wouldn't stop; all her attempts to quiet them down failed. Angela then stepped away from the podium and walked the stage. The crowd broke into a chorus. Half the crowd would yell, "Who can?" then the other half would respond, "Angie can!" This went on for a few minutes, then the coliseum crowd quieted down. Angela returned to the podium and resumed her speech.

"We have to let the nation hear the voice of Virginia, the voice of freedom, just like it heard that voice over 200 years ago." Angela asked, "What Virginian doesn't take pride in Patrick Henry and his words? He spoke to an assembly in the Old Church, just a few blocks from where we stand today, that old white church on a hill. His words launched hundreds of revolutions against tyrannies all over the world. I still remember those words by heart, words which were taught to me in a Virginia school as a little girl. "Is life so dear, or peace so sweet, as to be purchased at the price of chains and slavery? Forbid it, Almighty God! I know not what course others may take; but as for me, give me liberty, or give me death!'"

The crowd jumped to its feet, and they again chanted "Angela, Angela, Angela..." Boyd, caught up in the enthusiasm, thought, *Well, we're not in Manassas anymore so they can call her Angela.*

"Our liberty and freedom are under assault today, just as much, if not more, than they were when Patrick Henry gave that speech. Today it's our battle, our challenge. Will we fight?"

Pandemonium swept over the crowd. People were yelling different answers; some yelling yes, some were pessimistic saying that people wouldn't fight, they were all politically correct.

Once Angela got the crowd's attention back, she waved her hand and thundered, "Of course we will! We are Virginians; freedom and liberty are in our blood. The social justice warriors won't win. Liberty will win."

The crowd roared, "Angela, Angela..." Boyd closed his eyes and thought back to the 1978 convention, when he was a young Republican volunteer. He tried to test his memory, was the chant as loud as "Obenshain Obenshain"? He opened his eyes and muttered, "My God, it is. They love her as much!"

She left the text of her speech to add another issue. Ordinarily Boyd got nervous when she left the prepared text, but he felt this was fine. Parrish said, "Norton and the Democrats say no on the requirement to show a government issued photo ID to vote." The crowd booed.

Parrish continued, "They say it is inconvenient, to have to show an ID before you are given a ballot. I don't know about you, but I will happily take the inconvenience of showing my license in exchange for an honest election."

The crowd roared, "Ang L Ah, Ang L Ah!"

Boyd thought her performance was flawless; the crowd reaction confirmed his belief. He muttered, "She can win, she can win." He felt pure joy when the balloons dropped, so overcome with joy and pride in his young protege Angela that he sat down and wept.

The crowd loved the speech, but perhaps the most touching moment came at the end when Angela's family came on stage to join her. The crowd went wild when they saw Mrs. Parrish, Hank's widow, come out onto the stage. She hugged Angela and spoke into her ear, "I still remember telling your father that a daughter can grow up to be governor."

Angela then took to the floor shaking hands, while the sound system played the recessional hymn, "When the Swallows Homeward Fly," her fathers favorite hymn. The crowd remained on their feet. The spotlight followed her while the delegates quietly stood, watching their new leader, tears in the eyes of old and young. As soon as she received the Party's nomination, the state police formally assigned her a security detail. They gave her the code name "Heartbreaker."

There was some international press covering the convention. The British magazine *The Economist* described Parrish as "Donald Trump in high heels." The German magazine *Der Spiegel* ran a satirical cover with pictures of Angela Parrish and Angela Merkel and the headline, "Can the world handle two Angelas?" France's largest paper, Le Monde, declared Parrish to be a thoroughly European candidate because, they reasoned, "She borrowed her looks from Segolene Royal, her ideology from Margaret Thatcher, and her zeal from Joan of Arc."

According to the first poll taken after her nomination, Parrish was down by 15 points. Mark S. Boyd had his work cut out for him. He told senior campaign staffers, "She's a diamond in the rough." They had to keep her focussed and get her to bite her tongue on certain things—she tended to go on a rant at times—and to make her more likable. He told all campaign staff who traveled with her, "Keep her on message. Every day must be a rant-free day. Don't let her start claiming the schools are going to ban Dr. Seuss or something like that." Boyd jokingly referred to those occasions as "Angelarants" or sometimes an "Angierant."

The Parrish campaign started their caravan across Virginia, with Parrish driving across the state in a gray Chevrolet Traverse. (Boyd convinced her to put the red GMC pickup truck in the garage.) They had an entourage of press and campaign staff behind her. The caravan was known as the "Angela Express." They would stop in towns across the state and sleep in economy motels at night. Angela didn't need much sleep; she'd be back at it at the crack of dawn. Boyd rode with the press in the RV. The reporters were dazzled by Boyd's knowledge of the state. Every time they crossed into another county, Boyd would tell them all about the history of the county, its economic status, its voting history, and so forth.

To the young reporters, Boyd was like a knowledgeable uncle. Some even started calling him "Uncle Boyd" or "Professor Boyd." He didn't seem to mind. When the caravan entered a politically favorable country Boyd got excited. He'd perk up from his seat and yell, "Friends welcome to Parrish country! I guarantee we'll win big; we'll get at least 65 percent here."

Elections Have Consequences

The campaign made sure every reporter got some time to talk to Angela. At each stop a different reporter would get to ride shotgun with Angela in the Traverse. They rotated the entire press corps through that front passenger seat.

A campaign staffer sat in the backseat recording all conversations, so the media couldn't misquote her. At night in his hotel room, Boyd listened to some of the conversations. It was his bedtime routine. He'd lay in bed listening to the conversations until he fell asleep.

Angela could be very charming when she wanted to be. She got to know each member of the press. At one pit stop on the road, she bought coffee and donuts for everyone and passed them out to the press bus. Cohen joked, "Is that an attempt to buy us?"

Angela quipped, "No, Steve you were bought a long time ago, and for a lot less." Angela said it with a smile; everyone laughed. Cohen was in such a good mood he didn't seem to mind the dig, even one that had more than a little truth to it.

There was one thing the campaign didn't mention publicly. President Bush had called Parrish on a few occasions to offer advice and encouragement. The day she was nominated he called to congratulate her. "I caught the speech on CSPAN; it was beautiful. You are off to a great start," he told her.

And once when the caravan was just outside Danville, Boyd was informed through a text from the White House that the president wanted to speak with her. The campaign made an excuse that they needed to pull over in Danville. It was really to get a secure phone, but they told the press the reason for the stop was to deal with a "mechanical issue."

On the caravan the campaign got excellent footage and produced a series of commercials, titled, "On the Road with

Parrish." In these commercials she spoke on different issues while driving, with the cameraman in the passenger seat. The campaign even had a little fun by releasing a series of outtakes or bloopers. One of these had her talking, and being so deep into making a point that she missed her exit. The staffer in the back seat finally got her attention. Angela stopped speaking, looked into the rearview mirror, and said, "I missed the exit?" Then she exclaimed "Ah, (expletive)!" They did bleep out the word she used. But the campaign was having fun, and Angela was in her element.

The other aspect of Angela that the campaign played up was her love of the outdoors and shooting. She was an avid hunter and gun collector. The campaign decided to use a shotgun as a symbol, a symbol of cleaning up Richmond. Boyd described how her most famous ad was created. "It was by accident, really. We were getting shots of her shooting her rifle. Angela joked and said maybe she should bring this with her to Richmond after the election. Well, everyone laughed. And we said, let's work that into a commercial."

The first series of campaign ads ran in July, one with her outdoors, presumably hunting or target shooting, casually dressed in an L.L. Bean flannel shirt, while talking about the issues. The announcer said, "Send Angela Parrish to clean up Richmond." Then a pause. "She might even bring her shotgun."

It went over big with the focus group. A female candidate had promised to take charge from the big boys in Richmond, so with the good early response the campaign ran another ad, this one showing Parrish shooting at a target in the woods. She turned, faced the camera, took out her ear plugs, shook her head, let her long, beautiful, abundant brown hair bounce down and promised,

Elections Have Consequences

"I will go to Richmond and clean house." She then flashed her million-dollar smile, raised the shotgun to chest height, and said, "Who knows? Maybe I'll even bring this with me to Richmond."

The Norton campaign responded weakly, denouncing Parrish for wanting to bring a gun to Richmond when the city was "already riddled with guns and bullets."

The ad was considered one of the best political ads ever produced. It got national coverage and a video of the ad went viral. An advertising executive commented, "It is a brilliant ad for a number of reasons. Funny, if you just watch the ad and keep it on mute, you'd guess it's either a shampoo ad or a toothpaste ad."

Cohen jokingly summed up the race: the metrosexual male (Norton) against the alpha male (Parrish), both of them Northern Virginians, and he also pointed out that of the two of them, "Only Parrish was born in Virginia." Norton's family had moved to Virginia when he was young.

Momentum started to build for Parrish in early July. She drew huge crowds all summer; many waited in lines for hours to get a good seat. Her rallies were excellent productions, with a giant American flag in the background. She would come out on stage to Tom Petty's hit "American Girl," which became the campaign's anthem. The words blared, just barely above the crowd noise:

If she had to die tryin',
She had one little promise she was gonna keep
Oh yeah, all right
Take it easy, baby
Make it last all night (Make it last all night)
She was an American girl.

Elections Have Consequences

She gave the standard stump speech, calling for cutting government regulations, cutting taxes, stopping the indoctrination of kids in public schools, and protecting our history. She would also take jabs at Norton,

"Ronnie Norton is so far left he could get elected to the DC city council. He wants to turn our state into a high tax, anti-business state—a more beautiful version of Maryland. I won't let that happen." Parrish went on, "Our crowds are double and triple the size of his crowds. Perhaps we should just call him 'Little Ronnie.' On second thought we better not; that could be cruel. You know how sensitive men are about size." The crowd laughed.

"It's getting kind of desperate for him. He needs help from the celebrities, the progenitors of America's cultural rot. Yes, you see Ronnie is in a little hometown jam, so he set off for a foreign land—New Jersey." Laughter. "To be more precise, a little oasis, a slice of utopia really, called Asbury Park." More laughter. "So, he said, 'Bruce, I'm in trouble here, and like you I'm a woke social justice warrior. You were born to run, and well, so am I. I've been running here in Fairfax for a couple decades now.'" The crowd loved it.

"So, with guitar in hand, in his uniform of a t-shirt and blue jeans, the Boss came down to Fairfax, put on a show for Norton. And guess what, our crowd here today is bigger!" The crowd went wild, and Angela interjected, "I have a bigger crowd and I can't even sing a note."

As she finished the Wytheville rally, Boyd joined her on stage. Angela took him by the hand, leaned in and said, "Boyd, have you ever seen such a large crowd?"

Boyd responded, "No, I can't say I have."

Elections Have Consequences

It was a warm day, with not a cloud in the sky. Angela felt a strange sense of peace and calm. Her schedule was full, but she slept the whole night for the first time in weeks. She could feel victory; she was starting to believe it was possible. As she looked out at the big crowd, she saw a sea of American flags, "Angela" signs, the burnt orange, "Hokies for Parrish," "Angie Can!," and "Make Virginia Great Again." The campaign, perhaps to mock the left, had signs that said, "Believe All Women, Even Parrish." Pleased, Angela sighed, "Ah, Boyd, if every day was like this there'd be no stopping us."

The makeshift stage had one entrance and exit, in the back, that is backstage, and behind the stage one flight of stairs to the ground. Backstage there were a dozen campaign workers and press waiting for Angela. But before she talked to them she and Boyd needed to have a huddle.

So they headed backstage, passing the press and campaign workers, then took a flight of stairs down to where they could speak privately. The stairs were metal, rusty and wobbly. They were too narrow for two people to walk side by side, so Boyd went down first, with Angela right behind him. He could hear her heels hit the metal stairs with each step. There was a landing at the bottom of the stairs where they could talk. Staff waited several feet away, until they were done.

With the crowd noise in the background, the usually dour Boyd seemed genuinely happy, and said, "Good news! Our latest internal polls have us on the move, down just 4 points, an improvement from last week's 8-point gap. Norton's underperforming with women. His waffling on Right to Work is hurting him." Boyd also pointed out that Norton had trouble with his past support for Angela's filibuster proposal. To try to draw a

Elections Have Consequences

distinction, Norton modified his support on the condition that the rule would not apply to "voting or civil rights bills," or "positive bills" regarding undocumented resident aliens.

Angela responded, "Excellent, we are on the move."

Boyd replied, "We are indeed!" Perhaps he was influenced by the speech or caught up in the enthusiasm of the crowd, or Angela's charisma, but he became emotional. He felt the need to express his feelings. Angela was a gifted listener; she seemed to pay total attention to someone when they were speaking. Her brown eyes had a way of boring in, and she seemed to block out everything around her, as if nothing in the world mattered as much as what the person in front of her was saying. It was part of her charm. Her gaze was intent but in no way intimidating, rather it was a look of sincerity that induced a person to say more.

Boyd spoke. "This is my last campaign, and I want to say that of all the candidates I ever managed, you are the best, the most gifted." Angela stared silently at him. Boyd went on, "Kid, you are the best candidate I have ever seen." She blushed. "You have an ability to connect with voters like no one else. My God, what a crowd out there. They started lining up at 4:00 a.m. Heck, I'm the campaign manager and the park was so packed with people that even I had trouble getting in."

Angela was touched. She was about to cut him off, but Boyd went on, "Marshall, like you, was young and ambitious. He wanted to be Governor more than anyone I ever met, but he couldn't connect with voters like you can. You remind me so much of Obenshain. You have a strong ideological foundation, and no one since him can move conservatives like you, and like Obenshain you have that intellectual firepower."

Elections Have Consequences

Boyd paused, looked down, and then summoned the courage to go on, "I know your dad would be so proud of you. I can never forget all the times he mentioned you, and said how proud he was of you.

"I remember when you got accepted into law school. He told everyone. For a week, he would not stop saying how proud he was of you. I remember we thought he was going to announce on the floor of the House of Delegates, the oldest legislative body in the world, 'Hey ,everybody, my daughter got into law school!' Now you draw huge crowds, and *The Washington Press Democrat* attacks you every day. The *Press Democrat,* the mouthpiece of Virginia Democrats. I know he's smiling down from Heaven. He's saying, 'Go get 'em, Angela. Don't let the bastards get you down."

Angela didn't say a word. She just looked away, silent, for several seconds, and then she wiped a tear from her eye.

Boyd decided he said enough and concluded his pep talk, "Now, stay focused, stay on message. Every day the hacks at the *Daily Dispatch* and the *Press Democrat* will try to trip you up, try to make you mad, and make you say something you'll regret. Don't let them. We play error free and we win."

The media tried to downplay the size of the rallies, but to his credit Cohen corrected them. "I was at her Abingdon rally, and there were at least 15,000 people there. And in Martinsville it was about the same. The only gubernatorial candidate I can remember getting those types of crowds would have been Doug Wilder in 1989."

Despite trying, the media couldn't continue to deny or downplay the size of the Parrish rallies, so their spin focused on the makeup of the crowd. They claimed that the crowds, overwhelmingly white, didn't represent Virginia, and worse than that, the lack of diversity indicated that the Parrish message was

Elections Have Consequences

divisive. The *Press Democrat* ran a front page above the fold story by Bhavna Agarwal, "Lack of Diversity at Parrish Rallies Raises Concerns on Both Right and Left."

Parrish commented on the story the day it was published, on the tarmac at the A.L. Philpott Airport in Martinsville. Parrish, her voice raised to be heard over a landing plane, said, "My message of stopping the indoctrination of our kids in government-run schools, my message of tough law enforcement, my message of protecting our Right to Work law, and my message of standing up for law enforcement is an inclusive message to and for all Virginians."

To win, the Parrish campaign knew that they would have to separate suburban women from the Democrat Norton, and in an attempt to gain support among women, especially married women, they picked an obscure issue to drive as a wedge. The social justice warriors wanted the candidates to commit to allowing transgendered student athletes to participate in the sport of their "gender identity." Parrish disagreed, and decided to tar Norton with the idea.

The Parrish campaign's ad buy included, or some say created, the issue. It was so controversial, or perhaps so effective, that most social media companies stopped running it. The ad entitled "Girls Sports" raised an issue no one, at least no one in the Norton campaign, saw coming.

The thirty second ad started with an old home movie clip of Angela playing basketball for Stonewall Jackson High School. The family often took home movies, perhaps with a future campaign in mind. Hank might have even been the cameraman. The film showed Angela as a high school student dribbling the ball up the court, calling the signals for what turned out to be the final shot in the district finals against Osbourn Park. Then the video faded to State Senator Parrish speaking into the camera, dressed in a business suit with her General Assembly lapel pin, in an empty school gym:

"Growing up in Virginia, I was blessed with schools that offered girls' sports. School sports teams offer girls a great opportunity to learn about teamwork, dedication, hard work, and self-improvement, and help to boost self-esteem. I wouldn't be where I am today without this valuable program. Sadly, State Senator Norton and the social justice warriors want to adopt policies that will destroy girls' sports in Virginia public schools. They want to force girls' teams to accept biological boys, who identify as girls. No amount of junk science can justify such an idea. It is not fair to our girls. As your governor I will protect girls' sports teams in Virginia."

The commercial ended with her shooting a ball and making a basket. It took several takes to get the shot, but she hit it, flashed her million-dollar smile, and then came the obligatory voiceover: "I'm Angela Parrish and I approve this message."

Norton caught the ad one night while watching TV. He flew into a rage. "That nasty woman is lying about me! I have taken no such position." Norton got on the phone, called Beaman and Brand, and told them to come over at once." Steve Beaman and Ann Brand were Norton's two closest advisors.

Norton turned to his wife Paula. "Damn it, honey, how is this woman allowed to lie like this? I have never voted, or said one word in support of such an idea. I know politics is a rough business but that can't excuse lying and character assignation."

She tried to calm him down. "It will be fine, sweetie. The

media will hammer her for it. And Brand and Beaman will come up with a good response."

Norton replied, "I have to tell the people of Virginia at once I don't and will never support such a proposal." Norton shook his head and muttered, "Nasty, lying woman."

Brand and Beaman arrived within an hour, and Norton was still fuming. They huddled in the family study room to go over a response. Norton began, "Please tell me that I never took the position that public schools should force girls' teams to accept biological boys who identify as girls."

Beaman and Brand looked over at each other nervously, probably both wondering how to break it to him.

Beaman responded, "You didn't take a position on it, because it's a tough one. Actually, it's best for you not to take a position. Your base and donors are with the transgendered kids on this."

Brand pointed out that he did promise, through a written questionnaire from Moms United to Save Virginia, that he would fight transgendered discrimination in public schools. Brand claimed that denying a transgendered girl a spot on the girls' basketball team was discrimination.

An exasperated Norton explained, "Look, if I take a position like that, I will lose mothers and fathers even in liberal Fairfax County. Such a position is suicide."

Brand countered that abandoning the transgendered would cost him tens of thousands of social justice voters "Ronnie, we have received over 20 million dollars, much of it from outside Virginia, from LGBTQIA groups and individuals on the basis that you will fight discrimination."

Beaman added his view, "Ronnie, I agree Parrish is on the popular side on this one issue, even in Fairfax County, but they are not going to abandon you and vote for her over it. Plus, think of all those single women inside the beltway, in all those half a million dollar condos. They have no kids in school. They are not going to care. They want you to fight for social justice, to fight on behalf of the LGBTQIA community."

"What do you two advise me?" Norton asked.

Beaman had the answer. "Announce that you will appoint a commission of educators, psychiatrists, social workers, community leaders, and other such experts to dispassionately look at the issue and make a recommendation. And to appeal to the left, we can privately let our activists know that Reverend Brand will pick the members of the commission."

Norton made the announcement the next day in a press release. The media applauded the Solomon-like approach as "a mature and responsible decision." The Press Democra*t* praised Norton, for "taking the politics out of such a decision."

Parrish had a different view. "We elect governors to make decisions, not hide behind blue ribbon commissions." Parrish posed a rhetorical question. "Does anyone really believe that Norton doesn't have a position on whether biological boys should play on girls' sports teams? Of course not, but he won't reveal his real position."

The media denounced Parrish for running a "transphobic" and divisive ad. Cohen claimed, "The ad is perhaps the most hateful ad since the Willie Horton ads, but it's no doubt effective. Many people assume Boyd came up with the ad, but I doubt it. In all the campaigns Boyd has managed over the last couple decades, I can't think of one that hit below the belt. Sure, some were hard hitting, negative ads, but nothing like this. This is a direct appeal

Elections Have Consequences

to bigotry. This has the fingerprints of Parrish all over it."

Cohen added, "However offensive, this ad shows what Parrish is willing to do to win. In boxing terms, it was a headshot. Parrish wrote that ad and picked the issue with the intent to knock Norton out. It is Campaign Strategy 101: make your opponent defend an unpopular position."

This issue, however, was quickly exhausted. Norton and Parrish went on to other issues, but Parrish had gained on Norton. By the end of the summer Norton's lead was gone. The Real Clear Politics average had it within the margin of error; Robert Cahaly's Trafalgar Group actually had Parrish up by 3.

Beaman, Brand, and Norton realized they were in trouble. In an effort to assess the damage, Beaman ran a focus group of 24 undecided voters, demographically representative of Virginia. It didn't go well.

Beaman sat in on the focus group, nervously tapping his pen on the desk as he listened to the voters. As he became more alarmed, he tapped louder, crossing and uncrossing his legs. At the end Beaman came out to talk to an aide. According to the aide, Beaman left the room ashen-faced, a look of panic in his eyes, probably the same look Captain Smith had when he was told that his ship had hit an iceberg.

Beaman muttered to the aide, "We are screwed. That wretched woman will be the next governor of Virginia. Only a miracle can stop her."

5) Norton Takes Low Road to Governor's Mansion

The stunned aide listened as Beaman explained what the focus group indicated. "The women love her, they admire her, and the men lust after her. She has no gender gap! A Republican is running even with the Democrat with women voters. There were five black women and two Hispanic women that left the group saying they'll vote for her!"

The focus group found Parrish to be straightforward and honest. One respondent, a self-described independent from Suffolk, said of Parrish, "She's a woman that has something to say and she says it. No pretense, no ulterior motive. She's like a regular person, not a politician."

Another woman said, "Angela can't be bought by the special interests. She will fight for us."

One man said Angela reminded him of his favorite daughter-in-law. If Norton were part of the focus group, he might have said Angela reminded him of his first love.

The focus group also showed that Parrish, a 36-year-old woman, was considered tougher, in effect more masculine, than the progressive, sensitive Norton. This suggested that voters looking for strong leadership would go for Parrish. "Even on compassion and sensitivity she wins, and that's after they watched a commercial of her shooting a deer!" Beaman complained. "She shoots Bambi in the woods, and still, they still think she's compassionate."

The aide asked, "What do we do?"

Elections Have Consequences

Beaman responded, "Let's get Brand in on this. She may have some ideas." Beaman saw defeat coming. In order to avoid it, he had to swallow his pride and bring in Brand for help. Brand and Beaman met alone in the conference room at Norton campaign headquarters in Tysons Corner. As with all major events or crises in the campaign, the two preferred to agree on a common strategy first and then present a united front to Norton.

After going over the grim findings, Beaman said to Brand, "Ann, if you know how to cheat, start now."

Brand, a former state director of Moms United to Save America, seemed unconcerned. "Look, Steve, we haven't even begun to attack Parrish. She comes across as clean and as white as her pearly white smile, but we will have at least $50 million to use in campaign ads against her. When we're done with her, she'll be radioactive."

"Well, I like your positive attitude, but I was at the focus group and they loved her. I have never seen such a positive reaction to a candidate."

A confident Brand responded, "The focus group shows that right now Virginians like Parrish, I don't doubt it. And let's face it, Norton can't beat Parrish, so rather than run against Parrish, let's run against her voters."

Beaman asked "What do you mean, her voters?"

Brand explained, "We need to make it clear that racists, hillbillies, rednecks, and all other sorts of deplorables are voting for Parrish. Do suburban women really want to be voting alongside those deplorables?"

Beaman nodded, and Brand contiiued, "Women aren't turned off by Parrish but her voters will turn them off. So let's introduce those people and focus on exposing her voters."

Elections Have Consequences

Brand went on. "Also, we have to use that gun against her."

"How so?"

Brand replied, "Claim the gun is a racist symbol; the shotgun is like a noose."

"I don't follow."

Brand explained, "We have cases in Virginia of shotguns being used in hate crimes. Parrish as a one-time Virginia prosecutor must be aware of this. And she uses it to appeal to her racist followers, either because she is a racist, or she knows people that vote for her are racists. We need to press her to apologize, which she won't do, and agree to take down the offensive ads, which she won't do. The media will play along."

Beaman seemed to get it. Brand said "We get footage of people with Confederate flags at her rallies, and tell people in Northern Virginia, we pull the curtain back and say 'Here are Angela Parrish's supporters. Are you on their side?' No, so they'll vote for Norton. As I said, Norton may not be able to beat Parrish, but he can beat the guy waving the Confederate flag. So, the election is about Norton against racist hick voters and the Ultra MAGA people. We can win that matchup."

As luck would have it, they found a picture of Parrish at a rally with a rebel flag in the distant background. Now there were lots of flags at the rally; several Gadsden flags, a Trump flag, a Marine Corps flag, and more, but the rebel flag was the only one the Norton campaign needed or wanted to use.

Brand said to Beaman, "All pictures of Parrish must include the one with the Confederate flag in the background. Never use an image of her without a Confederate flag." Brand said with a chuckle, "Make the voters think the guy with the confederate flag is her running mate."

Elections Have Consequences

Beaman responded, "Well, running against a candidates' voters is Joseph Goebbles-like diabolical, but it may work."

Brand reassured him, "Of course it will work," and she bristled at the comparison with Goebbles, "The difference between us and Goebbles is that he ran against good people; we are opposing evil people. And again, when people learn that the guy with the Confederate flag is backing Parrish, her support will collapse. Voters can do the right thing if they are given the right information. Steve, it isn't right versus wrong, it's good versus evil. Conservatives are evil; they are against progress and equality. They must be destroyed, not just defeated. That is, defeated and silenced. They can live, but they must pay a price for spreading their views."

She emphasized, "Remember, Steve, if the ends don't justify the means, what does?" Beaman didn't argue; indeed, he agreed.

Brand then suggested that maybe they should look into her time at UVA. Maybe they could find some examples of racial insensitivities. "We already found out that at UVA she was the head of a MAGA club. There may be more stuff, and it doesn't have to be anything proven. Just a good charge can raise questions. Remember, they went through Brett Kavanaugh's yearbook. Do we have copies of both her high school and college yearbooks? They can be a source of damaging info."

Beaman said, "We have people looking into it. And I'm told a national magazine thinks they may have something." Beaman added, "I'll use the outside group I formed, Latinos for Social Justice, to do an ad with the truck she likes to drive, and the media can run stories on the history and the true meaning of the shotgun in Virginia."

Elections Have Consequences

Beaman then briefed the press about a case in Virginia of a black man being murdered by a racist with a shotgun, and shortly thereafter stories appeared in every major paper asserting Parrish must have known about the case, and the claim that she was incredibly callous to use such a symbol.

The Virginia news media saw Parrish gaining—indeed surging ahead—so they sprang into action. They agreed with the ridiculous "the shotgun was a racist symbol" narrative and at every turn they pressed Parrish on it.

One millennial reporter asked Parrish, "Now that you know what an offensive symbol the shotgun is, will you remove all ads using it? And if you keep using it, what message does that send to people of color?"

Beaman also created an ad for his outside group against campaign laws of a Parrish look-alike appearing to drive into a group of Hispanic day laborers. The urban legend that the ad played on was that President Bush had a plan to round up suspected illegals in paddy wagons and forcibly deport them. The ad had the Parrish look-alike driving the van. Rather than stop and arrest them, the Angela character decided to run the group over.

One camera shot showed what was supposed to be Angela's foot in a sandal, complete with pink nail polish, slam on the accelerator. In another scene, a mother with a baby in her arms screamed as the Angela character let out a horrifying witch's laugh. The shot cut to her foot slamming on the gas as she ran them over them both.

A brutal ad, which even the *Press Democrat* called "over the top", and in fact gave it four Clinocchios. In that rating system, four is the highest rating possible for a misleading ad.

Elections Have Consequences

The Parrish campaign objected, but the Norton campaign denied any involvement, and the media mostly ignored the story. Norton did answer one question about it, saying, "The ad was not in good taste, and of course my campaign had nothing to do with it."

In response to the day laborer ad, Steve Cohen offered in a chirp: "Campaigns in Virginia really have gotten nasty...it is sad." After the word sad was an emoticon of a frowning face shedding a little tear.

Bhavna Agarwal, with the *Press Democrat* and a loyal Democrat herself, continued the attacks on Parrish with a front page story pushing Brand's narrative titled, "Parrish's Shotgun Brings Back Painful Memories of the Old South."

Steve Cohen piled on, claiming that "Parrish's use of a shotgun is an appeal to the worst instincts of people." He added, "Real dog whistle stuff."

Moms United to Save Virginia also got in on the attacks. They decided to portray Parrish as a bigot and a racist. So, in an effort to come up with a clever line to make the point, they played on Parrish's last name.

The word "perish," which means to destroy or eliminate, sounds the same as Parrish. So the group printed bumper stickers that read "Parrish Hate." One Democrat consultant said, "You couldn't drive anywhere in Arlington County or Alexandria without seeing some of those stickers. However cute or clever the line might seem, I don't think it was a good bumper sticker. It may have backfired, and it raised Parrish's name ID." He went on to joke, "I think the people with a 'The Future is female' bumper sticker replaced it with a 'Parrish Hate' sticker."

Elections Have Consequences

The Parrish campaign didn't get into personal attacks on Norton. Sure, there were rumors of Norton's past and his business dealings, but Parrish said they were not going to go that route.

The Parrish campaign saw the polls and the internal numbers, which showed Angela had trouble with single women. Boyd told her, "We need to use the woman card. Remind young women that you are like them, a young woman."

Parrish didn't want to highlight her gender, or as Boyd called it "play the woman card," but she did add a couple of lines to her stump speech. One was, "Virginia was named after a woman. Isn't it about time we have a woman governor?"

The other, less direct, appeal was a phrase she used to deny a Norton charge. The Norton campaign claimed that Parrish had a secret plan to defund public universities' arts and history departments, since Parrish claimed they were "corrupted by the virus of political correctness."

Parrish said no, she had no such plan, "Ronnie Norton, like lots of men, can't handle the word no. Once again, no, I have no such plan."

***

The Norton campaign had another dirty trick. They convinced–it wasn't really hard–a former Republican congressman, Dan Danner, to run as an independent, with the hope of siphoning off votes from Parrish. Danner was a former mayor of Danville and a one term member of Congress. The main reason it was not hard to convince him to run was the simple fact that Danner was a petty and vindictive man. He lived by the motto "Don't get mad, get even."

Democrats funded Danner's quixotic campaign, and MNN gave him plenty of airtime. He made twenty-two appearances between June and November.

Elections Have Consequences

Danner never forgave Parrish for leading an effort to primary him. Danner won an election to serve as the congressman representing Virginia's 5th district. A moderate Republican, he quickly fell out of favor with Virginia conservatives. Parrish believed that since the 5th district was a reasonably conservative district, a moderate Republican wouldn't fit.

Perhaps, if Danner had represented the 11th or 8th or 2nd district, he would not have been primaried. But not in the 5th, so Parrish recruited an opponent and helped raise money to defeat Danner. He lost, and the Republican went on to win the general election.

***

The first debate took place on September 14th at the Homestead Resort in Hot Springs, sponsored by the Virginia Bar Association. The debate lasted ninety minutes, and the Washington Television station WJLA carried it. Based on the debate criteria, Danner didn't qualify to get into the debate since he was not over ten percent in the latest Real Clear Politics average of polls.

But still, Parrish really had two people to debate: the moderator and Norton. For the most part Norton got softball questions such as "What would you most like to accomplish as governor?" Parrish got, "Do you understand why so many people of color are concerned about some of the things you say?"

The panel pressed Parrish on a number of issues. Their main beef was her complaint that white privilege had nothing to do with her success in life, even suggesting there was no such thing.

Bhavana Agarwal asked, "With two hundred years of slavery, racism and misogyny, can you really maintain that in America success goes to those who work hard?"

Elections Have Consequences

Parrish responded, "Yes."

Agarwal then asked to follow up. "Don't you think that it is offensive, or at the very least out of touch, to people of color and women to claim that all you have to do is work hard and you can get ahead in America?"

Parrish responded, "No." Parrish then went on to use the rest of her minute to attack Norton on a previous answer he gave on taxes.

Maddy Clack asked Parrish, "Can you defend the fact that as a prosecutor in Prince William County, 74 percent of the people that you prosecuted were black and Latino? Is that just a coincidence?

Parrish responded, "Yes, because I only prosecuted people that I thought were guilty. I never prosecuted anyone that I thought was innocent."

Clack was befuddled; she had no idea how to respond. She shuffled some papers, looked around, and said "Okay. Well, moving on to our next question."

Matt Deeds with the *Roanoke News* asked Parrish, "What would you say to Virginians who feel that you are insufficiently pro social justice?"

Parrish responded, "I would say I am pro liberty. The two concepts, social justice and liberty, are incompatible. The quest for social justice will destroy liberty. When a bookseller stops selling a conservative book, they do so under pressure to advance social justice, but that is done at the expense of the liberty of the author and the readers. When the social justice warriors demand higher taxes, that is done to help advance social justice, but the price is paid by a loss of liberty regarding the fruits of one's labor.

These are but two examples among many of the threats to our liberties which come from the social justice warriors."

Norton sought to avoid culture war issues and instead sought to carve out a middle ground on a host of kitchen table issues. He claimed on education, "All 133 Virginia school superintendents are supporting my campaign." It was a lie, but one he believed he could get away with. While not all superintendents were publicly backing him, none were backing Parrish, at least publicly.

Many school superintendents privately told Parrish they would vote for her; but that they could not publicly back her. Going on record supporting, or even saying something nice about Parrish, would upset the unions, and many teachers and principals under the command of a superintendent. Norton believed that for the sake of school unity, and their career advancement, no superintendent would want to be on record backing Parrish.

Norton ran an ad with him talking in front of a school, saying "All 133 school superintendents are backing my campaign. Won't you? I am asking you, this November vote for me, Ronnie Norton. Because our kids deserve a great education." The media picked up on the same talking point claiming "All 133 school superintendents back Norton."

Norton did reasonably well, but he did make a gaffe at the end of the debate. Once both candidates finished their closing arguments, they waited for the moderator to officially end the debate, and as the crowd stood and applauded they were supposed to meet in the middle and shake hands.

However, Norton didn't turn to shake Parrish's hand. He just walked off the stage. For several seconds the viewers could see Parrish standing in between the podiums, in her white dress with

Elections Have Consequences

black stripes up the sides, looking for Norton. The TV director cut away to the pundits.

Norton explained later that he thought they would meet backstage to shake hands. The media for the most part bought his excuse.

One other attack took place two weeks before the election. This probably didn't originate with Norton and Beaman but they no doubt benefited from it. The *Metropolitan* magazine, based out of New York, was the political journal of the left, read by the elite. They knew a conservative woman governor of Virginia could have national implications, so in an effort to defeat her, they posted an expose, claiming that as a student at the University of Virginia she made derogatory remarks about black people. They claimed to have three witnesses to back up the story. However, they kept their names out of the story and protected their anonymity.

They justified it by claiming that if their names got out, they might not be safe, and at the very least the witnesses would get harassed online. As far as personal safety the magazine reasoned that Parrish and her supporters were mostly gun owners and bitter people, and that they might harm their sources.

The magazine's editor, Jeffrey Himmelfarb, explained on MNN's political afternoon show, *Both Sides with Myra Stone,* that "Ordinarily, of course sources should be made public, but with Parrish and her supporters' aggressive language and easy access to firearms, well, you can see why the sources would be afraid to allow their names to be released."

A new standard appeared to have been formed in the mainstream media. According to MNN legal expert Jeffrey Thomas, "If there is an anonymous charge made against a public official it is okay to publish it, if the person making the charge has reasons to believe that their safety could be in jeopardy."

In a talk before journalism students at William and Mary College, Steve Cohen was asked about the use of anonymous sources in this case. Cohen said, "Well, sure, I think ideally people making serious charges should go on the record, so we can size them up regarding their veracity, but these aren't normal times. We need to protect whistleblowers. Do I think Angela Parrish is going to shoot somebody making a charge against her? No, but she has lots of supporters, many who own guns. So, I understand the concerns of the whistleblowers. And if in college she made disparaging remarks about people of color I think we need to know that."

***

The second debate was originally scheduled to take place on the campus of VCC. However, the students complained that Parrish, who had a concealed carry permit, might bring a gun on campus. VCC has a gun-free policy on campus and all school property. Parrish, the students argued, could not be allowed to violate that policy.

In an effort to placate the students, the president of VCC, Veronica Ladson, asked Parrish to promise not to bring a gun on campus. Parrish balked, stating that she didn't want to telegraph to a would-be attacker that she was unarmed. So VCC, not wanting to upset the students, asked that the debate be moved.

The organizers of the debate found a new location, the Westfields Conference Center in Dulles. Boyd felt both debates went well. Parrish kept her cool, going toe to toe with the older, more seasoned Norton. Based on the polls, Norton felt he just needed to avoid a big mistake, which he did.

Elections Have Consequences

Parrish tried to avoid harsh counterattacks. She kept it highbrow; she quoted Reagan, Milton Friedman, H.L Mencken. Once when she felt Norton had misrepresented her position on something, she quoted Lincoln. Changing the gender, she basically used verbatim Lincoln's rebuke of Stephen A. Douglas in their first debate. She smiled, shook her head, and said, "When a woman hears herself somewhat misrepresented, it provokes her–at least I find it so with myself. But when the misrepresentations become so gross and palpable, it is more apt to amuse her." The crowd laughed.

By the time of the debate, the Norton campaign had spent 20 million dollars in ads, mostly negative, going after Parrish. He attacked her on abortion, her opposition to the ERA, the support of school privatization, her promise to work with the Bush administration on illegal immigration enforcement. Some of the ads were quite tough, even cringeworthy.

In response to a question about negative ads, Parrish said, "Ronnie Norton will say and do anything to get elected, but I think he has gone too far. His negative ads are insulting and offensive, and even worse, they are not true. He was for my filibuster proposal before he was against it, he was for protecting girls' sports before opposing it, he was for the right to work before he was against it, he was for protecting our monuments before he was against it."

Norton kept his cool throughout the debate. He said most of his ads were positive, and that his negative ads against Parrish "track very closely with her record and statements."

Beaman watched from backstage. When Norton came back, a relieved Beaman smiled and said, "You did great! No gaffes, you kept your cool. We fucking got this! She needed a knockout, and she didn't even lay a glove on you."

A confident Beaman told him, "Our lead will hold." Indeed, Norton avoided any gaffes. He made sure not to interrupt, or in any way come across as condescending toward the younger woman, and he remembered to shake her hand after the debate. He even held onto the handshake for five seconds to make sure all the reporters saw it. Then Norton pulled her close, leaned in, and through a forced smile said, "Just think, Angela, the next time you shake my hand you will be congratulating me on my election as governor."

Cohen, backstage, commented that the debates were pretty much a draw. "If you were with Parrish going in, you are still with her and same with Norton supporters. My bet, few minds were changed."

Not to be outdone by the *Metropolitan*, the Press Democrat ran a story less than two weeks before the election, below the fold, "Veterans Group Demands Parrish Apologize for Alleged Smear."

The campaigns were at a fever pitch that day in mid October when the story came out. Boyd sat in the lobby of the Econo Lodge outside Newport News, reading the paper. He muttered, "Another October surprise." He went up to meet Angela in her hotel room, but he only found her advance man, Bill Stevens. "Where is Angela?"

Stevens responded, "She's down stairs having breakfast. I can tell you she is not in a good mood. She's reading the *Press Democrat* front page story."

"Yes, I saw it. Typical *Press Democrat*. I'll go talk to her and then we'll be on to Richmond, for the Steve Cohen event." Angela

Elections Have Consequences

had the habit of marking the newspaper up as she read it. She always had a pen with her, and would happily use it. Campaign staff always knew she had read the paper because they found it marked up. She would circle, underline words, and sometimes she would leave funny comments in the margins. She liked and commonly wrote the expression, "WTF?" beside what she thought was a ridiculous paragraph.

One staffer suggested, "Maybe I should save one of her marked up newspapers. If she becomes Governor it will be worth something." He went on, "I'll have her sign a copy and once she is elected I'll put it up on EBay."

Boyd went down to the lobby, then turned the corner to the little dining room down past the vending machines. There he found Angela, all alone. her glasses dangling from her nose, coffee in hand, reading the paper. Boyd got some breakfast and sat next to her.

Angela didn't even say hello; she simply asked, "Did you see this? It says here that I said that the military is for 'suckers and losers and sheep." And Parrish went on, "They say they have an anonymous source. This is garbage!"

The story claimed that Angela, while in college, was asked by another student, who happened to be a military recruiter, if she would consider joining the military. Angela, according to the source, said no that the military was for "suckers and losers," and "sheep." Angela, the friend said, declared the military wanted people who couldn't think for themselves, people easily led and indoctrinated.

Boyd responded, "We have logged a protest. And the press is out front, probably waiting for you to make a statement, but I do think the voters will see it for what it is, yellow journalism. The group Veterans for Social Justice is a Norton front group. They probably gave the story to the Press Democrat.

"Angela, I understand you're upset about this, and it's wise to respond strongly, but I think voters will see through this, so let's not get off our main message with a rant against the liberal media."

Angela responded, "Norton must be behind this. This demonstrates that he's unfit for office."

A press contingent traveled with Angela, and out in front of the hotel there was a galaxy of cameras. On her way out of the hotel she stopped to make a statement.

"The latest story from *The Washington Press Democrat* is a baseless smear. I have never said such things about veterans; I have always had high respect for our men and women in uniform." Angela then went on to attack the paper. "The *Press Democrat* is acting as an unofficial arm of the Norton campaign. Well, I am not going to stand by and watch a person who is unfit for office glide into that office on a feel good message." The feel good message Parrish was referring to was the narrative that Norton was a son of a construction worker.

Angela then quoted Kipling: "If you can bear to hear the truth you have spoken twisted by knaves to make traps for fools, or watch the things you gave your life to broken, and stoop and build them up with worn out tools; if you can wait and not be tired of waiting, or lied about, don't deal in lies, or hated, don't give way to hating, and yet don't look too good or talk too wise."

She went on, "This poem was written by Rudyard Kipling. He wrote these words in a letter to his son, to be advice as he grew into a man. My father loved this poem, and while he didn't have a son to pass this advice on to, he believed it was just as good for a daughter to learn from. He taught it to me and my sister, and made us memorize it. I was 12 when I committed it to memory. I have faith in the people. I have faith that the truth will win out in the end."

She turned away from the cameras. Reporters then started shouting questions as she walked away towards the campaign bus.

***

Both candidates took a break from the campaign trail for an afternoon to attend a bipartisan event. In the basement of the capitol building, down past the snack bar, Chickens, at the end of the hall is the press room. The room is literally at the end of the hall because it goes right into the room. For at least a century, the major news agencies covering Virginia politics have used the room. First the big papers reserved it, then radio, then TV networks were given some space. For a fee they could reserve a desk and phone there in the capitol for their reporters, and there is also a little studio for radio and TV interviews. For decades legislators would come down to do interviews.

To honor Steve Cohen's decades of service covering Virginia politics, the legislature decided to name the room the "Stephen Cohen Media Room." A sign outside on top of the door would list his name, and in the capitol directory it would be listed as such.

Certainly it was quite an honor, and to mark the occasion a little ceremony and party were to be held. Both Parrish and Norton agreed to attend the party and make some light hearted remarks.

The room is not very big, so the party spilled outside into the hall. Chickens provided the hors d'oeuvres, cake and other light refreshments including their famous chicken sandwiches and peanut butter pie.

Chickens is described as a snack bar, but there are some seats in a little dining room. The walls are lined with pictures of Virginia politicians past and present. In fact, it is an honor for a Virginia politico to get their picture put up on the wall, usually out of reach for anyone below the rank of Attorney General or Lt. Governor. And an even greater honor is to have a menu item named for them, something that 99% of Virginia politicos could only dream about. But on that day the "Norton Nachos" and the "Parrish Reuben Sandwich" were introduced. Chickens is most famous for their Smithfield ham biscuits.

Norton and his entourage arrived first. He made the rounds, shaking hands and making small talk, while he and Cohen waited for Parrish to arrive. That moment that would soon become obvious to everyone in the room. They could hear some commotion outside, then an advance man said, "She's in the building now. On her way down."

About 20 seconds later, Parrish and her entourage came out of the elevator. A circle formed around her as she walked down the hall toward the media room. The noise of her confident strides echoed off the walls as her heels hit the floor. Norton, while talking to some people in the room, could hear a roar of cheers as Angela made her way to the room.

Then the speeches started, with Norton going first. He congratulated Cohen for his years of service and said, "You are a Virginia institution, and such a strong institution that no one would dare try to cancel you." The crowd laughed. "And the naming of this room is fitting. I can't think of a better reporter,

Elections Have Consequences

and I am not just saying that to butter you up. Even if I weren't running I'd still say nice things about you." More laughter.

Parrish went next. She joked, "I think it's fitting that this room is named in your honor, and perhaps Senator Norton will agree that this is one Virginia landmark that should never face a name change." The crowd laughed.

Parrish continued, "Steve, I have promised to protect the names of Virginia schools, roads, bridges, monuments and I think I will add the name 'Stephen Cohen Media Room' to the list." More laughter. "Steve, I promise you that when I am governor and the social justice warriors in the legislature demand that the name of this room be changed, I will bring out my veto pen." Even Norton laughed along with the crowd. Parrish went on, "Steve, the social justice warriors will push and I will say no, they will push and I will say no, they will push again and I will say to them, 'Read my lips. No name change.'" The crowd roared, reciting the chant often heard at one of Parrish's campaign rallies, "Angela, Angela."

Cohen thanked everyone, then told the story of a middle-class kid growing up in Petersburg who had dreamed that one day he could cover Virginia politics like his role models Guy Friddell and Tyler Whitley. This occasion was the pinnacle of his career. Not even Buster Carrico was given the honor of having the media room named after him. Cohen could have continued to write movie and theater reviews as C. Atwood Bellamy (his pen name), and probably would have become the greatest of reviewers. But he gave up Hollywood and Broadway to become the dean of Virginia politics, and finally he had received due recognition.

At the conclusion of the event the three got together for a picture. Parrish was on Cohen's right and Norton on his left. A jubilant Cohen joke, "How fitting, Parrish on my right and Norton on my left." The crowd laughed. Cohen had a smile from ear to ear. His arms were wrapped around the candidates' waists, Angela had her hand on one of Cohen's shoulders, and Norton's hand was on the other.

Cohen had his friends, including his longtime friend Professor Lawrence Seavers, family and colleagues in attendance. There were a couple of legislators, including Delegate and personal friend Kevin Mack but the group was mostly made up of members of the Virginia press."

All agreed that they had never seen Cohen happier, like a little kid on Christmas morning. A beaming Cohen joked, "This picture is going up on Bolshebook." Laughter. "Well, this definitely qualifies for a status update." More laughter.

That picture was as close as the two would get to each other before their final debate.

***

The Parrish campaign wanted a third debate. They felt Angela had done well, and with Norton holding a slight edge Boyd felt they had more to gain from a third debate. Norton would agree, but at a price. The Parrish camp had to agree to Willow Bush as the moderator. It would be nationally televised on MNN, lasting 90 minutes, with some audience questions. The audience would be "undecided" Virginia voters.

There were reasons why the Norton camp wanted Willow Bush as moderator. First and foremost, she leaned left ideologically. Second, as a woman she could go after Parrish in a way a male moderator could not, or at least probably wouldn't want to.

Elections Have Consequences

The Parrish campaign realized that with MNN host Willow Bush as moderator Angela would have to battle two Democrats. But the campaign still felt a third debate would be beneficial.

The debate was held on Wednesday night six days before Election Day, in Roanoke, at the Hotel Roanoke and Conference Center. Parrish did have a step stool under her podium to bring her up to Norton's height. It started vigorously, with both trading charges and counter charges on the key issues: right to work, transgender sports policy, taxes, education. Norton responded to Parrish's claim that schools were indoctrinating kids, claiming, "Our teachers are heroes. None would indoctrinate students," and he believed that politics must end at the "schoolhouse door."

Midway through the debate Norton did make a mistake, and Parrish seized on it. In lamenting Virginia's history of racism and sexism, Norton said, "What does it say that every Virginia governor but one has been a white male." Norton seemed to instantly realize the gaffe,

Parrish jumped in. "Ronnie, you are complaining about only white males as governors. We can fix that next Tuesday." Parrish's half of the crowd erupted with cheers.

Beaman, watching backstage, muttered, "Damn, he stepped in it."

Bush became alarmed. She knew that Angela had landed a major punch, so she said, "Ms. Parrish, it is not your turn to speak!"

Angela pushed back. "Ronnie complained about only white males being governor."

Again Bush stopped her, "Ms. Parrish, please, it is not your turn!"

Elections Have Consequences

Angela finished her point. "And if I am elected, Ronnie can be happy that a wrong has been righted."

Again, Bush snapped, "Ms. Parrish, please be quiet."

Whenever Norton went over his allotted time by several seconds, Bush would let him complete his thought, but once Parrish's time was up Bush would snap with the alacrity of Judge Roland Freisler, "Time's up!" Angela would finish, then Bush would admonish her, "Ms. Parrish, please stop. You continue to run over your time, and that is not fair to Mr. Norton."

Other than the one gaffe, most analysts considered it a draw. The next morning, Boyd had to be in Northern Virginia for various reasons. While there the campaign, without Angela, would hold a press briefing at the Key Bridge Marriott in Arlington. The purpose of the media briefing would be to debunk a poll that the *Press Democrat* would publish on Friday.

The campaign got tipped off about the poll, which Boyd said was pretty much fake. It oversampled Democrats and Northern Virginia turnout and underplayed Southwestern Virginia turnout in their models. Privately, Boyd said, "This is typical of the *Press Democrat*. They do this every election. In my opinion, it's done in an attempt to suppress Republican turnout." The poll had Norton up by 15 points.

Boyd flew out of Roanoke at 6 a.m. He hated being out of touch even for a couple of hours. He did some work on the airplane, but then he heard that familiar chime. Near takeoff, the voice of the captain said, "We ask now that all electronic devices be turned off and stowed as they may interfere with the aircraft's navigation and communications systems. Once airborne, we will let you know when you can turn them back on."

On the flight, Boyd looked out the window. There down

Elections Have Consequences

below lived the voters who would decide the fate of the campaign in just five days. He thought if the plane descended a little bit, he could probably see thousands of Norton and Parrish signs. In just over 90 minutes, they landed. Boyd grew impatient while the plane was pulling up to the gate. It seemed there were two planes ahead of them.

Boyd got off the plane, but before he left the airport he wanted to check the newsstand. He used to say, "I admit, I still like to see the newspaper, the physical paper and the headline. To me it's much more dramatic." He picked up his bag, and headed up the escalator to get to the newsstand. He again became impatient. He looked up the escalator and thought, *Why are people standing on the left side? Why in the world do people do that?* Finally, he got up to the concourse, moving at a quick pace, pulling his suitcase behind him. He could hear the squeak of the wheels. Approaching the newsstand, there in the window he saw a row of *Washington Press Democrat* papers.

On the cover, above the fold, were pictures of Parrish and Norton from the debate, side by side. The headline was "Candidates Make Final Pitch Before Tuesday's Vote." Boyd bought the paper, stood there, and read it as passengers rushed by him. Boyd had half his body inside the newsstand and the other half in the concourse, causing people to have to walk around him. But he was transfixed by the article. There was his candidate. He had spent months with her; she had become like a daughter to him. He was sure that Hank was counting on him and watching from Heaven.

The editors probably tried to use a bad picture of Angela, but that was impossible. They used one of her pointing at the

Elections Have Consequences

moderator, probably a moment when she was hitting back at Willow Bush. Angela wore a gray suit with a maroon colored blouse underneath, while Norton was in a dark suit with a bright tie.

Boyd felt confident. He saw the internal numbers showing a dead heat, and he knew that Republican candidates close late, in part because undecideds usually break to Virginia Republicans at the end. There was another theory, which years later would be taught in political science classes as the "Parrish effect." That is, many Virginia voters didn't want to appear politically incorrect, so they were less likely to tell a pollster that they would be voting for Parrish. This caused most polls to undercount her support.

***

The election results stunned most of the pundits. It was much closer than anyone thought, so close that the concession and victory speeches were not given until the next day.

Norton beat Parrish, 50.4⁻ 49.2. Third party candidate Dan Danner had no real effect on the race. Parrish won his old district, the 5th, and even won Danner's home precinct. Deb Foster did win in a slim margin, becoming the nation's first transsexual Attorney General.

Norton voted and spent election day in Northern Virginia. He and a select group of campaign staff planned to watch the returns at the Tysons Ritz Carlton. They arrived at 7, once the polls closed. The suite was packed and security was tight, with only about 25 people allowed in. They were milling around the TV watching the returns and grabbing food and drinks from the kitchenette.

Once Norton was assured of victory, he would come down and address the crowd in the packed ballroom. Beaman believed Norton would be able to declare victory "no later than 9 p.m."

Elections Have Consequences

After the final debate, the campaigns had exchanged phone numbers for the concession phone call.

The victory was delayed by three hours, but around midnight it appeared that no matter what happened with the Norfolk absentee ballots Norton would win.

Then the moment Norton, and everyone in the room would never forget. The clock said 12:06 a.m. when the phone rang. Everyone knew who it must be.

Then everyone in the room started shushing each other. Beaman yelled, "Quiet down, everybody, quiet down." After about the third ring Norton nonchalantly picked up.

Everyone in the room looked at him intently, holding their collective breaths.

Norton responded, "Hello." After a few seconds he flashed a smile. Paula started crying tears of joy. The staff remained silent but many started hugging and shaking hands.

Norton looked at his advisors and said, "Well, thank you, Angela. I think you ran a great and honorable race, a race I know your father would be proud of." Norton reminded her of the time they spent in the State Senate, and told her he looked forward to finding ways to work together.

He even made an attempt at humor, telling her that his only regret was that now he wouldn't be able to get her coffee and a donut at Chickens before committee.meetings. They both laughed; he even reminded her that he still remembered she took her coffee with a little bit of milk.

Once he hung up the phone the room erupted in applause.

Paula broke out the champagne. Norton hugged her and declared, "We won this thing! We did it!"

Elections Have Consequences

An exhausted and elated Beaman, who had served as campaign chairman, wanted to push through the crowd and hug his friend, now Governor elect. Beaman had never been prouder of anyone in his life. After Norton hugged Paula, he turned to find Brand. He walked past Beaman and said, "Ann, I couldn't have done it without you."

Norton believed that he might have lost the race if Brand hadn't come in to help. She was the one who suggested the get-tough-on-Parrish approach, and the claim that Angela's use of the shotgun was really a racist prop.

Beaman took notice of the snub. He determined he would work even harder for Norton in his administration.

6) Sandoval

One of the rising stars of the Democrat Party was a female legislator, Maria Salena Sandoval, a first-term state senator from Arlington. Her parents were "undocumented aliens" from Honduras. Why they were here illegally the press never asked, but Sandoval did mention them. She remarked to a reporter with the *Arlington Courier*, "I considered my parents to have been oppressed and exploited by a racist country." She was referring to America. So Sandoval said she got interested in politics and committed herself to fighting racism, inequality, and capitalism. She said she wanted above all to "change America."

At 27, she was one of the youngest senators and also one of only two members that claimed an affiliation with the Democratic Socialists of America. After she graduated from college, she came back home to Arlington and went back to work at the same restaurant where she had worked when she was in high school in Falls Church.

It was while working her normal shift at the restaurant that she met a leader in the Democratic Socialists of America movement, leader Hunter Jackson Carter, who was simply known as Jack Carter. Carter would later tell the *Washington Press Democrat* that meeting Sandoval that day was "pure serendipity."

It happened at a protest, or "demonstration" as it was called, that took place outside an Episcopal Church where Washington had once attended. Carter and his group were demanding that the church, a private organization, remove a mural of George Washington in front of the church, with a sign that said "George Washington Prayed here."

Elections Have Consequences

Now a church is a private organization and is on private property, so they can put up whatever sign, message or mural they want, but Carter claimed that the mural, which portrayed Washington in a positive light and failed to mention that he owned slaves, could be offensive to many people, who would involuntarily be exposed to it driving down Rt. 29.

Carter explained to an *Inside NOVA* reporter, "I understand Washington went to the church, but such a large mural, with such a false portrayal so near the road, is just being provocative."

The snarky reporter then asked him, "Well, is the Washington monument in DC unduly provocative?"

Carter frowned and then said, "Now you are just being silly."

While on her break at Applebee's, Sandoval walked across the street to the church to see what the commotion was all about. There she met Carter, who was a rather goofy looking guy about six foot tall, medium build, with brown hair in a pumpkin pie haircut. Carter walked into the restaurant wearing a button that said, "Ask me about socialism."

He sat at Sandoval's table. In the course of small talk, she noticed the button, and said she wanted to learn more about socialism; she was interested in it. Ironically, her parents escaped a socialist country. Since she only had 10 more minutes left on her break, Carter promised to swing back by later that afternoon to talk with her.

After the police came and broke up the demonstration, Carter went to the Applebee's bar to continue their talk. He didn't know it at the time, but the demonstration paid off. Several months later the church apologized for the offensive mural and agreed to remove it—and made a big contribution to Carter's social justice group!

Elections Have Consequences

Carter acted as a talent scout or recruiter for the socialist movement. His main mission: find viable candidates to run for state and local offices in Virginia. Sure, he would recruit members and raise money, but his primary job was to find socialist candidates. Carter would scour the state in search of candidates with potential. They didn't have to be particularly bright or intellectual, as much as have a certain look or background that might help them connect with voters. Carter bluntly admitted, "In fact, the less they know the better." Carter's maxim was "The more you think, the more you stink."

In an interview with the magazine *Today's Socialist* said, "I am not really looking for people who are totally conversant with the socialist philosophy; rather, I am looking for candidates who are committed to social justice and have the qualities of a winning candidate, the ability to connect with voters."

"Look, I would vote for Marx in a heartbeat, but let's face it, the average voter wouldn't. We need to appeal to the average voter." Carter went on to say in that interview, "It isn't what a candidate knows, or the depth of knowledge that matters; it is the conviction and passion they bring." Carter didn't mention it in the article, but the other attributes for a good candidate include race, gender, sexual identity, and generation.

Carter came back to that Applebee's several more times. He was fascinated by Sandoval's ability in dealing with customers of different religions, races, backgrounds—rich and poor, black and white, gay and straight. She seemed to be a bright, cheery millennial. She was good with banal statements. And she was the daughter of undocumented workers, so in his mind she had a great inspirational story.

Elections Have Consequences

He also was heartened to hear her once complain to a customer, "Why is it that in such a rich country there are so many poor people?" *Ah*, he thought, *she could be a promising member of the revolution.*

At another time she pointed out what she thought was some sort of a contradiction. "This country is happy to put someone in jail but is unhappy with even discussing providing free healthcare." He noticed that she wore a button on her lapel that read, "Love knows No Border" and "The System is Racist." He looked at her like a kid in a candy store. She could be perfect. Yes, he thought she should be in the Virginia General Assembly making laws.

He came back several times, taking the same seat in the corner of the bar, munching on free pretzels and drinking free refills of Sprite. Just staring at her for a couple shifts, like a Hollywood talent scout. He knew talent when he saw it. *Yes, yes she could be a star,* he thought.

He got up the nerve, walked over to her, and asked if she would like to consider a career in politics. She said she was "flattered by the suggestion," and would be happy to think about it.

Sandoval commented later about her fateful meeting with Carter. "I just thought he was some creep in a bar, but then I found out that he was a leader in the Democratic Socialists of America." She laughed, "I thought to myself at the time, boy, I was wrong."

Carter convinced her to run, and when an open seat became available, she won with nearly 80 percent of the vote running on the ballot as a Democrat in Arlington County.

In an effort to unify the party and convince skeptical

progressives that he was one of them, Norton came to Arlington to campaign with her one Saturday afternoon.

She introduced him at a rally, declaring, "Send Ronnie Norton to Richmond to help me end racism, bigotry, homophobia, hunger, and global warming." She then repeated the same banal mantra in Spanish.

Richmond Daily Dispatch political reporter Stephen Cohen came up to Arlington to hear Sandoval on the campaign trail. He wanted to see for himself what all the fuss was about. In her speech that day, she spent half of it condemning the fact that children at the border were being put into cages. She also said that once elected to the State Senate she would introduce a bill to abolish Immigration and Customs Enforcement agency. No one pointed out to her that the Virginia State Senate has nothing to do with border enforcement.

Certainly, Cohen didn't mention the gaffe in his column the next day; rather he gushed over Sandoval, describing her as brilliant and personable. He opined that she "could be the most dynamic political force in the State Senate since the late J. Sergeant Reynolds." Now in Virginia politics to say a young politician reminds you of J. Sargent Reynolds is a high compliment.

In explaining the comparison to other members of the press, Cohen said, "Reynolds was fearless; he would speak truth to power, as they say; he was a man of the left and he told the Byrd Democrats what he thought of their reactionary policies. For those too young to remember Reynolds, he was a force like no other in the history of Virginia politics. He had money, looks, intelligence, and charisma, but he was young. In his 30's, I think the same age as Angela Parrish. He probably could have become president, but he died young."

Norton, realizing his party's leftward shift, was very complimentary of Sandoval, and included her in one of his ads. Even after the election, whenever her name came up he would have a kind word for the young socialist legislator. Norton claimed Sandoval was a "breath of fresh air" and "full of youthful energy that Richmond needs."

Jack Carter felt Sandoval needed some tutoring on basic issues, so he got her a tutor: his old history teacher from Edison High School, Pat Linehan. Jack and Pat became friends at Edison and remained close after Jack graduated. Pat became politically active after he left teaching. Pat's students claimed that he believed in two things for sure: socialism and the need for the liberal application of Aqua Velva.

Linehan taught high school civics and history, and Carter decided he would be a great tutor for Sandoval. She could use a refresher on things like how a bill becomes a law, what the three branches of government are, the number of senators and representatives, who wrote the Declaration of Independence, what the constitution does, etc.

The two would meet once a week to run through textbooks, the same books that he used at Edison High School. They got along fine; however, Linehan didn't suffer fools gladly. Many of his students were on the receiving end of what became known as the Linehan Stare. It could be intimidating.

One of his former students described the stare: "When a student answered a question, or tried to, and it was not going well, Linehan would give them a stare. He would sort of squint his eyes, his mouth would open slightly, and he would just stare for several seconds. Rather than help the student out by giving some clues, he'd just stare instead. It was a look of pure contempt." The student went on. "And sometimes, once you gave the wrong answer, he would keep the look on his face, and slowly shake his head a few times."

After several weeks of study, they got through the books. Linehan thought she did well; in fact he said she would have passed his 10th grade civics class. Linehan liked her; ironically, he lived in her district and voted for her.

But Pat warned Jack, "Keep her away from reporters as much as possible. And tell her to keep her head down in the State Senate and just learn for a year or two. If she tries to spar with Parrish in the State Senate she will get torn up."

Carter reassured him, "The media loves her. She's not Parrish; they will never ask her a hard question—nothing but softballs right over the middle of the plate."

Carter then admitted to Linehan, "The fact that she is from such a far left county as Arlington gives her room to the left. She can help move the Democrat caucus in Richmond further in a progressive direction. And if from time to time she says something which may sound stupid, well, it doesn't really matter. She's a Democrat in Arlington; she can't lose." He added an analogy. "It's like being a Democrat U.S. Senator from Delaware; you can say stupid things for thirty years and as long as you vote right they'll keep electing you."

7) An Odd Occurrence in Damascus

An event took place which would shape the political landscape in Virginia—and the country—for years to come. Steve Cohen called it an "odd occurrence in Damascus."

It took place just weeks after Ronnie Norton's inauguration, in the little town of Damascus, Virginia in Washington County, in southwest Virginia. Damascus is a rural town; it is known to hikers, bikers, and outdoor adventurists, but most Virginians have never heard of it. A number of popular trails run right into the city, hence the nickname "Trail Town." It is beautifully nestled in the Appalachian Mountains.

For its anniversary, the town chose to honor one of its founders, Colonel John D. Imboden, with a statue in the town square. It seemed like a fine thing to do, and there might not have been a major controversy had one guest not agreed to show up at the statue unveiling.

President Marvin P. Bush probably first heard about the statue and the unveiling from a friend and supporter who happened to be on the Damascus City Council. As a courtesy, Bush was invited, but there was certainly not a real expectation that he would attend. It was almost like a couple sending the president or governor a wedding invitation knowing that it is not realistic for him to attend.

Bush was reported to have told an aide when he read about the event, "This is too deliciously counter-revolutionary for me not to go." Bush liked the idea of another monument going up, and despite growing up in Sherman Oaks, California President

Elections Have Consequences

Bush was a Civil War buff, and of course he knew the media would go nuts over his showing up.

In addition to being a founder of the town, John Imboden served as a state legislator, and in his youth fought in the Civil War with the Army of Northern Virginia, under Lee's command. To deal with this potential controversy, the town council designed the statue to show him in a business suit, not a military uniform, and the statue made no mention of his service with the Confederacy. It did, however, list him as a colonel.

Now, the statue made no mention of it, but Imboden in Damascus was known as the hero of Manassas. In all other parts of the state, people viewed Stonewall Jackson as the hero of Manassas. Great care was taken to focus the ceremony on Imboden's post-Civil War career. Instead of the words, "Hero of Manassas" on the statue, it read, "Father of our Town."

Yet the media blasted the idea.

MNN dedicated a whole hour to the resurgence of racism in Southwest Virginia. They had the headline, "Confederacy Making a Comeback in Virginia?" Several Hollywood stars promised never to set foot in Damascus again, although no one in the town ever remembered seeing a Hollywood star.

The population of Damascus is just under 1,000 people, and most people in the town had never met a president; there is no record of a president ever visiting the town. It was a cool crisp winter day and the whole town and a lot more were there. In fact the crowd was estimated to be just over 12,000. Never in its history had so many people been in the town. They were packed all along the streets and around the square, most coming in from neighboring counties.

Elections Have Consequences

The *Washington County Journal* found a 90-year-old resident, Ida Bell Turner, who had once met Colonel Imboden's granddaughter. She described the day as great for the town, thrilled that Colonel Imboden was finally being honored with a statue. She mentioned that the idea of a statue had been talked about in the town for as long as she could remember.

The media failed to mention the fact that after the war most Confederate soldiers went home and rebuilt their towns, served in local government, and many even got elected to the state legislature. John D. Imboden did all those things, and hence the town now wanted to honor him.

Most of the networks did not cover it, but it was quite the sight: the president in front of the podium, adorned with the presidential seal, the 9-foot statue of Colonel Imboden in the backdrop as President Bush gave a great and spirited dedication speech. At the beginning of the event, they unveiled the statue by cutting away the canvas covering. The crowd cheered. There he was, the hero of Manassas.

Under his arm he had a blueprint of the town, and in his hand he had a gavel. The gavel recognized his service in the House of Delegates as the chairman, or as we say today chair, of the powerful Rules Committee.

President Bush asked State Senator Parrish if she would introduce him at the unveiling. The two were, of course, political comrades, and also friends. They had first met when she attended Hillsdale College. In her introduction, Parrish acknowledged that she went to Stonewall Jackson High School, so she greatly admired Jackson, but then speculated, "Who knows what would have happened if Imboden didn't hold Henry Hill as long as he did?"

Elections Have Consequences

With that an old guy, and a longtime resident, stood up and bluntly yelled, "We would have lost the damn battle, that's what would have happened!" The crowd cheered.

On this, Parrish was taken aback, almost flustered. She flashed her smile and seemed to blush, but she was smart enough of a politician to know not to comment. She went on to talk about Imboden's post-Civil War work in the House of Delegates.

Parrish described Imboden as a "great son of Virginia" and she added, "My father served for 40 years in the House of Delegates, but to be clear, he never actually met Delegate Imboden." The crowd laughed. She went on, "He served at least a few decades before my father. John Imboden was a great Virginian, served our great state and after the War Between the States he worked to rebuild and unify our country. He settled in this beautiful spot and helped build a great town. Colonel Imboden was the type of Virginian we should honor."

One irony that went unmentioned: Angela's maternal great-great-grandmother, Ann Dogan, had watched the battle. She had property in Sudley Springs, near the battlefield, and from her backyard she watched Federal forces come down Mathews Hill and march up Henry Hill to push Imboden's forces off.

Angela then went into rally mode; she went on to attack the media. "The late-night comedians and chattering classes inside the Beltway attack Imboden's memory and you for honoring him. John Imboden built a great town. What did they ever build?" The crowd roared with cheers.

Then President Bush got up to speak. He commented, "What a beautiful statue." He went on to claim that it had to be the most beautiful statue since the Lee statue was unveiled in 1890. He

Elections Have Consequences

even managed to take a few digs at Norton, claiming Norton would have come except he thought "Damascus was a place in the Middle East. He said he didn't have time to renew his passport." The crowd roared with laughter. Bush continued, "Norton doesn't realize that Virginia extends beyond Roanoke."

He then attempted a joke, "We have always believed that Col. Imboden delayed the Federal advance. However, we must face the truth. Recently, new evidence has come to light that makes it clear what really held back the federal advance. It seems that there was an accident on westbound 66, two lanes were down, in fact traffic was backed up all the way up to 495!"

The laughter was polite, but many didn't get it. Bush added, "Well, I guess to appreciate that joke you have to be from Northern Virginia."

The president was supposed to just focus on Imboden's contribution to building the town–the laying out of the town plan, the irrigation system, and the city charter, but the history lover in Bush went back to history:

"If you are from Damascus, you already know this, but those watching us across the country probably don't know. At the battle of Manassas, the South's victory that day would not have been possible without John D. Imboden and his brave undersized force. You see, when the battle began, Jackson and his forces weren't yet in Manassas. So had Imboden and his brave forces not held on, Jackson would not have been able to stand on the plains of Manassas like a stone wall."

Well, that caused a media firestorm. They seized on his word "brave." MNN ran the headline, "Bush Calls Slaveholders Brave." Governor Norton issued a demand that Bush apologize, but he didn't.

Elections Have Consequences

Bush even added that in the war there were "good people on both sides." Of course, the news media interpreted this to mean he was saying there were good slaveholders. Todd Charles, host of the show *Meet the Press Corps* asked the ancient talking head Georgia Folger, "Does this statement morally disqualify President Bush?" Her answer went on for over a minute, but it was essentially yes.

Even the late-night comedians got in on the orgy of outrage. It didn't hurt ratings, far from it. To paraphrase Mencken, no one ever lost money virtue signaling.

On leaving Damascus, a reporter asked Parrish about the potential backlash to the statue. She responded with a dismissive gesture and said, "Let them wag."

8) Brand

One of the advisors closest to Norton was a female Episcopal bishop named Ann Lee Brand. Brand bore a slight resemblance to the late folk singer John Denver–short blonde hair, similar round face, and she even wore the same thick glasses. Brand, a newcomer to Virginia politics, quickly became one of the most influential activists on the left. Over a relatively short period of time, she became a kingmaker in the Democrat party. A negative word from her and a Democrat hopeful would be done. Democrats all across the Commonwealth felt an obligation to go to Alexandria and get her blessing to run. Had Norton never met Brand, he might have been a decent governor.

Brand's charisma did not come from a pleasing or winning personality; hers was definitely not pleasing or winning. Her temperament was usually brusque, and at times downright rude. Rather, Brand's zeal and commitment to the cause of social justice, and her strategic genius, moved people. Indeed, those traits created a devoted core of followers and admirers.

She usually wore a clerical collar, occasionally pink but for the most part the traditional black and white. Sometimes she would wear a Kente cloth. She would always do this on Columbus Day to show solidarity with indigenous people. Normally, though, she would be clad in all black, including Reebok black rubber soled sneakers, the kind school cafeteria workers wear. In the wintertime she wore a light blue North Face coat.

She never appeared in makeup, or even earrings. She believed such fashion accouterments were created to please a male dominated society, so no thanks for her. Reverend Brand radiated asexuality, which many found ironic considering that she had a degree in human sexuality.

From her position in the church, she made a name for herself as a champion for social justice, due to the fact that she invariably commented on the political news of the day from the pulpit. The liberal congregation didn't seem to mind her political sermons. Eventually church leaders allowed, perhaps even recommended, that she take a leave of absence to get involved in politics.

Brand became the executive director of the Virginia chapter of Moms United to Save America, and it was in this capacity that she met Norton. At the time he was a candidate for the state Senate. Brand impressed Norton with her passion for social justice and her ideas of reforming Virginia's educational system. Norton also found her to be politically very astute and intelligent. Her blessing, so to speak, would be necessary to get the Democratic nomination for governor, which Norton was eyeing. He needed her more than she needed him.

The group Moms United to Save America is one of the largest and most powerful groups on the left. One doesn't have to be a mom to be a member of the group or a donor; in fact it has nothing to do with motherhood. The organizers use the word "mom" because focus groups have determined that moms are very influential. Hence the name.

Each state has a chapter, and there are spinoff groups, such as Moms for Peace in Palestine, Moms for Truth (they want people banned from social media sites), Moms for School Safety (they want the police off school property), Moms for Free Choice (they want taxpayer funded abortion), Moms for Proper

Historical Preservation (they want to tear down statues and rename schools.)

As a bishop she would speak to campuses all across the Commonwealth denouncing racism, sexism, and white privilege. She didn't usually talk about religion on her campus visits; perhaps she believed that to be too divisive. Brand would draw big, adoring crowds. Brand listed with one of the largest speakers' bureaus in the country and her topics of expertise included "White Privilege, Social Justice, and Feminist and Queer theory."

The media also built up Brand with great fawning profile stories. The secular media always liked to highlight liberal members of the clergy. For the secular media, the best Christian is the one talking about social justice and advancing a leftwing agenda, and in Brand they had that activist, a social justice warrior with a collar.

Brand's view, not unique in the Episcopal Church, is that Jesus was a community activist and social justice warrior. Brand believed it is fine to go to church on Sunday and say prayers, but to really follow Jesus meant taking up his quest for social justice.

In an effort to promote her, *The Washington Press Democrat* did a big puff piece in their much-coveted Sunday "American Culture" section. The paper described her as "this generation's Father Drinan."

The flattering article had a picture of her with her arms crossed, the Church behind her, and was titled, "Can This Woman Save Christianity in America?"

The narrative of the secular media is that Christianity is dying, and to save it would require a woman, a pastor or bishop. To many on the left, this person could only be Reverend Brand.

Elections Have Consequences

In actuality Reverend Brand's church had experienced years of declining membership, an irony lost on the media. Her church bosses liked her, not because she brought in a lot of converts, which she didn't, but because she raised a lot of money from Hollywood and New York liberals, and she got great media. Brand became the face of the church to a secular world, while the church had lots of empty pews.

The leading feminist magazine *Today's Woman* did a whole cover story on her. The writer rhetorically lamented, "Why can't this woman be pope?" The article speculated that it would take a woman to save the church.

But controversies always seemed to surround Brand. Her critics accused her of distorting the Christian faith, trying to indoctrinate children, and even dishonesty. Brand's claim that certain vices were sins were dubious to say the least. In addition, her ideas of sins really blurred the line with politics. For example, her assertion that creating greenhouse gasses was sinful was even challenged by a few of her fellow clergy.

The other controversy was her name, specifically her ancestors. Her middle name was Lee. As a child she may have been led to believe that she was a descendant of the famous Robert E. Lee. She even told people she was related to him.

The media would occasionally describe her as a "Lee descendant,," or "indirect Lee descendant." She did not disabuse anyone of the idea of her being related to the Lee family.

There are no examples of her calling a newspaper to deny being a "Lee descendant." One friend asked her about the media's misimpression, and Brand responded, "Let them think what they want. All I have said is that I am a member of the Lee family of Alexandria."

Elections Have Consequences

One of her critics found a church bulletin that listed her as Reverend Ann Brown, but as she got more politically active, she changed the listing to Ann Lee Brand. One theory behind the change was that the Lee name might give her more credibility before the big push to remove Confederate statues, such as statues of General Lee.

The obedient media went along saying, "Even members of the Lee family want them taken down." Who were they referring to? Probably Brand.

Not everyone on the left was enamored with Reverend Brand. Steve Beaman never could understand why Norton was so taken with her. Beaman reasoned that she was 41, had never worked in the private sector as far as he could tell, spent time getting degrees in stupid subjects, and wrote nonsensical tracts on her theories of race. He would derisively refer to her as the "former female bishop."

Beaman also thought it was suspicious that she continued to wear a collar even though she was technically not a reverend. She was on sabbatical, and she continued to wear a collar when she went to work in the Norton administration. And everyone continued to use the honorific Reverend in front of her name. To that Norton responded that being an ex-reverend is like being an ex-president; you still keep the title.

First and foremost, Ann Lee Brand was a member of the clergy, her first big assignment out of the seminary came as pastor of a church in Alexandria that Washington was known to attend.

No quiet pastor, Brand started making waves right away. The first controversy: Brand took down an historic painting of George Washington, hung in the church in his honor.

Elections Have Consequences

One irony was that the church makes money off the Washington connection. Tourists come to visit the church, take a tour, buy souvenirs in the gift shop, and contribute to the church all because of Washington. Some thought attacking Washington was the equivalent of biting the hand that feeds you. However, it didn't hurt fundraising; the press coverage actually helped fundraising. Many non-church members, non-Episcopalians, started contributing some money in support of the virtue signaling Brand. The press described her as "brave" and "honest."

Brand also caused some controversy when she created a ceremony. She obtained a list of names that were purported to be George Washington's and his family's slaves and read them aloud. After each name was read, the congregation would bow their heads and have a moment of silence. Then she would go to the next name, parishioners would bow their heads, wait, and so forth. The service took over an hour.

She made this a tradition, a regular ceremony at the church. She wanted to make the Washington slave name reading an annual event on Washington's birthday. At first her superiors were okay with it, but then they said that would be in poor taste on his birthday, so they compromised and allowed it the next day.

Reverend Brand called the day, which the church made an official holy day, "National Washington Slave Remembrance Day." She wanted to make it a national holiday for the church, even possibly a Holy day of obligation. The church initially said yes, but dragged their feet on implementing it. In fact, they never did. Thankfully for them. they moved her out on the campaign trail and the idea was dead, at least temporarily.

Elections Have Consequences

She also taught an English class at the church's school and came up with an odd writing assignment. The children were asked to take the role of one of George Washington's slaves and were asked to write a letter begging for their freedom. The church higher ups didn't say anything at first, but even in liberal Old Town Alexandria parents started to complain. So that assignment got the ax. And the math class included questions such as, "If George Washington had 1,000 slaves and freed 35, how many slaves did Washington have?"

Mike McHugh with the local Alexandria paper did several stories on Brand and the church. "Publicly she was highly regarded. However, off the record it was a different story." McHugh talked to one of the former church secretaries and she had very different views of Brand. She told McHugh, "The diocese is afraid of her. Look, churches are like cable news channels. They have to appeal to their audience's prejudices. Churches need to please parishioners, but also their donors, and Brand was raising money from all kinds of left-wingers, all around the country; people that weren't even members of the church, or even Christians gave because of her. So, the church did not want to offend Brand."

It turned out there was a LGBTQIA advocate in New York that contributed $200,000 to the church out of admiration for Brand. As long as she raised money, her position in the church seemed secure.

Brand's other issue dealt with history and the interpretation of it. Specifically, she helped lead the charge to remove statues and monuments to the Confederacy in Virginia in Richmond. With a coalition of leftist groups, they went door to door getting signatures. The goal was to get every homeowner to sign a removal petition.

The groups included, Moms United to Save Virginia, VCC Law Students for Justice, Students Against Toxic Masculinity, Students for Racial Equality, other civil rights groups, Moms for the Proper Preservation of History, VCC Pride Club and LGTBQIA Virginia, among others. Volunteers would engage neighbors and, if necessary, try to convince them just how offensive the statues were.

One way they did this was to give personal testimony about how the statues made them feel. Volunteers would knock on the door and usually have a story about how angry and oppressed the sight of the statue made them feel. After the volunteer left the house, they would make notes about the visit and the conversation.

Brand would review the notes at the end of the week and decide which volunteer to send next. Brand practically knew the names and address of every neighbor on the famed Richmond street by heart. She knew which neighbors had signed the petition and which had not.

The total number of homes along the street, over the several blocks, would be a little more than a hundred. However, over two years there would be a few hundred door knocks, and in the case of some homes, several visits by different activists.

Finally, after a couple years, they received the signatures of all the homeowners. It was unanimous. Even Saddam Hussein had never won with 100%. Quite an accomplishment, and the Richmond media played it up for all it was worth. *Daily Dispatch* writer Steve Cohen claimed "The neighbors have spoken; there is no reason the statues should remain up."

Elections Have Consequences

But there was another element of the story that the media completely ignored, probably on purpose. That was the possibility that Brand's effort was an intimidation campaign against the owners. How would most home owners feel if people knocked on their door and said "We are against the racist statue out front; will you sign here to get rid of it?" In other words, "You are against racism, aren't you? So, sign here, and we will stop knocking on your door."

The media profiled some of the neighbors, that is, the ones willing to go on the record. The quotes used in the media stories could have been written by Reverend Brand, and they probably were. However, there was at least one homeowner they didn't quote.

Margaret Wilson, a retired government worker who had grown up in New York, bought a home on the street in the early 80's. She told the *Daily Dispatch*, "For two years literally 50 different people, activists, knocked on my door. Nice young kids mostly, many VCC students. I had no real problem with the statues, I guess I was indifferent really, but I was tired of all these kids knocking on my door. Some could be quite obnoxious.

"I complained to Reverend Brand, and she said that if I wanted the door knocking to stop, I probably should sign the petition. They used intimidation, they implied that I wouldn't want to be the last homeowner to sign."

That quote never made it into the *Daily Dispatch* story. The *Daily Dispatch* and the Richmond media refused to cover the possibility that there was an intimidation campaign, and once every homeowner was on board they reported the story as if there were a natural consensus. Perhaps it made for a better story, a positive story, that the neighbors weren't racists after all.

Elections Have Consequences

For Brand, the root cause of evil was not racism or bigotry, although those sins were pervasive throughout American society. Rather the root, or fount, of all America's sins could be attributed to the white male patriarchy

Despite being a minister, she was no fan of marriage, at least heterosexual marriage. She believed that it enslaved the woman and empowered the man. A former member of Moms United to Save Virginia, who later became a born-again Christian and left the group, described how Brand would start staff meetings off. "Brand would start every morning meeting with a series of questions:

Brand: "Comrades, what are we here to do?
Staff: "Advance the cultural revolution."
Brand: "And how do we do that?"
Staff: "Destroy the American family."
Brand: "And how do we do that?"
Staff. "By destroying the patriarchy."
Brand: "And how do we do that?"
Staff: "By destroying monogamy."
Brand: "And how do we do that?"
Staff: "By promoting sensuality, promiscuity, abortion, contraception, pornography, and homosexuality."

One week after Norton was inaugurated governor of Virginia, he appointed Brand to be Virginia's Secretary of Education, the cabinet spot she wanted the most.

***

Despite Norton's great confidence in her, there was some opposition in the State Senate. At her confirmation hearing,

Elections Have Consequences

Parrish pressed Brand on a number of issues. Parrish produced an article from an Alexandria paper and a quote from Brand claiming, "Parents have no business telling schools what to teach." Parrish confronted Brand, "Did you say that, or were you misquoted?"

Brand, in her priestly collar, seemed somewhat surprised that such an old quote, especially from an obscure newspaper, had come up, and responded, "Yes, Senator Parrish, I did say that, but the full context is missing from that article." Brand explained that while parents "do have a role" in the child's education, the schools must pursue "unbiased and objective truth." Brand, like others on the left, believe that parents, all parents and not just white parents, have prejudices and biases, which they can't suppress. Schools, especially public schools, are run by professional educators, who are trained to teach objectively, that is, to put aside prejudicial views when teaching.

Parrish rhetorically replied, "So professional teachers are like professional journalists, they are naturally objective?" The crowd in the hearing room laughed; even Brand smiled. She was confirmed on a mostly party line vote.

Brand told friends during the campaign that if Norton were to offer her a position in the cabinet, she wanted to be Secretary of Education. Brand, like her fellow progressives, believed in the socialist's maxim, "Gain the youth and you win the future." They believed that educating the youth properly was essential to ending racism, saving the environment, and replacing capitalism with a socially responsible economic system.

While schools were for the most part controlled by elected local school boards, the state can create standards and guidelines.

Elections Have Consequences

One hint into Brand's thinking could be found in the transcript of a speech she gave to a conference of Episcopal bishops in Washington. Brand claimed that to fight transphobia, the concept of gender fluidity needed to be introduced to children in earlier grades, as early as in elementary school. She told bishops, "We must not fail our children. If they are not familiar with the concept of gender fluidity, which like it or not is settled science, until middle school or God forbid until high school, it will be too late to eradicate transphobia."

The secretary could make recommendations that would shape legislation. Brand had a bold vision for Virginia schools. For starters, she wanted to change the names of dozens of schools, change discipline and suspension policies, and review curriculum from kindergarten to the universities.

She wanted schools to adopt radical policies. In addition to gender fluidity, she wanted to advance critical race theory, which claimed America was founded to exploit black people and native Americans.

She wanted to change the names of colleges such as George Mason and James Madison University for starters. Norton didn't really have strong positions on these issues, but he had respect for Brand's intelligence and her ability to help in reaching out to the progressive wing of the Democrat Party.

In addition, as Secretary of Education she would have a great influence on who the governor appointed to the Board of Visitors at Virginia's colleges and universities. The board runs the schools, so with the right appointments ideological control of the schools could be taken over by the left. Those Board of Visitors members would then pick the university presidents.

Elections Have Consequences

Brand dreamed of a day when every university and college had a truly woke president. Her other desire, indeed a goal of the entire left, was to change every school named after a Founding Father to the name of a woke social justice warrior.

Brand also wanted to reform school discipline procedures for one main reason: minority students, particularly black males, made up a disproportionate percentage of students suspended every year for disciplinary reasons. For Brand and other progressives, this indicated racial bias in the schools. Therefore, the state must lean on individual schools to get rid of suspensions.

The other thing Brand wanted to do as Secretary of Education was to stop schools from categorizing students as "boys" and "girls." Instead, students should be able to use the designation "X" for gender. She argued having to choose between being a boy or girl was unfair and discriminatory to non-binary children.

Brand had a great interest in the state's chartered magnet schools. There were several throughout the state that were set up for Virginia's gifted and talented students. These were places for them to excel, not to be held back by the distractions of average and below average students, a competitive environment for Virginia's best and brightest.

A good example could be found in Chesterfield County. The Matthew Fontaine Maury School for Science, Technology and Math had a national reputation of being one of the best schools in the country, but it lacked the racial diversity the left was demanding.

For years the county and state tried to diversify the student body, but it remained nearly 80 percent white. The Press

Elections Have Consequences

Democrat said "that while they have a well-deserved reputation for high academic achievements, that does not outweigh their lack of diversity, which is starting to turn the school into a national embarrassment."

Brand suggested that all state charter schools undergo a "holistic review of the admissions process," that is, getting rid of merit-based testing and instead imposing racial and ethnic quotas on the student body. While not opposed to merit-based testing, Brand wanted a renewed emphasis on equity, that is, students from diverse backgrounds,

In addition to admission standards and student discipline, Brand, like other social justice warriors, was concerned about the issue of "math equity." It seems boys do better at math than girls, generally speaking, so Brand didn't want more money allocated for advanced math classes since that would disproportionately benefit male students. So, while they couldn't eliminate all math classes, they could reduce and delay the offering of advanced math classes. Leave them for high school. Maybe just junior and senior year.

Perhaps the greatest power of the Secretary of Education is the power to determine what will be included in the curriculum of Virginia public schools. What will be allowed in the classroom and how can it be taught? Is anthropogenic global warming true? Can it be taught in school as fact? Ask the Secretary. Was there an attempted coup on the eve of the 2021 presidential inaugural? Ask the Secretary. Did Covid 19 come from China or Italy? Ask the Secretary. Shortly after taking office, Brand issued guidelines on all these questions.

Brand also wanted to move away from the "western classics,"

Elections Have Consequences

that is, she wanted schools to stop assigning students books from authors ranging from Shakespeare to Jane Austen; all the western classics should be purged from reading assignments. She believed that schools, although she didn't think it was intentional, actually promote white supremacy by a "nationalist exaltation of western civilization." She believed schools must move away from the western canon, and move to a more diverse set of literature, history and art. For example, she thought requiring a Latinx to read Jane Austen was absurd.

***

One curious favor Brand asked of Norton when he appointed her Secretary of Education was that she would have some input on his appointments to an obscure commission under the governor's control called the Virginia Commission on Fine Art and Historical Sites. Norton didn't really care or understand what the agency did so he agreed. In a couple years he'd find out why she wanted to pick the commissioners.

9) Beaman

A member of the House of Delegates is in Richmond for two months out of the year, and must find a place to stay while the assembly is in session. When Norton was elected in the 1990's, he stayed at Steve Beaman's house on Monument Avenue. Beaman's primary house was in Northern Virginia, but he also had a house in Richmond. The divorced Beaman had a daughter, who very few people saw. Norton met her only a couple of times; Beaman's ex-wife had really raised her. Beaman was mostly married to his career, and then when he retired he moved to help Norton full time.

Norton and Beaman were just a few years apart in age, Beaman being a few years older but basically the same generation, with similar interests and outlooks. Beaman, the more cynical of the two, shared Norton's desire for power and influence. However, Beaman realized he could acquire power through his relationship with Norton.

Norton was probably Beaman's best friend, perhaps his only friend. Beaman spent a brief time in the Army after he graduated from college. Rumor had it that the Army drummed him out of the service pretty quick. After being given a required psychological evaluation, the Army concluded that he was probably a sociopath.

It was said that analysts summed it up this way. If a store clerk informed Beaman that the store had stopped carrying his favorite brand of bread, or if an emergency doctor told him his uncle just died of a heart attack, Beaman would feel the same level of sympathy and sadness. In effect his feelings of disappointment would be the same in either case. Despite some investigation, those rumors never could be confirmed. Beaman received an honorable discharge and the Army sealed his records permanently, which barred anyone without a court order from accessing them.

Beaman then went to work for a local Washington DC television station, working his way up to an executive position. He had a knack for TV and media. Some possible reasons for his great success included a combination of intelligence, ambition, ability to work hard, and his lack of desire for personal relationships. He had no qualms about stepping over people, and also had a great knack for always finding out what other people knew while never revealing what he knew.

After decades in TV, he started to pursue his other passion, politics, working on the side to help Democrat political candidates. He met Norton when Norton announced his campaign for the Fairfax County Board of Supervisors, representing the Providence district.

Over the years they became close friends and Beaman earned Norton's trust. Norton appreciated Beaman's intellect, frankness, and his political instincts. Beaman would do anything for him; he had no moral qualms. He was a rough political brawler, in effect taking the role of Norton's son of a bitch, doing the dirty work needed.

On more than one occasion Beaman made the 91 mile trip to Richmond on a Friday afternoon, just to hang out with Norton for a weekend during the session.

The two were big movie buffs, so in their free time during the session they'd watch old movies at Beaman's house. They especially loved espionage movies. They watched all the Bond movies. each had a favorite Bond and Bond villain; they even had a favorite Bond girl. They also liked Cold War movies, especially *All the President's Men*, about the Watergate scandal in the 70's. Beaman used to joke, or maybe it was more in the realm of a fantasy, "Maybe one day Ronnie will be in a pickle and we'll have conversations in a secret location like an empty garage at midnight." This was a reference to the scene where Woodward and Bernstein meet their contact, Deep Throat, in a parking garage near the Watergate hotel.

Ronnie, who at the time was just a member of the House of Delegates, responded, "No, Steve, I don't think I'd have the power for us to have to go deep cover."

"Seriously, Ronnie, you never know. Maybe you'll be governor and involved in a scandal. We'll have to meet under deep cover to go over strategy."

While neither had served in military intelligence, they loved to talk in secret agent code. They decided that a very serious conversation which must be kept secret would be labeled "DEFCON 1" or that such a discussion must be under "deep cover."

Beaman said, "We should do a dry run sometimes."

Norton laughed. "What secret conversation do we need to have? And as a member of the House of Delegates, I have an office where we can talk."

Beaman explained, "Of course, but sometimes total secrecy will be necessary. We might not want people in the office to know we were talking privately at a certain time with the door closed. They might put two and two together. It is deep cover for an emergency."

Elections Have Consequences

Beaman and Norton were fascinated with the cloak and dagger movies they used to watch. Beaman believed that leaks were detected to a large extent when investigators would compare meeting logs and phone records.

Beaman said to Norton, "The Dreyfus affair was probably unraveled because French authorities matched schedules and phone logs."

They concluded that deep cover might not be necessary, but just in case they set up a system. Norton probably agreed just to please his friend.

They found a parking garage off Broad Street on 7th Street, the ground floor. Beaman added, "To be precise you go seven columns down to the right from the entrance."

The code was simply the words, "We need to talk." It could be spoken or written by either one, at any time. Norton played along, "Okay, Steve, we have a plan."

"Ronnie, we have to do a dry run."

Norton rolled his eyes and said, "Why?"

Beaman explained, "We have to go through it a few times to really commit it to memory. On a dry run we could discover any problems regarding security and privacy."

Norton went along. "Okay, we can practice once."

Soon they had a little excuse—a very little excuse. It was a small personnel matter, so they went through the drill. After a meeting in Delegate Norton's office in the General Assembly building on a Tuesday afternoon, Beaman slipped Delegate Norton a note which read, "We need to talk."

Norton nodded, and mockingly said, "Roger that," and they

Elections Have Consequences

triggered their deep cover operation. He then asked "Steve, do you want me to drive?"

Beaman frowned in disapproval, "No, we have to come from separate directions. If we go together to the secret meeting location it could undermine the secrecy." Norton just rolled his eyes.

They went through the dry run. There in the garage at midnight they agreed to fire a staffer and agreed on the rationale.

Standing there in the 7th Street parking garage, Norton concluded, "Steve, we could have made this decision at the office. I know it's a sensitive subject, but we didn't need deep cover. This is hardly the level of DEFCON 1."

Beaman responded, "Ronnie, this was a dry run, but don't you see the benefit? It's like this meeting never happened. No one, unless they followed us, would have any idea this meeting ever took place; it is totally off the record. We just made the personnel decision and we agreed on the rationale. There is no record of us having discussed it in a meeting, and no one could have overheard us." Beaman added with a little levity, "Well, maybe the mice and cockroaches heard us."

Norton, ever the neat freak and germaphobe, asked, "What's that smell?"

Beaman raised his head, flared his nostrils, looked around, and concluded "Urine." He explained that there was a concert at the Mosque last night. "The kids probably came down here, the lines to the bathroom were probably long." The Mosque was a popular concert venue in Richmond.

"All right, Steve, I guess there can be a benefit to this secret communication system, but only in rare circumstances, and I mean only DEFCON 1 level seriousness."

Elections Have Consequences

Beaman added, "Of course, but you see secrecy is sometimes necessary. I understand 7th Street is only DEFCON 1, but we need to drill a couple times a year."

Norton agreed. "Okay, but let's not over do it."

"Okay, just three times a year we do a practice run." Norton agreed. They kept this up while Norton was a delegate and then for Norton's terms in the State Senate.

10) Ask The Governor

The major news radio station in the DC area hosts the show called *Ask the Governor*. It is a long-running program; no matter if a Democrat or Republican is governor, they are on once a week when the legislature is in session. That makes it a perfect opportunity to talk to Northern Virginians, since the radio station is picked up as far south down 95 as Fredericksburg. The audience is fairly large, especially since the show airs during the morning rush hour.

The questions are fairly easy since the host of the show doesn't focus on Virginia politics, and the callers aren't allowed a follow up on their question. The caller may ask a good question, but is then hung up on while the governor responds. That response may or may not answer the caller's question, so it is easier for a governor to dodge a question without a follow up.

However, due to the popularity of the program the producers decided to bring outside guests on the show, such as Madyson "Maddy" Clack and Steve Cohen both known as leading reporters of Virginia politics.

Almost every week, at least one of them would be one of the guests. The others were a mix of radio employees from the news department. When the show first started decades ago, the host of the show was the former traffic reporter "Helicopter Bob." Since then, there have been a number of hosts.

Cohen, famous for his bow ties and hipster glasses, looked younger than his years. Despite being in his early 60's, he looked like he was in his early 50's. A native of Petersburg, he started with the *Daily Dispatch* right out of college. Since he was naturally a good writer, they hired him, but the editor didn't know exactly where to put him. A movie buff, Cohen kept talking at the paper about different movies he liked. The editor gave him two tickets for the Byrd Theater and said, "Write me a review." He did such a good job he was given the assignment of writing theater and movie reviews, with the promise that a couple of times a week he could work on Virginia politics.

However, for his reviews he used the pen name C. Atwood Bellamy rather than his real name. It is unclear why; perhaps Cohen thought theater and movie reviews were a step down from reporting on Virginia politics, or perhaps he wanted to be known exclusively as a political reporter.

His movie reviews were quite good; in fact, so good that they were picked up for national syndication. Everyone in the entertainment industry knew the name C. Atwood Bellamy, but few made the connection with Cohen. Doing the movie and theater reviews helped supplement his income, but he wanted nothing to detract from his reputation as a Virginia political reporter. As he used to say, "Buster Carrico never did a movie review." Melville "Buster" Carrico wrote for the *Roanoke Times*, covering Virginia politics for over 40 years before retiring in the 1980's.

The other frequent guest, Maddy Clack, worked in television for a Washington network affiliate. How did Clack become one of the deans of Virginia politics? It was really by default. When she graduated from the University of Massachusetts with a degree in communications and a minor in international relations, she came to Washington to find a job in media. Ironically, it was Steve Beaman who gave her a job at the NBC affiliate.

Elections Have Consequences

The only job opening they had, however, was covering the state capital. Not Capitol Hill. And most reporters didn't want to go 91 miles to Richmond to get stories about delegates that few people knew or ever heard of. Where's the glamor in that?

She did get some national exposure, though. It seemed court documents revealed that a prominent member of the House of Delegates had been involved in a little scandal. About 15 years earlier the delegate was accused by a business associate of sexual harassment. Naturally, it became national news and Maddy was on all the national news networks talking about what she uncovered.

In one day Maddy was on MNN, MSNBC, PBS, and dozens of other stations outside Virginia. For a day her extended family all over the country could see her on TV.

But for over 20 years Maddy had done a decent job, solid work. So she was given a spot on the *Ask the Governor* show when the old co-host retired from broadcasting. Interestingly, Maddy had a family connection to the General Assembly; her father represented Fairfax County in the State Senate.

Democrats retook the House of Delegates two years into Norton's term, and with that they took control of the General Assembly. Norton told Beaman on election night, "I got those bastard Republicans where I want them. They have no power, and I will never have to sign a Republican bill." He happily declared, "Just like Governor Harry Byrd, I won't need to work with Republicans." Norton asked, "Who was the last Democrat governor in Virginia that had as much of a partisan advantage as I will now have?"

Beaman thought for a second and replied, "I would guess Governor Albertis Harrison in the early 1960's."

Elections Have Consequences

Norton smiled and responded, "Just like good old Albertis Harrrison."

Beaman mused, "I think they named a school after him. Well, if so, it's probably been renamed by now."

Their only possible block was Republican Lt. Governor Jim Morrison. As long as there were no ties, Norton and the Democrats could get anything through that they wanted, things they never would have dared to try if Republicans had held either chamber. One example: the day after the election, he signed an executive order instructing Virginia public schools to allow students to play on sports teams based on the gender they identify with, not their biological sex. Any student who identifies as a girl must be allowed to play on the girls' teams.

Norton's handpicked commission had made this recommendation months prior, but he waited to make the announcement until after the election since he didn't want to jeopardize Democrats chances to take control of the legislature.

However, there was one downside to his party taking over the General Assembly. When he ran for governor, he promised Brand and the social justice warriors that he'd appoint a commission to come up with a new, more relevant state motto. He figured with Republicans in charge of the legislature, or at least the House of Delegates, the motto change would go nowhere. Now he would have to follow through.

A senior campaign strategist told Bhavna Agarwal, on the promise of anonymity, "To get the Democrat nomination Ronnie promised party activists three things: that he would sign a repeal of Right to Work, that he'd appoint the first gay justice to the state Supreme Court, and that he would appoint a commission to come up with a new state motto. Norton opposed all three ideas privately. But when he promised to do those things, Republicans controlled the House of Delegates, which offered him protection."

The strategist went on, "Ronnie was thrilled; he thought those concessions were a small price to pay for the Democrat nomination for governor. He later chuckled and told me, 'I thought Brand and the other lefties were going to want more.'"

Now he had to deliver, and now the cover of the Republican House of Delegates killing the bills was lost.

The commission on a new state motto would be chaired by Reverend Brand, and the co-chair of the commission would be Attorney General Deb Foster, the only transgendered attorney general in the country. Ironically, Foster, a self described "Joe Manchin Democrat," considered to be a centrist Democrat, would probably provide a good, sane balance to Brand. At least Norton believed that Foster would provide a brake on any motto too crazy.

The left didn't like the current motto "Sic Semper Tyrannis," which translates to "Thus Always to Tyrants," mainly because it was anti-government. To Brand and the social revolutionaries, government power and control was necessary to bring social justice and equality. They believed that limited government was the hope of white supremiscists, men, and capitalists. Also, the words are in Latin, which to the likes of Brand is the language of Western European civilization.

It was the first Wednesday in February when a thin, fairly goofy-looking Norton arrived for his guest spot on *Ask the Governor*. The interview program was broadcast from a studio in Arlington. Norton walked in with a modest security detail.

Nothing as gaudy as a rock star would have; simply three security officers and a couple of press people. His driver who would wait in the car.

Norton did fine in one-on-one interviews. He was always in command of the issues he cared about, but on issues in which he wasn't particularly interested he could be sloppy and overly glib. The questions asked on the show were the usual softballs provided to a Democrat. After all, both Clack and Cohen were basically Democrats, and the other rotating questioners didn't follow Virginia politics enough to ask a tough question even if they had such an inclination.

Officially, Vince Baxter hosted the show since it aired during his morning time slot. While Vince was thought of as a conservative, he didn't really follow Virginia politics, and anyway he deferred most questions to Clack and Cohen.

Maddy Clack started the show off by asking Norton if he was aware of Senator Sandoval's abortion bill, SB 1819.

"I am, though I can't say I have read the entire bill. I would add, though, that I am supportive of a woman's right to choose, so I am inclined to sign it."

Clack then went on to ask about another initiative the governor was pushing: his controversial educational initiative which required Virginia public schools to record incidents of racist jokes being told among the students. It asked students to report racist jokes they heard while on school property to teachers and school personnel. The school was required to tally up the number of these "incidents" and report the data to the state to be logged onto a state database. School systems could compare numbers and see if over the course of years there were increases or decreases.

Elections Have Consequences

"Ideally, once passed and with the website working perfectly," Norton said, "parents will be able to type in the school's name into the search engine and find out how many racist jokes were reported in their child's school during a semester."

If the number increased, the school system could apply for money from the state to institute additional sensitivity classes and training. One objection, among many to the bill, was that it would give the school system an incentive to overstate the number of racist jokes told in order to get more state money.

However, the racist joke would only be counted if it took place on school property. If the student told the joke on the way to school, but not on school property, it would not count, even if another student heard it and was offended. If the joke was told on the school bus, that would count because the bus was school property.

Clack asked, "Governor Norton, Republican State Senator Angela Parrish described your offensive joke initiative as 'stupid, asinine, ridiculous and unconstitutional.' She even suggested that such a proposal would only encourage students, out of rebellion and defiance toward the school, to step off school property and tell as many racist jokes as they could think of before they got to school. Your reaction?"

Norton smiled and said "Well, more hateful rhetoric from Republicans. Let's face it, they have no interest in making amends for their racist past and trying to move our state to a just, fair place. Racist jokes are a real problem. What alternative are they proposing? None, because they have no interest in stopping racism."

Clack followed up. "Parrish also said this amounted to a 'snitch hotline' where students would be encouraged to tattle on other students, creating hostile feelings between students."

"It is not snitching to report bad things going on in schools."

Clack then asked about a possible conflict with the First Amendment. Norton replied, "There is no violation of the First Amendment, since a student's First Amendment rights are in effect nonexistent. The state has an interest in creating a learning environment and racist jokes interfere with that mission. Look, I understand that in the streets or in their homes they are free to say what they want, but in a public school, conformity is required for an effective learning environment."

Norton even mentioned a story of a girl—although he avoided the use of the word girl by using the more politically correct term "female student"—in Goochland County whose classmate had a backpack with a Confederate battle flag sewed on. Norton pleaded, "Imagine how difficult it must be for a student of color to have to study and learn in such an environment!"

Clack then asked if obscene or so-called dirty jokes would apply. Norton responded, "No. While dirty jokes are not positive, everyone knows that 13-year-old boys are likely to express themselves with an occasional dirty joke. After all, boys will be boys, and we don't wish to stifle the creativity that might come by such an expression. And it's only natural that the boys will notice that the girls are developing in certain ways. So it raises their curiosity, and they might tell a bad joke or two. Now, I am just as concerned about toxic masculinity and the evils of lookism as the next person, but this bill simply, and I believe effectively, deals with racist jokes."

"Speaking of free speech, there is an issue on college campuses of MAGA clubs being formed at, according to the progressive Hate Group Watch, an alarming rate. For our listeners who don't know, MAGA stands for Make America Great Again. I believe that as a student at UVA State Senator Parrish organized a chapter. Does it concern you that these groups are popping up, and do you believe that the schools should recognize such groups?"

Norton responded, "I think conservatives should be free to get together to talk politics, I don't think anyone disagrees with their right to organize, but the controversy stems from the name of the group, 'Make America Great Again.' This implies America was once great, and to many Virginians of color, this is considered highly offensive and insensitive. Such a name could trigger anger. So I would suggest the group change their name, and I think that would help quell the controversy. Hopefully, a compromise name can be found."

"Those on the left have argued that conservatives have shown little willingness to compromise. What makes you think they might be willing to compromise on a name change here? And do you have any ideas on a possible new name for their clubs?"

Norton suggested, "Perhaps the Conservative Club. That, I think, would be fine with most people." Norton then jokingly added, "Or the Angela Parrish Fan Club." Others in the studio laughed.

Cohen asked, "This question deals with what can be taught as fact in schools. A teacher in Danville taught her class about the insurrection of January 6th, 2021. One parent complained that the teacher was expressing an opinion, not fact. That is that there was no insurrection. I know the Virginia Department of Education will release a ruling on this case, but can you update us on this?"

Elections Have Consequences

"Steve, I am glad you raised this question. Yes, the department will issue a ruling; I expect within days now. I would point out that they have a full docket of cases this year. There is no question that the then president incited an erection [no one corrected Norton, but several in the control room laughed] on that infamous day, January 6th. Most textbooks list it as the 'Great Insurrection of January 6th.' Heck, a police officer was killed, in part by defending democracy that day. So, there is no question about it. And I have no doubt that the department will find that it is indeed a fact." Norton made a comparison. "The Department of Education is like the fact checkers online, like Chirp and Bolshebook have, and like the DHS's disinformation board, their role is to keep false information out.

"So, I believe that the teacher was correct, historically, and I am confident the department will rule that. And I would point out that the Virginia Department of Education exists to teach truth no matter how painful, but also in part to back up teachers."

Norton went on: "Everything taught in our schools must be vetted through the Department of Education. This department is nonpolitical and non-ideological. They are the safeguard to keep politics outside the schoolhouse door."

Cohen asked, "Another education question, on the controversial Critical Race Theory curriculum. Are you in favor of mandating it be taught in Virginia public schools?

"No, I think it is theory and should not be mandated from Richmond. I realize many on my side will disagree with me, but I think the local school system should decide for themselves on this theory; again, it is not a matter of fact. So if it is not fact, it shouldn't even be in the classroom, in my opinion."

Elections Have Consequences

Clack asked about a breaking news story. "Governor, I don't know if you saw this, but this morning Moms United filed an emergency appeal with the Board of Education to block the assignment of Joseph Conrad's novel *Heart of Darkness* in Chesterfield County public schools. Your reaction? Do you agree that it should not be assigned reading, due the potential racial insensitivity of the novel?"

The novel is considered a classic and is actually quite critical of colonialism. However, the book uses harsh language and refers to the natives as savages. In their filing, Moms United cited the removal of Mark Twain's *Huckleberry Finn* as precedent for removal of novels that use racially insensitive language.

Norton really didn't want to oppose Moms United, a powerful group on the left. Teachers United also joined the appeal with an amicus brief, in support of removing the book. Norton deflected the question.

"I think the Board of Education will look at it and make an informed, sensible ruling. And they will have a decision soon on whether this book is to be allowed in school. Again, I would point out the board is nonpolitical and non-ideological; the people of Virginia can trust the board to vindicate the truth and remove errors from our schools." Norton then added, "Of course, I encourage our young readers to read all types of books that are inclusive, diverse, and reflective of our community."

The Board of Education had a nine-member panel that ruled on all cases where facts are in dispute; that is, what should be taught as facts in Virginia public schools, and also what books should be allowed. However, the majority can be overruled by the Secretary. An example took place in Norton's first year in office.

Elections Have Consequences

The board voted five to four to remove six of Dr. Seuss's books from the school's list of recommended books on grounds racial insensitivity. Brand was sympathetic with the reasons for the decision, but for political reasons overruled the board. During the campaign, Angela Parrish had claimed that the radicals who run Virginia public schools would ban Dr. Seuss. Norton said she was nuts for making such a claim. So as not to prove Parrish correct, Brand defended Dr. Seuss and overruled the board. In addition to the Secretary of Education, the governor also has the power to overrule the board.

Maddy Clack, with Channel 4, asked the final question. "Despite living in Richmond, you are still a resident of Fairfax County. What is your opinion on the push to rename Fairfax County?"

In order to out-woke each other in Fairfax County, one member of the Board of Supervisors, introduced a resolution to recommend changing the county's name. The argument centered on the belief that the Fairfax family didn't do enough to oppose slavery in the colonies. In doing some research, the Fairfax Chapter of Moms United to Save Virginia concluded that Lord Fairfax was not a social justice warrior; in fact far from it, so they joined the campaign to rename the county.

Some members of the Fairfax family in England made contributions to a group committed to fight the name change. To get a jump on the potential name change fight, the group produced several radio ads. Fairfax family members put out a statement promising to help combat all forms of discrimination. In a statement a family spokesman said: "Our family has not always done right by all people throughout the centuries, and for that we are very sorry, but we have, we believe, on balance made a positive contribution to humanity. We are committed to the cause of social justice moving forward."

Norton thought the idea of the name change was a stupid and unnecessary move, but again he knew he needed to be careful in his answer. "I don't support a name change. Two things I will insist on: first, I am willing to listen to the arguments for the change, and second, the people of Fairfax County must have a say through a referendum. It can't just be a vote of the Board of Supervisors."

"Looks like we have run out of time. Thank you and we will talk to you next week.

"I look forward to it," Norton said

"Now let's get an update on traffic, and guess what, Governor, no surprise, looks like there's a big back up on 66 eastbound."

Norton took a shot at humor. "Darn, it's about time somebody does something about 66 traffic." Light, perhaps polite, laughter erupted in the studio.

Before he left the studio, Norton recorded a public service announcement on his anti-racist joke school initiative.

A press aide leaned over and informed him, "Governor, just one change to the script."

"What is that?" Norton asked.

"Well, Governor, we cut out the term 'off color joke'; the kids probably won't know what that means, so we left it as simply as a 'racist joke.'"

"Okay, that makes sense," Norton agreed.

Norton looked into the camera, waiting for his cue and then read the teleprompter:

Elections Have Consequences

"Hello, friends, this is Ronnie Norton, governor of the great Commonwealth of Virginia. As governor there is no higher priority for me than the education of our children. I am convinced that to educate, our schools must provide a safe, non-hostile environment where our kids can learn, free from harassment and bigotry. And to create such an environment we must not allow racist stereotypes to be allowed to be spread through racist jokes. I am asking all students who hear such jokes to report them to a guidance counselor or administrator, or even the gym coach. If you are unsure if a joke you just heard was offensive, please consult with a school employee.

Racist and offensive jokes are not a laughing matter."

"And that is a wrap, Governor. Excellent! You did it in one take!"

Norton inquired about when the PSAs would start running. "They will start next week, and air state wide for the next month."

"Excellent," Norton replied. He thought, *That will keep my left flank happy.*

On the way back to Richmond, Norton checked in with Beaman. "Hey Steve, did you catch the show?"

"Sure did, Governor. Not bad, but you changed your position on abortion! A pretty big thing to do on drive time radio." Sandoval's bill allowed late term abortions.

"Steve, I didn't intend on it, but I wanted to praise Sandoval and the NARAL crowd, and state my support for a woman's right to choose. I'm sorry about the appearance that I support abortion through the third trimester. I would only support that for limited reasons, which I was referring to. I guess we need to backtrack."

"Yes, Governor, that bill got attention today because of

Angela Parrish grilling Sandoval about it in committee. Our hope was it would die a quiet death. Parrish's display today brought it up in the news. It may be best to backtrack this afternoon, with a clarification., I do think you should backtrack a tad. Reaffirm your support for abortion, but in the first trimester, not late term abortion."

Norton agreed. "I'll put out a statement reaffirming my support for existing Virginia law."

"Listen, Governor, I will be out of commission for the next couple of days. I'm having a gallstone removed and will be under the weather. Hopefully Friday night I'll be able to call again, so keep the commonwealth safe for the next three days."

"Sounds good, Steve, I'll talk to you Friday night."

11) An Old Picture in the Attic

Ronnie Norton went to college at VCC for undergrad and then off to Washington and Lee for law school. Norton's parents were very proud of their son. Ronnie was a good student and stayed out of trouble, for the most part. Sure, there was the occasional teepeeing of a house, a blown-up mailbox or two, but by most Virginia parents' standards, Norton would have been considered a good kid.

Ronnie wanted to become a lawyer. He was not interested in the construction trade like his father. In an interview with the *Washington Press Democrat,* Norton said of his career path, "I had a great interest in public service so I wanted to work for the federal government like most of my neighbors but I also had a great interest in politics, and I decided that I could do best by running for elective office."

At VCC, he joined a fraternity, since he was still a little awkward, and the fraternity would hopefully help him mature and meet people. At the recruitment table, he saw a big picture of General Lee. The recruiter said, "Lee was the spiritual founder of our fraternity." Naturally this appealed to the history buff in Ronnie.

Generally popular at VCC, he rushed the fraternity and became friends with Scott Miller, also from Northern Virginia. Miller fondly looked back at that time as glory days.

"I was one of his best friends [this was a bit of a stretch] at VCC. He and I were drinking buddies. Ronnie was a good guy, smart and funny," Miller would tell people. They went their separate ways after graduation.

Elections Have Consequences

Miller went to work for an insurance company in Fairfax, and Norton came back to Northern Virginia after he finished law school. Despite both being in Northern Virginia, they never got together.

Scott's wife Cindy knew that he had gone to school with Norton, but didn't think about him at all until decades later when he ran for governor. She never shared his politics, but had nothing against him. She would drive to and from work and see the big orange and blue campaign signs with "Vote for RONNIE" blazoned across them.

In the spring, ironically in the year Norton first ran for governor, she was going through the attic, to do some cleaning. In walking across the dimly lit attic she tripped over a box and fell pretty hard.

She looked back to see what she had tripped over. It was a box with Scott's handwriting on it marked "VCC college personal." She thought, *This is a perfectly good place to start throwing away junk,* but rather than just throw out the whole box she decided she had better go through it first.

She found his college notebooks, a scrapbook, a Rubik's cube, a few old textbooks, and a Playboy magazine (August 1982, missing the centerfold.) She muttered sarcastically, "Without the centerfold, I won't get much for it on eBay. Terrific!"

She also found his fraternity pin and a book with the name of his fraternity on the cover. The fraternity produced an edition every year, to honor its members and list what they have done as a group, including their charitable work. It was only produced for the fraternity, but sometimes they sent a copy to donors.

She noticed that they did do a good bit of charity work in and around Richmond. There was a picture of Ronnie and Scott

Elections Have Consequences

hauling away some junk, in what looked like a "Clean Up Richmond" beautification program.

In the index she looked up her Prince Charming husband, and she also decided to look up Norton.

She went to the index of Norton's pictures and glanced at page after page, until she got to page 73. She stared, flabbergasted by what she saw. It was a picture of a person who appeared to be Norton in blackface, and a picture of someone in Nazi regalia next to him, his arm extended in a Nazi salute.

Norton's name was listed in the caption under the picture. "Major Hans Rimmer and Ronnie Norton aka, Huggy Bear." Norton was dressed as a pimp, with plaid pants, a white belt, a white coat, and a tee shirt that read "Ask me about hoes and bitches." She couldn't tell for certain that it was Norton. Could it be some odd mistake? A misprint?

Two thoughts came to mind. First, she thought, *Why would any fraternity allow such a picture in a book with their name on it?* Even in the 1980's, that would be considered unacceptable behavior.

With the election just a few months away, Cindy had a dilemma. She thought, *Could there be some sort of honest mistake here? Could Norton be a closet racist? Could her husband be a racist?*

It was perfectly natural to be curious, and she decided to confront her husband.

As she got halfway down the stairs to his man cave in the basement, she could see her Prince Charming sprawled out on the couch, his feet on a table, staring at the TV. Most Saturdays Scott would binge watch murder mystery shows.

Cindy nervously started the conversation by clearing her throat holding the book in her hand, "Listen, Scott honey, we need to talk."

Elections Have Consequences

Scott was glued to the TV and pleaded, "Sure, honey, but this is not a rerun. Can we wait until the next commercial?"

"No, we need to talk now."

Scott reached for the remote control and turned the volume down, so he could still get the gist of the program while she spoke. He assumed she was going to give him another lecture about leaving his underwear all over the place and treating the place like a pigsty, or how he was spending way too much time talking to a female former coworker on social media.

"I wasn't trying to be nosy, Scott, but out of curiosity I looked at your old fraternity yearbook, and I found a picture of your old buddy, State Senator Ronnie Norton"

Noticeably relieved, Scott realized that he was not in her crosshairs. She was not going to launch a tirade at him; rather, she just wanted to talk about his glory days at VCC.

Excitedly, Scott got up and said, "Let me get a beer. Do you want one? And we'll talk about whatever you like. I am interested, I really am."

"No, Scott, please tell me, can you explain how this picture got there?" Cindy then slammed the yearbook down on the coffee table. "Can you explain this picture?"

"Oh, yes, Huggy Bear! That takes me back. I haven't seen this picture in years; where did you find the book?"

Cindy replied, "In the attic. Explain the picture, please!"

Scott went on, "Norton is in character; he used to dress up as Huggy Bear. And the other guy, Jack, is dressed as his character, Major Hans Rimmer of the SS."

"Scott Oscar Miller, you better explain this right now!" Cindy said as emphatically as she had ever said anything to him. The look in her eye signified that without a good explanation she might go talk to a divorce attorney.

"Well, the other guy was, I think I have mentioned him to you, Jack Villiers. Sadly he died about a few years ago, died young, way too young, about my age. He and Ronnie were best friends. Ronnie took the loss hard; he gave the eulogy at Jack's funeral, about the time Ronnie was getting ready to run for governor." Scott said, "But let me finish getting that beer. Sure you don't want one?"

While he was rummaging through the refrigerator looking for a beer, Scott continued the conversation, "Look, sweetie, it was years ago. In college at our fraternity house, we did some pretty bad stuff. The black face and Nazi dress up just happened. Ronnie was no racist; he was just in costume."

"What?" Cindy asked.

Scott said, "Look closely, can't you tell who he is impersonating?"

"No."

Scott said, "He's Huggy Bear."

An exasperated Cindy responded, "What is a Huggy Bear?"

Scott explained, "Huggy Bear, from the show *Starsky and Hutch*. Huggy Bear was a secondary character, and we gathered from the show that he was a pimp, although I don't think the show ever made it explicitly clear. It was just implied. Well, Ronnie was fascinated by Huggy Bear. So he started dressing up like him as part of a skit. He practiced Huggy's mannerisms, he asked the sorority sisters if they could help him apply shoe polish to his face—my shoe polish, by the way. Oh, and he learned to walk like him, dress like him, and speak in a jive dialect like him. My God, if he entered a national Huggy Bear lookalike contest he'd win hands down.

Elections Have Consequences

"I guess Ronnie used to watch the show *Starsky and Hutch* and decided he wanted to impersonate Huggy Bear, and Jack watched *Hogan's Heroes* and he wanted to dress as an SS officer." Scott remembered, "Jack would come into a room, dressed like that, snap his heels together, and then in almost a yell, extend his right arm forward and say 'Heil Hitler.'"

Cindy just shook her head in disbelief.

Scott added, "As far as Jack Villiers also dressing as a Klansman from time to time, well, he was in a character he invented. Major Hans Rimmer of the SS. He was good. He would have on a full uniform, burst into the room, and yell things like, 'Orders, orders which must be obeyed at all costs or I will have you shot.'"

Cindy sighed, "Oh, my God."

Scott responded, "The only other fascination was his interest in the Klan. He studied Klan by-laws and chapter rules and history; he searched for all kinds of first-hand source material; he scoured state archives; he studied how they formed cells and recruited members; he probably knew more about the Klan than anyone, even professors and historians. I don't think Jack was ever a member of the Klan, and he didn't try to recruit anyone. For Jack, I think it was an historical exercise and to dress up that way was done when he gave a lecture on the Klan. He did other characters, but Hans Rimmer was his favorite. Actually, this picture is not so bad."

Cindy said, "He dressed as a Nazi and a Klansman?"

Scott tried to respond, "Again, Jack had a historical fascination. Ronnie's costume was more innocent. He just liked Huggy Bear." Scott added, "Ronnie wasn't as deep or intellectual as Jack; Ronnie just thought Huggy Bear was cool. Huggy Bear got the ladies; he lived a charmed life."

Cindy simply shook her head and muttered, "Oh, my God."

Scott went on, "Ronnie was the best man at Jack's wedding, and gave the eulogy at his funeral." Scott said, "How sad! Imagine being the best man at a guy's wedding and also giving the eulogy at his funeral. Ronnie cried at Jack's funeral. He loved Jack; he always said he wanted to be just like him."

Scott tried to explain. "Jack could be kind of mysterious. He was, as the saying goes, an enigma wrapped in a riddle. We all admired Jack. He was the leader; he got both of us in the fraternity, well, first Ronnie then me. Jack was a man for all seasons. He was smart, he was a loyal friend, he had a certain charm and charisma. He also smoked and drank constantly, which probably contributed to his early death. I remember what a great dresser he was. Well, when not in an SS uniform or Klan suit."

Scott paused, took a sip of beer, then continued the story. "Well, Jack went into medicine. He became a doctor and set up a practice in Henrico County. And what a small world–do you know he delivered Lt. Governor Jim Morrison's kids. It's funny, because if you had asked me who in the fraternity was most likely to one day become governor of Virginia, I would have said Jack."

Scott went on, "Every Friday night we'd go to the fraternity house and have dinner, then we'd go into the basement and Jack would give a lecture.

"Jack was a polymath. He was interested in and conversant with all kinds of subjects. He would sit in an armchair in the center of the room and start a monologue, or you could call it a lecture. There would be 20 to 30 people there. For nearly two hours he'd talk without notes about a different topic. One night it would be on McClellan's peninsula campaign, the next the history of the Persians and the Greeks, colonization of southern Africa, the Norman conquest, the meanings of Shakespeare's plays and so forth. All kinds of subjects fascinated him."

Scott laughed, remembering another detail. "Jack had the nickname 'Jitters,' because he would sort of shake if he went too long without a drink or smoke. When he would sit up front and give his lecture, after about an hour his knee would start bouncing up and down. At first it was barely noticeable, but the longer he'd go on the more pronounced it would become. This indicated he needed a fix, and that the lecture would be ending soon.

"Jack used to give everyone advice; he always had an opinion. It was amazing how you almost had to book an appointment to meet with him to discuss a problem. He was in demand like a doctor. It's fitting that's what he became."

Scott went on, "Villiers could be very generous. Ronnie was obsessed with this chick from Mary Baldwin. Her name was Mary Louise or Mary Sue; I can't remember. She had some such hyphenated name. He kept asking us what he could do to impress her. And at the time he was driving around in his old klunker of a car, which he felt embarrassed about. He had his eye on a new white Chrysler LeBaron convertible, but being a college student, like most of us he didn't have the money for the down payment."

Scott smiled and gave an example of Jack's generosity. "One night Ronnie and a bunch of us were sitting in the kitchen. We were all finishing up dinner when Jack came in and said, 'Ronnie, you want to get laid, and I as your best friend want you to get laid, but you're driving around in that old jalopy. In that car you ain't going to get to first base. So here's what I'm going to do. I'm going to give you the money for a big down payment on that Chrysler convertible you have your eye on.

"Ronnie was thrilled, and told him he'd pay him back as soon as he could, but Jack said there was no need to pay him back. He told Ronnie, 'Just consider it your birthday and Christmas presents for the next 10 years.' Ronnie loved that car."

As he spoke Scott seemed to remember more about Ronnie's girl. "If Ronnie dated a seven, he'd be lucky, but this Mary Baldwin chick was probably an eight. Ronnie claimed she was a nine, but as I remember her, that was a stretch."

Scott continued, "Jack and Ronnie were inseparable. I'd see them all over campus together, all over Richmond together. There was this bar in Shockoe Bottom, I forget the name, but I swear I saw them there all the time. They had a corner table; I can still see them huddled together absolutely absorbed in conversation. My natural instinct, of course, would be to go over and say hi, but they seemed like they were in such deep thought that I didn't want to bother them."

"How does that justify Norton's behavior? Dressing in blackface?"

Scott responded confidently, "Look, Ronnie was no racist. You know how I know that?"

Cindy shook her head. Scott replied, "Ronnie genuinely liked people. All people interested him, he loved to learn about everyone he met. A racist is someone who dislikes people. That wasn't Ronnie. I may not agree with his politics, but I will say this, Ronnie is motivated with a desire to help people. And as far as Huggy Bear, well. Ronnie thought he was a great character to imitate. To my generation, Huggy Bear was an idol."

Elections Have Consequences

Cindy buried her face in her hands, then looked up and asked, "But why did you take the picture, and why did you get it into your fraternity's yearbook and list him as being in the picture?"

"Well, I was in charge of collecting photos for the yearbook. I got all the pictures from the brothers, and I had the picture I took at the party, which I threw in. Well, I thought what better picture would sum up Norton than a picture of him as Huggy Bear?"

Cindy responded, "I can't be drunk enough to understand this."

"Ronnie *was* Huggy Bear; it would seem odd not to include the picture."

"I am curious about one thing. Whoever wrote the caption, Huggy Bear aka Norton doesn't list Villiers by name. I wonder why?"

"Maybe because all the fraternity brothers knew it was Jack dressed like that. Major Hans Rimmer was so believable there was no need to list him as Jack."

"Scott, my dear, give me one good reason that I shouldn't take this to the press. One good reason I shouldn't run right downtown to NBC4 and give this to Maddy Clack."

"Ronnie has a right to a private life, a past, a youth and upbringing free from media scrutiny. In our fraternity we had a code: you don't rat on a fellow fraternity member. We all have embarrassing moments in college; they should remain private. And anyway, sweetie, he didn't know he would one day run for governor. I took the picture, and it was me who put it in the yearbook. How are we going to explain that to the press? I don't think anyone wants their college conduct examined. Trust me. I was 18 years old and I was a wild child. I did some stupid things."

Cindy sarcastically responded, "Really"?

"I am going to vote for Parrish and I assume most of the brothers are going to vote for Parrish, but we are not going to use this info against our fellow fraternity brother, even if it could guarantee our favored candidate wins. It just wouldn't be right." Scott took a sip of his beer and then earnestly said, "It's a matter of ethics."

Cindy kept the secret.

Several weeks later Norton was elected Governor. Neither Scott nor Cindy voted for him, and that was the end of it, or so it seemed.

Ironically, part of the reason he won big was because of his strong support among African American voters. The Norton campaign made a number of false claims, one being that the Republican candidate, Angela Parrish, would set the state back regarding race relations, and even suggested that Hispanic Virginians would not be safe if the Republican candidate won.

No one knew of Norton's membership in a questionable fraternity or his dress up games.

12) Hell Hath No Fury

Despite being a feminist and pro-choice, Paula Norton did think her husband's embrace of the Sandoval abortion bill was a step too far. That night over dinner in the executive mansion, she brought it up. "Look, honey, I listened to *Ask the Governor* today, and while I agree with your position, most people, even women, find late term abortions very controversial."

Norton responded, "No worries, the base will be happy. Social conservatives and pro-lifers don't support me anyway."

"Look I don't like the religious zealots who attack abortion rights, but there's no reason to anger them any more with these types of extreme bills."

"Nah," Norton responded. "Anyway, the story will be done by Friday. Might even be taken over by some other story."

Norton then reminded her of his school initiative. "My campaign to go after racist jokes in public schools is the first in the nation. No other state is working on such a database." He beamed proudly. "Virginia will be the first state! No other state would even consider such a thing. Once again we're a leader among states."

Later that afternoon, Norton's PSA on racist jokes in schools started getting radio play all across the commonwealth. It did have an impact, but not the impact Norton wanted.

Cindy Miller began her late afternoon commute home, a chore no one in Northern Virginia enjoys. Going down 66 toward Vienna, she could see red tail lights get brighter, and in the distance she could make out the sign, "Two right lanes blocked."

Elections Have Consequences

Over the next two miles traffic slowed to 25 miles an hour as those lanes collapsed and drivers moved over. To pass the time, Cindy turned up the radio and immediately recognized the voice she heard. It was Governor Ronne Norton, giving his public service announcement, imploring Virginia students to snitch on others in class for telling a racist or off color joke. Norton concluded, "Racist jokes are not a laughing matter."

Cindy grew angry. She thought for a moment, searching for a word to express her feelings. After several seconds, she blurted out, "What an ass!" As she said it, her hand slammed down on the wheel. The very idea of "Huggy Bear" calling others racist for telling bad jokes was infuriating. And not college aged adults, but kids. She thought, *I saw the picture of him dressed in an offensive costume next to a guy in a Klan outfit. Jack Villiers, a Neo Nazi. And Norton has the nerve to claim others are racists? Villiers was his best friend. No doubt he overlooked Jack's behavior. Now he wants kids to snitch on other kids, over a bad joke?*

The rest of the evening, the more Cindy thought about it, the madder she got. *In a state of eight million people, we have to be lectured to by Norton? We have gone from Patrick Henry as our first governor, now we have Ronald Milsap Norton. What a decline.*

She said nothing about it to Scott, who would no doubt try to defend him. She tried to conceal her anger, and fortunately Scott didn't pick up on her feelings. Over a dinner of Swiss steak, mashed potatoes, and peas, the two said few words to each other beyond the obligatory "How was your day?" Scott simply stared at his smartphone in between bites, using his thumb to scroll through one of his favorite social media sites. Every few minutes the silence was interrupted by a chuckle, which he made whenever he saw a funny meme. Occasionally he felt the need to share one with her. Turning his phone towards her, he would say, "Check this out. Isn't that hilarious?" She pretended to be amused at first, but eventually when he said, "Here, check this out" she wouldn't even bother to look. He didn't seem to notice.

In addition to anger, Cindy felt a twinge of guilt. *I could have gone to the press with this info before the election. I kept quiet and I saved him. I saved that bastard. Parrish probably would have won if this had gotten out.*

By bedtime she had made a decision. She figured since Norton decided to set up a snitch program to report racists, she would follow his lead. She would snitch on "Huggy Bear" Norton to the media.

She would make sure Norton paid a price for his hypocrisy. Cindy knew where the yearbook was kept and would hatch a plan to get it to the news media. She called her plan, "Operation Bust Huggy Bear."

The plan was to begin on her lunch hour the next day. Cindy would drive home, get the book, run it to the copy store, then return it safely to the box in the attic. Scott would be at work and would never know. She felt both nervousness and excitement. No one would have to know who had leaked it. There would be no way Scott would know for sure she did it; she could point to the fact that his fraternity book was still in the attic.

But then she thought, *How do I get this yearbook to the media? Do I copy the page and send it in the mail? Go right to the TV station, or the newspaper?*

She didn't want it traced to her. *I better not send it through the mail. They might find my fingerprints on it, and I certainly don't want to give a return address so the police, or Norton's henchmen, can track me down.* She concluded it would be better to drop the copy off. She wanted to be as careful as possible. A little paranoia began to set in. *"Might the state police figure it was me? Is it a crime?*

As for the news outlet, she picked *The Falls Church News Leader*. Their offices were on her way to work. It was in a small office building, just three stories, and she assumed it would go right to the editor, Bruce Dutton. He was the grandson of the founder, and took over the paper from his father. To survive, the paper had been subsidized for years by family money. In effect it was a loss leader.

Bruce Dutton, a true lefty, real kook and ne'er-do-well, ran the paper. As luck would have it, he really hated Norton. Cindy had no idea he couldn't stand the governor. Bruce had never forgiven Norton for saying in 2004 that he would not vote for Howard Dean under any circumstances, even if he were the Democrat nominee; Norton claimed he was a "Never Deaner." He also couldn't forgive Norton for his stance against gay marriage. At the time, circa 2004, most of the political world considered Dean to be on the left wing of the party. By the time Norton became governor the party had moved so far to the left that Dean would be viewed as a moderate Democrat.

Perhaps Norton, at the time masquerading as a moderate Democrat, wanted to create some distance from Dean. In addition, and perhaps with that end in mind, Norton upset Dutton when he said in an interview with the *Fairfax Journal*, "Look I have nothing against homosexuals, and if they wish to cohabitate fine, but not marriage." Dutton, single and by all accounts heterosexual, was nevertheless a strong advocate of gay marriage in the early 2000's. Most of his fellow Democrats didn't get on board the gay marriage bandwagon until after Obama gave the idea his blessing on the eve of the 2012 election. They understood and accepted the political reality that Obama couldn't endorse gay marriage during the 2008 election.

Cindy decided that the *News Leader* would be a good outlet to leak the picture to. Sure, it had a small circulation, but it had the ability and motive to disseminate the info. It also had a certain obscurity. The little office on the corner off Park Street wouldn't have cameras, or even a front desk, just a door to slip the info under. But just in case, she decided that if she went in disguise, dressed like Patty Hearst in the old bank robbery video, no one would recognize her.

The copied picture made a reference to Norton as "Huggy Bear." The picture clearly showed a man in a Nazi uniform and a man in blackface with the caption, "Ronnie Norton aka Huggy Bear."

She put on a black wig and glasses. To add to the disguise she had an overcoat and wore gloves. *No fingerprints,* she thought. Inside the envelope was a copy of the picture from the book, with a note:

"Take a look at Huggy Bear! Please tell Starsky, Hutch and Captain Dolby that if they are looking for him they can find him at his new crib - the Governor's Mansion in Richmond."

On Thursday morning she dropped it off. By Friday morning, all hell had broken loose. It was a political firestorm the likes of which had never been seen in Virginia.

***

Elections Have Consequences

That Friday began like any other. Norton's schedule started at 8 a.m., meeting with his private secretary, Mrs. Helen Winchester, and a couple of aides. They did a rundown of the day. Norton reminded everyone, "Now my meeting with the Fairfax Chamber of Commerce representatives can't run late, because I do have to meet with Marty Knowles at two."

Mrs. Winchester added, "And your meeting with Marty Knowles is a full hour." A full hour with the governor was quite an honor, signifying that a person was important. Even though Knowles was a Republican, Norton genuinely liked the diminutive and portly guy.

Also from Northern Virginia, Marty Knowles chaired an important transportation commission. He was not a Norton appointee, and due to the way the commission was set up, legally Norton could not yet get rid of him. Despite being from different political parties, they saw eye to eye on transportation issues and had a good personal rapport.

But an odd thing, which could be indicative of Norton's pettiness, was that while Norton liked Marty, he couldn't stand his wife. He would occasionally refer to her as "a nasty woman" or "that dreadful woman" to others, but of course not to Marty.

Norton believed any man married to such a woman deserves sympathy, so he referred to Marty as "Poor Marty." Originally, his nickname was "Little Marty." but after Norton met his wife, he changed it to "Poor Marty."

He once complained to Beaman, "How can Marty stand being married to that woman?"

Elections Have Consequences

Beaman responded, "Have you taken a good look at Marty?" That usually ended the discussion.

Whenever Marty's name came up, Norton would mutter under his breath, "Poor Marty," and shake his head. Marty never knew Norton couldn't stand his wife and referred to him as "Poor Marty."

Just then there was a knock at the door. Before Norton could respond, Chief of Staff Ronnie Jackson came in. "Governor, we need to talk."

Norton said, "Give us ten more minutes."

Jackson responded, "Governor, this is an emergency."

When Norton looked at Jackson, he saw a look on the man's face that he had never seen before. Norton silently got up and walked towards the door. It was like the slow motion feeling before the impact of an inevitable accident, the feeling you get when you see an out of control car heading right at you.

He could see a crowd of staffers in the hallway. As he got closer, he could see they were watching a block of TVs, tuned onto all the major networks. From the staffers, there was nothing but silence. Thirty people were standing around, with no one saying a word. He looked up and saw a picture which, though he had never seen before, he instantly recognized. The background in the photo showed an old couch and curtains by a window. It could have been taken nowhere else but his old fraternity house.

The picture, of a Nazi and a pimp in blackface, had been taken by his fraternity brother Scott Miller. But Norton didn't remember that at the moment, and if anyone had mentioned the name Scott Miller, he would have had no idea who that was. Scott Miller had long ago been erased from his memory.

Elections Have Consequences

The graphic on one network glared, "Virginia Governor Norton Fraternity Photo Surfaces." Another, "Awaiting a Comment from Governor Norton." A third said, "Governor Must Explain Racist Photo."

His staffers were silent; not angry yet, but rather stunned. He did notice Reverend Brand, staring at the racist photo on the screen, had tears running down her cheeks.

Norton felt totally deflated. His first thought was, "Who betrayed me?" He saw the faces of the staffers, many of them looking blankly at him. His face turned white; he turned back to his office and said loudly, "Get Paula. I will be in my office. No one is allowed in until I talk to Paula."

He shut the office door, slumped down in his chair, and kept thinking "Who set me up? Damn them, those racist Republicans. They found this picture."

A few minutes later, Paula came in. "Honey, this picture is all over Chirp and social media."

Norton started rambling, just trying to come up with an excuse: "Honey, I was in a fraternity at VCC that did some pretty bad things, including a few costume parties. The fraternity was an old Virginia fraternity; our spiritual father was Robert E. Lee. When I was a freshman, I saw the fraternity's recruiting table with a picture of General Lee on it. They seemed like a bunch of good guys, so I joined."

Paula interjected, "Hold on, slow down. Just tell me about the picture!"

Norton composed himself. "I was the guy in black face dressed as Huggy Bear. The other guy in the picture was Jack Villiers. You may remember he died a couple years ago. Obviously someone, I don't remember who, took a picture of me in that getup."

Elections Have Consequences

"Huggy Bear? Oh, that's right, I remember, your old impersonation. Why did you let anyone take a picture of you dressed like that?" Before Norton could answer she interjected, "But look, dear, there's no way anyone can tell that is you. No one can prove it. And Jack Villiers is dead. He is probably the only one who could credibly finger you, so you're in the clear."

She thought again of Villiers, a man she only met a couple of times, and got angry. She opined, "It was that damn Jack Villiers! What a bad influence—he got you to do it, I bet. He convinced you to put all that goop on your face and to wear that black fright wig on your head. Honestly, Ronnie, back then he probably could have convinced you to wear a dress."

Norton responded, "Oh come on, it was my decision to dress up as Huggy Bear back then. I developed that character."

Paula's face betrayed no concern, and she proffered her advice, "Okay, well, just say you weren't in the picture. And your name in the caption is a misprint, an editing mistake by the publisher. That happens."

Norton seemed unsure and responded, "Maybe."

Paula went on, "I have known you for over 30 years. I can't tell by looking at this picture that you are in it; how could anyone else? Heck, your own mother wouldn't recognize you!"

"I guess so. I hope nothing else comes forward."

"Well, dear, you have no reason to say you were in this picture, I am quite sure, so you can easily deny you were in it. Honey, someone sent this picture to the media. Some racist fraternity brother, probably a racist redneck from Southwest Virginia, leaked this photo to the media. They know as governor you are going to fight for social justice and will succeed now that the

Republicans have lost both chambers of the legislature, and that bothers them."

Norton asked, "What am I going to do?"

Paula became agitated, her voice rising. "Well, for the fourth time I am telling you not to admit you are in it! There is no need to! Just pull a Joe Biden—make a statement to the press and walk away without taking any questions."

After a pause, seeing him slump down in his chair, silent and seemingly despondent, Paula finally blew up: "You are not going to admit a damn thing. I put up with being a political wife for two decades. I raised your children while you were off to all kinds of political events, even one called a shad planking, an event in some God forsaken place called Wakefield. And every Labor Day is spent in the southwestern town of Buena Vista.

"Your son played high school football; you didn't attend one of his games! Not one! Our daughter was the homecoming queen; you weren't there! When my favorite aunt died you couldn't make the funeral because of a Fairfax Chamber of Commerce convention. In two decades, you never missed one Fairfax County Fair, yet you missed hundreds of family events. Every 4th of July was spent at the Fairfax Parade! We went years without having a single family dinner together. You skipped my mom's funeral because of a damn political event!

"So, I know I signed up for this crap when I married you, but on the condition that there might be a reward at the end. Something for me! That is four years of being First Lady of Virginia. We have a maid, a butler, an historic house in Richmond which is rent free; we are living the life of Riley, and you are going to risk it because you can't tell one little lie?"

Elections Have Consequences

Paula looked at her crestfallen husband; he looked defeated. She then grabbed him by the lapels as he just sat there. She was sitting on top of him, her knees on his thighs, her face inches from his. Spit was flying out of her mouth, her voice rising. "Okay, Beaman is not here to give you the plan, so here goes, You are not going to fuck this up for me! You hear me? You are not going to admit a damn thing. Nothing! You are going to go to the press and say you are not in that picture, the caption was a misprint; no, perhaps a setup by some hick fraternity brother, who probably lives in some place like Gate City. Then you are going to say you have nothing to add. Turn and walk out of the press conference."

Paula calmed down, took a deep breath, and removed her clenched fingers from his lapels. Then, in an effort to break the tension and defuse the situation, she sighed "Look, honey, there is nothing wrong with a little white lie. We all tell them from time to time." She moved in, hugged him, and said, "You remember the day we got married? I was already pregnant with our first child. Nobody knew, and I still wore white. Just a little white lie." As she said the word "lie" she put her thumb and forefinger about an inch apart. "Now you can tell one white lie, right?"

Norton gave a little smile and said, "I suppose." He put on a brave face. "Trust me, I think I know how to fight this– we will fight this."

She smiled, hugged him, and told him she loved him. Norton stood up, "Let's get Jackson, Reverend Brand and some communications staffers in here"

Paula said, "We need Beaman!"

"He's in surgery, I can't talk to him until tonight."

Paula added, "I have nothing against Rev. Brand; on social

Elections Have Consequences

issues and issues dealing with racial justice she is quite sensible, but on this you need the advice of a ruthless street fighter like Beaman, not a female bishop from a dying left-wing church."

Norton nodded, "I know, sweetie."

"Fixing things like this is a Beaman specialty." Paula added, "You remember when that congressman got arrested for roughing up his wife? Beaman made that story disappear. He can work wonders."

"Yes, I remember that."

Paula concluded, "Well, I guess this isn't just going to go away, but do me one favor. Please don't remind people that you even knew Jack Villiers. Just say you have no idea who was in that picture with you. Villiers was a bad guy in life, and I think even from the grave he can destroy us."

"No worries, mum's the word. No mention of Jack."

Before Norton went to face the staff, he excused himself and went to the restroom. He stared into the mirror and said to himself, *Think, Ronnie, how do I get out of this? I could deny it's me in the picture. Paula is right; it would be almost impossible to say it's me, but there are people who can verify it, But Huggy Bear is not so bad; it could have been worse.* He reasoned that at least he wasn't the guy in the Nazi uniform, so it might appear to most Virginians as merely an immature act by a college student.

The media will engage in their usual virtue signaling; that is to be expected, but most Virginians will forgive me. Norton remembered that his hero Bill Clinton had lied to the American people about his affair with an intern. *That was a mistake. If he had just admitted it the people would have forgiven him. Lying about it was what really got him in trouble. It wasn't the burglary that brought Nixon down; it was the cover up.*

Elections Have Consequences

Norton concluded that the people of Virginia would forgive him for dressing as Huggy Bear. *Honesty—to a point—is best in this case.* Norton took a last look into the mirror, straightened his tie, and said, "I can do this!" He remembered his football coach at George Marshall pushing him. "You can do it, Norton! I have confidence in you, Norton, you can punch it in."

The doors were opened. Norton started to explain to his staff, who were eager for an explanation. "I belonged to a racist fraternity at VCC. I was at a party where that picture was taken; in fact I was the one dressed as Huggy Bear, the pimp." This was a half truth; yes, it was taken at a party but his dress up was not a one time thing.

He went on, "It was not meant to be malicious. In my immaturity I thought it would be funny and please the fraternity brothers." This was a lie. He did it because he wanted to, and because he thought it was funny.

The staffers were silent for a couple of minutes. Finally, Reverend Brand, who was considered somewhat of the moral conscience of the staff, stood up to speak. The room was so silent you could hear a pin drop. Her eyes red from crying, she stared off into space, paused for a second seemingly to collect her thoughts, then wiped her eyes for a final time. "I am so disgusted right now," She paused again for a few more seconds and took a deep breath. "But I am also heartbroken. What is being blared on all the national news networks right now is truly shocking, and sickening. America has a history of bigotry and racism and hatred that is disgusting, disgraceful, and sad. You," she said, looking at Norton, "along with most of white America have condoned bigotry for centuries. You looked the other way! You said, and believed, that we were great. It is because of white privilege, in part, that you are governor, yet you deny any such privilege. It was your white privilege that enabled you to ignore the demeaning of black Americans who you didn't even recognize as people. And since you didn't see them as people, you were able to be at a racist party and not think twice about it. You had no pangs of conscience. You say you are not evil because you are not a Republican, but you condoned racism. This picture proves it. What are you going to do about it? Blame Republicans? Accuse them of even worse acts or even equal acts of hatred?" She continued, her voice shaking. "I feel shame and sadness for our country and state. I pray for healing. I hope you are able to atone, beg for forgiveness, and help our state recover."

She then started tearing up again, meekly said, "Thank you," and sat down. Just then a thunderous round of applause could be heard outside the office. While the meeting was starting the governor's mansion staff had come to the door to listen.

Then a member of the communications staff, a 23-year-old woman, recently graduated from Radford University with a BA in communications asked the governor directly, "Do you have any idea what it is like being a second-class citizen?" More silence.

Another millennial staffer asked the governor, "How would you like to be a slave for 400 years?" Awkward silence hung in the room. Governor Norton didn't respond. What could he say? He realized that for the next 24 hours at least, he would have to take a lot of abuse.

Steve Beaman, in his crude vernacular, used to tell him, "Sometimes in politics you just have to bend over and take it."

Elections Have Consequences

He tried to gain his composure, but he was speechless. Finally, Chief of Staff Jackson addressed the next steps. "We will need to prepare a response, and with all the national coverage we can't wait long." Jackson pointed out that without a statement by the governor, no one else from the governor's office could comment. "Okay, let me work on a statement."

The meeting broke up. Norton went to his secretary and said, "Well, I guess we have to cancel my meeting with Poor Marty–I mean Marty Knowles."

Meanwhile, Paula decided to get a rundown on the lay of the land with someone other than one of her husband's advisors. She wanted to hear what kind of trouble her husband could be in, from someone outside party politics.

As luck would have it, Radford political science professor Lawrence Seavers was in the mansion for an event. Seavers, referred to by the media as the King of Conventional Wisdom, was well known in Virginia political circles. That epigram was meant to be a putdown, but Seavers never objected to it; in fact, he embraced it. Though it wasn't a compliment, he decided to take it as one. When he did TV interviews, the networks usually labeled him the King of Conventional Wisdom, even creating a graphic of him with a little crown on his head. The crown looked like the producer had copied it off a Burger King ad.

Show hosts would often tease his appearance with, "After the break, we will be joined by the King of Conventional Wisdom, Lawrence Seavers." This was fitting, because Seavers had never had an original, nuanced, or perceptive thought in his life.

He was one of the most famous political science professors in Virginia. Most of his students thought he was brilliant, but the

Elections Have Consequences

smart ones mocked him behind his back. Seavers never really made definite political predictions; he would hedge everything. One way his students made fun of him was by pretending he was a weatherman. A student would say, "So, Professor Seavers, will it rain tomorrow?"

The imitation Seavers would answer, "Well, I'd say it is 70 percent likely; but, if the sun can peak through, even a little, the clouds might burn off, and it could be sunny and therefore no rain, and then there will be egg on the forecasters' faces, so I would say, to quote Yogi Bera 'Be careful about making predictions, especially about the future.'"

When Mrs. Norton tracked Seavers down at the mansion, she got right to the point:

"Professor Seavers, based on what you know, what are the worst- and best-case scenarios in this mess?"

Seavers replied, "I must say this is a unique case in American politics. The only thing like this that I can think of would be found in Canada, the blackface incident involving Prime Minister Justin Trudeau several years ago."

Paula interrupted, "Yes, and he survived."

"Yes, but Trudeau had established himself as a true champion of equality and human rights. He had a great deal of credibility with the public." Seavers went on, "It depends on if your husband wants to fight. He can resign and that may save some personal embarrassment. I don't know if there is another shoe to drop, but if he's willing to hang on, no matter what, he should survive. So far it doesn't appear that there is anything impeachable."

Paula optimistically interjected, "That's right, nothing impeachable."

"He also has an ace up his sleeve. There is a Republican Lt. Governor. The Democrat majority in the House of Delegates and Senate probably won't want to turn to him. But there might be a few Democrats who suggest your husband resign."

A shocked Paula said, "Resign? For a childish prank?"

Seavers clarified, "He didn't do anything impeachable, but there may be legislators that don't believe he still has the moral authority to hold the job, so they might call on him to resign."

Paula felt his words like a punch in the stomach. She knew a few calls for resignation were possible, but the idea was still shocking. Seavers went on, "At the very least the General Assembly may want to pass a non-binding resolution condemning his action as a college student. It would be embarrassing, and it would make it harder for your husband to govern. As far as the best-case scenario, well, hard to say. Perhaps if there are no more revelations, he can ride out the storm, in say a few months."

There was one curious thing about this scandal, specifically about the picture. Norton was pictured as a pimp, and as such he was wearing a shirt with the words, "Ask me about the bitches and hoes" written across it.

However, the media, for the most part, blurred this out of the picture. They rarely mentioned it or pointed it out, probably because they were pushing the racist angle in the narrative, not the misogynistic part of it.

Mrs. Norton thanked Seavers for his help. She truly felt the seriousness of the scandal once she heard Seavers use the word "resignation." However, she felt a little more hopeful after she spoke with him. Ronnie could hang in; she would demand it. She wouldn't let him give up.

Elections Have Consequences

If he explained it was a youthful, immature mistake, and if no more pictures appear, he would survive. And she wanted to shift blame to the racist fraternity, which no doubt was a bad influence on an otherwise good guy. In fact, she thought, *They probably talked him into posing in blackface.*

Her narrative, which Ronnie rejected, was to claim that he was not in the picture, and the fraternity put his name in the caption as Huggy Bear, to embarrass him. Actually it was the opposite. Most people in the fraternity knew of Norton's Huggy Bear routine, and kept silent even when Norton ran for office. They may have been racists and they may have been Republicans, and they probably voted for Parrish, but they kept Norton's Huggy Bear secret. All the fraternity brothers were loyal to Norton and protected his secret from the press.

Paula went back to his office to help him write his statement. Norton said, "God, I wish Beaman were here. I don't want to write it without him."

Paula replied, "Honey, we need a statement of apology, and then we need you to get on the phone and apologize to every Democrat legislator. Then go on statewide TV tonight and give a sincere apology. By doing that we should be able to head off any resignation calls."

A surprised Norton responded, "Resignation calls? For a stupid college prank? That's ridiculous."

"Honey, we live in very sensitive times. There are people who see a racist under every bed. So, apologize quickly and sincerely."

When Norton sat down to work on his statement, he wasn't the only one hard at work. Brand went back to her office, shut the door, wiped her eyes again, and sat down to absorb it all. On her desk was the maxim, "Never let crisis go to waste." She thought, *Can something good come out of this? Can the social justice movement gain something from this?* Brand's idea of good and Norton's idea of good were not necessarily the same.

After a few minutes the proverbial light bulb went off in her head. She audibly muttered, "That's it. That's it." She then called Delegate Richard Carwile. Carwile had been in the House for 30 years. An old red, he got elected back when conservatives dominated the state, so the snowflake legislators looked up to him, calling him a trailblazer. "Dick, meet me in Capitol Square in 10 minutes. I will be sitting on a park bench."

13) Never Let a Crisis Go to Waste

Everyone thought the tough infighter in the Norton administration was Beaman, but Brand could be every bit the schemer. The primary difference between Brand and Beaman was that she didn't come to Richmond for power; rather, she came to Richmond with a purpose—to enact a woke, socialist legislative agenda. If she had to turn on her boss to do it, she would. Brand had no loyalties to people, only a loyalty to a cause and a political agenda.

Carwile represented Henrico County and was elected over 30 years ago. He used to say, "When I came to Richmond my hair was dark and Republicans ran everything. Now my hair is gray and we control the General Assembly."

Like Brand, he put ideology above everything else, although he did have a sense of fair play and decency, which Brand lacked. He also had another virtue that she appreciated: he didn't like Norton.

Brand arrived at the park bench. Fortunately the rain had stopped; perhaps the clearing skies was an omen, Brand thought. The bench faced the capitol; the Virginia flag was gracefully fluttering above the building that Thomas Jefferson designed. Some people, not too many, were out walking back and forth from the General Assembly building. To her left she could see the Washington statue and behind that the old City Hall, a beautiful, ornate building built in the 1920's. The city had built a new City Hall and the old building was now used by the state.

Out of the corner of her eye, she could see Carwile approaching. A dignified looking man with gray hair and piercing blue eyes, he looked like a labor leader from the 1970's. A staffer once joked that Carwile was the only member of the legislature who wore galoshes and read the paper edition of the newspaper. And, sure enough, Brand saw him approaching with a newspaper tucked under his arm and galoshes covering his shoes.

Carwile sat down. Brand didn't even say hello. Not a word was spoken for several seconds; they just stared at the capitol. Brand then looked around, leaned in, and in a calm, even voice said, "I want you to call for his resignation."

A stunned Carwile said, "What?" He paused for a second, and through clenched teeth, said, "Certainly you realize I am a Democrat member of the House of Delegates and he is a Democrat governor. For me to call for his resignation is madness. It's political treason."

Brand reasoned, "I don't want him to resign and you don't either, but I have a plan you might be interested in."

Just then a couple approached, walking up the hill, nearing their park bench, walking within earshot. Carwile waited for them to pass, and then replied while staring straight ahead, "I am listening, Ann."

Brand explained, "If we can make him and the media believe that there is a genuine groundswell of Democrats in the General Assembly that want him to resign, we can have leverage over him. Remember, politics is about leverage."

Carwile seemed to reflect. "First, to attempt such a thing is as close to political treason against our governor as is possible. Second, I am not sure we could pull it off, just in terms of the credibility of a call for his resignation over this. What I mean is, sure, what he did was a hateful, racist act, but it happened decades ago, when he was in college, so won't the press question why this merits his resigning?"

Brand responded, "Do you remember the old fable *The Emperor's New Clothes?*" Carwile shrugged.

Brand recited the story. "As you might remember, fancy fashion designers created the clothes, which were nonexistent, and when the emperor was parading around buck naked all the adults said how wonderful the emperor's new clothes looked. Only the children spoke the truth. But the adults wanted to be, shall we say in today's terms, politically correct." Brand went on. "A child in Virginia would point out that Norton shouldn't resign for a decades old incident, but the Virginia press won't. Every reporter is concerned about appearing insufficiently woke, so they can't claim or suggest that calls for Norton's resignation are an overreaction. In fighting racism there can never be an overreaction. So, they will push the question, thereby lending it credibility."

Carwile replied, "Yes, but why would Norton believe such a move? He knows what we know, that if he leaves office then Republican Lt. Governor Morrison takes over. So why would he take a move by Democrats in the General Assembly to demand that he resign seriously?"

Brand reasoned, "He is at heart a politician. He will do all he can to avoid having a chunk of his caucus publicly suggesting that he should resign. That would be devastating. And look, he is a bit paranoid. And he knows his friend Morrison would make a capable governor. So he can't totally discount the idea that our party would dump him for Morrison. Morrison is no right winger like Angela Parrish; he can be fairly moderate. I would recommend you describe Morrison as capable, that's it, he would make a capable governor."

Elections Have Consequences

"Who have you talked to about this?"

"No one yet except you. I'm not sure we can count on anyone in the Fairfax delegation. Most of them will probably still stay loyal to Norton, and they might expose the plan. I would say don't go to Carrico on this. He's a goody two-shoes. He won't go along, and he might even tip Norton off." Carrico was Fairfax Democrat Delegate Bruce Carrico.

"Yes, let me think about who we can trust. Let me ask you, what is the end game?"

"We dribble out resignation calls, legislator after legislator calls on him to resign. We space it out hour after hour, day after day. In a few days you and the others make a deal. He signs the Critical Race Theory in Schools bill and in exchange the caucus drops the calls for him to resign."

Carwile stared straight ahead, looking at the Capitol building. He could hear the flag fluttering above the Capitol. He thought about Brand's plan, and muttered, "Oh, my God. Madness. Madness."

Brand moved in to close the sale. "Dick, this is our chance to get our bill passed, and who knows, maybe more bills to come. If we don't take this opportunity, Norton could go back to being a moderate Democrat. This is our chance. Do we want another Chuck Robb, or do we want Bernie Sanders? If progressive legislators start the calls for him to resign, then we come in and appear to save him. He will owe us big time when this is over."

Carwile conceded, "I see your point, but to go after a governor, our Democrat governor like this..." muttered, "Madness. Madness" After several seconds he said, "Okay, I will make some inquiries."

Elections Have Consequences

She smiled. "And of course leave my name out of it. I have to continue to appear loyal to Norton. And again, when you call for his resignation, say you think Morrison will make a capable governor."

Sensing another possible concern, Brand added, "Your calling on Norton to resign won't hurt you back home. Henrico County Democrats never fully trusted Norton anyway. They won't be too mad at you for calling for his resignation."

Carwile nodded, then said with a mixture of disbelief and admiration, "I must say, to manufacture a campaign of legislators calling for the governor to resign, even though they don't really mean it, in order to get leverage over him is Machiavellian in the extreme."

Someone came up the path by them, so they stopped talking. As the person neared they nodded and waited for him to pass so they could pick up the conversation.

Carwile began, "One thing, don't you think Beaman will sniff this out? He's loyal to Norton, and he's sharp. Very little gets by him."

Brand explained, "Steve is in surgery right now. He'll be out for several more hours, so we have a nice head start."

Carwile said, "Excellent."

Later in the afternoon Norton issued a press release:

"My Fellow Virginians, like most all of you I felt shocked and sadness when I saw that picture, released this afternoon by the *Falls Church News Leader* of two men in offensive racist costumes. What made it more shocking and sadder for me is the fact that I was in that picture. I was the man with the fright wig, darkened face, and loud clothes. I have since learned that this is known as

Blaxploitation that is a racist portrayal of a black person, in this case a black man. That picture doesn't represent me as a person. That picture represents a single moment of my life, a life committed to public service, equality and justice. I realize that because of my horrible conduct on that day, many Virginians now may be questioning my commitment to equality and justice. Let me promise today that I will recommit myself to regaining trust and respect, of you, all of you, the people of Virginia."

14) Beaman to the Rescue

By 4 o'clock Beaman was out of gallstone surgery, had been moved to a private room, and sleeping comfortably, but by 9 p.m. he began to wake up. He must have thought he was dreaming about work because he kept hearing Governor Norton's name being mentioned over and over again.

He tried opening his eyes. After several seconds of staring at the ceiling, he started to realize where he was. He felt little pain, just some grogginess.

But the television down the hall might have woken him up. He kept hearing his boss's name mentioned, things like, "Several Virginia Democrats are calling on Governor Norton to resign," "Norton released a statement and admitted..." Then what sounded like pundits discussing Norton, "Will Norton be able to continue as governor?"

Beaman blinked. He knew he was awake, yet he kept hearing all kinds of odd things from down the hall. Beaman got off the bed. He was in a hospital gown and didn't even bother to get his clothes from the closet. He walked out of his room, following the sound. By now he realized it was the cable news network MNN, which was usually friendly to Norton. He got to the open room. Other people were there, but Beaman paid no attention to them. He just walked up to the TV.

What he saw stunned him. On MNN, he read the banner, "Governor Norton Issues Apology, Says He Has No Plans To Resign."

Beaman, totally gobsmacked, stared motionless at the screen for five minutes, trying to take it all in. At that moment he

Elections Have Consequences

thought, *I am in the Twilight Zone.* Finally able to move, he went back to his room to retrieve his phone.

In the walk down the bright hall it sunk in. This was not a dream, it was all too real. He called the governor's private line, and his secretary picked up, "This is Beaman. Get me the governor."

She responded, "One second, Mr. Beaman."

While on hold, Beaman tried to take it all in. He thought, *Fraternity, racist photo, blackface, and several Democrats called for him to resign. What the hell is going on and how long was I out?*

After a minute Norton came on the line. "Hey, Steve."

Beaman opened with "Governor, please tell me I'm dreaming."

"Well, I guess you've seen the news. I am in a bit of trouble."

"Yes, I'll say. I woke up to it on the news here in the hospital. Governor, let's not discuss this over the phone. Do you remember our emergency deep cover plan?"

Norton paused then replied, "Affirmative on that–but can you get out of the hospital?"

"Yes, Governor, I should be able to get out of the hospital. Security is not too tight, and I don't feel too bad. The pain meds should last for a few more hours. Your driver Jasper should be able to get you out. Just lie down in the backseat with the blanket on top of you, in case the press is outside, and have Jasper make sure you are not followed."

"Okay, say 11 p.m."

Beaman said, "Sounds good. Our designated meeting spot."

The governor went into the bedroom to see Paula. "I'm off to see Steve. He should be able to advise me."

"How did his surgery go?"

Elections Have Consequences

"He didn't say. See you a little after midnight."

Norton called Jasper to meet him in the garage. Jasper didn't bother to ask who the governor was meeting or why. Norton then gave the State Police the slip, laid down in the backseat of the car, and told Jasper, "Make sure no one is following us."

Jasper pulled out of the mansion garage and checked the rear-view mirror. "Nobody's behind us."

The limo moved past Capitol Square, down Broad Street, and into the 7th Street parking garage. From underneath the blanket Norton asked, "Jasper, is anyone following us now?"

Jasper checked the rear-view mirror again. "No sir, still clear."

Norton uncovered his head. Still under the blanket, he remembered a story he had read from a history book. During the coup of 1953, when the US put the Shah of Iran back in power, Shah Mohammad Reza Pahlavi would be secreted out of his palace by lying down in the backseat of a car, and being driven to a secret location to meet with his CIA handler.

Beaman got rid of the hospital gown and put on his clothes, dressing in the dark; he didn't want to alert the nurses by turning on his light. He slipped down the hall, found the exit to the stairs, and ducked into the stairwell just as his doctor was coming around the corner. The rendezvous point was just about four blocks away, on 7th Street off Broad, but rather than walk it Beaman called for an Uber ride.

While sitting in the car, Beaman heard the news on the radio. What he heard shocked him. "The United News Service is reporting that Delegate Richard Carwile, a member of the governor's party, is calling on Norton to resign."

A horrified Beaman thought, *No, not Carwile. He can't be against us. Damn it! We're screwed, We're screwed!*

The radio report included a soundbite from Carwile. "I think Governor Norton has lost the moral authority to govern our commonwealth. I think Jim Morrison should step in. Despite my political differences with him, Morrison is a decent, capable man and will be a good governor."

Beaman now knew that his friend's governorship was on life support. He thought Carwile was the canary in the coalmine, because he reasoned Carwile was an old-time establishment liberal. He was no social justice warrior. Carwile was not rash, not a bomb thrower looking for publicity, or the type to grandstand and virtue signal. Beaman worried that Carwile calling on Norton to resign would lead other mainstream Democrats to do the same.

Sitting in the dark car in the backseat, Beaman felt about as bad as he ever had. It felt like the lowest point in his life. He felt he had let his friend down. He knew it wasn't his fault that he had surgery and was out for several hours, but he now knew Norton, his best friend, was in real trouble. He thought *Ronnie needed me all afternoon, and I wasn't around.* He also realized with Carwile's announcement they were behind in the game. He felt like a football player who arrives at halftime and finds his team down by two touchdowns.

An anxious Beaman looked out the window. He was now just two blocks from the rendezvous point. Beaman looked to his left and saw the back of the capitol building; beautifully lit up, always an impressive sight. On his right he could see the Virginia State Library. His mind began racing and he started getting angry. *Morrison was probably behind this. That bastard. I will fix him.* Beaman then realized. *That's it, I know how. I know how I can finish Morrison for good.*

Elections Have Consequences

The Uber driver dropped Beaman off at the corner of Broad and 7th. Beaman handed him money; the driver could see Beaman's hospital bracelet as he accepted the tip. Unlike the hospital gown Beaman hadn't ditched the hospital bracelet.

It was now just after 11 p.m. Norton walked down the aisle of the empty parking lot. He still had dress shoes on, and he could hear the click-clack echo of his steps as he continued past the columns to the end of the lot. There in the distance, by the last column, he saw a shadowy figure. Beaman walked around the corner and came in through the back pedestrian entrance.

Norton felt a sense of relief; his point man to the rescue. He thought, *This is how General Lee must have felt when he finally saw General Jackson at Chancellorsville, or when he saw AP Hill at Antietam. All will be okay now; the battle has been joined by my key general.* They came closer together. It wasn't pitch black so they could still see each other pretty well.

Steve started the conversation off with a little humor. "Well, Governor, looks like you are getting a little media attention. But Huggy Bear?" As he left the hospital Beaman had remembered the Huggy Bear story. He reminded Norton, "Well, as you may remember about ten years ago a cub reporter with the *Winchester Star* was sniffing out this story, and I got the editor to quash it. Now it comes back, but from a different outlet."

"Yes, it's a media feeding frenzy. They have all picked it up, and they're having me for dinner. Steve, who do you think did this? Who released the picture? Couldn't have been Parrish; she would have used it against me in the campaign. How did the *Falls Church News Leader* get it?"

Elections Have Consequences

"Governor, I have no idea how they got it, but no doubt that kook Bruce Dutton happily published it. Look, we can't afford the luxury of thinking about that now. We have to save your governorship. In the next ten minutes I am going to explain where we go from here. First, are there any other pictures? Do any of them have you pictured as a more offensive character?"

"No. It was just Huggy Bear."

"Okay, then do not admit to any other examples of you in blackface. If you were just imitating Huggy Bear you should be okay. If you must apologize, and I think you should, try to deflect with 'Gee, I really shouldn't have been at that party, being part of a racist fraternity, and having an obsession with a black pimp named Huggy Bear.' Heck, they may have put you up to it?"

"Steve. I don't want to throw the fraternity under the bus."

"Governor, blame them as much as possible. And what would the downside be? They're mostly Republicans; they won't vote for you anyway. But, as I remember, you said the sorority girls helped apply shoe polish to your face. Don't mention that. It can't appear that you are blaming a woman or women for this. Putting some of the blame of the fraternity brothers is okay, but not on a sorority. It's odd to me that there are some resignation calls over this, but we live in sensitive times." He added, "Just think if you were never convinced to join that racist fraternity you would be fine now. No doubt their horrible influence got you to do that. I wonder if we can go with the idea that it was an initiation, and that they forced you to do it?"

"No, it was a character I developed. Others know I did it on my own initiative; there are witnesses who can claim that. Paula wanted me to deny it was me in the picture, but I can't because there are people out there who know I was Huggy Bear."

Elections Have Consequences

Beaman cut in, "Okay, Governor, understood. The second thing is we have to tar the hell out of the Lt. Governor and damage him so much that a handful of Democrats won't join House Republicans on a vote for a resolution suggesting you resign in favor of Lt. Governor Morrison."

Norton winced at the prospect. "Steve, Jim Morrison is a friend of over 20 years, but he's a Republican, and therefore I doubt any Democrats will move to get rid of me for him."

Beaman shook his head and replied, "The heat is on; they may dump you like a hot potato. Our only hope may turn out to be making Morrison toxic. Then you're safe. We must take him out, as even a remote possibility to replace you."

Norton offered, "Steve, there is nothing impeachable, though, at least I don't think there is, so I don't see how they get rid of me."

"Yes, in a constitutional sense you can hang on but for what? Your governorship will be over. So for insurance we have to finish off Morrison." Beaman added, "And oh, by the way, I don't know if you heard the news but Carwile is already calling for you to step down in favor of Morrison. So Governor, you know what we have got to do right?"

The governor looked down at his feet, then in a near whisper said, "I think I know."

Beaman then started getting worked up, nothing seemed to please him more then when he was going in for the kill, about to finish off an opponent.

Every thirty seconds or so, lights from street traffic would enter the garage and Beaman's face would light up as he spoke. He'd be in the dark and then his face would light up, then go back to dark.

Elections Have Consequences

Norton knew what was coming. He and Morrison had become best friends in the House of Delegates years earlier, and Morrison had confided in Norton. He had told Norton a secret, something he told no one else, not even his wife. At the time Morrison was having an affair with a female student at VCC. He first met the girl when she was a senior at Almond High School. He knew it was wrong, and sought advice from Norton.

Norton got the Morrisons in touch with a marriage counselor. In time Morrison ended the affair with the woman and saved his marriage. He was grateful for Norton's guidance.

Beaman also knew of the affair. He had gotten copies of emails between Morrison and the girl from the mother of one of her friends. The two girls had a falling out, as teenagers do. The friend knew the girl's password and hacked into her account. She copied some of the lurid emails between Delegate Morrison and the student and gave them to her mother, who was a Democrat activist from Henrico. The mother, after offering them to local Democrat party activists and being rebuffed, finally passed them on to Beaman. He really couldn't do much with them at the time. But he recognized they were a political landmine and held onto them, saving them for the best (or worst) possible moment. Now he wanted to use the affair to tarnish Morrison and take some heat off Norton. He told Norton, "Well, Governor, let me spell out what we got. In the 1990's Morrison started an affair with a 17-year-old girl, more precisely a student at Almond High School. From what she said in her emails she was a member of the cheerleading squad."

Norton cut him off. "Steve, do we need to release the details?"

Beaman excitedly responded, "Well, Governor, the details are quite revealing. You know that yourself. While it doesn't seem that they were actually having sex until she was 18, at least there's no evidence of that, he did send her all kinds of sleazy emails. And Governor, guess what we got? That's right, we got copies of lots of emails!" Beaman's voice rose on the last sentence, as if he were hosting a game show.

Norton interjected again, "Steve, do they need to be released?'

Then Beaman displayed his evil, manipulative side, the side that made the psychologists in the Army conclude that he might be a sociopath.

Beaman paused and asked rhetorically, "Do you want to remain as governor, or do you want to protect a pervert?"

Norton responded, "Oh, come on."

"We will have to finish Morrison off. It may be our only hope." Beaman advanced a bluff. "I bet right now he is lining up support against you. He is probably calling every black lawmaker and asking them, 'Do you want that racist Norton to remain governor? Governor Huggy Bear?' And he already has Carwile's backing."

In reality there was no evidence that Morrison was angling for the governorship. Norton remained silent.

"So tomorrow, in about seven hours the media will be reviewing emails where Morrison tells the girl that he would like to 'spank her because she has been a very naughty girl.'"

Norton's last pang of conscience: "That seems like dirty politics."

Beaman quickly responded, "Oh, you want dirty? We have that! We have an email where he tells the girl that he wants to make love to her under the bleachers, while the football game is going on." Beaman then added, "But don't worry. In that particular email he clearly demonstrates what a gentleman he is. He says that after he makes love to her, he will make sure she is able to get back with the other cheerleaders for the second half! Presumably with a perfectly clean skirt."

Beaman went on with the plan. "In addition, releasing the dirt on Morrison will distract attention away from your impersonation of Huggy Bear. The media wants a scandal. And nothing sells quite like a sex scandal. So, we release the emails, and the media switches over to the Morrison scandal. Which takes the heat off you. It's a win win. What's not to love about it?"

Beaman seemed proud of himself. "Isn't it great I kept the emails? I knew they would come in handy one day." Then he asked, "Governor, is it fair that you should get all the media heat when you did nothing wrong? I mean really wrong, like Morrison? He's a pervert; you simply dressed up inappropriately, in a politically incorrect way."

Norton then said, "Steve, he has been a friend for over twenty years."

Beaman's response was classic deflection. "You can continue to be his friend, who is saying you can't? But he's to blame for trying to seduce an underage girl."

"I don't know, Steve."

"It's the only way to stay governor."

The governor paused for about ten seconds, then responded, "Okay, go ahead and release the emails to the press. Anonymously, of course."

Beaman replied, "Okay great. It's the right thing to do, and as General Jackson would advise 'We must attack.' Now one more concern. So far all your cabinet members have spoken out in your defense, except Brand. Can we really trust her?"

Elections Have Consequences

"Yes. I'm sure she will defend me publicly soon; she just may be upset right now." He continued his defense of Brand. "Look, Steve, I can't just surround myself with yes men. She has a good heart, and she's my connection to the religious community, and to the woke, progressive base. Heck, she did as much as anyone to get me elected governor. She deserves my understanding."

Beaman countered, "No, she must show her loyalty to you. If she can't defend you now, then she can't be trusted. She can't be a free agent. Frankly, I never trusted her."

"Oh, come on, Steve, she's just sore right now. She'll come around."

Beamon concluded, "Okay, enough about her. Now, this is very important. This deals with the media narrative. Our spin. Tomorrow, you emphasize the idea that you should not have joined that racist fraternity. And deny, if you can, the idea that you might have dressed in another costume. Make it clear you never dressed as a Klansman or impersonated a minstrel singer, Going as Huggy Bear is bad, but there are worse characters." Beaman asserted confidently, "I think we will survive Huggy Bear. Actually, he was kind of a lovable character. The press wants an apology, so give them one–'I am sorry I joined a racist fraternity party.'"

As Norton walked back to the car, he felt better than he had all day. *I will be fine,* he thought. As far as any moral pangs about releasing dirt against a friend, he didn't think too much about it. Never considered if the emails were genuine, or how Beaman got them. He learned early on in his political career that pangs of conscience had to be stamped out thoroughly, like old cigar butts.

Getting closer to his limo, he thought, *I have to do what I can to win. The state needs me, and the great men of history had to bend the rules a bit. What did Churchill say...what was that line? I think something like "The truth is so important that sometimes it must be surrounded by a bodyguard of lies."*

Norton rationalized that he must have to be willing to lie from time to time. That was part of the job. What did Beaman once say? "If you want a clean conscience, stay out of politics."

With confidence in his "old war horse," as he called Beaman, Norton was able to get a good night's sleep...but in the morning the feeding frenzy continued. All the cable networks were focused on Virginia politics, and thanks to Beaman's handiwork the glare shifted to the lieutenant governor.

***

Norton woke up at the crack of dawn, turned on the TV, and discovered it wasn't a dream. "What is going on in Virginia?" was emblazoned on the headline news with Willow Bush.

"In the latest bombshell from the Old Dominion, Lt. Governor Jim Morrison is confirming reports at this hour that he did have an affair decades ago with a student at Virginia Commonwealth College. The affair seems to have started when the woman was a student at Almond High School in Henrico County, but that cannot be confirmed. I want to turn to our own Lin Canyon in Richmond with the latest. Lin, shocking news to say the least."

"Yes, the affair seems to have begun when a woman—we are withholding her name for privacy reasons—met Morrison at a Young Republicans event. He was a member of the House of Delgates when the affair began. Sources say, however, that the relationship did not become physical until she was 18 and a student at VCC. Reports say he would sneak into the dorm and spend time with her. Legal sources don't expect charges to be filed, due in part to the statute of limitations, and also there has never been a police report filed regarding the affair, Willow."

"What a difference a day makes! Yesterday there was talk of Norton stepping down and Morrison taking over. I guess that is no longer a possibility, Lin."

"Yes, all that talk is over. And let me say, this was a well-coordinated attack. It most likely was coordinated by one of Governor Norton's supporters or friends, if not the governor himself. My sources say Norton okayed the attack on Morrison."

Norton was dispassionately watching the program over his breakfast of bacon and eggs, when he heard a ping, and noticed he got a text message:

Beaman: "Well, this should take some of the heat off us" (smiley face)

By late morning the media had found a picture of the student with her fellow cheerleaders. They blurred out her face, since she was a minor at the time, and to protect her privacy currently.

All the networks were running the picture now. It showed the cheerleaders in their uniforms of blue and gray, the school letters "AHS" emblazoned across their chests, all their beautiful smiling faces. In the picture the team formed a pyramid. It all looked so peaceful and innocent.

Norton continued to watch the TV with no emotion. He was going over his schedule, looking at the numbers of legislators who were now on record demanding his resignation. Like a virus spreading the number of legislators calling for him to go was rising. Hopefully the curve would flatten soon, Norton thought.

Despite his friendship with Morrison, he was greatly relieved that the pressure had shifted off of him. Norton thought

Morrison had a strong marriage and that he and Sally would be able to work it out. Not to mention that the media would greatly prefer to attack a Republican, and now they were.happy.

All in all, Norton thought it was a great development. "A win-win situation" as Beaman had described it.

Norton and Paula had spent lots of time with the Morrisons, and they always seemed happy together, so Norton concluded that they'd get past this.

Beaman and Brand were supposed to meet with Norton before he held his press conference to go over the story.

15) A Bizarre Press Conference

Norton spent the morning in his upstairs study, preparing for his press conference. He had gotten the plan from Beaman. He knew he had to keep his cool and not let the reporters get to him. Be apologetic, but don't admit anything else, use the phrases "I don't remember" or "That was just so long ago, I can't possibly remember." Perhaps even the line, "Sorry, I wish I could remember, but that was a lifetime ago." Norton was confident that the only one who could implicate him in any more college days controversies was Jack Villiers, and he had died two years ago.

The conference was to be held in the first-floor ballroom, the same room where Stonewall Jackson's body lay in state after he died at Chancellorsville. It would be where the body of his political career would end, if Norton had a poor performance at the press conference.

At about 11 o'clock the ballroom at the mansion began filling up with both local and national press. The scene outside was surreal. Capitol Square was filled with press trucks from all over the country.

As the hour approached, Norton left the residence on the second floor and met his wife in the hallway by the elevator. Paula expressed sadness regarding the news about Morrison. "I feel so sorry for Sally and the kids. News of the affair with the Almond High School cheerleader must be devastating for Sally."

Norton reassured her, "Sally and Jim have a strong marriage; they will be fine."

Paula responded, "The Morrisons have a daughter the same age as that Almond High School girl was at the time of the affair.

Elections Have Consequences

Think of how his daughter must feel!"

Norton just nodded as he looked at his notes. Not even looking up he said, "Yes, not good. So sorry to hear about it, so sad, very sad." They arrived in the ballroom to face the press.

All the national networks were on standby.

In airports and bars all across the country the scene on television was the same, a live shot of an empty podium where any second the governor of Virginia would appear. A man, Ronnie Norton, who up until yesterday had been almost totally unknown.

The press secretary gave the high sign. "Here comes the governor," a producer whispered into Willow Bush's earpiece.

"Okay, breaking news—we are going to Richmond for Governor Norton's press conference:

The camera shot was on the podium. Seconds later the doors opened and Norton walked in with Paula at his side in a blue dress, looking downcast. The ballroom was silent except for the click, click, click, click of cameras.

In a hushed voice Willow Bush said, "Let's go to the governor."

Norton started off in a somber tone. "In 1982, I was a student at Virginia Commonwealth College. I belonged to a racist fraternity at VCC, and there, in part to impress my fraternity brothers, I developed an alter ego, a character really. I would dress as a black pimp named Huggy Bear." Norton then gave the big sound bite that would be repeated all day and lead in many papers. "Yes, I am in the picture. I was Huggy Bear."

A slight groan could be heard in the room. Norton explained, "To get into character, I dressed like a pimp, complete with loud plaid pants, a white belt and white blazer, or sportcoat. In addition, I darkened my face with shoe polish." More groans could be heard in the room.

"As a young man I became obsessed with the show *Starsky and Hutch,* and specifically with a secondary character, a pimp—or at least that was his assumed profession—nicknamed Huggy Bear.

"I have since learned that this is known as Blaxploitation; that is, imitating and perpetuating black stereotypes, for which I am deeply sorry."

The show never claimed that Huggy Bear was a pimp; true, he was a nightclub owner and involved in criminal activity. The fact that people assumed he was a pimp was considered bigoted and an example of Blaxploitation.

Norton continued: "That was a long time ago, and I conscientiously believe that I am very much a different man, and like most I have matured over the years. I have committed my life to help people."

Then with a wry smile he added, "I have not even watched an episode of *Starsky and Hutch* in over 20 years."

Norton's opening statement lasted 20 minutes. He concluded with another attempt at humor:

"There have been some things reported in the media over the last 24 hours that simply aren't true. One major news outlet listed me as a Republican. Let me say as vigorously as I can that I deny the charge." To signify it was a joke, he leaned back and gave his Gomer Pyle-like smile.

He then took some questions.

"Thank you, Mr. Governor. Cassie Baumgartner. with WRIC. Just to clarify, do you believe you were in any other racist pictures, other than as Huggy Bear? And how can you not be sure? Most Virginians would remember if they were in a racist photo. Why can't you?"

Elections Have Consequences

Norton responded, "I don't believe I am in any other pictures, Huggy Bear was my only character. Sadly, I can't say for certain I am not in other Huggy Bear photos with other questionable characters in the picture with me. As far as why, well, part of the reason may be attributable to Pabst Blue Ribbon."

"Bhavna Agarwal, *The Washington Press Democrat*. During the campaign you claimed that your opponent, State Senator Angela Parrish, was insensitive to the views of black people and people of color. When you made that claim, did you forget that there was this picture of you in blackface? Or did you believe that it would never surface?"

Norton responded, "I had no idea there was a picture, and I stand by my criticism of Ms. Parrish."

"Governor, Milt Miller ABC7. Do you know who the man in the photo with you was, or who took the picture?"

"No, I don't remember. Honestly, I don't remember the event, but I did recognize my getup. The plaid pants and the rest of it were all part of my Huggy Bear costume. Also I remember the room it was taken in."

"And to follow up, you say you don't remember the person in the Nazi uniform. Do you remember if that person or anyone else tried to recruit you or anyone in your fraternity to join a hate group?"

"No. No one ever tried to recruit me." Norton quickly added, "If they had, I would have punched them in the face."

"Mr. Governor, Tahanee Cahill, Norfolk 11 News. Have you ever gone in blackface as any other racist character, and why again did you go as Huggy Bear?"

Norton shook his head. "No. As a young man I developed a fascination with that particular character. Well, I started to

Elections Have Consequences

imitate him. He had the funniest walk; if you ever watched the show, even just the opening of the show, you can see it." To be helpful he added, "If you go to YoutTube you can probably see the opening of the show. He does the walk there." Paula, standing next to him, rolled her eyes.

He went on, "Well, in an effort to look more like him I colored my face. That really is the only character I did in blackface."

As a side note, after the press conference the name of the actor who played Huggy Bear was trending on social media. Spending all day doing radio and TV interviews, he commented that this was the most attention he had received in 30 years. "I never heard of Ronnie Norton until today, but damn if he hasn't gotten me attention."

The questions continued, with Norton being both contrite and aggressive. He was aggressive in the sense that his history was one of tolerance and healing, and talking about his plans moving forward.

Basically 90 percent of the press conference was devoted to the picture scandal; there were some unrelated questions, however:

"Dan Davis, ABC channel 7. Governor, you are not attending the Jamestown celebration today because of the attendance of President Marvin P. Bush. Could you explain why you are not there?"

"I feel that because of the offensive and divisive comments that the President has made recently I would prefer to stay away, in a show of solidarity with Virginians of color."

An incredulous Dan Davis snapped back, "You are here admitting that you went to a party in blackface and got your picture taken next to a guy dressed as a Nazi, but you don't want to go meet and get your picture taken with the president of the United States today because you don't want to offend people?"

Norton replied, "I was in my early 20's then."

Mike Chavez with the Roanoke News asked, "Do you think President Bush is a racist?"

Norton knew his political base believed Bush to be a racist; Norton could not say otherwise so he responded rather carefully, "I saw a Gallup poll the other day that found 52 percent of respondents said that they can't say for certain that Bush is not a racist. I think I am stating that accurately. But yes, I am with that majority. I can't say for certain that he is not a racist, and that is really sad for our country."

Chavez shot back, "Can you say for certain that you are not a racist?"

"Yes."

"Lin Canyon, MNN. There were allegations made this morning, and indeed the Lt. Governor acknowledged an inappropriate relationship decades ago with a VCC student. Do you know who leaked the story?"

"No."

"To follow up, will you tell your supporters and friends to stop leaking negative information?"

"Yes. To my supporters, don't leak any more negative info on Morrison, who is a very good friend of mine; I would say he was one of my oldest friends in the General Assembly. Jim Morrison and I were first elected to the House of Delegates in the same year. In fact, we became seatmates. Funny story, we both suspected that Speaker Hank Parrish seated us together in a far corner of the chamber so he could claim from time to time that he didn't recognize us." Norton chuckled.

Speaker Parrish privately referred to Morrison and Norton as Tweedle Dumb and Tweedle Dumber.

"But we became good friends, and in fact our families vacationed together. We used to hike the Peaks of Otter, right outside of Bedford, every year for several years. He is a good guy and hopefully all this leaking of dirty laundry is over."

"Mike Forrest, National Public Radio. There are constitutional and other concerns with your initiative regarding school tracking of racist jokes. Angela Parrish calls the plan 'asinine, stupid, unconstitutional' and furthermore she alleges that it won't stop the telling of a single racist joke. Now one problem: how will the school system determine whether a joke told by a student at school is racist?"

The whole idea of the racist joke initiative was the brainchild of Rev. Brand. She theorized that if there were no racist jokes then racism would be eliminated.

"Children will be encouraged to report jokes that they may think are offensive. Whether they are in fact racist, and hence to be recorded, would be up to each school. I think all reasonable adults know what a racist joke sounds like. As far as a definition, well, I think old Judge Potter Stewart summed it up best when he said of obscenity 'I know it when I see it.'"

The final non-Huggy Bear question dealt with the budget: "Frank Myers, the *Charlottesville Daily News*. Republicans have attacked your proposed tax increases. They say if the tax hikes you are proposing go through, Virginia will have Maryland and DC-level taxes."

Elections Have Consequences

This was actually what Norton wanted, for Maryland, DC, and Virginia to have uniform tax rates.

Governor Norton responded, "Look, my predecessor shut down the state for three months due to a flu virus, which was unnecessarily long, and caused real damage to our economy and budget. My tax plan hits those that can most afford to pay. It is an increase, no doubt, but it is an equitable increase. It places the burden on the wealthy where it belongs."

The main soundbite to come from the press conference was "I am in the picture. I was Huggy Bear." Naturally, the national media ran with it. *The New York Post* carried a downcast picture of Norton with the headline "Yes, I was Huggy Bear." *The Boston Globe*, *The Los Angeles Times* and the other major papers also carried the headline "I was Huggy Bear."

In the crowd gathered in the ballroom was a reporter that already knew Norton was called Huggy Bear by his fraternity brothers. Gary Frank was with Universal Press Service and ten years earlier was in Winchester with the *Star*. While doing background on Norton for the *Star*, he learned that Norton had acquired that nickname. His bosses mysteriously put a stop to his investigation before he could find out why.

Frank had his hand up during the press conference, but Norton didn't call on him.

16) Morrison Responds

With Norton's press conference over, it was now Morrison's time on the national stage. All the networks went from Richmond to Jamestown. Never before had so much national attention been focused on Virginia. Since Norton refused to introduce President Marvin P. Bush at the Jamestown celebration, that honor naturally fell to the Lt. Governor. It was truly remarkable and unprecedented that national attention would turn to a Virginia Lt. Governor.

As Morrison sat in the waiting room, it dawned on him that millions of Americans would be hearing what he had to say. It would be the first time they ever saw him; first impressions are lasting impressions, as they say. No doubt it would be the biggest speech of his life. The media was carrying it only because they thought Morrison might use the opportunity to apologize for a sex scandal or resign, or both, but Morrison had other ideas. This was the moment of his life.

Willow Bush interrupted the panel discussion on the Norton press conference. "Okay, we are going to go to Jamestown to hear from Lt. Governor Morrison. He is approaching the podium; let's listen in."

"Wow, what a great crowd! Welcome to Jamestown. Look at all the press here. I didn't know the national press was so interested in our anniversary." The crowd laughed.

"For us Virginians, Jamestown is a sacred place. Many of you know PBS has a show called *Finding Your Roots*, and they profiled me last year. That, by the way, was the last time I got national press." More laughter.

Elections Have Consequences

"It was a fun show and through research they determined that I was indeed a native Virginian. A rare condition, especially in Northern Virginia." The crowd liked that.

"Boy, if I had a dollar for everyone who claimed that they were related to Robert E. Lee, I'd be rich. But it was nice to have my roots confirmed. For those of you who haven't seen the show, I am related to a woman by the name of Anne Hartford who came to Jamestown from England in 1637. When I learned that I wondered what she must have thought and felt. She was probably 20 years of age, with her whole life ahead of her. She must have anticipated starting a family and building a new life here in Virginia.

"But Jamestown was a rough place. From 1609 to 1610 we had what was known as the Starving Time, where over one third of the population died. In 1621, there was a massacre with over five hundred settlers killed. There was starvation, scurvy, yellow fever, malaria and freezing temperatures. There was lots of hard work. Captain Smith said if you don't work, you don't eat. But the amazing thing? People kept coming!

"I know of no other comparable example in all of human history of so many people who were willing to risk everything, including life, to make it to such an inhospitable place. But even in the 1600's Virginia was the place to be–it still is. So, on that fateful day when Anne Hartford said goodbye to her friends and family and all the scenes of her youth, she knew that she would never see them again. But you know what else she knew? She knew that she was the lucky one because she had the chance to make it to Virginia." He paused. "She wasn't going to pass that up."

"So today, all these reporters are here to see me crumble. To see me quit. They are not here to honor our ancestors, our state, our

Elections Have Consequences

heritage. The editors of *The Washington Press Democrat* and *Richmond Daily Dispatch* want to write 'Jim Morrison had a bad day.'"

"But when I think of what my ancestors and the other early Virginians did to make our state the greatest place in the world, compared to what they had to do – I have never had a bad day in my life!"

The crowd then became euphoric, going from dead silence to screaming and cheering. They jumped to their feet and started yelling, "MORR IS SON, MORR IS SON," and then "MNN sucks, MNN Sucks, MNN sucks!"

Morrison thundered "They–" he pointed at the bank of cameras–"want to focus on me, but we are here to celebrate the founding of the greatest state in the union in the greatest country on earth!"

Again, the crowd started yelling "MNN sucks, MNN sucks." At that moment you could hear the producer at MNN yelling "Cut away now, cut away, cut away!" MNN then went to a commercial. It seems Willow Bush was away from the desk so they couldn't go to her.

In the governor's office Norton and Beaman, watching on television, sat silently for a minute. Then Beaman turned to Norton and said, "Looks like we met our match.

***

True to form, Beaman had acted unethically and perhaps illegally, since there was no proof the emails were genuine. He released them out of desperation. No reputable news outlet should have run with the story. Luckily for Norton, MNN is not really a reputable news organization.

Just after the Jamestown speech Morrison released a statement:

Elections Have Consequences

"Decades ago, I was involved in an improper relationship with a student at Virginia Commonwealth College. I have made amends for it, and my family and I have put it behind us. I have nothing more to say."

He didn't admit any wrong doing with a student at Almond High School; rather, he cited her as a student at Virginia Commonwealth College.

Morrison handled the Jamestown celebration perfectly. He had a national audience, and certainly wouldn't have used the occasion to apologize or announce wrongdoing. In addition, because Norton and the Democrats boycotted the event, more of the tickets went to Bush supporters. So, Morrison had a friendly crowd; in effect it was a Bush rally.

He went after the "lying fake media." After his speech he became a rock star among conservatives. The speech went viral, and all the conservative media outlets wanted interviews with him.

Richmond-born James Stuart Morrison grew up in Henrico County and attended the famed St. Christopher's High School in Richmond. He went on to Hampden-Sydney for his undergraduate degree and finished law school at the University of Richmond. First elected to the House of Delegates as a Republican in the early 2000s, he served a few terms there until, like Norton, he moved over to the state Senate.

While Norton's political hero may have been Bill Clinton, Morrison's was a man he had met only once, as a little kid. Richard Obenshain, a Richmond lawyer, Republican party activist, and also a law partner of Morrison's father. Like Obenshain, Jim Morrison believed in limited government, that

Elections Have Consequences

government expansion posed a threat to individual liberty and the health of the economy.

Like the Nortons, the Morrisons had three kids, all about the same ages. Morrison's wife Sally was also a lawyer by occupation. Despite political differences, Morrison and Norton worked together on a number of issues, in both houses.

Norton liked Morrison in large part because Morrison had qualities he didn't. For example, Morrison had athletic talent. He played baseball at UVA; he even got a tryout with Norton's favorite team, the New York Yankees. Norton loved baseball but never got farther than Little League.

Shortly after her husband's election, Paula Norton did an interview with WBT Richmond, where she was asked about partisanship in the state capital. She pointed to the friendship between the Nortons and the Morrisons as an example of the potential for bipartisanship.

"One of Ronnie's best friends in the General Assembly for years was Jim Morrison, a Republican, and our families became friends. We even took some vacations together. We had a tradition for years of taking a joint vacation to the Peaks of Otter in the Blue Ridge mountains, outside of the town of Bedford. It's a great vacation spot. You have the three peaks, and there are trails to the top, a lake, and a resort at the base where our combined families would stay.

Ronnie and Joe loved the Blue Ridge mountains and hiking to the top of the peaks. A hike to the summit of one peak would take three to four hours, and you would go up to an elevation of nearly 4000 feet."

Elections Have Consequences

In his book *Notes on the State of Virginia*, Thomas Jefferson mentions the Peaks of Otter. "The mountains of the Blue Ridge, and of these Peaks of Otter, are thought to be of a greater height, measured from their base, than any other in our country, and perhaps in North America." In the quote he refers to Virginia as "our country," a point not lost on historians.

"Sally Morrison and I would make sandwiches, and all of us would hike to the top. The Peaks of Otter are quite famous and beautiful. Ronnie says it's the most beautiful site in Virginia. General Lee used to love to visit and hike the trails after the war. About halfway up, where the picnic area is, he'd dismount Traveler and hike to the top. You can see where he carved his initials towards the top. So, the six children would have this annual tradition. They would all race up to the summit and try to be the first one to reach General Lee's initials; the first one to touch them won. That kid would have bragging rights for the year. To make it fair, Joe and Ronnie came up with an idea.

"In the closing 50 yards or so, depending on age each child would get a head start, then the older kids would run to the spot. Those were good times. It became an annual tradition for our families."

17) Family Retreat

In order to stop the flow of resignation calls, Brand and Beaman came up with a deal. If Norton signed the Critical Race Theory bill, his party in the General Assembly would stop all calls for his resignation. The deal was agreed to by the House Speaker, Glenda Fox-Meadows, State Senator Steve Siebers, and Delegate Julius Jones.

Despite the deal supposedly being a secret, several in the press knew all about it, but of course didn't report on it. While sitting in the press room in the basement of the capitol, Stephen Cohen remarked to another reporter that this had to be "the first time in Virginia history that the legislature promised not to pass a resolution calling on the governor to resign in exchange for his signing a bill that he opposed."

Cohen chuckled. "They got Norton by the balls, and he knows it."

The other reporter asked him, "Steve, do you think Virginians have any idea of what a cuckold of a governor they have?"

Cohen thought about it for a second and smiled. Then he leaned forward and said in a low voice, "My lips are sealed. I won't tell if you won't." Cohen kept his promise.

Beaman, with Brand's okay, did get the legislators to agree to change the name of the program from Critical Race Theory to the nebulous and vague sounding "History with a cultural and historical perspective," but it was the same program. It still taught that the founding fathers broke away from Britain in part out of fear that the British would stop slavery and protect the Indians.

Elections Have Consequences

The bill mandated that all Virginia public schools, starting in middle school, include teaching the children that race was a critical component of the founding of the United States. The current conventional view is that America declared independence from Britain based on principles listed in the Declaration of Independence, ideas such as taxation with representation, the right to a jury trial, guarantees of freedom of speech and of the press, the right to peacefully assemble, limited government, and separation of powers.

The new required teaching didn't say those things were untrue; rather it required children to be instructed that the colonists also wanted to continue to exploit black people and drive Indians (or native Americans) into extinction. The colonists, led by white men who opposed women in positions of authority, were also concerned that England might try to stop them. Hence, the need for the American revolution and the founding of the United States.

Beaman tried to cheer Norton up with the idea, "You can still say that we don't teach Critical Race Theory in Virginia schools; that is technically true. It is not Critical Race Theory, it's 'history with a cultural perspective.'" As Beaman said this he made little quotation marks with his fingers. Norton knew everyone would see through that claim, so he dismissed Beaman's spin.

"Steve, the name change is too cynical. If I go along with it a part of my soul will die. And worse than that, I fear the people would buy it. The very idea that they could be led to believe that there is a difference between Critical Race Theory and 'History with a cultural and historical perspective' is heartbreaking. No doubt Cohen and most of the Virginia media would push such a

Elections Have Consequences

lie, but deep down if the people of Virginia accepted the argument that it's not really the same as Critical Race Theory then that would mean that they are stupid; they are sheep. I can't face that possible realization. So I will take the heat. I will sign the bill with no name change. I will call it what it is, Critical Race Theory, and I will admit to changing my position."

"Okay, I understand. I think that's very noble of you."

Norton paused, shook his head, and said, "But damn it, Steve, I don't like it. I don't like it one bit. I sign their bad bill, and they stop calling for my resignation. It seems like blackmail."

"Well, it is hardball stuff, I know, but you got something out of this as well. You put an end to the resignation calls, and now you can move forward with your governorship. Sure we lose on this one, but the bill is their priority. We do this for the progressives and they help put this Huggy Bear scandal behind us. Putting your signature on this bill will help get you back in the good graces of the party. Not all the way, but it will at least stop the resignation calls."

Norton protested, "Steve, I told people I was opposed to the bill. Now I have to backtrack?"

The ever cynical Beaman reassured Norton. "It won't be hard. Just say you took a second look at Critical Race Theory and believe it's fine to teach this as theory, not necessarily fact, to school children." Beaman seized on that point. "It's taught as a theory, so no one has to believe it. You can have a clear conscience."

Norton seemed to ignore what Beaman just said and added a new thought, "Sure, I think Parrish is a right wing nut, but on this one she is right. That Critical Race Theory is pure propaganda funded by taxpayers and spoon fed to their children."

"Well, never admit that."

"No, of course I would never publicly say that."

"As far as being accused of a flip flop, well, the media won't say that; they support the proposal. They won't even mention your promise to veto. Sure, Republicans will mention it, but the media never listens to them."

"Steve, why won't the media hit me on this obvious flip flop?"

"The media wants you to sign it. Heck they'll praise you for it. That tool Cohen will write, 'Governor Norton was willing to break a campaign promise, proving he is a true Virginia statesman, in the mold of John Warner.'" Beaman laughed. "You will get great press. The media only ridicules flip flops if it goes in a direction they don't agree with. Your flipping to the politically correct position is praiseworthy by their journalistic standards. It's like you're a Profile in Courage. It shows you have 'evolved.' In other words, you'll be a hero."

Beaman confidently predicted, "The media won't hammer you on the flip flopping, but as far as Huggy Bear goes, well, they have to hammer you there. It's called virtue signaling. Take Steve Cohen. He's a lefty, but even if he weren't he would still have to virtue signal. Cohen knows how to play the game. I remember he used to always go around quoting those old Virginia historians Douglas Southhall Freeman and Virginius Dabney, but the social justice crowd canceled them, so Cohen stopped mentioning them. Two of his heroes! Cohen is a tool. He believes he has to please his colleagues in the media. Remember he speaks at colleges and organizations around the state, collecting honeria no doubt, so to keep getting invited and receiving honoria, he has to do his share of virtue signaling. And more than that, to remain, the 'Dean of the Virginia Press corps' he will have to make clear he is an anti-racist. Remember in America today you are either a racist or an anti-racist." He rolled his eyes and went on. "Another thing, to understand the media you must realize that they cater to their readers' biases and worldviews, their perception of reality. Every day there's lots of news to report. The purpose of a newspaper is to shape the news into a narrative that will please their readers, a narrative that makes sense, a narrative that doesn't confuse the reader. Most newspapers are barely hanging on financially. To survive, they need to appeal to a younger demographic, ages 25-54. Those folks are woke, so the paper has to be woke. They play to that worldview."

Norton interjected, "You say that a newspaper must not confuse the reader. What do you mean?"

"So in the jumble of news that comes up every day, a paper must sift through it and piece it together in a way that seems consistent. That is, consistent with their editorial page, and consistent with what they have been saying over the last several weeks and months. Usually, this can be done through omitting some stories, evidence and even facts. For example, their narrative is that the Republican party is the racist party. Well, if they acknowledge Harry Byrd, a segregationist, was a Democrat it can cause confusion. So the *Daily Dispatch* implies Byrd was an Angela Parrish Republican. It's confirmation bias, and let's face it, confirmation bias is what sells newspapers. Now sure in the body of a story, several paragraphs in, they may acknowledge Byrd was a Democrat, but usually they will simply refer to him as a conservative.

"Now the sought after demographic group of readers are interested in the Huggy Bear scandal. They want to know if their

Governor is a racist like Angela Parrish. So they will buy copies of the *Daily Dispatch*, or I guess should say log on to the digital edition. Lots of clicks! That paper, and most other papers in Virginia, have to stay on this story for a couple of weeks. Then they will give you a clean bill of health." Beaman went on to make a prediction, "But Governor, once this dies down Cohen and the entire Virginia media will be singing your praises. Just be contrite, virtue signal, and sign some progressive bills, such as this Critical Race Theory bill, and you will demonstrate that you're okay, you are not a racist."

Norton sighed and nodded. "Okay, I will sign the bill, but I won't like it."

Beaman reassured him, "It's like having to kiss your sister; it's over in a second."

"Now, you implied that signing this bill won't totally bring us back into the good graces of the caucus and the media. What else do I have to do?"

"Not sure what totally gets us back, but I have an idea. Governor, you remember when our hero Bill Clinton was president. He played a game of small ball. He took little symbolic issues and got behind them to appear to be a moderate Democrat. For example, he pushed little things like school uniforms, minor reforms on education, a wimpy welfare work requirement, things like that. It didn't do much, but it recrafted his image as a moderate Democrat. Well, I think you need to do this in reverse. Throw some little bones to the left."

"I think I'm too old to reinvent myself now." Norton chuckled. "I can't imagine myself kneeling for the national anthem, or demanding gender neutral bathrooms in all public schools, or

Elections Have Consequences

campaigning that George Mason and James Madison Universities must change their names. But what do you have in mind?"

"Currently in Virginia, if a litigant owes money for court costs or outstanding tickets and fines, in time if it is not paid they could lose their driver's license. How unfair."

An unimpressed Norton rolled his eyes and sharply responded, "They are given plenty of time to pay court costs and tickets. A small interest rate is charged, and it is not more than a few hundred bucks. And anyway, the percentage of Virginians who have had their license suspended over unpaid tickets or court fees is infinitesimal. The odds are similar to getting beaten up by a police officer or struck by lightning while walking on the boardwalk at Virginia Beach."

Beaman persisted. "Exactly, it is a small BS issue in the sense that it doesn't have much legal impact, but symbolically, it says you care about people, mostly minorities, who are caught up in a racist legal system. You can argue to moderate and independent voters, look, If they don't have their driver's license, how can they get to work to pay their court costs?" Beaman gave a confident "case closed" smile.

Norton just stared at him with a look that said he was unimpressed. An undaunted Beaman continued, "This is an issue where Virginians can see the obvious social injustice. Someone caught up in an unfair justice system, and then stripped of their license. As I said, it's a small but symbolic cause you can take up."

"Okay, I'll think about it. Maybe that could help with the base. Look, Steve, I know I will have to appease the base, but I don't want to be rolled over."

Beaman nodded and said, "Exactly, that is why this little court cost bullshit reform is perfect. It's small and won't do any real damage to the state, but it will please the base. You throw them this little bone."

Norton seemed to appreciate that and insisted, "I am willing to sign some of their little bullshit bills, but I still want to be the moderate centrist Democrat that I promised on the campaign trail." He then reflected, "Funny, a Republican controlled General Assembly, or at least one house in their hands could have helped me resist the far left."

"I know, but elections have consequences, as you like to say." Then he laughingly pointed out, "The people of Virginia sent two socialists to Richmond. They both make Henry Howell look like a moderate."

"I'm worried about what they may send me. I have my limits. For example, laws requiring police officers to survey everyone they stop. Ask them what gender they identify with. They may pull over someone for a busted tail light, in the middle of the night, write them a ticket and then have to ask, 'Now what gender you identify with?'"

"It's just a survey question to make sure police don't have a bias against transgendered. No big deal."

"It's a waste of time and demeaning to the police to have to ask such questions. Seriously, it's at night, a motorist has a tail light out; does anyone seriously believe she or he was pulled over based on the gender they identify with? Either the tail light is out or it's not!"

"Governor, don't worry. We can kill a lot of that type of crap, and most, but not all, of the kookiest bills. We have enough moderate Democrats on the Courts of Justice committee and the Education and Health committee in the Senate."

Elections Have Consequences

A skeptical Norton shook his head. "I don't know; maybe Parrish is right. We need a filibuster in the State Senate to stop a lot of bad legislation."

Beaman laughed, then with a serious look said, "Don't say that publicly."

"I won't, but we need to stop a lot of this crap in committee. Keep it off my desk. Steve, your main job is to be like a goalie and keep those lefty crap bills off my desk."

Beaman pointed out, "Well, the first test will be SB1619. That is Sandoval's bill to prohibit the prosecutors from charging shoplifters of merchandise up to 950 bucks; that is shoplifters can only be charged criminally if they go over that amount. I know you prefer to veto the bill.

Governor, this is a kooky bill, but I don't think we can kill it outright. Probably the best we can do is amend it. If we don't try to at least amend it, it may pass as is, and you will be in the tough political position of having to veto it. So we may have to settle, with an amended bill."

Norton sighed. "Really, that bill has the votes to pass?"

"I think so. The social justice legislators are complaining that the overwhelming number of people charged with shoplifting are minorities, and hence, such shoplifting prosecutions are unfair. It's what they might claim is an example of systemic or institutional racism. But we could probably water it down with some friendly amendments, and lower the threshold to 200 bucks."

Norton, seemingly frustrated, said, "Well, I can't really stomach any threshold over $200. I prefer to do symbolic stuff, like wishing people a happy Kwanzaa, or pushing to remove a statue, or school name changes, than to signing bad bills or creating another state holiday, like making January 6th Democracy Day. You know, when I looked into the cost of creating a state holiday, I was shocked at the price. It costs millions of dollars!"

Beaman nodded. "Well, virtue signaling can get expensive. But at some point we will have changed all the school names, so we have to give them some love on their bills."

"Still, a filibuster would be nice in the State Senate." Then in a mocking voice Norton said, "Sure, State Senator So and So, I'd love to sign your bill defunding the police, paying slave reparations, offering free college tuition to illegal aliens, and demanding that Israel get out of Palestine but that damn Angela Parrish in the Senate keeps filibustering." They both laughed.

"Well, that's not the case. We have to keep you as a moderate centrist Democrat, and at the same time satisfy your left flank. Not easy, but we can do it."

Norton stopped laughing. The smile left his face, and he simply nodded. Norton realized that he sat in the governor's chair, but his hold on his party's caucus was weak.

Beaman went on, "Look, Governor, now that the session is almost over I recommend that you take some time off and relax. When you come back after a long weekend we'll get back to work and put the Huggy Bear scandal behind us."

"When I come back I'm going to meet with Reverend Brand. She's going to give me a crash course in woke theology."

Beaman laughed and sarcastically said, "Sounds like fun. Better you than me, but Governor, the fact is we are all going to have to drink the Kool Aid at some point. In America today you can't go anywhere without demonstrating a certain level of wokeness. Every industry and profession requires a certain

Elections Have Consequences

amount of compliance with political correctness. Jobs in the federal government or even in corporate America require a certain ideological conformity. And as I said a few minutes ago there are now two camps, racists and anti-racists. We are all going to have to prove we are anti-racist or risk getting canceled. Just get used to the Kool Aid."

Beaman then realized an irony, "You know the derivation of the expression drinking the Kool Aid?"

Norton shook his head.

Beaman replied, "It was a socialist, Jim Jones, who forced his followers to drink Kool Aid spiked with poison."

***

Several years earlier, the Nortons bought a house in the Outer Banks of North Carolina. They bought it as a vacation place, and later they discovered that they could rent it out. In the late 2000's they turned it into a little money maker; they would rent for weekends on BRNB and other internet sites.

Norton and his family decided that a little break for a long weekend would be a good idea, and before he left he agreed to do a Public Service Announcement. Brand had come up with the idea for a campaign to promote "unity." Norton liked the idea, because it meant he would get some free statewide exposure—at the party's expense.

The campaign was titled "Unity–Pass It On." Norton did a spot which would run as an ad all across the Commonwealth. The PSA had him reading into the camera:

"This is Ronnie Norton, governor of Virginia. I wish to speak with you today on an important subject, unity. A beautiful word and a wonderful concept. We are all different in some ways. Some of us like the Commnanders; some of us like the Ravens. Some of us like marmalade; some of us like jam. Some of us like hip hop; some of us like country. Some of us like cafe lattes, and some of us like Dr. Pepper. But despite our differences we work together on the really important things. We know that to achieve great things in life we must be united. Together, without rancor and prejudice, we all can succeed: black, white, brown and yellow, male, female and transitioning, but we must put aside our differences. We must stay united on our fundamental principles." Then the tag line: "Unity. You and I know why—Pass it on!"

Ronnie then flashed his Gomer Pyle-like smile to close. Because of the length of the commercial and basic TV commercial formatting, there was an extra three seconds at the end used as filler. So the commercial would run and then the viewer would be exposed to 3 extra seconds of Norton frozen in his goofy smile. One TV executive commented, "At the end of the clip Norton's face lights up in a broad smile so quickly that it's like he just realized he sat on a whoopie cushion."

The state Democrat party agreed to pick up the cost of the unity PSA. After three takes Norton was finished and he and Paula left the Governor's Mansion for the Outer Banks, in his unmarked blue Chevy Malibu.

The Norton house was of modest size, three floors, not a huge yard, but it had a deck on the roof, and from there you could sit and watch the tide roll in. Ronnie and Paula were joined by their three kids. The house was very private and a special place for the family to gather at special times. Governor Norton could walk the streets of the small town without being bothered. There seemed to be an unwritten rule in the Outer Banks: they left visiting celebrities alone. He could go to restaurants and bars and no one would say anything to him. For a few days he could be just Ronnie Norton, a lawyer from McLean, Virginia.

Adding to his feeling of normality, the State Police would need a small contingent to be in the area, but they would be discreet and give the family as much privacy as safely possible. Norton could drive his car and the State Police would lay back; in fact, Norton could barely see them in the rear-view mirror.

The family gathering, organized by Paula, was designed to show support for and to try to cheer up their embattled husband and father. The kids also brought with them some ideas and strategies for salvaging Norton's governorship. But it was just immediate family, no significant others.

To Mrs. Norton, Ronnie complained half-jokingly., "How can I be a racist? I'm from McLean!"

Paula soothed him. "When the people of Virginia really get to know you over the next two years of your term, they'll understand that you're not a racist or a bigot; rather, they will see you as a kind, progressive man."

Norton complained, "I don't like being called a racist. I don't know how Angela Parrish does it. She's called a racist every day and it doesn't seem to bother her."

"That Parrish girl has no heart, just ice water running through her veins."

The family's favorite place in town for dinner was a seafood restaurant, Mickey's. Norton loved the place because they offered all you can eat crab legs. Over dinner, the kids offered all kinds of advice on how to change his image and get over the past.

"Dad, take a look at some of the bills State Senator Sandoval is working on. She has a bill to require that public corporations

Elections Have Consequences

in Virginia have boards of directors that are at least 50 percent women. You need to get behind good bills like that," daughter Susan implored.

Norton sarcastically responded, "Does it include a 50 percent quota on condo homeowners association boards?"

Susan made a funny face. "Be serious. Look, Dad, I'm trying to say you need to push progressive, forward looking policies."

Norton lamented the failure of his racist joke school tracking bill. "Sadly, it got tabled in committee; there were concerns on the definition of a racist joke. What if school officials disagreed on whether the offensive joke was as racist or not? For example, what if the gym coach says it's not racist, but the soccer coach says it is? Does it get recorded or not? In addition, opponents claimed it would encourage kids to snitch or tattle on others. So, we'll try to address the concerns of enough legislators and get the program passed next year. If we add an arbitration panel to judge disputed jokes, maybe it will pass."

His son Robert Lee Norton said, "Well, you got Kevin Mack on the State Supreme Court, the first openly gay judge on the high court. A significant step."

Paula raised her glass and said, "Here here."

Norton looked down at his plate and responded, "Yes, I thought he'd be a great addition to the court." He seemed to try to reassure himself. "He will be an excellent addition."

Delegate Mack ran against Norton for the Democrat nomination in the governor's race. He stayed in the race all the way to the end, splitting the progressive vote. Some pundits even maintained that had Mack dropped out, Norton might not have won the nomination.

Elections Have Consequences

Susan asked, "Dad, Virginia has some of the oddest, racist, and most sexiest traditions. How did the Hollins vs. Mary Baldwin prettiest girls debate start?"

Norton smiled and replied, "Of all the great Virginia traditions, this has got to be my favorite. Both Mary Baldwin and Hollins College are women's colleges that go back to the Civil War era, so the debate over which school had the prettiest girls may have started in the late 1800's. It probably just began naturally, organically. It was the pride of the alumni, mostly the parents of the alumni. In the early 20th century the actress Tallulah Bankhead attended Mary Baldwin, which may have fueled the debate. She was considered the most beautiful woman in all of Hollywood.

"Well, one of Bankhead's publicists or fans stated, "Well, of course Tallulah went to Mary Baldwin. That's where all the beautiful girls go. That was interpreted as a not so subtle dig by some of the Hollins folks. There was a time when you couldn't go anywhere in Virginia and not be asked 'Which school has the prettier girls, Hollins or Mary Baldwin?' Most every Virginian would give you an opinion. Today we talk about a partisan divide, but we had a passionate divide between Hollins and Mary Baldwin proponents, that's for sure."

Norton stopped for a sip of water before continuing. "The debate spread naturally because people, everyone really, knew a girl, say a daughter or granddaughter, or niece or maybe a pretty girl down the street, and they would think 'Well, she is the prettiest girl in all Virginia, and she went to Hollins or Mary Baldwin,' so they would come to a conclusion that the prettiest girls must go the that school. I always used to say that Mary

Elections Have Consequences

Baldwin is where most of the southern belles went. Honestly, my view was that Mary Baldwin produced the more beautiful women, that is until I met your mother, since she's a Hollins graduate."

With this the kids rolled their eyes, and son Mark mocked throwing up.

Norton went on. "Even at candidate forums, it was a common question, usually at the end of the debate. Perhaps to ease the tensions of a sharp debate, someone would ask each candidate to weigh in on the Hollins vs. Mary Baldwin question."

Susan looked angry. "How sexist."

Norton responded, "Look, little girl, it could be a tricky question. I always had the perfect answer. 'My wife went to Hollins College, so obviously Hollins produces the most beautiful women.' Some candidates were in a bind over this question."

Susan interjected, "Very smooth, Dad."

Norton laughed. "It was so funny. A questioner would go to the microphone and ask, 'Candidate So and So, there is a raging debate taking place all across Virginia, and I'd like to know if you have a position on this. Which school produces more beautiful women, Hollins College or Mary Baldwin?' The crowd would laugh and applaud. But anyway, it was an old Virginia tradition; it was something candidates had to anticipate. Were most of your female supporters Hollins women or Mary Baldwin women? But as the state grew and more people were educated out of state, the debate lost a personal connection and finally died out."

Susan responded, "Nice spin, Dad, but it was pushed by the parents trying to marry off their daughters. They're both good schools and the schools had nothing to do with the debate, but enough parents from both schools were saying, `Hey Virginia gentlemen—preferably wealthy ones—the prettiest girls go to say, Hollins College, where our daughter goes to school, so please go meet her."

"Well, most parents get involved in trying to marry off their daughters."

As the crab legs were being passed around and the alcohol was flowing, Norton's oldest son, Mark, chimed in. "Dad, African Americans, who have not been welcomed, indeed since 1619 have been treated like second class citizens, are looking for a governor who is trying to be inclusive. You can be that governor, just if I may say, think of them in everything you do."

Susan responded, "I think tearing down racist monuments and looking at removing out of date names for schools and buildings is very appropriate. It's ridiculous that Richmond's international airport is named the Harry Flood Byrd International Airport. What kind of message does that send? Not just in Virginia, to people of color, but also around the world. Our airport is named after a segregationist. The airport even has a big statue of him out front waving."

Norton said, "Well, they say Byrd helped get it built."

Susan responded sharply, "He was a segregationist, but we should overlook that because he built an airport? That is like saying 'Other than that, Mrs. Lincoln, how was the play?'"

Norton gave a quick humorous response. "Well, little girl, maybe we should name it after a cutie pie like you." As he said this he pretended to give her a punch on the chin. Well, in the case of the Byrd Airport the airport authority likes the name, in part because in many parts of the world the name 'Byrd Airport' is well known. They don't think it's good business to change the name. Supposedly a huge portion of the Chinese business community thinks of Virginia when they hear the name 'Byrd airport'."

Susan spoke quickly. "All the more reason to change it to something more inclusive. Virginia, probably more than any other Southern state, holds on to racist school names and traditions longer than necessary. Heck, it wasn't until the early 2000's that Virginia got rid of Lee-Jackson Day.."

"I didn't mind Lee Jackson Day. I think it made Virginians think about the Civil War, and its origins and aftermath."

Mark added his two cents. "I think all these name changes can get a little absurd. The Almond High School nickname is the 'Travelers,' named after Robert E. Lee's horse, so they are pushing to change it to the 'Runners.'

Robert Lee chimed in, "Actually, it had nothing to do with the controversy of Lee's horse; rather, the basketball team doesn't want to be called the 'Travelers.'" Laughter.

Norton returned to the statue issue. "The state has given powers to the local governments to decide, and for the most part the statues will come down for the simple reason that the cities are fairly progressive. But there are some exceptions. The town of Damascus put up a statue of John D. Imboden who founded the town. He was a Confederate soldier before he settled the town. But that is the only one that will go up, and almost all of them will come down soon. As far as school names go, that's up to the counties and cities. Here are my thoughts on Confederate statues. After the Civil War, Confederate veterans came back home and helped rebuild their towns and cities, and many of the veterans got elected to the legislature. Can we honor them for what they did after the Civil War? I think so, but understand on

Elections Have Consequences

my side of the political spectrum I am in the minority. There were good people who fought for the Confederacy."

Susan interjected, "Good people on both sides, Dad?"

"Little girl, do you realize that after the war the next seven Virginia governors were confederate veterans, including Fitzhugh Lee, General Lee's nephew. James Lawson Kemper, the pride of Madison County, was the Speaker of the House of Delegates. General Lee's right hand man Col. Walter Taylor got elected to the State Senate, and of course Col. John Imboden got elected to the House of Delegates. I guess we can just go along with the social justice warriors and cancel all of them. But that probably won't go far enough. The next non-Confederate veteran governor was Andrew Jackson Montague in the early 1900's. He was a progressive Democrat, so he might be okay, right? Well progressive Democrats in the early 20th century had some really bad ideas, so bad that Democrats stopped calling themselves progressives for 100 years.

"Governor Montague and progressive Virginia Democrats made changes to the Virginia constitution in 1902 which basically disenfranchised black people. Why did progressive Democrats do it? Well, they were very paternalistic; they believed that if black people could vote they would vote for demagogues and charlatans. Those progressive Democrats believed that they would do what is right for black people—after all they were progressives—so black people didn't need to vote and risk making bad choices, which could hurt their interests.

"So Montague and all the Virginia progressive Democrat politicians would have to be canceled, and then we would have to cancel all the Byrd governors, who were conservative Democrats, and so forth. I estimate that every Virginia governor in the 20th century would have to be canceled, and that cancellation would not stop until the 1960's. So the first governor who would not get canceled would be Linwood Holton, and he was a Republican!"

Norton continued, "So, reluctantly, I realize that the Confederate statues will have to go, and maybe it could be a step to help bring unity, and move them to museums or battlefields, but where does it stop? I fear it won't stop with just Confederate statues and school and street names. As I said, are all governors to be canceled before Linwood Holton? Probably so."

Robert Lee said, "Dad, I know you will never be canceled, and will be considered one of the greatest governors ever."

"Thanks, son. When I was a kid, people would say 'Andrew Jackson Montague was Virginia's greatest governor,' the next generation after me would say 'Mills Godwin was Virginia's greatest governor.' I suppose now most people say Jerry Baliles was Virginia's greatest governor. Not that he was so great, but that almost every governor before him has been canceled."

"When I leave office, if people wish to pay me the compliment of saying I was a great governor, they can probably only go as far back as Jerry Baliles. 'Ronnie Norton was the greatest Governor since Jerry Baliles.'"

In an attempt to lighten the conversation, Mark finally asked the question everyone was dying to ask. "Dad, why Huggy Bear? Of all the characters of the 70's you had to impersonate Huggy Bear?"

Paula then broke in, "Be thankful, kids, I spared you from ever seeing him do his Huggy Bear walk."

Mark interjected, "Yeah, Dad, why couldn't you have been the Fonz?" Then Mark leaned back in his chair and did his impersonation with an "AAAaaay."

Susan added, "Dad, you could have impersonated Starsky or Hutch; heck, with your dark hair you could have been Starsky."

Paula suggested, "You could have been Joe Mannix. All you need is a loud sports coat. And he'd be perfect; you always had a man crush on him."

In addition to the Huggy Bear scandal, Virginians all across the Commonwealth were also talking about the new Miss Virginia. It was a first: the new Miss Virginia was a transgendered woman from Norfolk. Susan opined "I think she's beautiful, with that beautiful hair and those big beautiful brown eyes."

Mark wondered, "When was the last time Virginia had a Miss America winner?"

Robert Lee responded, "I don't remember her name but I think she was the one Chuck Robb was messing around with." Everyone laughed.

Robert Lee mentioned a column in the *Richmond Daily Dispatch*. "The article was by Professor Brockenbrough from UVA. He claims that the only way for beauty pageants to remain relevant in the Me Too era is to promote transsexual contestants and biological women with non-traditional figures. In other words, lookism practiced against trans women is more acceptable than lookism practiced against biological women. Professor Brockenbrough said that trans candidates may very well come to dominate beauty contests. Sad. First women's sports, now beauty contests. I am for social justice, but I do worry about roles for biological women."

Susan countered, "Look, I am a proud feminist, but biological women don't need beauty contests. Leave them for the trans women."

Elections Have Consequences

Robert Lee responded, "We have to look at male beauty contestants? That's not fair."

Susan said, "What difference does it make whether someone has a penis or a vagina? Can't we all be open minded enough to accept their decision to identify as a man or a woman? Why is gender identification pushed on people? Well, I for one think the new Miss Virginia is beautiful. So she is not a biological woman. So what?"

Mark responded, "Yes, he, I mean she, is beautiful and attractive, but wait until she's in a swimsuit. It will become obvious she's a dude." Mark and Robert Lee laughed and high-fived each other.

Susan replied, "They have done away with the swimsuit portion of the contest, but of course we know, Bobbie Lee, why you like that–because that's the closest you will ever get to seeing a half naked woman."

"If there are dudes competing for Miss Virginia, I don't want to look."

Norton chimed in, "On this issue, I agree with your brothers. Biology is a fact; you are either male or female. No matter what you want to identify as, you can't overlook biology. However, I haven't seen her yet. When we get back to the house I'll check out the story." Then he concluded, "Well, if everyone has finished stuffing your face, why don't I get the check and we can get out of here."

After dinner, the family decided to head over to a bar off the main street that had live music. Norton liked jazz; actually, he could be described as a jazz aficionado. As luck would have it, that night's performer was a famous jazz musician. Norton used to say, "I have two passions outside of politics: the Yankees and jazz."

The bar was close enough to walk, and as they were walking down the block Norton had got an idea. "Honey, can I do it?"

Paula knew exactly what he meant. "Honey, there might be cameras around."

"No, it's dark, and so a camera won't pick it up no matter how close it is."

"Honey, it's still light enough for people to see."

The kids figured out what he was talking about and egged him on, "Come on, Dad, do the Huggy Bear walk! Do the Huggy Bear strut!"

Norton said, "Okay, here goes." The family gave him room on the sidewalk and no one was coming in either direction. The two State Police officers were a block away; they could probably see him doing the walk, but they were discreet enough not to mention or film it.

Norton, flashing a Gomer Pyle-like grin, started. He took a deep breath and stepped forward, swinging his hips, rolling his shoulders back and forth, shaking his head from side to side as he walked several feet, turned around and continued. The family started laughing and clapping. Norton felt like a kid again. After weeks of hell, he loved seeing the laughter on his kids' faces.

Susan asked incredulously, "Mom, he really did that on your first date?"

Paula rolling her eyes said, "Yes, he did. Okay, honey, very nice, now you got it out of your system."

Sitting in the nightclub, Norton felt like a normal person again, just a regular guy out for a night on the town with his

Elections Have Consequences

family. The Outer Banks are just over 200 miles from Richmond, but for Norton it seemed like a world away.

Later, back at the house while watching TV in the living room, out of the blue Norton announced, "You know, I have an idea, something that you all brought up at dinner. This case with the new Miss Virginia, well, maybe I should send out a chirp offering congratulations."

Susan and Paula both liked the idea. Susan said, "Yes, Dad, that's a simple way to show that you are tolerant and inclusive."

Norton concurred. "It won't cost anything and it can be a positive message, which my political base will like." He laughed. "Maybe this will show people that I can be as woke as Sandoval and Brand."

His sons weren't so sure. Robert Lee asked, "Since when does a governor congratulate a beauty contestant? And anyway, Dad, this is radical! It might go against your Christian faith, and no civilization has ever claimed a man to be a woman, then declared her to be beautiful."

Susan responded to her father, "Don't listen to him. Since this beauty contestant has made history, this is indeed an historic achievement, a great breakthrough for humankind. And Dad, you need to show you're on the right side of history."

Norton thought, *Yes, this is the little, inexpensive bullshit type of virtue signaling I need. And I like the sound of the phrase "the right side of history."* As a politician he could see no political downside. *Sure, some traditionalists won't like it, but they won't vote for me anyway. The Catholic church won't like it, but I'm not Catholic; I'm an Episcoplian."*

Norton got on his computer, opened up his Chirp account, and with Susan's and Paula's help composed a chirp:

Elections Have Consequences

"We have a new Miss Virginia! I think I speak for most Virginians when I say va va voom! Lurleen Bennett is one beautiful woman. I am confident that all Virginians will be rooting for Lurleen when she competes in Atlantic City for the title of Miss America. Go Lurleen! Bring the title back to the Old Dominion!"

That weekend, Norton and his family avoided watching the news as much as possible, but later that night a bit of disturbing news caught their attention.

The cable TV channel the Memory Lane Television Network, which air reruns of old sitcoms and dramas, released a statement that they would stop airing reruns of *Starsky and Hutch*. The social justice warriors, and the left in general, were no fans of the oldies network. To them the network represented America in its heyday of white privilege. Norton liked to watch old shows which were popular in his youth, but he knew he shouldn't publicly admit he was a fan of the network.

Despite the hostility, the network tried to curry favor with the social justice warriors, so they would give in at every opportunity. With the Huggy Bear scandal dominating the news, the network made a decision. They announced in a statement, "Due to the stereotypical portrayal of the character 'Huggy Bear,' we will drop the show from our lineup. The racist phenomenon known as 'Blaxploitation' is all too real and in moving to a more just society we must stamp out this form of stereotyping. We apologize that we did not make this change earlier."

The family heard it and started laughing, "Dad, you canceled Huggy Bear! The show will never be seen again!" Laughter. "You have erased Huggy Bear from American history!"

Elections Have Consequences

Paula said, "Well, you left your mark, though I'm sure reruns of the show will survive in a museum vault somewhere."

Norton frowned, shook his head and said, "Imagine that, I canceled Huggy Bear. A great show, part of American history, and now it will be virtually wiped away,"

Susan responded, "Oh, Dad, don't be so sentimental. By getting rid of offensive and demeaning programs, there will be more room for other, socially responsible, shows. More shows written and directed by women and people of color. Think about it. We get new TV shows, just like we can get new statues. It's called progress."

Ironically, the Huggy Bear scandal had renewed interest among the public in the old show reruns, but since Memory Lane Television Network canceled it, viewers had to turn to other video streamers to get the show.

One media analyst with the blog, TV Junkie Dot Com explained the network's view. "They knew they would lose some money at first, but they're counting on the idea that by canceling the show they could earn some credibility with the social justice warriors. The network figured it was better to cancel the show than to risk being canceled themselves."

Most of the major Hollywood studios did a search of their current and former shows to determine which films had characters that could be viewed as examples of Blaxploitation. The Huggy Bear scandal created a national dialogue, and for Reverend Brand and others this was a good and needed development.

In addition, an internet retailer announced that they would no longer sell the Huggy Bear doll. The doll was no longer being

Elections Have Consequences

manufactured, but there was a market for second-hand dolls among collectors.

In bed, before going to sleep the Nortons would usually watch *Late Night Comedy with Lawrence O'Connell.* The show, known for light comedy and snarky comments about the news, was a favorite among the intelligentsia. In effect, O'Connell was their court jester. The Nortons were only casual fans, and had not seen the show since the scandal began. They didn't realize that O'Connell was having a great deal of fun with the whole Huggy Bear scandal.

Two of the most popular features of the show were the opening monologue, which consisted of a few unfunny jokes, and then his top ten list. Both of these usually pertained to some subject in the news. That night, the subject of Huggy Bear and Virginia came up.

First, in the monologue, Lawrence asked his audience: "What is going on in Virginia?" The crowd started laughing "Are you following this?" The crowd applauded. "First the Governor, Ronnie Norton, seems he liked to play dress up in college. He put shoe polish on his face. Now, I have never done such a thing, but geez, I bet that has got to be hard to get off." The crowd laughed. "And he had a friend who liked dressing as a Nazi. Okay, then we find out the Lt. Governor, as a legislator, had an affair with a high school cheerleader." More laughter. "Now, you think it can't get crazier in Virginia? Well, it just might have. It seems the new Miss Virginia's pageant talent is singing in baritone."

Paula said, "Come on, Ronnie, turn off the TV and let's go to sleep."

Norton, crestfallen, replied, "Well, usually O'Connell is funny, but not tonight."

Paula concurred. "Well, turn him off."

Elections Have Consequences

Optimistically, Norton said, "No, I'll give him one more shot. Maybe the top ten list will be funny." For his top ten list, O'Connell stuck with the Huggy Bear subject. With a graphic of New York city in the background, he announced "The top ten things Huggy Bear will do as Governor of Virginia."

Paula again implored, "Come on, Ronnie, just turn it off."

"Maybe there will be a couple funny ones." Norton just listened, expressionless, to number after number, joke after joke, staring at the TV. Then, " Number 3, Model all the State Police cars after the Zebra 3." The crowd laughed and Norton chuckled. The Zebra 3 was Starsky and Hutch's unmarked police car. It was a 1970's souped up Gran Torino, red with a white stripe across it.

The thin, blond, geeky looking O'Connell, with his thin lips and creepy smile announced, "Number 2, Make Hutch Secretary of the Commonwealth." Norton laughed at that.

Then with a drumroll, O'Connell announced "The number one thing Huggy Bear aka Ronnie Norton will do as governor, Turn the Virginia Governor's Mansion into a whorehouse."

The crowd laughed and laughed, and the laughter seemed genuine. They probably would have laughed even without the benefit of the flashing prompt sign reading, "Please Laugh."

Ronnie frowned and said, "You're right, he wasn't funny tonight." He clicked off the TV.

In the dark, Norton simply stared at the ceiling. Paula sensed something was wrong, "Ronnie, you are no racist, and soon you'll make that clear to the people of Virginia. I have no doubt about that. You shouldn't either." Paula kissed him and jokingly said, "Good night, Huggy Bear."

***

Elections Have Consequences

The next morning, after breakfast with the family, Norton called to get an update from Mike Jackson on the status of legislation. Paula noticed the alarm on her husband's face.

"Mike, that is the best we can get, a high $800 threshold on shoplifting charges? Mike, I thought they wanted 950; they only came down 150." Known as SB 1861, the bill required that no one could be prosecuted for shoplifting under $800.

Jackson responded, "They seemed stuck on 800; I know we offered 250."

"Yes, and they only came down 150? That is not acceptable." Norton concluded the conversation by telling Jackson he would be back on Monday to get involved in the negotiations.

After Norton hung up, Paula asked, "What's up now?"

"SB 1861 may be headed to my desk. It sets a threshold which must be crossed before a shoplifter can be charged with theft. The threshold is $800."

Paula shook her head. "What insanity. If you steal from a store you should be prosecuted. Even if it's just a candy bar."

"Well, you could still be charged with trespassing and banned from the store, and have to return what you stole."

"I'm a strong Democrat, but even I cannot support such a bill. Stealing is stealing! There should be no threshold which allows a person to steal up to a certain amount before they can be prosecuted."

"Well, the belief is that people charged with shoplifting are disproportionately minorities, and therefore such prosecutions may be biased. I want to make a deal on this. I really don't want to veto the bill, especially with the Huggy Bear scandal still in the air."

Paula simply said, "I support you; just do what you think is right."

Elections Have Consequences

There was some good news. A few hours later, while walking hand and hand on the beach with Paula, Norton got a call on his cell phone. "Governor, it's Ann Brand. Can you talk now?"

"Yes, how are things, Ann?"

Brand replied, "Well, I talked to Mike Jackson earlier and he raised your concerns about SB 1861." Brand wanted the bill, but was worried Norton might veto it, no matter how low the threshold turned out to be. To her relief, Norton said he could be flexible.

"Look, Ann, $800 is too high. I can't sign that."

Brand moved in for the kill. She quickly and wisely threw out a number before Norton said he would veto the bill, "Well, Governor, could you accept $500?"

"Yes Ann, I could accept that."

A relieved Brand said, "I can get it done. I'll talk to Sandoval and make the change when I see her on Monday."

Norton hung up the phone visibly relieved. He told Paula, "Good news, Brand can get the deal, so I don't have to risk a veto fight."

Paula said unconvincingly, "That's good, dear."

Just then a Frisbee landed in front of them; some kids were playing on the beach. Norton playfully picked up the Frisbee and threw it back, but it went over the kid's head. "Oops, sorry, I guess I'm out of practice."

He turned back to Paula. She stood there looking at him. Obviously something was on her mind. Norton looked at her and said, "What are you thinking?"

Paula was not the type to get into her husband's business, but then said, "Honey, I know you like Reverend Brand; I like her as well. Heck, she was our reverend before she got into politics, but

Elections Have Consequences

she's the Secretary of Education. Why is she involved in legislation not even related to her department? It doesn't seem like a good idea."

"She's just pitching in on this. I appreciate the help, but she knows her role."

Paula responded, "Brand was an Episcopal bishop; now she is running Virginia education and negotiating legislation on crime. That is quite a lot of power."

"What, are you questioning my cabinet picks?"

"No, I'm not. I like her, I consider her to be our friend. It just seems she has outsized power. The only one in the administration who seems to have as much influence with you as she does is Beaman, and at least he has proven his loyalty. Remember, it took Brand 48 hours to publicly defend you over the Huggy Bear scandal. I'm sorry, but that doesn't show loyalty."

Norton pushed back, "First, I have the most influence in my administration. She was just a little sore after the scandal broke, but she is loyal."

"Okay, Ronnie, I just don't want anyone, including Brand, to forget that they work for you, and that they know there is only one agenda—yours. Does Brand know that?"

Norton said emphatically, "Yes, she knows her role, and I won't let her exceed it."

Brand didn't like the idea of the police arresting people for shoplifting. For the most part she felt stores should hire their own private security, and the police should concentrate on other matters. She believed retailers had insurance to pay for shoplifting losses. And she had no sympathy for insurance companies having to shell out claims because, in her opinion, they had been allowed to make "obscene profits" for years, so let them pay.

Elections Have Consequences

True to her promise, Brand met with Sandoval at the General Assembly building first thing on Monday morning.

Sandoval got to her office at 7:40, and Brand was already there, sitting at Sandoval's desk talking on the phone. Brand made no effort to wrap up the phone call, and Sandoval waited outside until Brand called her in. "Change the shoplifting threshold from $800 to $500." Brand explained, "Look, when this process started Norton wanted no threshold. He wanted all shoplifters prosecuted, for the smallest of cases, as small as prosecuting someone for swiping a nudie magazine at a newsstand. Now he has agreed to a $500 threshold. A huge victory for us, so we take it and avoid a veto." Brand got up from Sandoval's desk ready to walk out, but she could tell Sandoval was unconvinced.

Sandoval didn't really get how it was a good deal, and stammered, "But $500 is less than $800."

Brand didn't lose her temper and explained one more time how the progressives had gotten a great deal. "Norton couldn't have gotten a worse deal if John Kerry flew in on his private jet and negotiated it for him."

Sandoval still didn't really get it, but agreed to make the change. As Brand was leaving the General Assembly building, she ran into Delegate Bruce Carrico coming up the steps. Despite both being progressive Democrats, Brand and Carrico were not close. "Hey Bruce!"

Carrico stopped and replied, "Hey Ann, what brings you to our building?"

"Just had to come talk to Senator Sandoval. Good news! Looks like we can get SB 1861."

Carrico seemed pleased. "Well, that is good. I must say it's a sign of the times. That's a bill that until recently could probably only pass in a deep blue state like California or Massachusetts."

A beaming Brand responded, "Bruce, this is no longer Hank Parrish's Virginia. We are a progressive, forward looking Virginia. A Virginia committed to social justice."

Carrico paused and looked around to check who was in earshot. He moved closer and said, "Ann, you are not the governor. It is not your agenda."

A defensive Brand responded, "Excuse me?"

"You heard me. Sometimes I think you forget your position. No one elected you; your role is at the Department of Education. Look, I agree with you on a lot of issues, but you have no business coming to the General Assembly building to negotiate on criminal bills."

"I am doing the Governor's bidding."

Carrico retorted, "Ann, Norton is a guilt ridden white liberal from McLean, so he's easy to manipulate, but that doesn't make it right."

Brand became angry. "I am not manipulating him."

"Really, Ann? You didn't have a hand in a campaign to get legislators to ask for his resignation, for something he did in college?"

She feigned disbelief that he would claim such a thing and said, "Of course not. Legislators were outraged, as all decent people should have been. I didn't pressure legislators to call for his resignation."

Carrico was unconvinced. "Ann, you are a liar."

Brand became indignant. "How am I a liar?"

"The media claimed you were related to Robert E. Lee. You knew that was false and you didn't correct them. And fundamentally You're wrong, Ann. The ends don't justify the means. We have to win honestly, not through lies, deception and manipulation, but by the logic of our ideas."

Brand was speechless. No one had ever spoken to her that way, certainly not her superiors in the Episcopal Church. Indeed, nobody was that blunt. She decided to walk away but she figured she had to get a last word in. "Screw you, Bruce." She blew past him, ramming into his shoulder as she went past, walking into Capitol Square.

Carrico stood on the steps and responded, "Very mature, Ann! And perhaps you forgot what the Good Book says, 'Thou shall not bear false witness.'" He then added mockingly, "See you in church."

18) Safeguard the Statues or Not

Very few Virginians understood the importance of an obscure little agency called the Virginia Commission on Fine Art and Historical Sites. The legislature's main reason for creating the agency was for the purpose of protecting Virginia history, mainly from counties and cities that might want, sometime in the future, to bulldoze an historic site in favor of commercial real estate development.

With just over a dozen commissioners, it had the responsibility of protecting monuments, identifying and protecting historic sites, and making recommendations on changes or additions to the list of state historic sites. Brand knew just how valuable the commission could be in the culture war.

Brand helped choose the members of the commission. If a candidate was known to be in favor of protecting Confederate monuments, they would not be selected. However, two years into Norton's term there still was not a majority who would drop the designation of those statues as historic monuments.

Brand got more involved and discovered three holdouts on the commission. These members still stuck to the view that the so-called Confederate monuments had "historic, cultural and artistic value." The state could still tear down a monument, but without the blessing of the commission it would not seem legitimate, and Norton had said early on that he didn't want to destroy those monuments without a majority of commissioners being on board.

After weeks of trying to persuade the three obstreperous

commissioners and getting nowhere, Brand tried another approach. She doxed them–leaked their home phones and emails to her supporters. The social justice warriors then bombarded them with calls and emails, asking them why they were protecting racist statues.

Still the three were holding out. Brand took it up a notch. The commissioners were then informed that if they didn't go along, their home addresses would be released to the public. Brand told an advisor, "I wonder how they might like demonstrations outside their houses?" She added rhetorically, "They may not want their neighbors to know that they are protecting racist statues."

Brand was right. They agreed to a statement, which Brand wrote, claiming that the Confederate statues had, "No real artistic, cultural, or historic value."

The press reported the statement from the commission, and seemingly had no idea there had been any holdouts. The final vote was unanimous. Norton, as well, was unaware of Brand's behind the scenes arm twisting.

After the vote and statement from the commission, Cohen wrote in the *Daily Dispatch*, "No doubt about it. This is a game changer. The commission has just debunked the right's claim that the statues have some artistic or historic value."

Beaman came to Norton's 3rd floor Capitol office to discuss the matter. Norton decided not to invite Brand to this meeting. He knew her feelings on the statues, but hoped Beaman would have a plan to save some of the monuments. However, he was disappointed. Beaman didn't think they could be saved.

Norton began by stating his position, "Regarding the so-called Confederate statues, my policy has been not to have a policy. However, I think we will have to move on the issue. The mob is now turning their rage towards the statues. Steve, as you may remember, I took the position during the campaign that I wanted them moved to museums and battlefields, and I meant it. That is what I'd like, but I am not sure it's possible. I don't think we'll have time to find homes for them.

"And now that the Virginia Commission on Fine Art and Historical Sites has found that the statues have no significant historical, artistic, or cultural value, I think that they will be almost impossible to save. Their destruction is now likely. I don't want that, but with the commission's finding, how can I argue against destruction? How can I hold out to find a new home for them? In many ways the commission's finding doesn't give me a free hand on the statues, it binds my hands." That is what Brand wanted.

Beaman replied, "Yes, you may be right. And look, Governor, the reality is that they will have to be destroyed for a number of reasons. Square miles of battlefields are shrinking, so just from a logistical standpoint it is unlikely that they will have room to add monuments, and what museums will want to take them? If the objection is that the monuments glorify the Confederacy, why would it be okay to keep them up on a battlefield? Your political base would argue that they are not acceptable there either, and with the statues up the battlefields might become a shrine to the Confederacy. A politician who says he will remove monuments must know that their destruction is the most likely outcome, but saying so explicitly might not be a good idea. At least it wasn't a few years ago when you ran."

"True, but I do want to preserve history. Surely tearing down monuments won't help people understand their history or inspire them to learn. On the campaign trail I promised to move them, not destroy them. Don't tell Brand or our friends on the left, but

Elections Have Consequences

I like the statues—the history, the beauty, and the craftsmanship. I used to like seeing them when I would come to Richmond. You know it was in my district that General Beauregard designed the battle flag for the Army of Northern Virginia. There's a marker along the side of the road, where it's said he designed the flag. All of that is part of history."

In an effort to offer a way around a campaign promise, Beaman offered a possible rationale. "Governor, we want people to have a proper understanding of history. And statues of Confederates will not help people achieve a proper understanding of history. So for people to get a proper understanding of the Civil War, Confederate statues must come down."

"By proper understanding of history you mean the understanding that the North was right and Lee was a traitor? Well, I must say I think it's absurd, the notion that if someone sees a statue of a Confederate soldier, they are more likely to be supportive of succession or slavery. People can judge for themselves." Norton concluded that he could go along with the proper understanding of history argument, but if some monuments could be saved, he'd like to see that accomplished.

Beaman said, "We can try to find new homes for some of the monuments, but I'd say 90 percent will be destroyed, thrown into the James River. Governor, it's inevitable; whether we like it or not they will all come down. Your political base won't stand for any remaining, not even on battlefields."

Norton, with a look of resigned incredulity, responded, "You're probably right."

Beaman added, "But I've come up with the perfect line. Virginians are relatively traditional, and may feel uneasy about the destruction of a historical monument. So to get people on board we need to convince them that the statues should not have gone up in the first place. Add that to the commission's finding that they have no significant artistic or historical value and it will be easy, at least politically, to tear them down."

Norton seemed to understand the talking point, "Okay, so if they were not put up legitimately, that is for legitimate reasons, then there is nothing wrong with taking them down."

Beaman quickly said, "And they have no artistic or historic value; don't forget that line."

A suddenly curious Norton asked, "Why did they put them up in the early 1900's?"

"The generations of Southern men who fought in the war were dying off, so their children, mainly their daughters, helped raise money to put up statues before they died. The soldiers started coming up to Richmond when the foundation stone to the Lee statue was put down, which I think was as early as the mid 1880's. The Daughters of the Confederacy promised they would erect a statue of the matchless Lee. They raised the money from all over the South, and decided to get the world's greatest artist to make the statue. Nothing was too good for the boys of the South. So they got this artist in France, I forget his name. Anyway, that statue went up in 1890, I believe.

"Well, it was such a hit that they raised more money for more statues. In fact, they had a whole street in Richmond designed for one purpose. It would be lined with statues, and in effect the street would become the parade route. Confederate reunions became a Richmond tradition. I think they had something like 42 major reunions in the city, and probably at every one the

Elections Have Consequences

governor and the mayor showed up to greet the soldiers and make speeches.

"I bet it was quite the sight, the old soldiers with gray hair and old gray coats parading around the monuments and spending a week exploring the old battlefields."

"It seems to me that the last reunion was in 1932. Douglas Southall Freeman wrote a famous book about it, *The Last Parade*. I read it when I was at Hampden Sydney. Due to their age, by then many of the soldiers were unable to walk the entire parade route. So they just sat and watched."

Beaman added, "But that was then. It's a new day in Virginia. The Daughters of the Confederacy are no more. They can't vote for you. Today, the people, at least your base, want them gone. And like it or not, we need to move forward with statue removal quickly. Counties and cities are changing the names of schools, streets, and parks; monuments can't last much longer. The outrage among your base is such that you can't hold them back. And at the rate things are going, one day soon the names of cities and towns in Virginia will be changed."

Norton simply sat and listened quietly.

"Look," Beaman said, "Politics is all about narratives, competing narratives. Parrish argues that a previous generation of Virginians put up the statues, so they are historic, and she is a daughter of Virginia, so she will protect them. Our narrative should be that the statues are monuments to white supremacy and to heal the divisions in Virginia they must come down. That is what our base wants." With a confident smile Beaman opined, "On this we have the winning narrative. The media will push it, and it can be one of our talking points. The vast majority of Virginians don't care about history. Fundamentally, though, it

Elections Have Consequences

shows that you are trying to heal the racial divisions in Virginia. The statues are low hanging fruit. There are like 3,000 in Virginia. Getting rid of them shows you are committed to racial healing and tolerance."

A resigned Norton leaned back in his chair, looked at the ceiling and sighed, "Well, I guess you're right. No need to delay."

Beaman shook his head, "It's over. The statues are well past their expiration date. We should move as quickly as we can, legally and practically. Dump them in the James River as fast as we can."

Norton thought the comment was a bit insensitive, but he realized Beaman was correct.

***

Later that afternoon, Mark Thompson asked to see Beaman alone, and told him it was urgent. Beaman cleared some time on his schedule. Beaman had a nice office on 9th Street, at the corner of Ninth and Broad. The main tenant of the building happened to be the Attorney General. Beaman joked, "I have to share the building with the Attorney General."

Thompson and Beaman were allies, in a way. Both were considered more moderate Democrats. They joined the party before the younger social justice warriors took over. And they both intensely disliked and distrusted Brand.

"What, shoplifting cases are up 453 percent?" Beaman asked Mark Thompson.

"Sadly yes." said Thompson, and added, "We both know why. Sandoval's bill limiting shoplifting prosecution cases for anything for under $500, which the Governor signed against my advice. So the word is out that you won't get prosecuted for stealing stuff under 500 bucks, and there is a mad rush on stealing."

Elections Have Consequences

Beaman shook his head. "Yes, this was one of Brand's horrible ideas, that and her school database for racist jokes. Norton fell for them. Unbelievable. Funny thing, I talked to him months ago, and he told me he would probably veto it; the most he would go is the $250 dollar threshold. Then weeks later I found out that he had agreed to the $500 threshold. I have no idea what happened, unless he just got confused about the dollar figure."

Thompson replied, "I think we both know why. Reverend Brand got to him. She convinced him that this would make him popular with the media and the social justice crowd. Like all politicians, I guess he craves popularity. Well, if the press gets a hold of this, it will be embarrassing."

Beaman, who knew the press well, responded, "I doubt the press will get this on their own, but if the Republicans get it they will make a big deal of it, and who knows, there may be some less mainstream news outlets willing to run it."

Thompson said, "Well, we will have to tell the Governor."

"Yes, of course we will have to, and I have an idea how and when to do it."

"What do you mean?"

Beaman replied, "I say let's hold this until the next full cabinet meeting, when Brand is with us, and then announce it. The governor will be pissed, and Brand will have to respond on the spot, with no forewarning."

Thompson thought for a moment, then said, "I love it. What does Norton see in Brand? She has his ear, there's no doubt about it. She's his Rasputin. But why does he listen to her?"

Beaman speculated, "Norton, like a lot of white male Democrats, is sensitive to the charge that he is not fully with the social justice movement, that he doesn't understand the problems people of color face. So they compensate by listening to race hustlers like Reverend Brand. I concede that Brand is very smart; she has good instincts, and remember, he was falling behind Parrish in the campaign. The idea to use Parrish's shotgun prop against her as a racist symbol was a brilliant idea."

Thompson added, "Yes, and let's face it, she was instrumental in his getting the nomination." Beaman didn't comment. His expression indicated that he was done complimenting her and said, "You know that saying, good humor always has a little bit of truth in it. Well, Brand reminds me of the joke about the Episcopal priest who one day discovers that he is a heretic; he no longer believes in what his church teaches. So he goes to his old seminary teacher for advice. He says, 'Father, I am a heretic. Must I leave the church? The old man tells him, 'No, you can be a heretic and remain in the church. However, if you go public with your heresies, the church is liable to promote you to bishop."

Thompson laughed. Beaman responded, "Well, that is exactly what happened to Brand. They made her a head pastor of a prominent Church on the false notion that she would then moderate and conform. But she did just the opposite; she got even more radical, turned into even more of a Bolshevik. She wrote what became a bestseller, *If You Are White, Chances Are You Are a Racist.* The book, by the way, is required reading at a number of colleges. Most of these mainline Protestant churches promote radicals like Brand. They are like newspapers and corporate America; they try to appeal to the woke, especially the kids. But she got too radical; heck, she was quoting the Koran in church. Well, the leaders of the church urged her to go into politics, and eventually she met Norton when he was running for the State

Elections Have Consequences

Senate. Sadly, she is now the Secretary of Education here in Virginia."

Thompson, searching for some optimism, said, "Well, when she's confronted with the facts on the results so far of the shoplifting law, we shall see what she says. At the very least Norton will clip her wings." That was the hope.

***

It was a peaceful few weeks, and the governor was enjoying a nice, blissful summer. He had put the Huggy Bear scandal behind him, so it seemed, and finally started to get invitations to different events. Because of the scandal, none of the universities invited him to give a commencement address, and even his fellow Democrats had shunned him, indeed treated him like a pariah. By July that started to change; he could sense the thaw.

However, things soon took a turn for the worse. It began on a Thursday morning, when Richmond police officer Darren Driscoll and his partner were on patrol cruising down Broad Street, just a few blocks from the Capitol building.

They spotted a late model white Toyota Camry with expired tags. Officer Driscoll turned on the siren, and pulled the car over. The driver, James Sayers, appeared to be impaired. Officer Driscoll and his partner had suspicions that there might be drugs in the car.

They asked the driver if they could search the vehicle, and Sayers consented. As the officers were checking out the vehicle, Sayers took off running. One officer stayed by the car and radioed for help while Officer Driscoll ran after Sayers and tackled him. Sayers and Driscoll fell to the ground, and as they hit the ground Driscoll's service revolver came out. It slid a few feet on the ground, in between the two men. Driscoll and Sayers both reached for the gun and struggled for control of it. In the melee the gun went off. Sayers slumped over; he had been shot.

The officers called for an ambulance, which transported Sayers to the VCC Medical Center on Broad Street, the same Hospital where Steve Beaman had his surgery several months earlier, the same hospital where Dr. Jack Villiers used to work. Sadly, Sayers was pronounced dead at the hospital.

That morning at about the same time. Norton chaired the weekly cabinet meeting. This was to be the meeting where Mark Thompson and Steve Beaman would confront Brand on the early results of the shoplifting prosecution limit legislation. All the cabinet secretaries would give their reports. Beaman sat excitedly, knowing what was coming Brand's way. To build potential anger towards Brand, neither Beaman or Thompson had given the governor a heads up. Finally, Norton called on Thompson, "Okay, Mark, what have you got?" He joked, "The Commonwealth is safe, right?"

Thompson started his report, and then dropped the bomb. He didn't even try to sugarcoat it. "As compared with this time last year shoplifting complaints are up 534 percent." Everyone in the room just stared at Norton. waiting for his reaction.

Norton, at first, didn't seem to get it. His first words were, "As compared to last year?" Norton instantly knew that the bill SB 1861 had led to the increase. He looked around the room, scanning the reactions of his cabinet, scanning to see if anyone had any other answer.

Everyone knew it had been Brand's initiative, so Brand spoke up to put a good spin on it, or at least try. "Governor, there is an increase in shoplifting cases, and yes, publicity about the new law creating a threshold at which no prosecutions will take place is mostly responsible, but the spike is simply a temporary blip. I say temporary, because within communities when word spreads that people are taking advantage of the law, there will be a corrective backlash. Through peer pressure from parents, siblings, relatives, neighbors and friends, people who engage in such behavior will be chastised, and if they don't stop they will be shunned. They do not want this, so they will conform and the shoplifting spike will dissipate."

Norton asked, "Secretary Brand, so you feel this increase is a temporary blip?"

Brand nodded and said, "I do believe it is temporary."

After the meeting, Norton asked Beaman to stay behind. Beaman said, "Sorry about the news. I don't want to kick you when you're down, but frankly, I never knew why you signed the bill in the first place."

"Well, I figured the bill would probably lead to a slight increase in shoplifting, but not 534 percent! Most of the shop owners are Republicans, and the big box stores are run by Democrats, and they are big enough to afford a small increase in shoplifting. I figured it wasn't a big risk, but this is not a small increase."

"I think very little of the Virginia press corps, but they can't miss noticing this."

Norton, looking for a reason to stay positive, said, "Maybe Brand is right; maybe it is temporary."

Beaman added, "Maybe something will come up to swamp this story."

Norton again muttered as if trying to convince himself, "Maybe it's just a blip, just temporary."

"Well, Governor, if we're done, I have to get ready to take my granddaughter to the Diamond to watch the Richmond Braves game."

Norton smiled, "Sure. I envy you; I haven't been to a Braves game yet this summer."

"Well, come with us."

Norton shook his head. "No, Paula has plans for me tonight. Oh, also, a Richmond police lieutenant has asked to see me. Says he needs to brief me on something important, so I have a meeting with him in an hour at the Governor's Mansion." Norton seemed puzzled by the request. "Steve, do you know why they want to see me?"

"It probably has something to do with the shooting on Broad Street earlier this morning."

"Yes, probably."

Beaman reminded him, "It took place on Broad Street so close to the Governor's Mansion that the shot probably could have been heard in the main ballroom."

Norton concluded their meeting, "Well, Steve, enjoy the game."

***

Lieutenant Jake Knotts of the Richmond Police came to the Governor's Mansion, and was taken upstairs to the governor's study.

"Come on in, Officer Knotts," Norton called.

The officer took a seat and began speaking. "Good evening, Governor. I wanted to brief you on a shooting that took place this morning on Broad Street."

Elections Have Consequences

"Yes, I heard something about it."

Knotts described the situation. "A couple of Richmond police officers pulled over a motorist with expired tags, and it looked like it would be a routine stop. However, the motorist seemed impaired, and the officers asked if he would step out of the car. He consented, then they asked if they could search the car. The motorist said 'yes' again, but then fled the scene, just took off running, so Officer Driscoll chased him and caught up with him. They fell to the ground, at which point the motorist grabbed for Officer Driscoll's gun, and in the struggle the gun went off. The motorist was shot. He was taken to the hospital where he died."

"Do you know why the motorist fled?"

Officer Knotts responded, "No, sir, we didn't find any drugs and there were no outstanding warrants. He has had some run-ins with police and had a rap sheet, but no current warrants. The car is registered to his girlfriend. She says she gave him permission to drive it, so it wasn't a stolen car. Why he fled we don't know."

"Well, you never know. My guess is there's some reason he didn't want to get arrested; he must have had something to hide. Perhaps he thought the officers were about to arrest him for something, and figured maybe he could run away. Especially since the car was not his, not registered to him. He may have thought that if he ran away and just left the car, he couldn't be connected to it, and he could probably get the owner, his girlfriend and probably baby mama, to cover for him. Well, sorry about the shooting but these things can happen; police work can be dangerous. I'm glad the officer is okay."

"We'll check the body camera video, and see if there is video from the stores along the street showing anything. I just wanted to keep you informed."

Norton concluded the meeting. "Thanks for the report. I know you and the Richmond Police are doing an excellent job in keeping us safe, but please keep me updated on the case."

All was quiet the rest of the afternoon and into the night. There was no mention of the shooting on the news, and Norton forgot all about it.

19) Take Me Out to the BallPark

"Take me out to the ballpark,
Take me out with the crowd,
Buy me some peanuts and Cracker Jack,
I don't care if I ever come back,
So its root, root, root for the BRAVES
If they don't win it's a shame
Because it's one, two, three strikes you're out
At the old Diamond."
(As modified and sung by Richmond Braves fans)

Beaman rarely talked about his daughter, his only child. Their relationship was basically non-existent. But through her he had a granddaughter and he was allowed to see her every once in a while.

So on this Thursday night, he took her to the Diamond for a Braves game. Beaman and Norton spent many nights at the Diamond watching baseball games; both were big baseball fans. Beaman hoped to pass on his love of the game to his granddaughter. The new owner of the team had done a lot to improve the fan experience. *What a great atmosphere,* Beaman thought. As they entered the Diamond, they could see Herbie, the Braves mascot, making the rounds to greet fans and take pictures with the kids, and out front a barbershop quartet sang "Take me out to the ballpark." All the concessions anyone could want were available, from hotdogs, hamburgers, fries, and funnel cakes to cotton candy.

In Richmond, and indeed all across America, baseball is part of summer. And what better place to be than at the iconic

Elections Have Consequences

Diamond Baseball Stadium. As a triple A affiliate of a major league baseball franchise, a number of future major league stars have spent time playing in Richmond.

The Salem Redbirds were in town that Thursday night for the opening of a three game homestand against the Richmond Braves. About 5,000 fans were in attendance, which wasn't bad for a July weeknight game, especially considering that the Braves were in second to last place in the mid-Atlantic division.

It started like any other night game at the iconic Diamond. The umpire, Donnie Stitt, called the managers up to home plate to exchange lineup cards and get final instructions.

Stitt noticed several people in center field. Based on the way they were dressed, they weren't members of the grounds crew. They seemed to be waving signs and trying to get attention.

"Who are they?" Stitt asked. Neither manager knew. "Well, let's get them off the field, so we can play."

As they were waiting for the people to be removed, Stitt, a minor league umpire for over 20 years, started reminiscing about instances of fans coming onto the field,

Stitt always had great stories of his life in the minor leagues, so many stories many of his friends encouraged him to write a book. He spit out his gum and started one such story. "Early in my career as an umpire, I did games in Danville, at the old American Legion Field, and as I remember one season something funny happened, with a fan coming onto the field. It happened usually by the 5th inning. This lady, in a tee shirt, and fairly well endowed, would run onto the field and kiss the 3rd baseman or sometimes the pitcher. Well, I would run over and tell her to get off the field. I just thought it was some crazy groupie, which happens with some of these teams even in minor league ball, but you want to hear something funny? It was the darndest thing. It was not just a random fan, it was a planned event. I later found out it was a promotion. The owner of the Danville club paid her to do it. You see, the team's owner thought it would help with attendance; that is, he assumed that if word spread throughout the town of an attractive, well-built blond blond kissing bandit at the ballgame, it might get more people to turn up. The word would spread around town, it would be free advertising. Well, the team's general manager didn't bother to give me a heads up, and you think he would have, so I had no idea it was a staged promotion. But I finally found out by word of mouth. And it's the funniest thing, I found out the identity of the woman. At the end of the season we had our annual awards banquet, and I saw this attractive blonde-haired lady at the head table sitting with the team's general manager. I said to a fellow umpire that lady looks so familiar, that lady sitting next to Steve, the general manager.

"Well, after the dinner I was introduced to her. She was the general manager's wife. My jaw almost dropped. I looked at her and it dawned on me, she was the kissing bandit!" Everyone laughed. Stitt concluded, "I guess it saved them money to have her do it."

The chief of the grounds crew went to tell the protestors in centerfield to leave, but that resulted in an argument. The group of protesters now numbered about a dozen.

The signs read "End Racism Now," and "Black Lives Matter." The grounds crew chief made the mistake of saying, "All lives matter, but we're here to play a baseball game."

This angered the group. "We don't care about a baseball game! We're making the demand to end racism in the Richmond Police Department and in this country!" The crowd of protesters asked him, "How can you live in such a country that kills and persecutes people?" They then told him his silence equaled tolerance of police brutality and racism.

As the discussion continued, more protesters were coming over the centerfield fence. It looked like they were students from VCC, or at least college-aged kids. "Get the hippies off the field so we can start the game!" some fans were yelling. Most of the fans became restless and started booing. Some even yelled "Play ball!"

Both teams were just sitting in the dugout. The grounds crew chief came back to Stitt with an ominous look on his face, "They say they're not leaving, and will be happy to have the police come and arrest them."

The number of protesters in centerfield was growing; it was now up to 25. Stitt responded, "What's their complaint?"

"They say an unarmed motorist, James Sayers, was murdered by a police officer yesterday while driving down Broad Street."

Stitt responded, "What does that have to do with us? I'm sorry if someone got into a fight with a police officer and was shot, but that has nothing to do with us. We have a game to play, and this is private property. They have to leave."

"I think they want the police to come and deal with them."

Sttit mockingly said, "Oh, great, now we aren't going to get this game done till after 11! God forbid we go into extra innings. Okay, we'll call the cops." Stit informed both teams, "Stay in your dugout until the field is clear." An announcement came over the

Elections Have Consequences

stadium loudspeaker: "Please exit the field. You are trespassing. If you don't leave, we will be forced to call the police. No one but team personnel are allowed on the field."

About fifteen minutes later two cop cars arrived. However, by then the crowd of protesters in centerfield grew to nearly 35 people, holding more signs: "Cops are Pigs!" "End Toxic Masculinity" "Justice for Sayers" and "No Justice, No Peace." What appeared to be college students, probably from VCC, had signs, "White Silence Equals Violence."

Stitt looked out into centerfield and thought, *This is starting to look like Woodstock, without the good music.*

The police assessed the situation and called for backup. This went on for a good 30 minutes; the crowd of spectators was getting restless. The police determined what the ground crew chief had thought, that many in the mob were trying to get arrested in order to make a point.

Police officials didn't want to arrest them; rather, they preferred to postpone the game. The team agreed, so, it was announced over the loudspeaker, "Tonight's game against the Redbirds has been canceled. Please go to the ticket office to get a refund, or exchange your tickets for a future home game." Stitt told the managers, "Okay, boys, no game tonight." For Stitt and the crew it was a night off. Stitt then went back to the Super 8 Motel where he was staying.

Some fans went over and joined the protesters, which now numbered just over 50, but most just quietly walked to the exits and box office. The police were correct that eventually the protestors would leave centerfield, but they didn't all go home. The primary reason the protest started at the stadium was for the simple reason that protesters, all protesters, want a crowd.

Elections Have Consequences

They knew several thousand Richmonders would be gathered at the ballpark, so it was a captive audience. As the crowd left, so did many of the protesters. They spilled out into the streets, yelling and chanting. "Shame on the Richmond police department," "Justice for Sayers," "Justice for James," and "Prosecute racist cops" were probably the most common chants.

The police were out in force. There was no real violence. Some of the protesters and motorists got into heated arguments, but by about 10 o'clock it was mostly quiet. At one point the number of protesters rose to about 80 people. That evening the local news picked up the story and for the first time the name James Sayers was in the news.

Mayor Stoney Case had been notified of the incident by Police Superintendent George Boulden. They knew they had a very explosive situation on their hands with the death of James Sayers, and decided to hold a press conference in the morning to lay out the facts for the public and go over the next steps in the investigation. By morning it was all over the news.

20) Commonwealth of Disorder

Norton arrived at his 3rd floor office in the Capitol Building by 8 a.m. As soon as he walked into his office, Jackson and Thompson were there to brief him on what had happened the night before at the Diamond and the unrest that had spilled into the streets of Richmond.

Norton had no idea what was behind the controversy. A motorist fled the scene, then got in a fight with an officer. He went for the officer's gun and the officer shot him. It was tragic, but Norton didn't understand what he was missing.

As he was getting a briefing on the unrest, he could see the TV tuned to MNN, his favorite news channel, and was stunned by what he saw. Emblazoned on the screen was the crawl, "Unarmed Black Man Killed by Richmond Police." He said, "When did this happen?"

Thompson replied, "This—"pointing to the TV screen—"is what we're talking about."

Jackson spoke, "I thought you were briefed. I sent Officer Jake Knotts to the Mansion to give you a briefing."

Norton leaned back in his chair, stared blankly ahead, and then said, "This is the shooting that Knotts was talking about? Knotts never mentioned the motorist was black, or the fact that he was unarmed!"

The only weapon involved was Officer Driscoll's, which they were wrestling over when it went off. Norton added, "This is the problem, the police are so insensitive that they don't understand the importance of race. I am a politician, I know the importance.

Elections Have Consequences

They didn't mention Sayers' race. As if it didn't matter." Norton started to panic and thought, *I don't need this now, I don't need this now.* As he continued to watch the news, he grew more pessimistic, he muttered, "Why is the world against me? I got past the damn Huggy Bear mess, now this!"

Norton then ordered, "Mike, get me Mayor Case on the line." As he was waiting for the mayor to come on the phone, Norton looked at Jackson and Thompson and said, "I ..We don't need this right now!" Norton, visibly concerned, repeated, "We don't need this right now."

The mayor came on the phone and outlined the facts of the case, which Officer Knotts already explained. The mayor said Officer Driscoll was on administrative leave until the investigations were complete. Later Discoll would have to go into hiding. The mayor also said it appeared that the officer had acted within the law and operated within proper guidelines.

The governor followed up by offering the assistance of the State Police and other resources if necessary. Norton reiterated, "We need to keep this under control. Nothing wrong with peaceful protesters, but we can't let riots break out. Anything I can do to help, let me know. If you need help, I can bring in the State Police to help." In making an offer of assistance Norton didn't say what he was really worried about, what would keep him up at night. That was the horrific possibility that the National Guard would be needed. The thought was too negative for him to even contemplate. He turned to Thompson, his friend for the last 20 years. "Mark, what do you think? Does this unrest spread?"

Thompson looked down, thought for a second, and replied, "We'll get a better sense of where this is going tonight, after close of business and it gets dark. What happens tonight, especially if

Elections Have Consequences

protests move to other cities." Into the afternoon some small and peaceful protests had started to crop up in Richmond. Ominously, they also started in other cities, although still peaceful.

MNN started airing live video from the Arlington courthouse showing a dozen people with signs reading "Justice for James." This slogan became the rallying cry. In the days and weeks to come, the slogan would be on signs of protest all across the state. In the coming weeks Justice for James rallies would take place all over the country. There were big rallies in New York, Los Angeles, Detroit, St. Louis, Denver, and Austin among other places.

Governor Norton and his family were going to spend the weekend in the Outer Banks, but considering the brewing crisis Norton decided to stay in Richmond. Friday afternoon Norton huddled with Beaman, Brand, and Mike Jackson. Outside the window he could see a small contingent of protesters in Capitol Square.

Ironically, the previous night Norton had watched a movie about the fall of the Romanovs in Russia. Looking out the mansion window reminded him of the scene from the movie where Nicholas looked out the palace window at a crowd of demonstrators. As he stood looking at the small protest from the bedroom window Paula came up to him. She hugged him and said, "Don't worry, honey. It's a small protest. And they can't blame you for what happened to Sayers." Norton seemed crestfallen and told her, "I don't want Huggy Bear thrown back at me. I really want to help unite the state racially. I want Virginians to know that and believe I am sincere."

Paula offered her husband some advice. "Remember Lincoln during the dark days of the Civil War. One of his most famous quotes, I think I have this right, 'I desire to so conduct the affairs of this administration that if at the end I have lost every other friend on earth, I shall at least have one friend left, and that friend shall be deep down inside of me.'" Paula seemed proud that she had remembered the quote and added, "I take from that, do what you think is right, whether it's popular or not. I'm not saying be heartless and taunt the kids like Parrish would, but understand that the mob out on the street doesn't necessarily represent the majority of Virginians." Norton appreciated her advice.

***

That night brought several incidents of violence and looting in Richmond, and a few disturbances in Norfolk, Virginia Beach, Petersburg, and Portsmouth. Saturday morning brought more peaceful protests, commonly referred to as "Justice for James" rallies.

At a Saturday afternoon meeting at the Governor's Mansion, Reverend Brand pressed him. "This is more evidence that the police are fundamentally and systematically racist. They would not have tackled James Sayers had he been white, they would have let him run away. Governor, you need to make it clear that you are on the side of the protesters and will do everything possible to bring about changes in the law to make sure this never happens again. You need to acknowledge that the police force is systematically racist."

Beaman challenged, "Governor, James Sayers was resisting arrest. He fled the scene and he assaulted the officer, which is a felony in this state."

Thompson agreed with Beaman, saying "Governor, in this case we have seen no evidence at this time that race had anything to do with this tragic action."

Brand pushed back. "It should not be a felony, and there was no reason to arrest him. They should have let him go. They had his car's license plate number."

Beaman said, "Don't be ridiculous."

Brand made a concession, "The officer may have followed the letter of the law, but Governor, we need to make changes in the law to stop these types of arrests in the future."

Norton asked about the status of the protests. "Thompson, are the protests mostly peaceful?"

"They are now, but the night isn't here yet."

Beaman optimistically claimed that since it was Saturday the news coverage would be lighter. Fewer people would be tuning in, so perhaps the protests would be light and not turn violent.

Governor Norton kept peering out the window looking to see if the crowd was growing.

Brand said, "Look Governor, put out a chirp expressing sympathy with the protestors and for what happened to James Sayers."

"I agree, I'll do it."

Beaman again offered pushback. "James Sayers did attack the officer. I'd be careful about expressing too much sympathy."

"Steve, I see your point, but I understand the protesters and the view that the police have been unfair to people of color. To quell the protests and to prevent this from getting out of control, I must speak out."

Thompson countered, "Speaking out and showing some sympathy is fine, but you're in charge of law enforcement in the state, and if the police acted properly you need to stand by them. If not, there will be a big problem with morale."

Elections Have Consequences

After the meeting Governor Norton made a symbolic statement by placing a "Black Lives Matter" sign in the bedroom window facing Capitol Square and asked aides to inform the press that he had done this. He even opined that maybe the press would publish a picture of the sign in the window.

He then went to his office to record a statement to air statewide: "Thousands of Virginians are raising their voices this weekend in a collective, and I think justified, cry of anguish and anger. The death of James Sayers has distressed me greatly. I understand the concern of many that people of color have not been treated fairly by our legal system. I have ordered a State Police review of the case, and I urge patience and calm while we find out exactly what happened. We must respect our legal system and maintain patience in the investigations. Also, please remember that there is no excuse for the destruction of property."

What Norton didn't acknowledge in his statement was that when he was first told of the incident, he asked no real questions. He accepted the police explanation, and now he wanted "to find out exactly what happened."

While peaceful protests dominated during the daytime, in many places in Virginia night time brought looting and vandalism, millions of dollars of damage in Richmond alone; windows were smashed and cars destroyed. Many businesses boarded up with the hope of reopening Monday. Protesters in Virginia Beach smashed several windows on Atlantic Avenue.

There were dozens of major "Justice for James" rallies planned for Monday, and no doubt others would pop up unplanned. Norton would hold an emergency cabinet meeting first thing Monday morning.

Elections Have Consequences

Monday morning started off bad and quickly got worse. It reminded Norton of a stock market crash. "By noon the market was down 500 points, and by the end of the day you look back and realize noon was the high point," Norton later wrote in his bestselling memoir.

The first bit of bad news: many colleges started canceling classes to allow students to peacefully protest the death of James Sayers. Virginia Commonwealth College President Veronica Ladson started the ball rolling by chirping, "All classes have been canceled today to allow our students to peacefully protest the killing of an unarmed black man by the police. Sadly, this has become all too common in our state and country."

This prompted Old Dominion University and University of Virginia to cancel classes as well. Other schools such as James Madison University followed suit.

Mike Jackson informed the governor, "So far 25 public colleges and universities have canceled classes." But on an optimistic note Jackson said that so far Longwood College, Washington and Lee, and Hampden-Sydney were holding classes as usual. Norton didn't appreciate the subtle joke.

Norton said, "Damn it, these overpaid university professors are trying to screw me over." He took it personally; almost all the university presidents had voted for him in the general election. Norton complained to Jackson, "We have given them almost all the money they asked for and this is how they repay me. These university presidents are making it worse. They released these students, most of whom have no firsthand knowledge of any discrimination in their short privileged little lives, to run wild in the streets. I guarantee you, watch MNN's coverage and you will

Elections Have Consequences

see mostly white kids who have lived charmed, privileged lives now take to the streets and disrupt people working and doing productive, positive things."

Jackson, in defense of the university presidents, declared, "No, Governor, it's nothing personal, it's just that these students are the constituency of the presidents. They have to answer to them. The students are upset and want to protest, so the presidents are not going to stop them."

Beaman had a more cynical view. "These university presidents know many of the kids are going deep into debt, for an average education. Better direct the anger of the students away from them."

Norton angrily responded, "The kids want a day off from school so they can join their friends in the streets where they all can make asses of themselves."

Brand was angry too. "These young people, the future of our country, are outraged by the racism and oppression they see all around them. I for one am thankful for their spirit and energy."

Norton retorted, "Seems to me that the inmates are running the asylum, and if those kids, who by the way gave us Taylor Swift and Justin Bieber, are the future then we're in deep trouble."

Tuesday started off just as bad as Monday. In his morning update Thompson told the Governor, "Some high school students are starting to demand that they also should be allowed out of school to join the protest."

Jackson went on, "Most school superintendents have denied the requests, but Arlington County, Henrico, Prince William, and Loudoun County schools have granted their students' request for the day off from school to join Justice for James rallies."

Elections Have Consequences

At this news a frustrated Norton simply rolled his eyes.

During the rest of the week, most of the progressive legislators joined in the street demonstrations. State Senator Sandoval helped organize a Justice for James rally in her district, and with the high school kids off from school the attendance at the rally was just over 250 people. The national media covered the event; since all national networks have offices in the DC metro area, it was easy for them to cover it.

Once the tragedy of the death, or as Carter would say murder, of James Sayers hit the news Carter began organizing rallies all across the commonwealth. Carter was the one who had come up with the slogan "Justice for James."

The left has an extensive communications network to reach out to followers. They have unions, gay rights groups, teacher organizations, student leftist groups, feminist groups, environmental groups, Moms United to Save Virginia, they have names from numerous petition drives, names from Green Party and Democrat volunteer lists.

Carter knew that many of Virginia's colleges and universities would let students out for a day or two because the colleges are run by left wingers who want to fight for social justice—and they know they have to placate the students. His goal was to have half a million people nationwide to attend a "Justice for James" rally by the end of the week. According to Carter, "That would send a powerful message."

He explained at an Alinsky Society seminar, "The rallies are a great opportunity to sign up more activists. For many young social justice warriors, a protest is their first encounter with our movement. So obviously we need to collect contact information at every rally, and we also need to find reasons to hold rallies. Not too long ago I had a rally outside a church, protesting a mural honoring a president who was the largest slave holder ever to occupy the White House. At that rally I met a great woman, a Latinx, who ended up joining our movement, running for and getting elected to the Virginia State Senate, so rallies are great recruitment opportunities."

At the Arlington rally, a black-clad Sandoval took to the stage and gave a fiery speech. "We demand justice for James, and for all people of color who have been murdered by the State of Virginia over the last 400 years." She also bragged, "Justice for James rallies are taking place in every region of the state. Even in rural, less diverse parts of the state there is a recognition that racism and injustice exist."

In a matter of days the issue of calling up the National Guard, something Norton had been reluctant to do, became an urgent topic of discussion. One political reason came from the White House. President Bush chirped:

"Virginia is now burning as Norton, aka Huggy Bear, dithers. Sadly, Virginia could have had a strong, decisive leader in Angela Parrish. But Norton has got to bring order and peace to Virginia. And if he can't, or is unwilling to, I will."

The story of the riots and peaceful protests in Virginia dominated the national news, and "Justice for James" rallies were spreading all across the country. By the middle of the week, Norton agreed to call up National Guard troops. Beaman and Thompson were pushing for it; Brand and everyone else in the cabinet opposed it.

Brand believed that the police could handle most of the looting and vandalism, which she felt was being exaggerated, and anyway the damage being done was still relatively small. Besides, business owners had insurance policies which would cover most of the damages. And in addition most of those insurance companies had experienced record profits over a decade.

Days went by, and Norton believed the presence of the National Guard on streets across the Commonwealth had helped restore some peace. Police and National Guard presence was particularly strong in the major cities.

There is no doubt the students on the streets made the unrest worse. Many of the students joined in the peaceful protests, others engaged in looting at night, and some engaged in what was called confrontational engagement with citizens. This involved approaching white residents on the streets and asking them things like, "Do you renounce racism?" The responses varied; some out of fear might reply, "Yes, I do," or "Of course." Others might brush the kids off, and even say rude things to them. The mob might respond by leaving them alone and going on to the next white person, or they might be more confrontational. In some cases they would surround a white person and ask them to denounce white privilege. They might threaten them, or sometimes they would surround the person and chant, "Shame, Shame, Shame." Their other chant while marching down the street was "White silence equals violence."

There were hundreds of examples of these confrontational exchanges, all throughout the Commonwealth. Dozens of fights came from these exchanges, although very few arrests. The media never reported these incidents. They really only talked about the peaceful protests, and only video of peaceful protests would be shown on the news. The media declared the protests were "mostly peaceful" so all their coverage had to back this narrative. One reporter said on the promise of anonymity, "The press didn't report on the confrontations taking place all across Virginia, because of a fear of a potential race war."

***

In every major city in Virginia there were impromptu white privilege atonement prayers taking place on street corners and in parks. Usually led by a college student or liberal priest, white people would take a knee, bow their heads and repeat a prayer. Ironically, it was the same prayer Reverend Brand used to recite on Sundays from the pulpit after communion:

"Do you support racial justice, equity, and compassion in human relations?"

"Do you affirm that white privilege is unfair and harmful to those who have it and to those who do not?"

"Do you affirm that white privilege and the culture of white supremacy must be dismantled where it is present?"

"Do you support racial equity, justice, and liberation for every person?"

"Do you affirm the inherent worth and dignity of every person?"

"Therefore, from this day forward, will you strive to understand more deeply the injustice and suffering white privilege and white supremacy cause?"

"Will you make a greater effort to treat all people with the same respect you expect to receive?"

"Will you commit to developing the courage to live your beliefs and values of racial justice and equality?"

"Will you strive to eliminate racial prejudice from your thoughts and actions so that you can better promote the racial justice efforts of our church?"

The supplicants would respond with "yes" to all questions, then rise off their knees and go on their way.

***

The autopsy on James Sayers was finally completed. The toxicology report indicated that he was high on several drugs. The report did nothing to quell the protests.

Elections Have Consequences

Just as things seemed to calm down a bit came a bombshell from Headline News Network. In doing a check on Officer Driscoll, the reporters discovered a piece of information, something that Norton should have known about. He should have remembered the officer.

21) The Latest Bombshell from MNN

Willow Bush came on the air; the big graphic blared "Breaking News." "Shortly after taking office, Governor Norton wrote a letter of commendation for Officer Driscoll."

The staff was gathered by the TV; Norton could see the commotion. *What's going on*, he thought. Mike Jackson came in and told him he might want to turn his TV on to MNN. Norton had it on mute.

Norton stared at the TV and read the breaking news crawl: "Governor Norton Letter to Officer Driscoll Surfaces." Norton felt like he had been punched in the gut. He went back to his desk, slumped in his chair, and thought, *Why me? Why do all these bad things keep happening to me? Is the whole world out to get me?*

Norton started to remember Officer Driscoll; it all came back to him. *That was the officer. I knew the name sounded familiar.*

On a December evening, a month before Norton was sworn as governor, Richmond police officers were dispatched to the 600 block of 25th Street in the Church Hill section of the city. The police were responding to a 911 call about unconscious people inside a home. The lead officer in the case was none other than Darren Driscoll.

When the police arrived, they were advised by other first responders that the carbon monoxide levels in the residence were dangerously high, so high that the officers were warned against going inside without the necessary protective equipment.

Officer Driscoll and Officer Jack Kowalski were met by a man who said his elderly father was inside. The father was disabled and the son didn't have the strength to pull him out. Officers Driscoll and Kowalski knew the risk, but immediately agreed to go in right away to save the people inside.

Driscoll said that there might still be time to prevent loss of life but no time to waste. "It is worth the risk if it saves a life. Who's coming with me?" In fact, they were able to pull out three people, and two survived, including the father.

It was a big story; it led the evening news in the Richmond metro area. Governor Norton, Governor Elect at the time, heard about the story and in response to the heroism asked his staff to write up a letter of commendation to each of the officers.

Once he was sworn in as governor, he wrote a nice letter to each. He waited to write the letters until after he was sworn in so that the commendation could be signed by a governor, which would increase the honor. In his letter he wrote:

"Officer Driscoll made the decision to go in fully aware of how dangerous and life-threatening the situation was. He and Officer Kowalski knowingly put their lives at risk to help others. They did so without hesitation. We should all be incredibly proud of them, and thankful that Virginia has such dedicated officers.

"In fact, our officers routinely put their own safety at risk to help others and protect our state. Officer Driscoll is a 20 year veteran of the Richmond Police force, and his contribution to our safety has been awe-inspiring.

Signed, Governor Ronald Norton."

The media really just ran the last sentence and signature. There was very little coverage on the facts behind the commendation. Most of the media didn't recite the story of officer Driscoll saving three lives, the lives of people who were not white. It didn't fit the narrative of a racist cop.

Elections Have Consequences

In watching the cable news, Norton could see the feeding frenzy. The press was having a field day; their narrative was that the cop was either a racist or dirty, and now the governor was caught praising him.

Norton demanded to see Beaman and Brand. He started off with a rhetorical question. "Why did I need to give a commendation to a city police officer?"

Jackson interjected, "Governor, you mentioned the case and wanted to write a letter praising the officers, including Driscoll. You may have forgotten because you never met them, you simply signed a letter of commendation."

Norton responded "Yes, yes, I know, but now what am I going to do? The media and the mob are going to lynch me for this."

An angry Brand responded, "Governor, that is outrageous language to use, a lynching? Are you serious?"

"It is just so frustrating. I did nothing wrong; how on earth can the media twist a commendation for saving a couple of people in Richmond into supporting a racist cop?"

Beaman responded, "The media always twist things to fit their narrative, and the mob wants to use this to put extra pressure on you. The Republicans, who have no power, will just watch from the sidelines as those of us on the left engage in a circular firing squad. No doubt they'll be laughing the entire time." He added, "We have to change the narrative. Focus on the positive things you are doing. Governor, we don't know that the police officer did anything wrong. He was enforcing the law. The motorist resisted arrest; it could have been an honest accident."

Once the story of Norton's commendation of the officer

Elections Have Consequences

became public, the protesters started to turn their anger toward Norton. At Justice for James rallies, the crowds began to use the slogan "Hey hey, ho ho, Huggy Bear has got to go." The mob was turning; Norton now felt a sense of panic.

In Richmond there were protests at police headquarters and precincts. The chants included, among others, "Every city, every town, every precinct, tear it down." There were calls by a few members of the City Council to abolish the Richmond City Police.

Norton dodged this controversy by saying it was a local matter and not for him to decide. He believed that getting rid of the police was a reckless idea, but he didn't want to say so and risk angering the mob and his Democrat voting base.

Monday night was very bad; the police had to block off several blocks downtown near the Capitol. There were disturbances up and down Broad Street.

The presence of the National Guard helped considerably, but there were three areas that were under the most assaults: police stations, stores (although that was diminishing with National Guard troops), and Confederate monuments.

The monuments were increasingly under assault. Thompson explained why they needed to be protected. "The monuments are high profile targets, and if we fail to protect them it is only going to embolden the mob to cause more violence and destruction. I realize there is a desire in this room to take them down, but not this way. We must send the message that law and order must prevail. "

Brand expressed the opinion of most everyone in the cabinet. "Defending the statues will do the opposite. It will increase the feeling of injustice from the protesters." Brand used the word

Elections Have Consequences

"protesters," never "looters," and she hated the word "mob."

Norton agreed to meet with Brand alone, something Beaman and Thompson were always concerned about, before he left work for the day. A frustrated Norton said, "Ann, I admit I am at a loss as to what to do next. Sure, the National Guard has helped a good deal, but the unrest continues, and I can't see it ending anytime soon. At some point the National Guard will have to stand down. What do I need to do to get the riots to stop? My God, there was even some looting in Danville last night. Looters hit a T.J. Maxx." Sitting at his desk, with Brand standing in front of it, he commented, "I can understand some rioting in Richmond or Norfolk. But Danville!"

Brand resisted the urge to roll her eyes or accuse him of making a racist comment and moved to some constructive ideas. "First, Governor, you have to stop sounding so white when addressing the people of Virginia."

Norton, taken aback by the comment, responded, "Excuse me? I am a white guy from McLean. How else can I sound?"

Brand maintained a diplomatic tone and replied, "Forgive me, Governor, what I meant is that in your words you say things only a white person would say; that is, someone who doesn't understand that our legal and justice systems are racist."

A curious Norton responded, "Give me an example."

Brand said, "Okay, when the disturbances broke out, you chirped a call for people to remain calm and respect the decision of the legal system etc."

Norton snapped, "Well, of course. What's wrong with that?"

"Everyone wants calm and no one condones looting, but to people of color such calls show a tone deafness to the real problem, that is injustice. So that is what I mean by sounding

Elections Have Consequences

white. You don't need to speak out against looting; rather, you need to focus on establishing justice."

Norton seemed to get it. He asked, "Well, what are some concrete things I can propose?"

"First," Brand said, "why not propose a special session later this fall to look at a criminal justice package?"

Norton seemed skeptical. "As you may remember, in the past I have opposed special sessions. My predecessor used one to ram through his tax increase, and other things, using the excuse that the virus required emergency measures, so we had to have a special session. Of course we could have waited a few months for the regular session. My problem with special sessions is that proposed legislation doesn't get adequate scrutiny during a special session." Unbeknownst to Norton, this was one of the main reasons why Brand wanted a special session. The package she had in mind would be so radical that it could only be rammed through and the less scrutiny the better.

Brand, using all her efforts to be persuasive, told him, "Well, think about it. Telling the people of Virginia that needed reform can't wait, that you are calling the legislature back in session, will help calm the people and show leadership."

Norton thought maybe a promise of a special session could calm the mob in the streets.

Brand added, "Maybe call Seibers and get his opinion."

"Okay, I will give it good consideration and talk to Seibers."

"The other thing emphasizes all the procedures that you have put in place that will bring down about 3,000 Confederate statues." Norton nodded. Brand, sensing Norton's skepticism about statue removal, added, "Getting rid of the statues won't improve anyone's life directly, but it is important symbolism. And removing the statues will help our schools teach a proper view of history."

Norton nodded and softly muttered, "Yes, a proper view of history."

Brand went back to the idea of a special session. "But with the symbolism of statue removal, coupled with real legislative changes in criminal justice laws, we can bring about calm, peace, and most importantly justice."

Norton seemed to be moving Brand's way. "Okay, I will call Siebers and get his views on the possibility of a special session."

Fairfax State Senator Steve Siebers, who took Norton's Senate seat after Norton became governor, was an ally of Brand's and would help her push for a special session.

Siebers had made a name for himself as Commonwealth Attorney in Fairfax, when he posthumously charged Robert E. Lee with treason. The case was ultimately laughed out of court, but for six months Siebers received national attention and praise. One prominent commentator on the left described him as "a true social justice warrior, in the best sense of the term."

Such a bizarre charge should have made Siebers a laughing stock in the legal profession, and it might have, but it seemed to have helped him with the general public, and Fairfax County voters rewarded him with a seat in the House of Delegates, then State Senate.

As the weeks of rallies, riots, and looting continued, Thompson began to fall out of favor with Norton. The key event took place with the burning down of the 13th Police Precinct in

Elections Have Consequences

Richmond. Thompson failed to get a heads up. By the time the mob, many of them from outside of the state, gathered and circled the building it was too late to stop them. The police evacuated in time, but the building burned to the ground.

Cohen commented on the event, "After that event, Norton increasingly turned to Brand for advice. I like Mark Thompson, but with his background he was never really suited to be Secretary of Public Safety,"

22) The A. P. Hill Statue

At around 9 a.m a crowd started gathering in front of the A. P. Hill statue. At first it was a peaceful, almost festival-like atmosphere, with music, dancing, and plenty of marijuana.

Members of the media came early in the morning to file the day's story.

There were chants of "The statue must fall" and "End racism now." The main groups organizing the protest were Students Against Fascism. Black Lives Matter, and Moms United to Save Virginia. Feminist groups were also represented, and had printed up signs for the occasion reading "End Toxic Masculinity Now." There were lots of VCC students, and college students from all over Virginia.

As the morning turned into afternoon, the crowd grew and became more agitated. Many started throwing objects at the statue and spray painting the pedestal. They wrote all kinds of things. Some started climbing the statue, and urinating and spitting on the pedestal.

Reverend Brand, wearing a black shirt and her Reverend's collar, showed up and gave a fiery speech. She praised the crowd of mostly young people. With a megaphone in hand Brand ranted: "You are the pride of Virginia, demanding a just society, reminding all of us that racism must be stamped out, or should I say torn down." Brand was always a favorite with young social justice warriors. They cheered her, but they were not happy with Norton. Many in the crowd started yelling, "How can you work for Huggy Bear?" More kept yelling, "How can you work for Huggy Bear?"

Elections Have Consequences

Some kids yelled, "Huggy Bear is a fascist!" They finally broke into chants of "Hey hey ho ho, Huggy Bear has got to go!"

Brand tried to ignore the interruptions and continue her speech. More and more in the crowd then picked up the chant. "Hey hey ho ho, Huggy Bear has got to go, Hey hey ho ho, Huggy Bear has got to go!"

While she generally liked and trusted Norton, she didn't want to be in a position of defending him, especially not to a potential mob. Brand concluded the speech, raised her clenched fist, and yelled, "Power to the people!" She got out safely. The crowd was growing, but the Richmond Police and State Police had no plans to break up the demonstration. The students denounced Norton, but ironically it was Norton who told Mayor Case not to break up the demonstration.

Later, back at her office, Brand came to the conclusion that she would have to walk back her fiery speech. Her concern was that the crowd could spill out into the neighborhood and cause damage, thereby it could no longer be considered a peaceful demonstration. So she took to Chirp and posted, "I know many young people are going to peacefully and patriotically express their views." Brand wanted to see a large crowd, but to cover herself she wanted to use the word "peacefully," just in case. She didn't use that word in her speech at the demonstration.

Senator Sandoval spoke as well. She claimed that this must be a wake up call for the "white power structure in the state." She went on to complain, "White people have run the state for 400 years. Isn't it time to consider a change?" The rhetorical question drew huge cheers from the mostly white audience of college aged kids.

MNN covered much of the protest. They had a panel

discussion; of course the panel was made up of sympathetic voices. One of the panelists was a former Democrat congressman from Charlottesville. Beaming, he said, "Can I just say on a personal note, I am from Virginia, and I have never been so proud of my native state as I am today. These young people, mostly young people, are the conscience of Virginia. For years white Virginians, even myself, have looked the other way at racism, sexism. homophobia, Islamophobia, and transphobia. Now these brave young people have taken to the streets to say 'NO MORE. We won't stay silent any longer.'" The one moderate Democrat on the panel warned, "I do worry that it could get out of hand." However, the consensus among the panelists seemed to be that these young people were the voice of Virginia, and should be praised.

The panel included one sort of plausible Republican voice: Bob Sharp, once a minor Republican campaign strategist in Virginia, and host of *The Sharp Edge* podcast. In addition, he was listed as a "Senior Contributor" with the political news website *The Daily Gruel*. Sharp possessed a third rate intellect, but a sunny personality. He served a specific purpose for the producers at MNN. Indeed Sharp found a niche. The network needed at least one Republican on every panel discussion. The ratio usually consisted of four members of the left, and one nominal Republican. As part of the MNN formula, the one nominal Republican was usually a weak debater.

The world of punditry is a lot like professional wrestling. In professional wrestling there is a term for someone who is supposed to lose a match in order to build up the credibility of another wrestler, to take a fall. This person is known as a "jobber." In the industry of political pundits Sharp was a jobber. He would criticize conservative Republicans while claiming to be a Republican, and of course the network billed him as such. But Sharp would acknowledge that Republicans had gone off the rails on "this one." On almost every appearance he would say something like, "I am a lifelong Republican, but on this I am very disappointed in my party..."

The vain Sharp didn't care about being used; he just wanted to be on TV. Sharp belonged to a very small group; it was shrinking with every great Bush achievement. The small fraternity was known as "no Bushers." They attacked the pro-Bush activists calling them "Bush leaguers."

The panel went to Sharp, and on cue he uttered his usual banal thought. "Look, I am a Reagan conservative, and spent most of my career campaigning for Virginia Republicans. But my party left me, so I sympathize with all these young people rallying for racial justice at the A. P. Hill statue. It becomes clear to me that my party has to decide whether we are to become the party of Jefferson Davis, or the party of Abe Lincoln. As my hero Ronald Reagan would say, it is a time for choosing."

Even the lefty snowflake moderator seemed stunned by Sharp's vacuity. "Okay, thank you, Bob. Now let's return to Richmond, where the crowd is growing. You can see the live video there on the screen."

Indeed the crowd continued to grow throughout the afternoon, swelling to several hundred. Most of the demonstrators arriving were young; many were from VCC and Randolph Macon. Stephen Cohen even showed up to see for himself. Many protesters arrived with tools; someone even had a blow torch, all to try to take the statue down. One witness described it as brazen disregard for the police. As one witness said, "Many protesters walked right by the police with sledge hammers and rope. The police just stood there."

Norton monitored the protest from his desk. Public Safety Secretary Thompson called to discuss what the governor wanted to do, if anything. Thompson urged the governor to break up the demonstration, telling Norton, "This is already getting out of hand."

However, in consultation with Brand and Beaman, Norton stood by his earlier decision. There was no need to intervene. Norton told Thompson, "They will get tired and go home to Mommy soon." He quipped, "Mom might be making meatloaf tonight and they wouldn't want to miss that."

Norton later explained to Beaman, "I know Thompson wants me to intervene, but I can't break up their fun. Those students are not happy with me right now, so it's probably best to have the police back off. I don't want the crowd to say 'Huggy Bear broke up my party.'"

Beaman agreed. "Let them have their temper tantrum and take their frustration out on a statue. They can't do any real damage. In a way the statues are good; they are the source of all our country's problems or so the kids believe, and once we take them down we will be heroes." Beaman smiled, "It's a win-win!"

All afternoon the protesters tried everything. It took awhile, but they got ropes around the statue. Hundreds of students spent hours rocking back and forth, until around 9 o'clock the statue was loosening from its moorings on the pedestal.

MNN brought on engineers to discuss the best ways to tear down a statue. All evening, while airing other stories, the screen was split showing the live feed of the protest at the A. P. Hill statue.

All the while there was a self-described "wall of moms" linking arms around the crowd, for the purpose of protecting the kids from the police. The moms were a motley crew of hags, Karens, and old biddies. Unbeknownst to them, they were not needed because the mayor and governor weren't going to protect the statue, although Norton did check on the situation every 30 minutes.

According to eyewitnesses, "The police were just sitting quietly on the street, just observing. The crowd was yelling, louder and louder. They had ropes around the statue, and tried to rock it. They had dozens of students on each side."

The statue then seemed to loosen from its moorings. They kept bringing in different people to replace the ones who got tired and would start pulling again. Then it started visibly rocking. The crowd went wild; it spurred them on. After an hour of this, the statue came down, making a huge thud. Thunderous cheers erupted from the crowd. Most of the news networks came back on with a live shot of the scene, and many networks interrupted regular programming with a special report.

Protesters, most of them described by the media as "peaceful," rushed in to get a selfie. In all the commotion nobody noticed, but a female protester was down on the ground, bleeding and unconscious.

The protestor, Zoe Kingston, had been yelling and screaming with the crowd. A VCC art student, she was there most of the day, working her way to the front during the evening. She tried to stay out of the way of the millennial males who had been working all day to tear the statue down. It was dark, and in all the commotion no one saw what happened to her. As the statue fell and hit the ground a piece of the statue broke off and hit her in the head. She lay on the ground, bleeding and unconscious.

Elections Have Consequences

The police were just sitting quietly on the street observing. In all the commotion no one saw what happened to her. As she lay on the ground, her head and shoulder were wedged between the cement and part of the statue. The oblivious crowd continued yelling and screaming. Many then started coming up to urinate on ol' A. P. Hill, and more selfies were being taken.

The police remained inactive.

The mob wanted to set fire to the statue, so they attempted to drag it out onto the street. At last, about 20 minutes after the statue fell, someone noticed the girl on the ground. They tried to get her up, and then they noticed that she was unconscious and bleeding. A fellow student tried to call 911, but it was hard to hear. After a couple of attempts they made a report, but getting the crowd back and opening a space for the ambulance was a real challenge.

An eyewitness explained how hard it was to get the ambulance to the downed statue to get to Zoe.

"The wall of moms were yelling at the police, chants, like, 'Pigs, pigs, pigs, shame, shame. shame,' and 'Hands up don't shoot, hands up don't shoot.'"

The police got a megaphone to try to explain the situation, but it took about 15 minutes to convince the crowd that the girl was down and needed medical attention. When medics got to Zoe, they had to walk through puddles of urine left by the protestors.

She was pronounced dead at the hospital. Her father had tough words for the Richmond Police, and Governor Norton for holding back the police and National Guard. "It never should have happened. The police were standing on the sidelines all afternoon, as the crowd was growing. The National Guard was told to stand down by the Governor. Will anyone be prosecuted for my little girl's death?"

The media, for the purpose of a sound bite, simply took his quote, "It never should have happened." The media spin became that it never should have happened because the statue should have been taken down years ago.

The statue went down shortly after midnight, which was just after Norton turned off the TV. It seems he had seen that episode of Mannix before, so he went to bed. Just as he was falling asleep the phone rang. "Governor, it's Mike. Bad news; the statue went down."

Norton, wiping the sleep from his eyes, responded, "Okay, I hope not too much damage was done to the neighborhood. I hope no one was hurt."

"Governor, the bad news is that a girl was killed, hit by the falling statue. By the time they got her to the hospital it was too late. She was dead on arrival."

Norton felt the blow like a punch in the gut. "Okay, get me Beaman and Brand on the phone. We will work on a statement, and Mike, tomorrow morning first thing, I want you, Beaman, Brand and Mayor Case in my office. We will discuss our response."

A dispirited Norton hung up the phone. Paula saw something was wrong, "What is it, Ronnie?"

"A girl was killed at the protest tonight at the A. P. Hill monument. It seems the statue came down and she was hit by it. The hospital did all they could but they couldn't save her."

"Why on earth would they be allowed to try to tear down a

statue? Why the hell didn't the police intervene? What type of nincompoops are running that city?

"The Richmond police have a limited number of officers; it was determined that the police were better utilized protecting businesses and homes." He didn't mention his part in the decision.

The next morning, Norton decided that he needed bold action. He agreed to a statement that Brand and Mark Thompson wrote: "The death of Zoe Kingston is a tragedy that never should have happened. It is time for the removal of all Confederate monuments in the Commonwealth. To stop future injuries and death, and to help heal our state, we need to remove them as soon as possible."

This statement drew a sharp response from Angela Parrish, who in a chirp said:

"The tragic death of Zoe Kingston could have been prevented. The mayor of Richmond and Governor Norton failed to defend the statue, which is public property, and put a stop to the anarchy which caused the death of this young woman. I call on Norton to do his job and stop the anarchy taking place in Virginia. I would like to know when we can expect arrests to be made in the death of Zoe Kingston?"

However, Norton stuck to his guns. He told Mayor Case the next morning that there was no need to change the policy of not protecting monuments. "We should continue to focus on protecting businesses and property."

Norton rationalized that such a tragedy wouldn't happen again. He also knew that even if he wanted to protect them his political base would not accept the police, whether state, local, or the National Guard, protecting Confederate statues. As Brand would say, such optics would look horrible, and "only excite the crowd even more."

At 11:00 a.m. Norton held a press conference in the Governor's Mansion, in the same room where he had faced the press over his Huggy Bear scandal. In his opening remarks, he announced an executive order directing the state to remove the rest of the Confederate statues in Richmond as soon as possible.

"In order to prevent another tragedy, I have directed the Parks Commission to remove all Confederate statues on state land and under state control as soon as possible."

Behind Norton were Brand, members of the clergy, and a number of civil rights leaders from Richmond.

Norton's opening statement had been well crafted by Brand and Thompson in an effort to soothe the mob. "It was a mistake, indeed a great wrong, to put the statues up in the first place over one hundred years ago, but today, at this hour, we are doing the right thing by removing them. We are correcting a historical atrocity."

Norton's position in the campaign had been that the statues might have made sense a hundred years ago but not today. Beaman and Brand convinced him to change that position. He knew he would have to say that they shouldn't have been up in the first place, if they were racist symbols.

Norton continued his pleas for calm. "There is nothing wrong with peaceful protests, but the destruction of statues by a group of citizens, without proper tools and equipment, can lead to injury and death, as we learned in the tragic case of Zoe Kingston. When it comes to the removal of monuments, that is best left to the government."

Elections Have Consequences

No one in the media asked how getting rid of century-old statues helps people "unify or heal." Norton promised that the state would remove all the Confederate statues as soon as they could, but he encouraged protesters not to try to tear them down.

Several news outlets pointed to Ann Lee Brand's leadership in the campaign to remove the statues, claiming, "Even members of the Lee family want the statues to come down." The media loved to emphasize her middle name.

In Capitol Square smoke from the fires of protests that had taken place overnight could be seen, and sirens from police and fire crews could be heard inside the mansion.

Parrish chirped later in the afternoon, "Virginia's Secretary of Education took part in the protest which led to this tragedy. She should be charged with incitement. She encouraged kids to cut class, and to engage in reckless and violent protests. While she was speaking, protesters walked past her with sledge hammers, drills, ropes, and explosives, yet she thinks it was a peaceful protest? Secretary Brand should do the right thing—resign immediately. She has no credibility when it comes to educating Virginia's children." Parrish went on to say that if Brand didn't resign, she would introduce Articles of Impeachment "as soon as Monday morning."

Many Republicans in the legislature agreed with Parrish that Brand's words at the rally, "Racism must be stamped out, or should I say, torn down" amounted to incitement, and that she should resign.

Steve Cohen said of Brand's comments, "Well, legally it doesn't amount to incitement, and Republicans, for political reasons are blowing this way out of proportion." He pointed out that Brand had even said, "Peacefully make your views known," but added, "I do think it was a mistake for her to be there, and it certainly wasn't wise for her to address the crowd." For the most part the media ignored the incitement claims against her.

Brand, Beaman and Case insisted this tragedy proved the need to move faster on removing the statues. Thompson, however, offered a different point of view in the cabinet. "Secretary Brand advocated taking down these statues years before today, before these events. The statues are not the problem. We do have problems—social problems, problems with our educational system, problems in our justice system. We may need to take down the statues, but only in the cool atmosphere of a reasoned discussion, not in the heat of mob violence."

Brand argued that symbolism was important, and removal could calm the mob, though she didn't use the word mob.

Norton felt real fear. His aides knew it was based in part on his obsession with the numbers of protesters at different gatherings around the state. Norton monitored the increased number of protesters on a daily basis. Indeed, the mobs were getting bigger. While he agreed with Thompson that the statues were simply symbols, perhaps Brand was correct and taking them down would calm the mob.

In the early evening Norton, Brand, and Beaman turned on the news anxiously. The media didn't place any blame on Norton for not breaking up the demonstration. Few in the media asked why the police didn't break up the protests. In addition, the death seemed to accelerate the drive to remove the statues. Beaman breathed a sigh of relief, telling the governor and Brand, "This may well work out in our favor." Brand nodded.

Elections Have Consequences

The ancient Gloria Folger on MNN suggested that after this tragedy there could be no possible excuse for allowing the statues to remain up. "The death of this young woman must be a signal that all these statues must come down. If the statues do come down, then this young lady, Zoe Kingston's, death won't be in vain."

Watching the news coverage throughout the next day, it became clear simply by looking at Beaman's face that things were going to be okay. "Well, it looks like we will survive this."

Norton responded, "Yes, thank God." Brand claimed this was a great opportunity to push forward their plans to remove all Confederate statues. Everyone agreed. Norton, now fully on board, commented, "The sooner the better." They all nodded.

Beaman then optimistically added, "Actually, we will come out of this in a stronger political position."

Still, Norton was not so sure. Visibly glum and downcast, he went back to the mansion for lunch, and there he was met by a smiling Mike Jackson. Norton perked up. "What? You have some good news? I'll take any good news you have; it's in short supply these days."

Jackson told him, "We have a taker for the Lee statue!"

Norton said, "Excellent! Thank God! Who wants it?"

Mike paused, and thought of the best way to tell him. "A museum in Paris, and not Paris Virginia, or Paris, Texas."

The Lee statue had been made in France by the artist Antonin Mercie. His works are considered national treasures in France, and much of his work is displayed in the Louvre.

The French government had watched in horror as the kids tore down the A. P. Hill statue and were frightened that the "les enfants d'Amérique " would destroy one of Mercie's masterpieces. That morning the French government had found a museum in Paris that would take it, and then called the White House to formally ask for it.

Later that evening at a hastily assembled press conference in Foggy Bottom, the Secretary of State and French Ambassador Jean Marie Favreau announced the deal. They laid out the time table for the transfer. They cut Norton out of the deal completely, not even bothering to talk to him.

Bush sent out a chirp expressing sadness at losing the "beautiful statue," but said he was relieved that it would have a good new home.

Angela Parrish chirped that it was a sad day for Virginia. She asked, "What other Virginia treasures is Huggy Bear willing to have destroyed?"

***

Jean Marie Favreau bore a striking physical resemblance to former Senator (and author of the Iran nuclear deal) John Kerry, but Favreau politically aligned with the right. The media liked him because Favreau could be blunt, bordering on undiplomatic, and he could make clear his anti-American views at times.

Favreau, like many Frenchmen who look down on America, believed that Americans were allowing the destruction of their country, their heritage, and their history through political correctness. The French have a term for political correctness: "la maladie de l'Amérique."

Some speculated that the French merely wanted the Lee statue to display it as a metaphorical middle finger to the United States, but that is probably not true. Mercie's work was very good, and as an artist he was considered a national hero. Indeed many people have visited the Louvre and other museums simply to see his work.

Favreau, who spoke perfect English, spent a semester at University of Virginia as an exchange student. He was a popular guest on public affairs programs in the States, and on the night of the statue announcement he went on *The Charlie Baker show* to discuss it. Baker and Favreau had been friends for years, and Favreau was a regular on his show. One media critic said the two of them had such a natural rapport that they could probably host a talk show together.

Favreau did the interview and talked about the statues and other issues: the upcoming G7 meeting, trade talks with China, foreign policy. He didn't say anything about the riots going on in Virginia, or really anything controversial, at least on air. On air Favreau seemed relatively tame; he seemed to have perfect control of his tongue, which was rare, and he took no digs at Norton or America. He simply said of the Lee statue, "Virginians and all Americans will soon have the opportunity to come see the Lee statue in Paris." He then added, "Without any graffiti on it."

Baker ended the show with his usual line, "Until we meet again America, good night," then stared awkwardly into the camera for three seconds. The producer finally announced, "And that's a wrap."

The interview had ended and the cameras were turned off, or so they thought, and the two continued their conversation.

Baker said, "Well, thanks again, Jean, for doing the show. I'm glad you found a home for the Lee statue."

Favreau replied, "Well, Mercie was a great artist, so we are happy to have his work even if it is of Robert E. Lee. It's sad but

Elections Have Consequences

not surprising that Americans won't stand up for their history."

Baker asked, "In your opinion, why won't they?"

"Well, let's take Virginia, for example. After all, that is the source now of the great unrest, for a couple of reasons. Virginia indoctrinates their kids in school from kindergarten all the way through college. I believe that political correctness saps a person of their ability to think, or reason, or put history into context. And the public schools don't teach children to debate, argue and fight. The little history a Virginia student gets is wrong, and it is by design."

Favreau pointed to an example, "Remember that young student from North Korea? She and her family got out, came to America, and settled in Virginia. She said that the indoctrination in Virginia schools was even more pernicious than in North Korean schools. I believe it. Let's start with the Lee statue controversy from today. Why would anyone want to remove a statue of Robert E. Lee? What did he do wrong? As far as I can tell, nothing morally indefensible. He had to choose: fight against his family. friends and relatives, or take up arms in their defense. How can anyone criticize him for not being willing to go to war against his family? In what universe is that okay?"

Favreau continued, "They say, well, Lee didn't fight for the Union. Well, the Union was a compact between the States. Lee's state left the Union. Lee defended his home, his family. Where is the Union on a map? Nowhere."

Baker tried to push back. "But some would say Virginia and Lee fought to preserve slavery."

Favreau dismissively responded, "Well that person probably went to a Virginia public school, as that is ahistorical nonsense. Virginia initially voted against secession, but then Lincoln asked for every state to produce 75,000 volunteers to put down the rebellion. So the leaders of Virginia..."

Baker interrupted, "Leaders who were all white."

Favreau conceded the point, and continued, "So it was a constitutional issue. Virginia didn't feel they, or any state, had the constitutional power to force a state to stay in the Union."

Baker said, "Well, what about the charge that Lee was a racist?"

Favreau conceded that also but said, "Lee was a man born in the 1800's. I am sure by our standards he was, but that is hardly a reason to take a statue down. Actually, Charlie, you hit on the rationale for taking down this and other Confederate monuments. For decades the Yankees moved south and they noticed all the monuments. Well, they objected to them on the grounds of succession and slavery, but that didn't work. Those arguments repeatedly failed throughout the 20th century. Into the 21st century, more decades removed from the war, the opponents of the monuments found the argument that worked. They claimed the statues were racist. Well, I still don't believe a majority want them to come down, but enough do, and the most influential people do–those who run the schools and the media. Then the support was there to take them down. And in Virginia, which has lots of monuments, Norton can't stand up for the monuments.

"When the Lee statue was put up in 1890, my understanding is that 100,000 people showed up for the unveiling. An amazing number even by today's standards. Just think, Virginia is about six times larger today, and there were no cars to drive to Richmond in 1890. People then would have to walk, take a train, or ride a horse; for many it would take days to get there. You could argue that adjusted for population growth and cars and roads, 100,000 in 1890 is the equivalent of 600,000 today." Favreau then rhetorically asked, "Could you imagine 100,000 people going to Richmond for an event? I am not positive, but I doubt that will ever happen. The Lee statue unveiling attendance record will never be broken by anything that ever happens in Richmond. So when the People's Committee on Statues in Virginia recommends that the state build a monument to Dr. Anthony Fauci, how many people will show up 50? 100? And the lying Norton will tell the people of Virginia, with a straight face, that of the two monuments only one of them should have been put up. Only the Fauci monument is legitimate?"

Baker laughed and said, "I don't think they are going to build a statue of Doctor Fauci."

"Well, whoever the People's Committee comes up with will be artificial. In other words, Lee's statue had real organic support. No one on the People's Committee on Statues list will actually have real support, that is, organic support for a monument to be erected in their honor."

"Don't you think Norton has to respond to the public he serves?"

Favreau replied, "Look, I spent enough time in Virginia to know who runs the state. Excuse me, Commonwealth. I once said to this Virginian that he had a beautiful state, and he looked at me and said, 'It is a commonwealth.'"

Baker laughed. "Yes, Virginians are funny about that, but you said you know who runs Virginia. Who?"

"The old maxim of Virginia politics is that 75 percent of the ideas that come out of the VCC faculty lounge eventually make it into state law."

Elections Have Consequences

Baker interrupted. "Who told you that, Professor Travis?"

"No. By the way, I am told VCC in Richmond is mainly an art college." Favreau joked, "Those students wouldn't know art if it fell on them."

Baker groaned. Holding back a laugh, he shook his head and said, "That is so inappropriate."

"Well, I would amend the maxim. I wouldn't say 75 percent of the laws are coming from the faculty lounge, I would say they're coming from the student body. These kids are indoctrinated all their lives and no longer have much power to think or reason, but they know how to make demands. The colleges who are ripping them off with virtually worthless degrees probably don't want to upset the kids any more, and the politicians don't want to upset them either, so they humor them, and much of the time vote for their stupid ideas. All to placate the kids."

"You think the schools are afraid of them?"

"Must be," said Favreau. "When Johnny comes to school and says he is a girl, well, he must be, so don't challenge him. You remember that teacher who wouldn't go along with it? The school fired him and made an example of him. Now all the teachers are on board, yes, Johnny you are a girl. Let's carry this forward. Johnny then says he doesn't approve of the school's mascot. The school responds yes, Johnny we will change it. Johnny then discovers he doesn't like the name of the school. He does a google search and discovers the namesake is a racist, so the school agrees to a name change. Johnny then discovers he doesn't like the name of the street, also a racist namesake. It goes on. Johnny knows nothing about historical context, or policies, or life, but by God he is going to govern the Commonwealth of Virginia. So Johnny has his demands and the teachers and school will comply. Maybe not happily, but they will.

"And just like the schools and politicians want to appease Johnny, so does the media. They need Johnny as well, as a viewer and reader. So they print the news that Johnny wants to read."

Baker pressed on why schools are so compliant to the students. Favreau theorized, "American kids today are coddled. You don't want to challenge their views, because that could be bad for their self esteem. And they are also the products of indoctrination. In a way the public schools created their own little Frankensteins. They filled the kids up with anti-American propaganda, and when the kids got to college and decided to tear down monuments. Well, what can the college professors and administrators do at that point? Nothing really, it's too late to challenge the kids' views and feelings. So they have to sympathize; they tell them they're right.

"And at the state level, the politicians have to go along as well. Norton doesn't want to challenge such a big voting block, and rather than admit that Virginia schools filled the kids' heads with nonsense, he takes the easier, politically correct route and agrees with them." Favreau concluded, "In politics, it's easier to go along with the mob than to try to persuade them."

Baker asked, "Well, maybe Governor Norton agrees with them?"

Favreau shook his head. "No, I think the student mob got Huggy Bear in a compromising position. They've got the poor bastard where they want him. It isn't just Confederate statues, it's all kinds of symbols of the Ancien Regime, Old America. It's like our revolution, the French Revolution; all the old things must be torn down for the new, to build a new society, a new man. This is what socialists do. They want to remake a country based on their utopian dreams. Here's an example. I used to fly into John Wayne Airport in southern California, but the last time I flew out there I discovered they had changed the name."

Baker interjected, "Yes, that had to do with some of Wayne's racist remarks."

"He may have made those remarks, but removing his name was for deeper reasons. Wayne represents an old America, a proud, bordering on arrogant America, a powerful post-war capitalist America, an America at the heyday of white privilege. So Wayne had to be canceled."

Baker tried to downplay the culture so dominant in America. "Well, we're not yet burning books."

"Well, almost. There was a writer, Mark Twain. He was considered, for many decades, the greatest American writer. The schools in Virginia got rid of him. He wrote a novel, titled *The Adventures of Huckleberry Finn,* considered, by Hemmingway, Mencken and others, to be the greatest American novel. It is no longer assigned. Did Americans fight to defend the great American writer? Did they say his work must be assigned in schools? No, probably because Americans won't defend their literature, any more than they will defend their heritage or history, either out of ignorance or weakness. I suspect both. What was Jefferson's line? 'Americans fear thinking more than hunger, thirst and cold'? I believe that's right. And it's gotten worse since Jefferson died. Today Americans are true sheep. They will allow the schools, the media and entertainment stars to tell them what to think. And the truly dumb ones will be influenced by a football or basketball star."

Elections Have Consequences

Baker laughed and corrected him, "I think he said, 'Pride costs more than hunger, thirst and cold.' Well, you do seem to talk a lot about Virginia politics. How do you know so much?

"Well. you mentioned her a minute ago. No, I never took Professor Travis's class, but remember I live in McLean since I work for the embassy, and when I was young I was an exchange student at UVA. I met a guy there who later got elected to the State Senate from Chesterfield County. I keep in regular touch with him, so I get an education in Virginia politics. He's a devout Baptist and is always trying to convert me. He is always talking about either Virginia politics, or the Bible. I told him, 'Steve, I am a lapsed Catholic and am religiously devoted to that.'"

Baker laughed. Favreau added, "And I was here for the Parrish-Norton race, which got worldwide television news coverage. That race was watched by millions of people around the world. By the end of that campaign a YouGov poll found that Angela Parrish was something like the 25th most recognized woman in the world."

Baker nodded and said, "Yes, I saw that poll. Amazing."

"She was not a bad candidate, perhaps a little too young. But let's face it, she has far bigger balls than Norton. She would have stood up to the mob." Baker suggested that Morrison would have been a stronger candidate. Favreau responded, "Norton and Morrison made a deal when they were in the legislature. They wouldn't run against each other for governor. Each would take a turn. They told each other, ``One term for you and one for me."

Baker laughed, shook his head and said with his voice rising, "Man, this would have been a great interview. Why didn't you say these things on the air?"

Elections Have Consequences

"Look, Charlie, I am in the diplomatic corps. I can't totally speak my mind in public."

Someone in the studio copied the recording, and three days later it was on the internet. The interview went viral.

23) Jack Villiers Returns

Unbeknownst to Norton, there was a new cloud on the horizon. Steve Beaman came to the Governor's Mansion in the late afternoon for a staff meeting, but he also had to meet privately with the governor afterwards.

As the meeting was breaking up, Steve Beaman slipped Norton a note. "We need to talk." Norton immediately recognized the code, which was deep cover at the 7th Street rendezvous point. Norton looked at Beaman, and silently nodded. Norton had no idea what it was about, but "We need to talk" is the most serious, DEFCON 1 alert. It requires a deep cover conversation.

As usual, Norton snuck out of the Governor's Mansion. Jasper drove him a few blocks to the 7th Street garage. No one was around, so Norton got out of the backseat. He could hear protesters a block away down Broad Street. Wearing jeans and tennis shoes, Norton walked the 50 feet to the last column and saw Steve come out behind it. As he got closer he noticed the look of concern on Beaman's face. Beaman was the eternal optimist, but ominously the familiar smile was gone. "Okay, Steve, what's the latest crisis?"

Beaman avoided the usual banter and simply said, "Governor, does the name Jack Villiers ring a bell?"

Norton responded, "Of course. He was an old fraternity brother. I gave the eulogy at his funeral. But why would his name come up now? He died a couple of years ago."

Elections Have Consequences

Beaman responded, "Governor, he's not totally dead."

"Excuse me? What the hell are you trying to tell me? I helped bury him. He is dead."

Beaman tried to explain. "Yes, he died a couple of years ago, but he sent us a present from the grave."

Norton just stared at Beaman, a quizzical look on his face.

"Yes, he died, but in his will he directed boxes of materials to be donated to VCC, your mutual alma mater. They were put in a warehouse off campus, where they've been since his death, but in the past few days VCC has started to open them." Beaman looked at Norton and in a calm voice said, "Do you know what they found?"

Norton hesitantly asked, "A bomb?"

"In effect, yes. He left Klan memorabilia and regalia. At the last count it was at least a hundred robes, hoods, insignias, patches, merit badges, bylaws etc. Over 30 boxes. It is estimated that it is the largest cache of Klan memorabilia EVER DISCOVERED."

Norton was stunned. "Dear God."

Beaman replied, "And that is not all.?

Norton blurted out, "There's more?"

"Yes. He left a manifesto, a five-hundred-page rant presumably on his views of race and other thoughts. It is in effect the ideology of the Klan. Maybe he wrote it, or it could be just the writings he collected. Either way it is a huge stink bomb. Governor, this could be serious. You remember what brought the spy Kim Philby down? It was his relationship with Donald McLean. A find like this may get out, and a good reporter might put two and two together and ask how this guy could be your best

Elections Have Consequences

friend for years and you never discovered that he was an avowed white supremacist? A good reporter, but thankfully we are blessed not to have any good ones here covering Virginia politics."

Norton, now flustered, responded, "Oh, shoot."

Beaman then imitated a reporter, "Governor Norton, how is it that your best friend in college was a neo-Nazi, but you are not?"

Beaman then went on, "If Angela Parrish had such a friend or even just a friend of a friend of a friend of a friend, who happened to have a friend who just might have been a neo-Nazi, that commie rag the *Press Democrat* would make it a front page story. MNN would spend hours on it, and that virtue signally ass Stephen Cohen would be all over it. The Virginia media is on our side so we should be okay, but we can't take any chances. Governor, is there anything else I should know about your relationship with Villiers?"

"No, we were just friends in college. Sure, I knew he had some odd views, but he never tried to recruit me into a secret society, or any group."

"I can't understand why he'd leave it to VCC. Who would do such a thing, to leave such a collection to his college?"

Norton suggested a possibility. "It was probably Jack's way of giving the middle finger to the school. He always felt underappreciated there."

"That's quite a way to screw your school over–leave them a Klan collection and hope the media finds out about it. Who the hell would do that?'

Norton ignored the question and suggested, "Can't the school just burn the stuff?"

335

Elections Have Consequences

"That's what I told them to do, but I can't order them to do it. I guess they have protocols for donated material. When the boxes were opened, several people probably witnessed the discovery. They've gotten everyone to keep quiet for now because our state and country are on the verge of a civil war, a race war. So everyone agreed to stay silent for a bit, until a final decision is made, which will probably be to burn or destroy the stuff. Or who knows, maybe there is historical value and it needs to go to a museum. But I think they can be persuaded to burn it."

Norton became emotional. "Steve, we don't need this discovery now; the state and the country are on the verge of war! We must destroy this! Can't we send some people into the storage unit, take it out and burn it?" He had an idea. "I know Veronica Ladson, the university president; she endorsed me for governor. I'll call her tomorrow and ask her for the sake of the country and state to burn it all."

Ladson was a Democrat as were most of the other university presidents in the Commonwealth. In fact, the only known conservative was Mason's Lenny Milstein.

"Okay, she will no doubt agree. But here's my immediate advice. Don't mention Jack Villiers. If his name comes up, downplay your relationship with him. Pass him off as no more than an acquaintance."

"Good advice, I'll take it. Ironically, Paula said to me when all this insanity started that Jack Villiers could kill us from the grave."

Beaman smiled and said, "We will be fine, Governor. The media is lazy and liberal. But we can't take any chances. We need to destroy the material and erase any ties to Villiers."

As Norton was driven back to the Governor's Mansion, lying

under the blanket on the backseat, he kept thinking, *Why would Jack do such a thing? How could he do it?*

Typically, Norton used his morning hours to put out fires from the day before. He had known VCC President Veronica Ladson for years. As a university president she didn't usually get involved in politics, but she was generally known as a supporter of Norton's and up to now had not suggested that he resign.

Just after 8 o'clock he called her. "Hey, Veronica, good morning. Ronnie Norton here. This has to be one of the oddest calls I've ever had to make, but it came to my attention recently that your university received a gift from an alumnus named Jack Villiers."

"Odd to say the least. Thirty-seven boxes of Klan material–garb, papers, insignias etc. We have received some weird stuff in the past, but nothing like this."

"Frankly. I'm deeply concerned about this getting out. At this tense time for our state and country, if news of this gift gets out it will become national news, and that would be a calamity. Let me be blunt. Destroy it, burn it all."

Ladson replied, "I understand, Governor. News of this material would also be bad for our school. Maybe that was the reason Villiers left it to us. Destruction would be best."

"What Villiers left is a gift and now your property, so you can do what you please. That can be to take the boxes and treat them as trash, toss them right into the incinerator. The sooner the better. This can't be allowed out."

"I agree. We will take care of it."

"I thank you, Veronica, and our commonwealth and our nation also thank you."

Elections Have Consequences

Norton hung up the phone and felt a great sense of relief. *Thank God. One potential media firestorm extinguished.* He shuddered thinking about what the media would do with this find. *Just imagine the 24-hour cable news talking about the largest Klan memorabilia cache ever found anywhere in the country, left by a guy who was my best friend in college. Damn that Jack.* The more Norton thought about it, the more he was convinced that Jack had meant to play a sick practical joke from the grave. Jack probably spent decades building the collection, putting it into boxes, putting it into storage, and then putting in his will a direction that the boxes be given to VCC at the time of his death.

Norton shuddered at the thought of a reporter with a copy of the eulogy he had given for Jack. The words "I wanted to be just like Jack" would be devastating, perhaps as bad as "I was Huggy Bear." Norton believed that he had extinguished this fire.

24) The Byrd Airport

Another target for the social justice warriors was the historic Harry Flood Byrd International Airport just west of Richmond. It was just an airfield when Harry Byrd was governor, but he envisioned that one day it could be a valuable asset to Virginia as a major airport.

As Senator Byrd helped to facilitate the growth of the project, it was used for military purposes, but Byrd knew commercial traffic would be more beneficial. In the early 1960's the airport really took off, so to speak. It started with a few major carriers, and by the early 1970's the airport had become a major US airport. As the home of American Airlines it developed into a major Richmond-area employer.

Byrd died in 1966, and the airport commission felt it would be fitting to name the airport after him. It didn't become controversial until a few decades later. By the 21st century there was strong support for a name change.

The airport was governed by a board of commissioners, who would have the sole authority to change the name. However, they were not inclined to do it. For one thing, it would be expensive to change the name, and the Byrd Airport was well known throughout the world. A rebranding could be expensive and risky. Those were two main concerns of the board

Nearly a quarter of all flights from China to the US come through the Byrd Airport. International travelers were not clamoring for a name change; no one canceled flights based on the name of the airport.

Elections Have Consequences

Jack Carter and the other social justice warriors saw the death of James Sayers as offering a great opportunity to take another crack at forcing an airport name change. Carter wanted to stage a Justice for James rally at the airport, but there are numerous logistical problems with that. In an interview, Carter explained to the online magazine *Socialism Today* how they were able to stage a protest and get a name change:

"Changing the Byrd Airport has been our dream for decades. However, it has been hard to get that done for many reasons. The commissioners are fairly insulated politically; that is, they are not elected and they have a set term, so it's hard to pressure them. Sure, we could stage protests outside their homes, and I have on a few occasions, but it's not always easy to find out where they live, and anyway, staging a protest at an official's home tends to do nothing more than upset the neighbors. Also, it's hard to stage a protest at an airport. First, the airports don't have room for staging or gathering of protesters. There is no place for protesters to really march or stand. Security is tight, so as soon as a dozen or so protesters are gathered, they are forced away, and if you don't have a ticket you can't enter the main areas of the airport. So, I had to come up with a new idea, something innovative. We had 100 protesters buy plane tickets. They then went into the concourse, and they had protest signs and materials in their carry-on bags. After a day of making a lot of noise, the Transportation Authority relented and agreed to change the name."

Thanks to the beneficence of Hollywood and a couple of Wall Street billionaires Carter's organization was flush with money, so they were able to buy plane tickets for over 100 protesters. Once there the protesters staged a sit-in, calling it Occupy Byrd

Elections Have Consequences

Airport. They demanded that the airport change its name, or there would be no peace and quiet.

Through Carter's fundraising, more tickets were given to more protesters, so the original occupiers could be replaced. There were enough tickets purchased to last for weeks. The message was perfectly clear: change the name or we won't go away.

After two days of occupation, the authority waved the white flag of surrender and announced that they would change the name. A blue-ribbon panel would be formed to find a suitable name. The authority also promised that the panel would be made up of a diverse group representing all of Virginia. They even offered Jack Carter a seat on the panel!

Jack commented on how easily churches and businesses cave to his social justice protests, "I stage a protest, the press shows up, and the target capitulates pretty quickly. They usually then hire me to help them find a new name! Lenin, who I did have my differences with, was right about at least one thing. The capitalist will sell you the rope to hang himself with," Carter laughingly declared.

The panel agreed to Jack's three conditions the new namesake of the airport would have to meet. First, the person could not have owned slaves or helped the slave industry; second, the person must have demonstrated a belief that black lives matter; third, they must not have abused Native Americans in any way. A reporter pointed out that under this standard the airport could not be named after Abraham Lincoln because he had fought Indians, and there was no evidence that Lincoln believed black lives mattered.

Elections Have Consequences

As a courtesy to Governor Norton, the airport authority gave him a heads up that they would cave in to the protesters and make a name change. Norton asked Beaman, "Why are they giving me a heads up? I don't care about a name change. I am not pushing for it."

"They're giving you the opportunity to publicly call for the name change first, so you can look like the hero for getting it done. You get the credit."

While he didn't really mind it being named after Byrd, Norton did understand the politics behind a name change. "Okay, maybe it's best to get in front of this caravan, Steve."

"That's a good way to look at it. Politics is like a caravan or a parade. When it gets long enough it's best to join in."

But Norton did ask for a favor. "Look, I have some concern that the name will be over-the-top politically correct—and stupid—so how about this. They give three names and I pick one."

"Okay, I think they will go for that."

Even before a new name was chosen, the Airport Authority removed the name Harry F. Byrd, and they even put a giant tarp over the statue. The tarp was borrowed from the Richmond Braves baseball team; they used it to cover the pitcher's mound at the Diamond during rain delays.

To stop the occupation, the airport promised to keep the statue covered until it could be removed. The hope was that with the Byrd statue covered, passions and tensions in the city could be calmed. An odd sight, no doubt: tens of thousands of commuters every day would see a giant beige canvas tarp draped over a statue.

The main expressway, known as Harry Byrd Drive,

Elections Have Consequences

temporarily changed to Black Lives Matter Drive. On the exit sign for the airport it looked like VDOT simply took black paint to cover the name, but left the word airport.

Carter said the combination of the death of James Sayers and the influx of money from Hollywood and New York helped make the name change campaign victorious.

Six months later, the Airport Authority sent the names to Norton. He was nervous about having to make the final decision. All his life he had known it as the Byrd Airport; now he would be responsible for a new name. Sure, the commission would give him some political cover, but he genuinely felt trepidation that the woke board would come up with three bad choices. Then what? Did he really want to upset his base by vetoing all the names? His hope rested in the co-chair of the commission, Attorney General Deb Foster. She was moderate and fairly sensible, or so Norton believed.

On a Monday morning, Beaman came to the governor's 3rd floor Capitol office to give him the news. A nervous Norton tried to feign disinterest. "Oh, have they already made a decision?"

A smiling Beaman responded, "Yes. Any guesses, before I open the envelope?"

Norton nonchalantly shuffled some papers, looked around, and said with a look of indifference, "I don't know, Harry Reems?"

Beaman frowned. "Oh come on, Governor, be serious. This is a huge decision. The Richmond airport is one of the busiest airports in America. It is nationally known."

Norton got more nervous as Beman opened the envelope. He read the names silently to himself. A look of relief came to his face.

Elections Have Consequences

Beaman, as if he were announcing the Oscar winner said, "The top choice, the Anthony Stephen Fauci International Airport!"

Norton audibly breathed a sigh of relief. He silently thought about it for a couple of seconds. On one hand he was glad the commission hadn't picked Fidel Castro or Colin Kapernick, but at the same time he was not thrilled with the choice.

"I don't know about this, Steve," a skeptical Norton said. "I'm sure he was a good doctor, but it seems to me that he made a number of big mistakes during the pandemic. Mask, no mask, and heck we were funding that lab in Wuhan where the virus may have come from, and Fauci was involved in that."

Beaman responded, "Governor, the board looked into it, and determined he did a good job. And he is a unifying person; he is one of the most admired men in the country. He is the one person whose name can unify people from all walks of life."

Norton seemed unconvinced. He pointed to another issue. "I realize that international travelers don't care if the airport is named after George Wallace or Henry Wallace, but it seems to me that the name must resonate with Virginians while also assuring them that we are committed to social justice. So why not a Virginian?"

"It's an international airport, so it doesn't need to be named after a Virginian. Naming it after Fauci would be acceptable to Virginians, and Dr. Fauci is greatly respected around the world, especially in China. Fauci's approval numbers are through the roof in Northern Virginia. Last poll I saw, single women in Fairfax County love him. He's like a rock star, and they stuck with you big time over Parrish. Your naming it after Fauci is a recognition and a thank you to your political base."

Elections Have Consequences

Norton, who had a veto on the final choice, optimistically asked, "Well, who's the runner up?"

"Someone we know, Leslie Byrne. She was the first woman elected to Congress from Virginia."

"I worked to get her elected, but I don't think we should name an airport after her. She served just one term, I believe." "Yes, but she broke the glass ceiling."

Norton seemed less than thrilled, to say the least. "How about the third choice?"

"Well, Governor, when I tell you the third choice, you'll be happy that Dr. Fauci was the first choice."

A curious Norton perked up and asked, "Who's the third choice? "

"Colin Kapernick."

Norton paused for a few seconds, thought about it, and replied, "Okay, Dr. Fauci it is. We already have a high school in Leesburg named after Kapernick; surely that should satisfy the social justice warriors. We'll go with Fauci as the namesake of the airport."

Beaman shook his head. "Well, the social justice warriors won't be satisfied until every name, of every school, every street, and every monument is changed, to reflect the ideology of social justice, but I think Fauci will be acceptable to the mob."

While Fauci was not considered a social justice warrior, he was viewed favorably by the left, for two main reasons: he is a scientist and a career federal employee. Beaman explained why Fauci was the best choice. "Voters who had a high opinion of Dr. Fauci were 80 percent more likely to have voted for you than for Parrish. His fans are your voters. So pick Fauci and you're honoring your political base."

Elections Have Consequences

Norton issued a chirp about the name change:

"The Airport Authority has recommended that the Byrd Airport in Richmond be renamed in honor of Dr. Anthony Fauci. I wholeheartedly agree with this decision. A great choice! Indeed, an inspired choice! While not a Virginian, Dr. Fauci provided expertise, strength and calm leadership to help our country cope with and come out of the Great Pandemic of 2020. Anthony Fauci Airport–I love the sound of that!"

The name change caused one fun debate. Angela Parrish chirped: "Will the statue of Dr. Fauci out front depict him wearing one mask or two? Will he be depicted with his sleeve rolled up ready to take another jab?" To avoid that controversy the board decided to go without a mask, but to depict him with a stethoscope around his neck.

The process of the name change would take a couple of years, and by the time of the statue unveiling Norton was out of office. However, he was invited to the unveiling. He was even given the honor of pulling the rope that uncovered the statue. The crowd of about 50 people marveled at the 10 foot statue of Dr. Fauci. It had a dark gray patina and it was thick. Reminiscent of an old Soviet statue of Lenin, Fauci had an heroic pose, gazing into the heavens, a stethoscope around his neck. His right hand was clenched into a fist, and at the base of the statue in bold letters a prayer:

"May Science Always Trump Superstition."

25) The Left Takes Over

Reverend Brand convened a meeting of progressive Democrats from the House of Delegates and the State Senate to agree on a common strategy moving forward. Now, as a member of the administration, a cabinet member, she probably shouldn't have been there, let alone leading the legislative effort. But in or out of the cabinet, she had become the de facto head of the state Democrat Party and the social justice movement in Virginia.

She once said privately about any conflict of interest between being a member of the executive branch and advocating legislation, "I am a member of the cabinet 9-5 Monday through Friday and in my free time I am a social justice warrior fighting to change Virginia."

The legislators met in Thornburg, right off 95 at the Best Western. The hotel offered space and a convenient location, between Richmond and Northern Virginia. There were about 25 progressive Democrat legislators in attendance. Brand insisted that the meeting be off the record, and everyone in attendance had to check their phones, and any recording devices at the door. Brand sternly told legislators, "When I say off the record, I mean off the record."

Brand started off the meeting with her take:

"In every crisis comes an opportunity. We, as progressives, were all upset and shocked to learn about Norton's past, and his commendation of a police officer involved in a questionable abuse case, but let us acknowledge that he has signed most of our bills to date. And with all the pressure he is now under, I think we can push for our boldest proposals yet. Indeed, at a moment like this we have an obligation to be bold. And let's not wait until next year when the General Assembly reconvenes. Let's push for a special session. We can use this opportunity to change Virginia forever."

Legislators applauded.

She then went around the room to allow every legislator to have 10 minutes to speak. Each legislator named the priorities they would like to see advanced in legislation. However, some legislators strayed into other areas.

Delegate Glenda Jones of Norfolk said she wanted to see same-day voting registration, even suggesting that without such a needed reform injustice and "a feeling of alienation" would continue.

Many suggested that new gun control measures were needed, especially bans on high capacity magazines. Delegate Richard W. Stump pointed to the riots, although he used the word protests, as reason to move forward with additional "common sense" gun control measures. He said, "There is violence in the streets. We need tougher gun control measures as soon as possible. Without the state getting a firm control of who is getting guns, we can't get a handle on gun violence."

Others suggested the need to expand Medicaid and make more money for school lunch programs available. State Senator Sandoval said something about global warming, environmental racism and defunding the police. Most recommended getting rid of bail. Delegate Stump denounced bail as the equivalent of a "modern-day debtors prison."

Delegate Sally Jenkins of Lynchburg touched on the thorny issue of the "Defund the Police" movement. She had taken over her husband's seat when he died. "Red" Jenkins was a good old southern Democrat. As conservative as they come, he was no fan of liberals, especially those who came from, as he called it, "occupied territory," referring to Northern Virginia.

Sadly, he died and his wife ran on his name. She won, and 20 years later she was still holding the seat, despite being one of the most progressive members of the House. Known as "Aunt Sally" to most of her constituents, she was considered by most pundits to be an incredibly good politician. She voted with the progressive wing of her party almost right down the line for nearly two decades, including abolishing Right to Work, "reforming" police immunity protection, divesting Virginia retirement funds from Israel-based companies, against requiring minors from getting parental notification before getting an abortion, in favor of giving people an option of not reporting their gender on drivers licenses, for college tuition subsidies for descendants of slaves, for free legal advice to ilegal aliens, and other far left initiatives. One political pundit compared the two saying, "Red was to the right of Attila the Hun, and Aunt Sally is to the left of Karl Marx, yet their constituents in Lynchburg always thought of them as moderate Democrats."

However, despite having a voting record that only the far left could love, Aunt Sally Jenkins had an ability to come across as a moderate, reasonable, and intelligent person. She could show up on voters' doorsteps, talk politics, and charm the heck out of them. The voters, unless they saw her voting record, would close the door and think, *She seems like a reasonable moderate.*

Delegate Jenkins, however, did concede, "This Defund the Police nonsense is going to get us killed at the polls. Two things

Elections Have Consequences

I don't want to hear: we Democrats are for socialism and defund the police."

Brand responded, "Delegate Jenkins, I agree completely. We are not going to defund the police. No county in Virginia is going to do it, and no city is going to do it. The point of the Defunding the Police movement is to put pressure on moderate Democrats, mostly, to move them our way on police reform. So we say to moderates like Norton, `If you are not going to defund the police, then at least move towards making the police force 50 percent minority. That could be a happy compromise."

The others generally agreed that defunding the police would not be in the reform package.

Sandoval conceded that this round of riots had nothing to do with global warming but "There is a sense of unease among the people of Virginia, because they know we are destroying the planet. Such destruction is causing angst, and if it's not reversed, we'll have panic and despair."

Reverend Brand brought them back to the crisis at hand. "I like all these ideas, but we need to focus on the present emergency and how we progressives can gain from it. There is systemic racism in our police forces here in Virginia, and a lack of fairness in our criminal justice system. To calm the protests, we need reform now. I am suggesting here, and I will suggest to the governor, a special session be called to deal with this crisis."

Sandoval then chimed in. "But Madam Secretary, when are we finally going to address environmental injustice? If not now, when, and by whom?"

Brand just glared at her with an unmistakable look that said *Shut up or I will reach across the table and strangle you.* Sandoval seemed to pick up on the signal and meekly kept quiet.

Elections Have Consequences

Brand outlined her strategy. "We need the special session by the end of this summer to push criminal justice reform, and then we push voting reform in the regular session."

All agreed that would be a great plan, but Delegate Jones expressed doubt. "Norton has expressed opposition to special sessions, and several years ago he criticized his predecessor for calling one. So for him to do it would be an obvious reversal. For political reasons he probably won't want one."

Delegate Carwile pointed out that this would not be the first flip-flop for Norton. He opposed Critical Race Theory mandates for schools and then signed the bill. Several legislators optimistically chimed in, "That's right."

Senator Siebers said, "Look, we know Norton opposed his predecessor's call for a special session, but the circumstances are fundamentally different this time. We have a real emergency, not a flu outbreak." The legislators applauded.

Everyone agreed with Brand's plan. The focus of the special session would be limited to the issue of criminal justice reform, and all talk of abolishing the Electoral College and other issues would be left for a future regular session.

The group put out a confidential memo of understanding for other Democrat legislators who could not attend. It declared that people of color, more specifically black males, are disproportionately convicted and sentenced to prison. Therefore, the criminal justice system must be "systematically racist." To counter that, they wanted to reduce sentences for all criminal offenses and even a reduction of criminal laws. In short, they wanted to do everything they could to keep people out of jail. The police must have their power diminished. While they didn't support abolishing or defunding the police, they did believe that some money should be redirected to programs designed to keep people away from crime, such as more money for after school programs and other investments. They concluded that a special session must be called to address the present crisis.

As Brand outlined in the memo of understanding (which later came to be known as the "Thornburg communiqué"), "We need four or five bills to present during the special session. We can't overreach by talking about other issues. All these bills must be related to criminal justice and police reform. Then, once criminal justice reform is passed in the special session, we will move to election reform, which will include same-day voter registration, no excuse absentee voting, and ballot harvesting."

It was agreed that State Senator Scott Siebers from Fairfax would be in charge of writing a criminal justice reform package. By profession he was a criminal defense attorney and former counsel for the ACLU. The legislators were united on the need for a common strategy. They would petition the governor to call for a special session in order to get meaningful criminal justice reform passed. In effect, no special session, no peace.

In the early afternoon, they took their final 10 minute break. Brand asked Delegate Julius Jones, Delegate Carwile, and Senator Seibers for a moment in private. They moved out into the hallway.

Jones was one of the most influential African-American leaders in Virginia. In the early 1960's his father, Delegate Julius Jones Sr., became the first black member of the House of Delegates, and had also clerked for Justice Thurgood Marshall.

Brand said, "I want to talk privately with you three for a few minutes. You are the leaders, and I have confidence in you. The only reason Sandoval is here is to help us sell this package to young people, so feel free to ignore her in writing the bills." The three legislators nodded. "You three are the brains behind this, and the leaders. Look, we have a real opportunity here, and let's remember we don't need to be timid. We can press for as progressive a package as possible."

Siebers asked, "What do you think the governor will accept?"

Brand replied, "He'll accept what he's given. For the most part, the only things I don't think he will accept are eliminating limited immunity for police officers and defunding the police. However, I think we can move him much nearer our positions on those things as well. In other words, we can still fund the police, but it will come with strings. Other than that, the sky's the limit. The Huggy Bear scandal and now the James Sayers killing has him really scared. There might even be the possibility of another scandal."

Carwile wondered, "Another scandal?"

Brand was bluffing; she wanted to raise the optimism of the legislators that Norton would remain weak as governor, and therefore easy to roll.

"I have no concrete information, but from my experience in any scandal there is always a second shoe to drop. Maybe Beaman knows if there's more, but he won't tell us since he's loyal to Norton, who is probably his best—and maybe only—friend in the world. But I think there is something else that Norton knows might get out. It's just a hunch, but Norton is probably scared that there is something else, so he'll need to cling to us. We are his lifeline. And he, like all governors, wants a legacy, some accomplishments to point to. He wants to be called a transformational governor by the overpaid, underworked professors and scholars who wear tweed jackets with patches on the sleeves. Well, if he signs on to what we want, he can have his legacy. He can have that headline, 'Ronnie Norton: The Greatest Governor Since Jerry Lee Baliles.' The fawning praise of Willow Bush. The adulation of the editorial boards of the *Daily Dispatch* and the *Press Democrat*. Well, he can have that. All he has to do is sign our bills. So let us proceed on the basis that he will do what we want. Be bold!"

Brand feared, based on remarks that she was hearing from the legislators, that they were softening their views on Norton. Brand continued, "Look, I know he signed the Critical Race Theory mandatory instruction in public schools bill, and that's great, but that doesn't mean all is forgiven or forgotten. We progressives must remember that. No let up, no quarter. He must be aware that with us progressives he is still in the doghouse. As long as he is governor he must prove that he is an anti-racist. Sure, he's not a Republican, so he's not really a racist, but that's not good enough. He must prove he is an anti-racist. So Julius, we need to apply some more pressure on him."

Jones responded, "Yes, I agree, but how do we do that?"

"Julius, let it be known to the press that so far you don't think Norton has proven that he's much better than a Republican. Heck, even say a couple of nice things about Morrison. That will get Norton's attention. Morrison is a friend of Norton's, but despite their friendship I suspect that Norton has always been a little jealous of him. So saying a nice thing or two about Morrison will sting."

"Okay, but I can't say we would back Morrison." Brand nodded, but Jones said, "I would be willing to say that he could be an 'able governor.'"

Elections Have Consequences

Brand smiled and said, "Excellent, or say he has a lovely family, or that he's a good man. That will do the trick."

Jones wasted no time in advancing the bluff. "I have an interview this afternoon with Maddy Clack at my office; I will float it then."

"Excellent. When Norton hears the interview tonight on the news he will freak out." Brand smiled, rubbed her hands together, and muttered one word, "Excellent."

She then went back to reconvene the meeting and closed it with a prayer. She asked the members to bow their heads. "Lord, we thank You for this blessed day. We ask, as did Your faithful servant John Brown, who You sent to us nearly 200 years ago to try to save our country, we invoke his name and his prayer that You have mercy on our guilty land. We beg for forgiveness and we ask for Your guidance that we do Your will in ending racism, homophobia, transphobia and all other forms of bigotry. Help us do what is right and avoid all sin." She ended with "Amen and Awomen."

Raising her head she said, "Thank you all for coming. We will meet again soon, and long live the revolution." She then raised her fist into the air. Only a couple of legislators did the same.

***

Delegate Jones had an impressive office overlooking Capitol Square, the very office that Hank Parrish once occupied. Jones, because of his seniority, was able to get it when it became available.

The walls of his office were lined with pictures from his distinguished career. There were pictures of him with Ted Kennedy, Thurgood Marshall, Nelson Mandela, John Lewis, Doug

Wilder, framed letters, news clippings, and plaques. Behind his desk was a bust of Martin Luther King.

As they were about to start the interview, Jones noticed Maddy Clack looking out the window, admiring the view. The large window provided a panoramic vista of Capitol Square, from the Governor's Mansion to the Capitol building to the General Assembly building. Right outside the window was the statue of George Washington pointing south.

Jones said to Clack, "Do you know why the leadership is given offices facing Capitol Square?"

Clack thought it was obvious. She responded, "Because it's a great view; certainly better than looking out at 9th Street."

Jones laughed and said, "Yes, true, but the real reason is strategic. It's for the purpose of gathering intelligence." Clack didn't understand.

Jones explained, "The Speaker of the House and Majority Leader can see all the delegates and senators walk between the General Assembly building and the Capitol building. They can see who walks next to each other and who stays far apart. It can give a hint as to which member gets along with which. Over the course of a session, the leader can identify cliques, which can be important. And the view goes all the way to the Governor's Mansion, so they can see which members are going to talk to the governor."

As Jones spoke, he could see that she was looking at the iconic statue of Washington. Jones said, "That statue is of Washington pointing south. It was under Washington's arm that Jefferson Davis was sworn in as President of the Confederacy. In fact, that statue was displayed on the seal of the Confederacy. When Winston Churchill came to stay with the governor in the late

Elections Have Consequences

1920's, he took a walk around Capitol Square and stopped right in front of that statue to admire it, much like you're doing now. Well, a lady came up to him, a politically active Richmonder, and she was in favor of Prohibition, the temperance movement, that wanted to ban alcohol, and she said to Churchill, 'Will you put in a good word for the temperance movement while you're here in America meeting with lawmakers?' Well Churchill, who was a man who loved alcohol, turned to her and said words to the effect of 'Madam, on this issue we will have to agree to disagree.'"

Clack and Jones laughed at the story. As they stood silently gazing out the window at the statue, Jones quoted some of Churchill's most famous lines. "We shall fight them on the beaches, we shall fight them in the hills, we shall fight them on the streets. However hard or long the road may be, we shall NEVER surrender." They remained silent, contemplating the Washington statue.

As they were gazing out the window, they could see Angela Parrish walking from the Capitol to her office. She was met near the Washington statue by Republican Delegate Neil Matricardi from Culpeper, who was on his way to the Capitol when they stopped to talk. Jones and Clack watched for a few seconds. Neil was clean cut, in his mid 40's, always well dressed. He looked like an Eagle Scout. Despite being in different houses, Matricardi usually helped get Angela's bills passed in the House. Angela had supported his first race, and her PAC "Angie's List" provided lots of campaign cash. With her help he won the nomination and had managed to keep his seat for several terms.

At first Angela seemed happy to see him, but it didn't take long for them to notice that Parrish and Matricardi were getting into an argument. Neither had pleasant expressions. Parrish's campaign smile had left her face. Of course, they could not hear what Parrish was saying, but she was speaking fast. Matricardi assumed a defensive posture, shaking his head and throwing his hands up. Angela also started waving her arms, seemingly pointing back at the Capitol building in making a point. She became more agitated as she spoke and then started jabbing her finger into his lapel. At one point she seemed to stomp her foot.

Jones chuckled. "I like seeing disarray on the Republican side of the aisle." They then sat down for the interview. Jones explained his thinking to Maddy Clack for nearly 30 minutes. Jones was always generous with his time to reporters. At the end of the interview he dropped the intended bomb on Norton.

"I think with all that has come out about Norton's past and the news that he gave a commendation to the officer involved in this recent horrible shooting, well, it causes many to doubt Norton's ability to govern. I rarely agree with Morrison, but he is an honorable man, and one who can lead the state at this darkest hour."

Clack followed up, "So you think Norton should have stepped down?"

"I didn't say that, but I think Norton still has a ways to go to reestablish trust with progressive Democrats, and as far as his legacy, he does not have much to show. We shall see what he does over his last two years."

The governor finally came around and agreed with Brand, going against the advice of Beaman, Thompson and Jackson, and called for a special session to take up criminal justice reform.

26) Operation Macacca

During the gubernatorial campaign Beaman became obsessed with the idea of catching Angela Parrish in what is known as a Macaca moment. In Virginia politics, that is where you get your opponent on tape saying imprudent things that the media could twist into something offensive.

The origin of the term dates back to Senator George Allen and his run in with a supporter of his opponent, who had a video camera. Allen used the word "macacca," which was viewed as a slur. Democrats and the media used it against him.

All during the gubernatorial campaign, Beaman tried to catch Parrish making a gaffe on camera. He had teams of volunteers following her around with recording devices, but he never got anything. Parrish was more disciplined than Beaman thought; for the most part she kept on message and stayed on script. After all, she was a daughter of a politician so she knew how the game was played.

However, even after Norton won, Beaman still kept trying. Most would have moved on after the election; in fact, it is an unwritten rule of politics that after the election recording devices are turned off. But the tenacious Beaman continued to send out volunteers with tape recorders and video cameras to her district in Manassas, trying to get something at her town hall meetings and at public events.

Beaman got his volunteers from a pool of young Democrats, eager to get involved in politics. He found volunteers who would be willing and discreet, or so he thought. For Beaman, it was more than just opposition research, more than just catching someone

Elections Have Consequences

in gaffe. Beaman told one volunteer his view of oppo research, a view that he acquired from the novel, *All The King's Men*. He said, "As Jack Burden discovered in that novel, everybody has a history. So I guess you can say we are historians. We find that history. And because man is naturally sinful, there will be some things he or she doesn't want others to know. But call me curious. I like to find that history."

For over two years he got nothing, so Beaman decided to take it up a notch. Instead of following her at public events, he tried to catch her on her off time, running errands and going to the store. He even decided to use hidden cameras. Public events where recording devices are out in the open is to be expected, but hidden devices in non-public settings is sleazy and unethical. In many states it is illegal.

Beaman put together a team of operatives who were trained on how to hide the recording device or camera. They would follow her, find her routine, and then when she was in a store they would go up to her and try to egg her into making some intemperate remarks—remarks that might not be too bad, but bad enough to be twisted. Oftentimes they would go in teams. One would ask her a question and the other would record her from nearby.

After months of work, Beaman and his goons got a break, and they found a pattern. On Saturday mornings, Parrish would go to Manassas Battlefield and jog for a couple of hours, then go to Starbucks for a coffee. Angela loved the Battlefield. It provided miles of beautiful space to run, and it also had a special meaning to her and her family. Angela's mother's side were Dogans; they owned some land where the Battle of Manassas was fought.

Elections Have Consequences

Beaman thought this could be a great opportunity for an operative to question her in Starbucks. Her guard might be down, unlike at a town hall meeting. He also gave them an incentive: a volunteer who caught a gaffe would get a photo op with Governor Norton in the Governor's Mansion.

One operative was to follow her to the battlefield and when she left he'd alert the operative at the Starbucks. This operative, Brad Gray, sat in his car in the parking lot, binoculars trained on Angela as she engaged in her stretching routine, leaning against a cannon near the Stonewall Jackson statue.

He couldn't take his eyes off her. One thing struck him, other than her pleasing form. People kept walking by Angela seemingly oblivious to her, as if they didn't know who she was. Joggers passed by her, and families with kids walked by her, and yet they said nothing to her, or even seemed to pay any attention to or acknowledge her. That's Angela Parrish!

He thought, *Do they not realize that the woman stretching before them is Angela Parrish? A woman who came within one point of becoming the first woman governor of Virginia?* Perhaps they knew and were just respecting her privacy, but somehow it seemed odd to him that Angela could simply blend in with the crowd.

About an hour later, he could see Angela coming back from her run, out from the woods, the same woods Jackson and his reinforcements came out of during the Battle of First Manassas. She was not running anymore, but walking back past the row of cannons towards her car in the parking lot.

As Angela got closer to her car, the operative sunk down in his seat to avoid being seen, just in case she might recognize him. According to the plan, once she left the park he would follow her and alert the next operative if she was heading to the Starbucks, but something alarmed him.

She had been in the car for at least five minutes, and yet still had not turned on the engine. She just sat there. *Why is she just sitting in her car?* The operative started to become paranoid, *could she be calling the police?* Gray's heart began racing; an idea flashed into his mind. He wondered, might she have sensed he was following her, and now she was calling the police?

And as soon as the police arrived she would come out and identify him. A few more minutes passed, and the operative thought, *Should I just leave and get out of here to avoid arrest on a stalking charge?*

But then he could see her tail lights illuminate. *Oh, thank goodness.* She started to back out of her parking spot and drive out of the park. Gray then informed the next volunteer, who would be at the Starbucks where Angela went to buy coffee.

Parrish made it to the Starbucks, ordered her drink, and as she was waiting, Beaman's operative went up to her. He claimed he was a Republican constituent who was upset with all the unrest, as well as upset that the priceless, historic statues were being torn down. He also expressed outrage that the Byrd Airport would undergo a name change. All these things were designed to get a rise out of Parrish, to induce her to rant.

The video and audio were not of great quality, but it was clear enough that it was her, and it was also clear enough to make it obvious that even without makeup, sweating and in jogging clothes, Parrish was still beautiful. Parrish was not in a good mood that morning and she let the rioters have it:

"We have to tear down some of the most beautiful and historic statues, because these spoiled, privileged kids throw a

Elections Have Consequences

temper tantrum? What happened at the Byrd Airport was outrageous. These smelly kids, many of whom live at home with their parents, tried to shut down commerce to change the name of an airport, which was named after the guy who built it. These kids never built anything of note."

She got madder. "I am sorry this girl got killed, but why did she (inaudible)..it was okay to tear down a several ton public statue? I have no idea. Norton should have stopped it, should have dispersed the crowd, but he didn't. He doesn't have the guts to stand up to the mob and his left wing. He is not a leader, he is a sheep. What a disgrace."

The operatives checked the video. Eureka, we got it, they declared. Beaman was in the office on that Saturday. As a special advisor to the governor, Beaman was given an office in an historic building, which was once the famed Hotel Richmond, across from Capitol Square. The state ended up buying the building and renovating it. General Lee had visited the Hotel Richmond, and in the 20th century the leaders of the Byrd political machine would gather at the hotel on election night to watch the election returns.

Beaman had a couple of phones in his office, and one was reserved for what he called "black ops": special projects like following legislators and secretly recording what they said. His "black ops" also included having legislators followed in search for potential blackmail information. Beaman got the money for his operation by diverting some Executive Branch operations money and from private donors.

The phone rang, and Beaman picked up. The voice on the other end simply said. "Operation Macaca, mission accomplished."

Elections Have Consequences

Beaman breathed into the phone, "Excellent... Excellent. Send me the recording."

The video and audio weren't of high quality, but there was Parrish. Her hair was up; she was still trying to play the politician and smile, yet you could tell she really just wanted to get her latte and leave. In the background you could hear the sounds of a store, "Gary, your order is ready" and "What can I get for you?" A chime would sound as new customers entered the store.

Beaman watched it, and while there was nothing too damaging the friendly Virginia political media would certainly air it, and probably at least try to enhance the audio.

Beaman thought it would at least take the heat temporarily off Norton. *The media jackals will have this distraction for a day or two.* Indeed, all the Virginia media and some national media ended up running the Parrish Starbucks video.

The Washington Press Democrat ran a front-page story, below the fold, "State Senator's Off the Cuff Comment Sparks Outrage." *The Prince William Times* tracked her down for a comment.

The media seized on three things: her claims that the protesters were smelly, privileged, and unemployed. Parrish told the Times and the media in general:

"I was referring to the protesters at the airport who were trying to block commerce for 48 straight hours. If they've been occupying the airport for 48 hours, they have not had access to a shower. So I did use the word smelly. If you haven't showered in 48 hours, it is reasonable to imagine a person might smell. In addition, if someone can take two days off in the middle of the week, odds are many if not most of them are unemployed or underemployed. Governor Norton has allowed rioters to run wild, to turn our state into a college campus. Sure, I resent it, and I am angry."

Steve Cohen commented on Chirp, "State Senator Parrish lost her cool. Name calling is never okay. The young people are right to speak out against racism and injustice."

Ironically, Operation Macacca was not what the press used to go after Parrish. They used her own words spoken to a reporter, words twisted and edited in a campaign to have her censured by the State Senate. This would take place a few weeks later during a special session in Richmond.

***

It's only natural that legislative members engage in some heated rhetoric from time to time, which can happen when discussing emotional subjects, and sometimes rhetoric turns into demagoguery and outright falsehoods. Such a thing happened in Richmond during the special session. One morning, State Senator Sandoval released a chirp: "Many police officers are willing to shoot people of color in the streets like dogs. Sad. We need criminal justice reform now!"

The media, for the most part, didn't spend much time decoding Sandoval's chirps, because they knew that they were embarrassing to Sandoval. The media's narrative was that Sandoval was brilliant, a narrative which must always be upheld, not debunked.

But a Virginia reporter from the United Press Service and a few other reporters spotted Angela Parrish walking down the hall of the Capitol Building on her way to a meeting. With a microphone in hand, the reporter asked Parrish, "Did you read State Senator Sandoval's chirp critical of the police this morning?

Elections Have Consequences

Do you have a comment?" The reporter didn't care about the substance of the chirp. but knew it would get a rise out of Parrish.

Ordinarily, Parrish, like most people, ignored Sandoval's chirps. They learned the maxim "Never get into an argument with a fool," but this morning was different. The chirp was a hot topic at the Republican legislators morning breakfast meeting. So with the chirp fresh in mind, Parrish replied, "If the Senator doesn't like it here she can always go back to where she came from.

And the other thing about her chirp. I can't think of a single case of a police officer shooting a dog in the streets."

With that Angela smiled, turned her back, and started to walk away. Then several feet down the hall, she turned her head back towards the reporters, smiled again, and gave a little wave as she continued walking. One of the reporters turned to another reporter, and said, "That, my friend, is what is known as a 'kiss my ass wave.'"

The hypersensitive media saw some potential here. In the Stephen Cohen Media Room in the basement of the Capitol, reporters were brainstorming the latest news. One reporter, no doubt a rising media star, perhaps even a future *Press Democrat* contributor, suggested, "Didn't Parrish suggest that a legislator of color leave the country?"

His colleagues were impressed. "By golly, I think we have something here," said a reporter. But since the guy asking the question was a young cub reporter, this great angle had to go to someone higher up the totem pole.

So, with a promise for a favor in the future, Bhavna Agarwal chirped out the story with the comment "Angela Parrish tells Sandoval, Go back to where you came from." It took off, not just

Elections Have Consequences

in Virginia, but nationally. Many outlets carried the story "Republican Legislator Tells Woman of Color, Go Back to Where You Came From." MNN had a whole round table discussion on the scandal.

The story fizzled after a couple days, but Democrats brought it back at the end of the special session.

27) Lord Fairfax Community College

In addition to his *Daily Dispatch* column and his radio and TV appearances, Cohen regularly spoke to political science classes across the Commonwealth. In fact, he almost always accepted invitations to speak at colleges and universities. Since pretty much all the professors were progressive Democrats, they loved having him. His lectures would combine Virginia political history with today's politics.

One affectation that Cohen acquired from being around college kids was the knowledge and use of their key slang terms, such as "No cap," "Lowkey," "Highkey," "Keeping it 100," "Clap back," and his most overused and annoying "I know, right?" The ever politically correct Cohen wasn't above a little cultural appropriation of his own. For example, if he had to seat students he might tell another student to "budge up," which means scoot or move up. Another common expression: a student might make a point and Cohen would often reply, "I def tote, I def tote," which translates to "definitely I totally agree."

Cohen's other affectation involved his clothes. When he went onto a campus he almost always wore the same Hart Schaffner and Marx tweed jacket with patches on the sleeves. He thought it made him look like a professor; he once saw a picture of one of his heroes, Virginius Dabney, wearing a similar jacket. He liked the jacket even more when a store clerk at Franco's assured him, "Yes, I sold this very jacket to Professor Dabney."

He mixed in banal cliches and non sequiturs from time to time, to show that he understood and agreed with the woke

Elections Have Consequences

justice revolutionaries. He would say things like, "I am a capitalist; I just think the rich should pay their fair share of taxes," or "I have many European friends and I have a tough time defending or even explaining our healthcare system. We need to make healthcare a right like every other civilized country does."

Cohen accepted an invitation to speak to a class at Lord Fairfax Community College. His message on that particular day included a summation of Cohen's belief that each generation fights essentially the same battle, on the same ground as the previous generation. The specific issues might change, but it is essentially the same fight between left and right. Cohen, a movie buff and former movie critic, could not help but use a movie to make a point. He asked the students, "How many of you have seen the movie *Groundhog Day?*"

Most of them were born after 2000, so no one raised their hand. He explained that the movie was about a guy who kept reliving the same day over and over again. "Virginia politics, indeed all politics, is like that movie. It's the same battle over and over. No defeat is ever permanent and no victory is ever final." Cohen joked, "I sometimes feel like I'm Bill Murray. In covering Virginia politics, for me every day is Groundhog Day." The kids didn't really get the joke.

Cohen digressed from his lecture to tell the students a story. He liked to sprinkle his lectures with anecdotes and Virginia political stories to make a point:

"Okay, since you don't remember the movie *Groundhog Day*, I am not going to ask how many of you were alive in 1978." The students laughed. "I, by the way, was just a kid," more laughter, "but that was, for a previous generation of Virginia conservatives,

Elections Have Consequences

a pivotal year. In 1978 I was a young person just starting to follow politics. But 1978 was the year of the Obenshain tragedy.

"That was the year where Virginia conservatives finally took control of the Republican party and nominated Richard Obenshain for the United States Senate. Obenshain was special, a firebrand conservative, but not a knuckle-dragging reactionary. He was smart, principled, and articulate. He was part of the New Right, part of the Reagan and Goldwater wing of the party.

"At the time, the Virginia Republican Party was dominated by moderate Republicans, like Godwin, Holton and Dalton. But with Richard Obenshain, the right took over. They had finally arrived, or so they thought.

"Obenshain was nominated in a state convention held at the old Richmond Coliseum, which was packed to the rafters. And Obenshain won! But for conservatives, the dream turned into a nightmare, the greatest nightmare for Virginia conservatives since July 3rd,1863. Several weeks after he won the nomination, his campaign plane crashed, just a mile short of the airport's runway in Chesterfield County He died, at only 42. The party had to have a new nominee, and beyond the personal tragedy of the death of a 42 year old man, was the realization for conservatives that Obenshain was irreplaceable. Now according to state law, the state Central Committee of the Republican party had the power to select a new nominee.

"Then, like today, the Republican Party was divided. The Obenshain people were bound and determined to find a conservative, and not to nominate another RINO, or what we might call today an establishment Republican." Cohen joked, "Or a Republican that would go on MNN."

Elections Have Consequences

The joke went over the kids' heads. "Well, there were enough Obenshain people on the state central committee to block a RINO, or so they thought. The logical choice, it would seem, would be just to nominate the runner up from the convention, John Warner. Right? After all, if something happens to Miss America and she steps down, the runner up takes over, or as happens here in Virginia, if Miss Virginia has to step down for any reason the next transsexual in line takes over." Cohen smiled and said, "Sorry, just a joke." A couple of kids laughed, but most either groaned or booed.

Cohen continued the story. "Well, the runner up for the Republican nomination was former secretary of the Navy, John Warner." In order to be clear for the students, Cohen reminded them that it was "John, not Mark Warner, but to the Obenshain folks John Warner was a RINO. Totally unacceptable."

All kinds of names were mentioned to replace Obenshain. The first choice was Mills Godwin, the popular former two-term governor. But Godwin didn't want the job. Other names came up: Nathan Miller, Wyatt Durrette, Congressman Caldwell Butler. I am not sure if Stan Parris was mentioned or not." Cohen tapped his fingers on the lectern as he thought. He asked himself a question, "Was Parris mentioned or not? Well, anyway, none seemed right.

"Warner made the most sense; he could fund the campaign, and as I said he was the runner up at the convention and he had a statewide network of supporters. So the Warner people started lobbying the state Central Committee. They needed to persuade enough conservatives, that is, Obenshain people, that Warner could be trusted to advance the conservative movement, that he

Elections Have Consequences

was not too much of a RINO. The Warner people set up a meeting between Warner and members of the state Central Committee. It took place in a suite at the old John Marshall Hotel. And for a couple of hours members of the committee came in to question, really to interrogate Warner, in an attempt to make sure he was sufficiently conservative and could be trusted."

Cohen then got to the point of his story. "Now there is one little known part of this episode in Virginia political history that I want to tell you about. One of Warner's aides with him that day was a young volunteer by the name of Henry Parrish. I don't think Henry was in the legislature yet, but he was a GOP activist from Manassas. He helped set up the meeting and also helped brief Warner. You are probably too young to know who Henry, or as most knew him Hank, Parrish was, but I am sure you have heard of his daughter." Cohen paused and then in a low voice said, "Angela Parrish. Now think of the irony. Today the leader of Virginia's conservative movement, in effect today's Richard Obenshain, is Angela Parrish. Hank Parrish's kid! The guy that briefed John Warner that day at the John Marshall Hotel on how to answer attacks by conservatives. Hank knew Warner was no conservative; he and Warner were moderate Republicans." Cohen added reflectively, "Virginia conservatives would walk over broken glass to vote for Angela Parrish. I think about that irony and I get goosebumps."

For the final ten minutes of the lecture Cohen agreed to take questions from the students. The College Republicans had prepared for Cohen's appearance. Actually, they prepared for an ambush. They had their members scattered throughout the room, not bunched together as normal, and to throw Cohen off; that is, to make sure he could not tell which students were College Republicans. They had members who were non-white and female ready with questions. Each member had six questions written on a card. When one question was asked, they checked it off and moved on to the next.

The first question was, "Mr. Cohen, you said regarding the governor's race that the media, 'Played it down the middle,' that there was no 'obvious example of media bias.' Then how do you explain the fact that we heard stories, unsubstantiated and anonymous, that Angela Parrish made disparaging remarks about black people during her days in college, but we heard nothing about Norton's taste for putting shoe polish on his face and dressing up as a black pimp named Huggy Bear, whom he called his 'alter ego.' No media bias?"

Cohen smiled and with a confident wave of the hand explained, "When I said we, I meant the Virginia media, and in that I include the DC media, and of course my paper. We didn't dig up stories of the candidates' activities in college or high school. The story of Parrish making derogatory remarks about black people while in school at Charlottesville were aired by a left of center, non-Virginia source, *The Metropolitan*."

The student pushed back, "No, *The Washington Press Democrat* had five front page stories about the charge."

Cohen responded, "Yes, but only talking about the effect of the story on the campaign, not assessing whether the story was true or not."

Another student also asked about media bias. "I grew up in Fairfax, and I am old enough to remember the DC sniper case. When Parrish handled the prosecution, the media heaped praise on her all day. Then she ran for office as a Republican and the media turned on her. The media is not biased against Republicans?"

Cohen again kept his cool. "Well, there is a difference. A prosecutor is different from a political candidate. Everyone, including the media, wanted to see her succeed in the prosecution of the snipers, so the reports on her were somewhat glowing, I admit, but once she became a candidate for public office, well, the media had to become somewhat adversarial. I don't think the media was any less tough on Norton." As evidence of the media being tough on Norton Cohen added, "The media reported on the failure of Norton to properly report his stock holding in the Virginia company Pocahontas Energy."

That story lasted 48 hours. Norton owned the stock, but he did not report it, because he thought the value of his stock was under the threshold. He said it gained in value, and he didn't realize it in time to make the report.

One student asked Cohen, "Two weeks before the election the *Press Democrat* used unnamed sources to say Parrish called veterans 'suckers, losers and sheep.' That is yellow journalism, but even if you think it's okay to use anonymous sources, doesn't the fact that the story was run two weeks from election day prove the *Washington Press Democrat*'s bias?"

Cohen didn't want to criticize another newspaper; the unwritten code is that reporters, especially print reporters stick together, but he conceded, "Well, I wouldn't have run the story, but the editors of the *Press Democrat*, an excellent credible news source by the way, had a different view. Look, the *Press Democrat* said they checked out the source, and this person they consider to be impeccable."

The student shot back, "If there are no sources on the record, then the paper can make up anything."

"Yes, but their reputation could be damaged if people don't believe them. I will say the *Press Democrat*, according to a recent survey, is a highly respected news source. And for good reason, because they earned a great reputation in Northern Virginia for accurate, unbiased and fair coverage."

One student asked sarcastically, "Are you a reporter or commentator?"

"I have done both, but today I write news analysis pieces. That is, my interpretation of Virginia political news. Look, you and other Republicans can call me a partisan hack if you want, but I am not a liberal Democrat. I have spent my career playing it right down the middle."

Cohen quickly turned to a student with blue hair and a ring through her nose. He assumed she would have a friendly question. From his experience he found that students whose gender isn't immediately apparent to him are almost always progressives. The question was, "Mr. Cohen, who do you think released the Huggy Bear picture to the media?"

Cohen smiled and said, "I must admit I have given some thought to this question." The students laughed. "Well, I would guess about 24 people knew of Norton's alter ego Huggy Bear. They kept quiet during the election campaign and well into his term. I would assume most are Republicans, but out of loyalty to the fraternity, they didn't want to hurt Brother Norton, despite political differences. I would speculate that Parrish was so far to the right and out of the mainstream that some of the fraternity brothers may have sided with Norton. So any idea of helping her campaign was out of the question. Another reason, in my opinion, why Republicans should have nominated a more moderate candidate. So the question, why did it come out halfway through his term. I think once Democrats took full control of the legislature, it was clear that Norton was going to move in a more progressive direction; after all, now he had the votes. So in an effort to embarrass him, and possibly keep him from moving in a more progressive direction, a Republican out there somewhere took the picture to the media."

Just then someone in the class yelled, "You're a hack! You guys held the story to help your fellow Democrat Norton win."

Cohen shook his head, "You Republicans push this theory that we in the press sat on the story. What nonsense. No news organization would sit on this. It is like a news organization in the 1990's sitting on the Clinton-Lewinsky affair story. It's too big to sit on. I would point out that this story came from the *Falls Church News Leader*. The publisher of that paper, Bruce Dutton, can't stand Norton. Certainly he'd publish it the minute he got the picture."

Cohen took another question. The student turned out to be another College Republican. "Mr. Cohen, you continue to claim your paper has no bias. Can you explain what seems to be a contradiction to that claim? Reverend Brand said, from the pulpit of her church, quote 'It's not God bless the USA, it's God damn the USA.' I didn't read that quote in your paper, but I did see your paper had a front page story attacking Senator Parrish for saying that James Sayers should not have fled the scene. Why is Parrish's suggestion offensive, but 'God damn the USA' is not?"

Elections Have Consequences

He smirked, shook his head and cooly replied, "Reverend Brand's comment was made years ago, when she was not a public official, like Parrish is now. Reverend Brand apologized right after she said it. She explained that she spoke out of frustration over US foreign policy, which she believed was contributing to the misery of Muslims. Parrish, a sitting legislator, chirped that Sayers should have done such and such. This was viewed as incredibly insensitive, so soon after he died. And some, not necessarily me, were offended that a privileged white woman would tell a black person what they should do and feel when confronted by a police officer."

Cohen then added, "You conservatives like to go after Reverend Brand, and I admit she is a little out in left field on some things, but look, Governor Norton has also appointed some moderates to his cabinet. For example his Secretary of Commerce and Trade, Mike Garvey is actually quite conservative. So I think he has a fairly balanced cabinet, some progressives and some moderates."

He then, glancing at the clock said, "This will have to be the last question."

He called on a student who asked, "The Parrish-Norton race was closer than people thought it would be. Why do you think Norton won?"

Cohen seemed visibly relieved that he could end on a softball question. "The people of Virginia are tired of partisan bickering, and they elected Norton because they viewed him as more moderate than Parrish. They felt Norton could bring back bipartisanship, as we used to call it the Virginia Way, and also that he would do a better job uniting the state. Which is, I think at this time, the most important thing. I think Parrish hurt herself with outlandish claims, like schools are indoctrinating students. Look, if that were so all 133, basically all 133 school superintendents, would not have endorsed Norton. Surely school superintendents would not be involved in indoctrinating children. So her claim was so ridiculous that she had no support from teaching professionals, who know what is going on in the classroom."

He cut off the questioning and thanked the audience. Cohen had never faced tough student questions before, especially a College Republican ambush. However, Cohen's appearance did cause some controversy and the demand for an apology.

One of the snowflakes complained about Cohen's Miss Virginia joke. "You have to chirp out an apology Steve." So said Cohen's editor at the *Daily Dispatch*. In addition to the chirp, the paper also posted the apology.

"Recently I addressed students at Lord Fairfax Community College, and in an attempt to be funny I told a very inappropriate joke. In my heart and mind, I meant no harm, but sadly what I said was offensive and immature. The worst thing I can do as a human being is to be offensive. I have asked the students, and the trans community, for forgiveness, and I will try in the future to be more sensitive."

The *Daily Dispatch* did not print what he said; rather, just his apology, causing great confusion and speculation. Everyone involved in Virginia politics asked, "What did he say?" But the paper decided not to print the joke and risk re-offending people.

28) Off The Record

On the eve of the special session, Norton decided to give an off the record interview to Maddy Clack, Steve Cohen and Bhavna Agarwal. This is something Norton did from time to time to clear the air with a select group of reporters.

The conversation would not be reported, and in exchange Norton would be more candid. The reason for these off the record chats was the belief that Norton could help shape the narrative and win favor with leading reporters by confiding in them. Beaman would usually sit in on the meetings with a notepad.

They met at the Governor's Mansion for drinks and refreshments and afterwards they went up to the governor's second floor study to chat. The study was lined with books; it had been turned into a library by former Governor Tuck. Norton started off with a few thoughts on the upcoming special session, and he preemptively answered a question he was sure was coming:

"The common attack is that I am pushing the special session so I can get bills passed that couldn't get to my desk in a regular session. I believe the six bills could pass in a regular session, but I don't think we can wait. The people of Virginia demand action now. The public (more accurately his party) will demand more progressive action if we don't do something now. By agreeing to these fairly moderate reforms now, I can hold off the left wing of my party. It's like FDR making liberal reforms to save capitalism. I am making changes that balance reform with protecting law enforcement."

Bhavna Agarwal pressed Norton. "You think these reforms are moderate?"

Norton attempted to backtrack. "Moderate relative to what the left wing of my party wants. Some of them want to get rid of the police altogether, get rid of their legal protections and turn personal injury lawyers on them and sue them as a way of getting them out of the force. So I may give in a little here, but compared to what they want I am standing strong."

Agarwal asked, "So the argument that Republicans are making, that you can't stand up to your own party, in particular your left flank, is false?"

Norton snapped, "Yes...Yes, of course it is false."

Agarwal followed up. "The common argument Republicans make, and I'm sure you've heard it, is that a special session is designed for your party's political advantage. They say there is no time for law enforcement organizations to mobilize opposition, and that the bill to get rid of bail could never pass in a regular session with the opposition mobilized. They say, `Why can't we wait a few months for the regular session when the bills can get a full hearing?"

Norton shook his head. "No, I am confident I could get these measures passed during a regular session."

Steve Cohen asked, "Governor, Virginia has traditionally been a strong law and order state. These proposals are very progressive; can't they hurt you and your party?"

"It seems to me that at this point Virginians are more interested in social justice and criminal justice reform than law and order. You look at all these major cities around the country that are cutting their police budgets. It's clear crime is going up, yet people in the cities are accepting of the budget cuts to police departments. I heard the other day that Portland, Oregon's murder rate is up over 500 percent, and I'm sure rapes. robbery, burglary, auto theft probably have risen about as much. Will the people demand change? Will they remember when they vote? Probably not.

"Now, Virginia is not Portland or New York, but I think for good or ill Virginians also are willing to accept more crime, that is, they have a higher tolerance of higher crime in exchange for more social justice. Now whether these measures get you closer to social justice we don't know yet.

Norton went on, "Like inflation, people will put up with a little bit of it, if they feel it helps the economy grow. Well, if police must let lower level crimes go unpunished in order to spare a wayward kid getting caught up in a justice system that many Virginians feel is racist and unjust, that's fine. I'll give you an example. I signed legislation establishing a threshold for prosecution of shoplifting cases at $500. Now, since then sure, shoplifting cases are up a bit, I admit, but I think most Virginians (although probably not shop owners) are willing to accept that."

Agarwal cut in, "Well, will that increase require a change in the law?"

Norton responded, "I don't think it will be necessary. The experts say the spike in shoplifting is simply a temporary blip. I say temporary, because within communities when word spreads that people are taking advantage of the law, there will be a corrective backlash. Through peer pressure from parents, siblings, relatives, neighbors and friends, people who engage in such behavior will be chastised and if they don't stop they will be shunned. They don't want this, so they will conform, and the shoplifting spike will dissipate."

Agarwal asked, "But isn't there a chance that it won't and Democrats will pay a price at the polls?"

Norton explained why he thought the state was shedding its pro-law enforcement reputation. "When I first started in politics the endorsement of police organizations was a must. For example, in the first campaign I worked on, Wilder vs. Coleman, my candidate Doug Wilder didn't get the endorsement of the Fraternal Order of Police, but he negotiated to get a nice letter from the board saying that despite not getting their endorsement, he was still not soft on crime. The FOP's endorsement was the gold standard for all candidates. Today is a new day. Many, if not most, Virginians don't like the police. Getting their endorsement doesn't seem to help, especially in my party. In fact, I doubt most candidates from my party would even meet with police groups."

Maddy Clack asked, "Could you expand on what you just said, that at this point Virginians are more interested in social justice and criminal justice reform than law and order. Don't you think it could hurt your party to get the image as soft a crime? A position that hurt Democrats in the past?"

"As I said, the crime issue doesn't resonate like it once did. And I suspect many, if not most Virginians are willing to err on the side of more liberal criminal penalties and fewer police officers. Now if crime goes up just a little, it won't be a political issue, but if crime spikes, well then Republicans might be able to make some hay. So when I say it could pass in a regular session, I'm saying that even if police groups and Republicans had more time to mobilize opposition to the bills, I think they would still pass. Take Officer Driscoll. Twenty years on the force, a clean record, yet all the media wants to talk about is the tragic altercation on Broad Street, and how the police are racists, or at the very least indifferent to the suffering of black people. Now, I think James Sayers should have cooperated with the officers that day on Broad Street. And it was best not to run and go for the officer's gun, if that part happened. However, at this point I can't say that publicly. Maybe when tensions die down."

Maddy Clack asked, "At some point do you think the pendulum will swing back to law and order, and perhaps the endorsement of law enforcement will be coveted again by candidates?"

"Two ways that could happen: if crime spikes, which I doubt, and another way which I doubt as well, if police officers vote like a minority group. For example, gays make up just a few percent of the population, yet for decades they have had a disproportionate amount of political power for their numbers. Why? Well, because they voted in a block, but just as importantly many of their friends, family, co-workers, and others voted with them. Like, a sister may have a gay brother so she votes for candidates that will help gay people. Imagine if police officers had similar backup from their friends, neighbors and relatives. They'd have real political clout."

Maddy Clack asked, "Governor, the 800 pound gorilla in the room, the Huggy Bear scandal. The charge that if it had not been for an old picture of you in blackface dressed as Huggy Bear, you would not have drifted to the left; rather, you would be the moderate Democrat that you ran against Parrish as. What do you say to that?"

Elections Have Consequences

"Well, bigger than the Huggy Bear revelations was the fact that before that, Democrats took over both houses of the General Assembly. And I would point out that a couple of socialist got elected. So my party's caucus is even further to the left. I have stood up to my party's left flank. I have said no to defunding the police, and I have stood firm in favor of keeping limited immunity for our police officers. Heck, some in my party wanted to stop the police from pulling anyone over for anything. I think they would have banned police officers from pulling a driver over for not having working headlights." Everyone laughed. Norton repeated, "I have stood up to my left flank. When I was inaugurated, the committee wanted to play the black national anthem. I said no. It disappointed many progressives, but I held my ground because it was not appropriate."

Stephen Cohen asked, "Governor, do you remember who the guy was pictured with you in the Nazi outfit?"

Norton turned his head toward the window, paused for a second, and then brushed off the question. Gazing out the window he said, "Well, some questions I may leave for my memoirs, or for the grave."

Cohen then asked, "This political turmoil must be tough for Dr. Norton. How has she been holding up? And what advice did she give you when the Huggy Bear scandal broke out?"

Norton smiled and said she had been very supportive. Norton loved his wife, and knew how lucky he was to have such a great partner. That is what she was, a political partner. Norton replied, "She just said to tell the truth and trust in the understanding of the people of Virginia."

Paula Norton really wasn't a doctor. She obtained a PhD from Baylor University in multicultural education, so the patronizing media made a point of referring to her as "Dr. Paula Norton," because she had a doctorate degree.

Norton went on to relate details of the day the story broke. "Paula was shocked, concerned about the political ramifications, however still level headed. She helped me draft my statement."

Agarwal asked, "Do you have any idea of who released the fraternity picture to the media? And why?"

"I would be lying if I said I hadn't given it some thought. The picture didn't come out before the election, because the Republicans never had it. Certainly, that is a logical conclusion. Otherwise, they would have used it then. Why now? Well, my party took over the House of Delegates at the beginning of the year, and months later this came out. I think that whomever released this knew that I would be pushing a social justice agenda, especially with my party in charge of the General Assembly. So, by releasing the Huggy Bear picture, there was hope that it would deter me from advancing my fight for social justice. That is, to undermine my credibility as a progressive. They could say, 'He is not a progressive forward thinker, he is Huggy Bear.' Well, they failed. I stuck to my guns to fight for social justice."

Cohen, always interested in Virginia political history, then inquired, "When you first got elected to the House of Delegates, Hank Parrish was the speaker. What was your relationship with him like? What was your impression of him?"

"Well, I was a freshman Democrat when I first met him, so he didn't pay me much attention, but he was always kind to me. And if I remember correctly, he retired after my first term in the House, so I didn't serve with him long at all. Funny story though. Before I got elected to the House, I was on business in Richmond, and I was on Broad Street heading to the exit to get onto 95 to come back to Fairfax. Well, ahead of me was Hank Parrish. I could see his Speaker of the House of Delegates license plate and his Parrish bumper sticker. As we got on 95 he was zooming, doing at least 75 up the ramp. Well, I wanted to make good time to get home too, and I figured the State Police were not going to pull over Hank Parrish, so I thought that with him as a screen I could speed along with him, a few car lengths behind." Norton started laughing. "Well, I was making great time; I was in effect riding his coattails. How ironic, a Democrat riding Hank Parrish's coattails! It went great for awhile, but nearing one of the Fredericksburg exits, I saw Parrish's turn signal light up and he got off, so I slowed down, and went the rest of the way to Fairfax at a normal speed."

Cohen followed up, "Did you ever tell that story to Speaker Parrish?"

"No, but I did tell Angela that story when I served with her in the State Senate. And that's a funny story as well. I told her, thinking she would laugh, perhaps even say yes that was just like my father, but no. She looked at me earnestly and declared, 'My father did not speed.'"

Everyone laughed. Norton added, "This is her main weakness as a candidate. She has no sense of humor. A sense of humor is necessary to be successful in politics. Her father had a great sense of humor, always laughing, but God, he could tell the dirtiest jokes."

Bhavna Agarwal brought the conversation back to present issues. "Governor, are you worried that as public schools adopt more social justice teachings, or as Angela Parrish would say indoctrination, such as mandating Critical Race Theory being taught in high schools, the censoring of jokes, and all Virginia colleges required to conduct a workshop on 'white privilege' and the 'the roots of America's racisms,' more parents will decide to send their kids to private schools or homeschool them?"

"No, I don't think Virginians will abandon our public schools. Some can afford private schools, but for most that's not an option, so we must do the best we can to improve the public schools. I say, let's fight to make our schools good. Sure, we may not all agree with the curriculum, but most will get used to it. It's like generations ago when schools started teaching the theory of evolution. Parents didn't like it, but they accepted it. Now, our schools teach that America may be a racist country and was founded by racists. Kids can get the info and make decisions on their own, and in time some ideas won't be so controversial. When I was a kid, I learned in school that George Washington never told a lie. Then kids learned he told some lies; now they are told George Washington was a racist. So over time the conventional thinking changes; we learn more about people, or at least our thinking about them can change."

Bhavna Agarwal added, "So you don't see a mass exodus from public schools here in Virginia?"

"Now, I think some conservative parents will move their kids to private schools or homeschool, but most parents will continue to send their kids to public schools."

Agarwal asked, "Do you think the changes to the state's elite magnet schools, such as the Matthew Fontaine Maury School, discarding merit-based admissions in favor of a random lottery, will hurt the school's academic quality?"

Norton shrugged. "No. Because our changes will make the student body more diverse, which is good and fair, and I think the schools will for the most part maintain high, or relatively high, academic standards."

Maddy Clack was next. "Do you regret not trying to defend the Confederate statues? Angela Parrish said if she were elected governor she would have."

Norton laughed. "No, and the reality is there was no way to protect them. The public didn't want them. The Yankees that move into the state don't care, the folks from foreign countries don't care. Anyway, how would Angela have saved them?" Norton asked sarcastically, "By standing in front of one with her shotgun?"

In conclusion, Bhavna Agarwal asked, "Governor, what do you want your legacy to be? Governor Baliles was known as the education governor; what do you want to be known for?"

Norton pretended to think for a minute and responded, "I think I want to be thought of as the governor who started the process of racial healing, and bringing our great Commonwealth together."

Cohen noticed the time, and speaking for the reporters said, "Well, thank you, Governor, for your time."

"You're welcome," and added with a degree of sincerity, "I think I will miss these get-togethers once my term is up."

***

A few blocks away from the Governor's Mansion is the section known as Shockoe Slip. In one of the tall buildings, on the top floor is an exclusive club known as the Old Dominion Club. The club formed in the early 1900's. Originally it met in a mansion downtown, but in the 1980's it moved to its current location on the top floor of one of Richmond's tallest skyscrapers. Cohen used to point out, "From the steps of the Capitol you used to be able to see the James River, but in the 1980's they built this building and blocked the view."

Becoming a member of the Old Dominion Club was very difficult. The only one guaranteed membership is a governor or former governor. Everyone else had to be nominated by a member and approved by the board in a unanimous vote. Both Cohen and Professor Lawrence Seavers were members.

Cohen had a lunch meeting at the club with his long time friend Seavers. As he walked to the club from the Governor's mansion he thought, *How long have I known Lawrence? It's been so long since I met him, so long since we became friends, that I can't remember the beginning of the friendship.* By the time he reached the club he concluded that it was in 1989 that they first met.

The lunch crowd had left; the clock said 3:30. They had the whole restaurant to themselves. The waitress seated them at a table by the window; the restaurant had big windows, almost floor to ceiling. They had a perfect view of Capitol Square.

The two met for lunch for no particular reason; they were old friends who tried to meet for lunch every few months.

Seavers genuinely cared for Cohen, loved him like a brother, and his interest in talking with Cohen had more to do with genuine friendship than their shared interest in Virginia politics.

Seavers started talking politics, but it soon became clear he was driving at a secret, a dark secret which was hurting his friend Cohen.

"Steve, one thing I still can't totally understand, and that is how a moderate like Norton won the nomination of a party which is pretty darn woke."

Cohen resisted the line of questioning, "This again, Lar? It's simple. The progressives had three candidates, well, originally

Elections Have Consequences

four until Sally Hutchison dropped out. Norton slipped through with a plurality. It's really not hard to believe."

Norton won the primary, and as luck would have it, didn't have to face a runoff. Democrats didn't like the idea of a runoff election, which would require the top two vote getters to run again, because in the party's view runoffs were used to help block minority candidates from winning the nomination. Their belief was that the concept of runoff elections, like the filibuster, was a "relic of Jim Crow."

Seavers pressed, "But the three stayed in, guaranteeing Norton won. Was that just a coincidence? A lucky break for Norton?"

Cohen continued to push back, "Well, Norton had the support of Reverend Brand; she is very influential with progressives. Her endorsement of Norton put him over the top."

Seavers seemed unimpressed. "But if Kevin Mack had withdrawn, Norton would have had a tough time, Brand's endorsement notwithstanding, getting the nomination, correct?"

Cohen knew what Seavers was driving at. He believed his friend knew the secret that he had been carrying around with him for several years now, a secret that made him question his worth as a reporter, a secret that kept him up many nights.

Seavers had no desire to expose or embarrass Cohen; rather, he wanted him to be able to confess, to get the secret off his chest, a secret which had seemed to age him. He didn't want his friend to have to live with a burden of guilt. Seavers' caring face said as much to his friend; it reminded him that confession is good for the soul.

Cohen gazed out the window, and said in a voice which implored understanding, "You understand I couldn't say anything...Because of my relationship with Kevin."

It seems Cohen and Delegate Mack had become lovers during the campaign. Cohen violated a basic rule of journalism: he became romantically involved with a person he was covering.

Cohen again implored, "You understand, these things can happen." He looked out the window, and collected his thoughts, "My marriage had ended, and Kevin was there for me. He understood me. He made me feel happy again. I know it sounds trite, but he made me feel young again. It just happened, one of those things." He looked back at Seavers, "You understand, don't you?"

Seavers simply nodded.

Cohen then added vehemently, "But look, I didn't know anything about a quid pro quo." Shortly after Norton took office he appointed Kevin Mack to the state Supreme Court.

Seavers simply let Cohen speak, to confess. Seavers' compassionate face said, confess my friend, get it off your chest.

"Kevin told me Norton didn't offer him anything to stay in the race. And I believed him."

Seavers asked, "Why did Mack stay in the race?"

Reflecting, Cohen said, "I don't know, really. He told me he was going to drop out and hold back any immediate endorsement. Well, Brand got wind of it, and she was constantly calling him. She even drove to Roanoke to talk to him."

Cohen confessed he had a near scare of getting caught, "I was with Kevin at his house in Roanoke, and we heard a knock on the door. It was Brand. I went into another room and stayed until she left. I don't think she knew I was there. At least I hope not."

Cohen reiterated, "All Kevin told me is that Brand believed Norton would be sufficiently progressive and that he could win.

Elections Have Consequences

Brand kept insisting that Parrish would beat either Baker or Salazar. She said Mack needed to stay in to get Norton nominated. Otherwise Governor Parrish would be on his conscience. Brand told him, `Kevin, you have a bright future, but this year we must back Norton.' Brand told Kevin that Norton could be surrounded by progressives and kept on a progressive path. She told Kevin, `We can control Norton.'"

Cohen paused and then again insisted, "I had no idea that he had been offered a judgeship to stay in. You have to believe me."

Seavers then asked the big question, a question that was designed to help Cohen restore his soul and his pride as a reporter, a question that would give him absolution. "If you had known there was a quid pro quo offered to Mack to stay in the race, would you have reported that?"

Cohen thought, and replied, "Yes, I would have."

Seavers completed the absolution by telling him, "We will speak no more of this."

29) Special Session

The Democrat leadership in the House and Senate chose a total of seven legislators to write the bills. Four Delegates, including Julius Jones, and three state Senators were tapped. The Speaker of the House, the Majority Leader, and Reverend Brand picked the team. There were some staffers, including Jack Carter, who were also included to help write the bills.

Senator Steve Siebers became the leader of the group. Other Delegate members were Lynchburg Delegate "Aunt Sally" Jenkins, Fairfax Delegate Dan Daniels, and Roanoke Delegate Kevin Dabney. Daniels and Dabney were lawyers and both had spent time as defense attorneys. In the Senate, in addition to Siebers, was Virginia Beach Senator Mike Lanning, a personal injury attorney by profession, and Arlington Senator Sandoval. She really had no input on the bills, but since she was the designated sponsor, they thought it best that she be there for the writing of the bills.

The only two non-lawyers were Sandoval and Sally Richards. There were political reasons for adding those two, Sandoval because of her star power with the college aged and young 20-somethings and Richards because of her association as a moderate Democrat.

The team met at the Best Western in Thornburg. Many of the Virginia press set up shop there covering the historic meetings. Steve Cohen compared the secrecy to the Constitutional Convention in 1787 in Philadelphia. Cohen said he got goosebumps thinking of the historic significance that might come out of the meetings.

Elections Have Consequences

On the first day of the conference Siebers, over breakfast, told reporters he'd had a dream. In the dream, when it was all over, he walked out into the Best Western parking lot, and with the noise of 95 in the background a reporter asked him, 'What did you create, Senator?,' and Siebers replied. 'A more just Virginia, I hope.'"

The only stipulation Norton made was his promise to veto any bill that stripped police officers of criminal and civil immunity. That is, they would retain their immunity from most prosecution. The trial lawyers wanted to be able to sue them and the left wanted to drive the police out of the profession, so for many of the social justice warriors this was a great disappointment. However, hope did exist for some smaller, yet still fairly radical, measures.

The legislators came up with six bills. The first bill, known as the "James Sayers Law," basically banned hot pursuit of a suspect. Unless the suspect has an arrest warrant or is an imminent threat to the community, if he or she runs from the police the police have to let them go. It was designed to make it tougher to arrest anyone without a warrant. Another example: if someone were pulled over for drunk driving or impaired driving, they would have the right to call for an Uber ride or cab. They would still get a ticket, but they could leave.

The second bill was a cap of 10 years on all criminal counts. All prior convictions were grandfathered in. The legislators belief was that 10 years was sufficient per count; any more was overkill. With time off for good behavior and time served before and during trial, a murder convict would likely serve no more than six and half years.

The third bill was a ban on the bail requirement. For most charges, once a suspect was processed they would be free to leave. Rape and murder were exceptions; for those charges a defendant could be held until trial.

The fourth bill banned the use of tear gas for crowd control. This was in response to what happened in Portsmouth during a riot. The bill was titled "Ban on the Use of Poisonous Gas Against Virginians Act."

The fifth bill reduced the charge of attacking a police officer from a felony to a misdemeanor. Siebers, a defense attorney, had been pushing this proposal for years; now he felt it was the time to get it through. Siebers felt that the felony charge was held over the head of people of color, who were in many cases simply protecting themselves against a racist police officer.

The sixth bill dealt with the issue of defunding the police. No local entity or county was going to do such a thing as defund their police force, and Brand knew that, but she still wanted some sort of victory on funding. So they came up with a plan tying state support for local law enforcement to certain measures. The bill demanded that for a jurisdiction to get state money for their police force, all new hires must be reflective of the county. In effect, it was a quota system for police officers. Norton won a couple of concessions. The current employees would be grandfathered in, and gender was not a factor; that is, the police force didn't have to be 51 percent female. But going forward the police force would have to be racially and ethnically diverse. This was one bill that many constitutional scholars thought would be struck down as unconstitutional.

In addition they threw one other bill in. Lee Jackson Day had been retired by the legislature, but many on the left wanted to

Elections Have Consequences

come up with a new holiday. So the legislature came up with Democracy Day. It would be a day to reflect on American democracy, how it had failed in the past and how it can be improved. It would provide a paid day off for all state employees. The sponsors envisioned that at least it would be a day where voter registration drives would take place all over the Commonwealth.

It took a week of work, but Siebers went to the cameras in the ballroom of the Best Western on a Friday just after midnight to say, "We did it. We have a set of bills that will make all Virginians proud." The crowd of reporters started clapping and whistling.

Siebers looked exhausted but happy. He had the look of a new father in the hospital waiting room telling family members that the newborn baby was a girl, and that mother and daughter were resting well. The tieless, unshaven Siebers outlined the proposals in the ballroom. Virginia and some national press were there.

As soon as he was done, reporters scrambled to file their stories.

30) Arm Twisting

Norton agreed to sign all bills if passed, and even to put in some effort to get them passed. However, he did want something in return. He and the Democrat majority agreed that next year the legislature would pick up on transportation-related bills and funding.

Norton and the legislative caucus were in agreement for the most part, except on the main thing he wanted–his prized item, something he always sponsored in the State Senate. He wanted to expand the Silver Line of the Metro, to add one more Metro stop in Tysons. The board that ran Metro said they would agree but Virginia would need to fork over $115 million. The proposed stop would be the Dogwood Grove Metro stop.

No Republican would vote for such a waste of money and even downstate Democrats were skeptical of the idea. The Metro had a long history of poor management, waste, inefficiency, a poor safety record, poor service, and declining ridership.

However, the saving grace for many Democrats was the fact that the Metro paid the prevailing, or union, wage to their employees. So downstate Democrats were willing to give in and spend the money. Brand described it as "a small price to pay for a criminal justice reform bill." One progressive Democrat said, "It's a great deal. We get rid of bail, and Norton gets another Metro stop."

Once Siebers announced the bills, Beaman and Norton gathered with aides to start counting votes. In the Senate, a tie would fail because Republican Lt. Governor Morrison would cast the tie breaking vote. So they needed 21 votes, and in the House they would need 51. The Democrat majority named the criminal justice package the "For the People Act." Republicans referred to it as the "For the Criminal Act." Angela Parrish described the bills as "the greatest transfer of power from law-abiding citizens to criminals that has ever taken place in human history."

Once the bills had gone to the governor's desk, Norton would have to decide if he'd sign all or any of them. He had reservations about both the capping of sentences at 10 years and the reduction of the charge of assaulting a police officer from a felony to a misdemeanor. However, on balance he didn't want to deny his political base a win, and more importantly he wanted to build a legacy for himself as the criminal justice reform governor. This historic package would guarantee he would be considered a transformational governor.

A veto of one or two of the bills would be viewed as a letdown to his party, no doubt, and signing all six would be seen, as Beaman said, as a "grand slam." On three of the bills they would have no problem getting the votes. The two bills that could prove to be the heaviest lift were downgrading assaulting police to misdemeanor, and capping all criminal sentences at 10 years.

The debates in the legislature were aired on local media. Parrish led the opposition. On the bill to reduce the charge of assaulting a police officer, Parrish pointed out that Siebers had a bill last session that increased the penalty for animal abuse from a misdemeanor to a felony. She asked rhetorically, "Don't our police officers deserve the same protection as our furry four-legged friends?"

Parrish also attacked Sandoval's bill, the "Ban the Use of Poisonous Gas on Virginians Act." Specifically, she attacked Sandoval's statement that "the Nazis used the same type of tear gas on inmates in concentration camps in order to stop uprisings." Parrish called it an "invidious and outrageous comparison."

Sandoval responded, "It is not invidious. I have documented proof; it's made from the same compound."

Parrish snapped, "You moron, do you even understand what I just said?"

Lt. Governor, Jim Morrison, presiding over the session, slammed the gavel, "The gentle lady from Prince William County will suspend. It is not okay to insult a member of this body. That violates Rule 57, a member is not to attack or demean another member."

Parrish asked, "But it's okay for her to insult the police? To compare them to Nazis?"

Parrish also attacked the bill requiring diversity in the police departments. She called it a "racial quota bill, pure and simple." She mocked the Democrats, saying "Why stop with the police departments? What about hospitals? If you don't trust a white police officer with your life and safety, why would you trust a white doctor?"

The debate raged for another couple of days. Beaman and Norton were nervous; they were still short on the two most controversial bills. They could afford to lose no more than three in the House and two in the State Senate. It went down to the wire. Finally, a break: they got Delegate "Aunt Sally" Jenkins to agree to vote yes on all six and that put them over the top in the House. However, they were still down four in the Senate.

In announcing her support, Jenkins issued a press release. "I have always been a strong supporter of law enforcement, and as a legislator I have always been tough on crime. I believe this criminal justice reform does both. It keeps Virginia a tough law and order state, and advances social justice. As one of law enforcement's strongest supporters in the General Assembly, I can vote for this package of laws."

Two bills, downgrading an assault on a police officer to a misdemeanor instead of a felony (which some called stripping police of protection), and capping criminal sentences at 10 years, were in trouble in the Senate. Norton thought of asking the Senate Majority Leader to pull the bills; actually that was quickly turning into what he wanted.

However, Brand implored him to keep fighting. "Our base wants this, our state needs it, and your legacy as a leader in the fight for criminal justice will be indelibly etched in history."

Norton felt he needed to go to the mat. And if he lost the base couldn't be too mad at him, he reasoned. *I could tell them I did my best.*

They were having problems with McLean State Senator Charlie McCade. As a former prosecutor, he knew such legislation would increase crime and make Virginia's streets more dangerous. Norton and Beaman had an idea on how to get the final votes on these bills.

Beaman briefed Norton several weeks before on some helpful intel. McCade's wife, Linda Page McCade, had been appointed by Norton to the George Mason University Board of Governors. This was done to get McCade's vote on a bill Norton wanted a couple of years earlier. His sources said that she had now expressed an interest in becoming president of the university.

Elections Have Consequences

"Didn't I just appoint her to the board?"

"Well, two years ago, and she is doing a super job. She may deserve a promotion."

"Hmm...I do know Brand thinks the world of her." Of course Brand did, for one reason in particular. Linda Page McCade had publicly stated that she favored renaming George Mason University in Fairfax to Ruth Bader Ginsburg University.

Norton paused and thought for a moment. "Okay. I am willing to appoint her President of GMU, if McCade votes for all the bills. Do you think he'll agree?"

"I'll find out."

***

After a late afternoon meeting Beaman stopped by the governor's office and said, "We need to talk."

Norton nodded and said, "Yes, indeed." Beaman indicated that he had some important developments to report on.

Norton left the Governor's Mansion around 12:40 a.m. Paula was asleep; the two usually watched *Late Night with Lawrence O'Connell,* with Paula usually falling asleep after the opening monologue. Norton wore jeans, a sweatshirt, and a New York Yankees baseball cap.

Beaman got to the 7th Street parking garage first. No one was around. As he waited by the 7th column, he could hear the traffic off Broad Street and in the distance he could hear the faint sound of some protesters. Then he could see the headlights of Norton's car coming into the lot. As usual, Jasper pulled in and dropped him off. He would wait by the entrance and Norton would walk the 30 yards or so to Beaman. The secret was so tightly held that even after a few of these rendezvous Jasper still had no idea who Norton was meeting.

Elections Have Consequences

Norton walked over to Beaman and smiled, but before he could say anything, Beaman said, "You know, Ronnie"—he had never once called Norton Ronnie since Inauguration Day—"I am going to miss these midnight meetings after you are out of office."

Norton, not really in a joking mood, responded somewhat sarcastically, "Well, maybe for old times' sake we can keep them going, but once I'm out of office, I'll have nothing to hide. Look, the session is almost done. We only have a few days left and we're still three votes short in the Senate."

A smiling Beaman said, "The Senate shouldn't be a problem. McCade is fine with the deal. He will vote with us on all six bills, and in exchange, his wife becomes president of GMU at the first of the year."

"Okay, and you don't think the press will find out about this?"

A confident Beaman replied, "No way. By the time of her appointment, they will have forgotten all about this vote. Steve Cohen and the rest of the media will praise Lisa McCade as an excellent choice. They will say it is about time GMU gets a woman President."

Norton replied, "You are probably right, well, by my count we still need two votes in the Senate."

"Steve, do you have any more ideas you have that can only be discussed here?"

Beaman replied, "Yes, Senator Hamilton's wife wants a judgeship. If you appoint her, he will come over to our side on the two bills."

This was, of course, illegal but Norton responded by asking, "How can I do that? It will be transparently obvious even to hacks like Maddy Clack and Steve Cohen, who can then rightfully claim it was a payoff for voting for these bills."

"Again, all we have to do is wait six months. Everyone will forget about it, and if not we'll deal with it then. Heck, you could say you're choosing her only on her merits; her husband's vote had nothing to do with it."

Norton was relieved. "Okay. done. One more."

Beaman smiled and said cryptically, "Don't worry, I'm pretty sure I've got you one more."

Beaman's legislator surveillance operation had some potential dirt on Senator Kirk Rothrock of Petersburg. Rothrock, a married man, was spending a lot of time at a house owned by a single, attractive young woman.

After months of following him, they discovered his pattern. Rothrock and the woman rarely left the house. Beaman's staff referred to them as "the lovers." They ordered in and ate, and spent several hours together a few nights a week. To keep their affair a secret, the two lovers never left the house together.

Beaman's goons finally got a few compromising pictures of the two of them. It was not easy though; the curtains were usually closed so even from the bushes it was impossible to get a good picture. However, one night the lights were still on and the curtains were slightly open, so the goon—probably a VCC student volunteer—was able to see the Senator and the woman in an embrace.

As luck would have it, the woman was topless. She walked Rothrock to the door and it opened just enough from the operative to snap a couple of photos.

Beaman said to Norton, "It's kind of hard to explain how you are in a picture with a topless woman who is not your wife." Beaman was ebullient; his voice was loud enough to generate an echo in the empty garage. "I mean what the hell is he going to say? 'Gee, honey, it was perfectly innocent! This woman just needed help getting her bra off." Beaman broke into his sophomoric laugh and concluded, "So I think he votes our way."

Norton smiled and said, "Excellent, then we've got it." He gave the okay, so Beaman would go forward with their plans to get those votes.

Beaman had the envelope with the pictures in them. He said, "Would you like to see the pictures? Take a look, I'm sure you'll agree with me that her tits are perfect."

Norton demurred. "No, Steve, I don't need to see the pictures. I'll take your word for it."

Beaman then became emotional and opined, "With this criminal justice reform, you'll go down in history as one of our greatest governors." Norton started to speak, but Beaman interrupted, his voice rising. "No, I mean it, man, one of the greatest governors in Virginia history. I mean like Jerry Lee Baliles-level great."

Beaman said earnestly, "Governor, it has been such a pleasure and the greatest honor of my life to get to work for you," and choked up with emotion.

Norton responded in kind. "Steve, I have always valued your friendship. I could never have accomplished this, or heck, even been elected governor without you." Norton placed his hands on Beaman's shoulders. "You were with me from the beginning, all the way back to my first campaign for the Fairfax County Board of Supervisors. In fact, when I decided to run, you introduced me to Mrs. Roper and helped me put together a campaign team. I will never forget your help."

Audrey Meadows was a long-time Democrat and Chairman of the Fairfax County Board of Supervisors. As such she was a major power broker in the Fairfax Democrat Party for a period of time. Beaman and Norton thought she was a nice, competent person, and jokingly nicknamed her "Mrs. Roper" because of her resemblance to Helen Roper from the sitcom *Three's Company*.

Beaman continued the trip down memory lane. "Do you remember that constituent, when you were on the County Board of Supervisors, that guy who complained that his neighbor's dog kept crapping on his lawn?"

Norton seemed to remember. Beaman added, "He expected you to come over and clean it up." Beaman laughed, "As if you, the Providence County Supervisor, had a pooper scooper in your office for such incidents. Like it was a supervisor's job." Beaman marveled, "Now you are a successful governor."

Norton smiled and said matter of factly, "Well, even as governor that guy would probably still expect me to come over to clean up the poop."

"Forget that guy. I'm just saying look how far you've come. The anchors on MNN are now calling you 'America's Governor' in anticipation of the reform package passing, and the *Press Democrat* and *Daily Dispatch* are saying the same thing."

"Well, that's nice, but don't know about that."

Beaman interrupted, "Well I do, and I guarantee you Cohen will have to acknowledge the historical significance of this reform package and will be writing 'Norton is the greatest governor since Jerry Lee Baliles.'"

Beaman started to tear up as they had a quick final embrace. Norton turned to head back to his limo. Beaman just stood there frozen; he watched Norton walk down to his limo, get in, and close the door. An echo reverberated in the empty garage. Jasper turned on the car; the engine noise filled Beaman's ears and then the headlights illuminated the garage. Jasper turned the car around to exit, and a beam of light washed over Beaman. The car then drove away and silence and darkness returned to the garage. Beaman stood there in the dark for a minute. He thought, with tears running down his cheeks, *He is a great governor...He is my friend.* Then he sighed, pulled a handkerchief from his pocket, and wiped the tears from his eyes.

Working for Norton had been the greatest experience of his life. For the last several years Beaman had been on call for Norton 24 hours a day, 7 days a week. Beaman would remember these as his happiest days.

The next day, Beaman sent a copy of one of the pictures to Senator Rothrock with a note that said. "Voting for all six criminal reform bills stops rioting and it also stops affairs from being exposed. Do the right thing. Signed, a friend."

Later that day Rothrock announced publicly that he would vote for all six bills. In the governor's office there were cheers and high fives. It seemed that the entire staff was there. Champagne was served; Reverend Brand also had a glass. She quipped, "Even Jesus drank wine."

31) Legacy to be Proud Of

Because of the great demand by both the media and public to witness the historic event, the signing ceremony took place in the rotunda of the Capitol. The national cable networks aired the signing and then Norton's brief remarks.

Norton used several different pens, and once he was done he handed them out to the legislators standing behind him. There was sustained applause. He stood for several seconds as the applause grew louder. He then turned to Senator Sandoval and hugged her; the Capitol erupted with applause. Even the staid media was overcome with emotion; many had tears in their eyes.

Norton made a few remarks. "This is not the end of the process of criminal justice reform; rather, it is the beginning of a process. Virginia won't achieve perfect justice by these bills, but I am confident that Virginia will become a more just place with the passage and implementation of these bills."

Norton went on to taunt his Republican opponents, all of whom voted against all six bills, with even a majority voting against the new state holiday making January 6th Democracy Day. "To the opponents of criminal justice reform, I say elections have consequences."

After the ceremony, Jack Carter went over to congratulate Sandoval. They hugged, both on the verge of shedding tears of joy. Jack said to Sandoval, "I am very proud of you. You have done so much in such a short period of time."

Sandoval thanked Jack and said, "I couldn't have done it without you."

Elections Have Consequences

No doubt about that. He recruited her to run for office, and now she was a star and a media darling. Steve Cohen commented on her success. "Not even J. Sergeant Reynolds accomplished as much in his first term in the State Senate."

With these bills Sandoval had to be considered an accomplished legislator. Most thought the young, inexperienced socialist would remain a backbencher, but in Ronnie Norton's Virginia a young socialist could sponsor bills that might be signed into law. No other governor in Virginia's history would have signed any of her bills.

She did, however, keep her part time job at Applebees for practical reasons: she could make a lot of money, because lobbyists could sit at her table, order a carafe of Sprite and some appetizers, tell her about their problems, and leave hundred dollar tips. They didn't report it, since it was not technically a gift or donation, and Sandoval wasn't required to list those who gave her tips at a restaurant, or even release her tax returns.

The Virginia media would continue to call Sandoval a working-class champion, because she worked in a restaurant. What they didn't know or report was that she was the only server in Virginia getting hundred dollar tips from lobbyists on orders of nachos and sodas. In just over a decade, she'd become a millionaire, all while being "the champion of the little guy."

More good news for Norton came later that afternoon. Once he signed the legislation, a member of the Norwegian parliament, Jens Goering, nominated Norton for a Nobel Peace Prize. In a statement Goering said, "By signing and doing the work to pass this historic criminal justice reform bill, Governor Norton has taken a giant step towards true social justice. This legislation can be a model for other states, indeed other countries, to follow. For such an achievement, Governor Norton should be recognized as a leader in the movement for justice and peace. Therefore, I nominate Virginia Governor Ronald Milsap Norton for a Nobel Peace Prize."

***

Norton went back to the mansion and watched the news with his family. The media coverage, of course, made Norton into a national hero, a champion for social justice. Pundits were calling him "America's Governor;" a Susan Constant University poll had him at a 57 percent approval rating.

Paula had a copy of Steve Cohen's column proclaiming that with this criminal justice reform legislation Norton would become the most consequential governor since Jerry Balilies. In addition, Cohen pointed out, "Through Norton's effort about 3,000 monuments in Virginia will be torn down. It took generations to put them up and in just under four years Norton will tear them all down. I don't think any governor, in any state, at any time in American history, can say that."

At that moment, Norton couldn't remember the last time he had seen his wife so happy. She hugged him and said, "Ronnie, I am so proud of you. You made your mark, the greatest Governor since Jerry Baliles."

There were just five days left in the session, and the Democrats had a surprise. Rather than take their historic victory and adjourn early, they decided to try to run up the score.

Anticipating that Angela Parrish would be the Republican gubernatorial nominee in two years, Senate Democrats decided to take a preemptive shot at her.

Elections Have Consequences

A few weeks earlier, Parrish said if Sandoval didn't like it "here she could always go back to where she came from." The media dropped the "she could always" and simply picked up with, "go back to where she came from."

The media had the video of what she said, but they never showed it. The reason was because they could not edit it; it was too quick, and any edit would be detected. So they simply repeated the last part of her statement, purposely taking it out of context.

And the media concluded the edited comment, telling someone to go back where they came from, was inherently racist. So Senate Democrats decided to pass a resolution censuring Parrish for "making a racist comment in the Capitol Building."

As Tucker Wilkins, a GOP activist said, "This is pure politics. They want to officially censure her, so they can always claim that the Virginia State Senate condemned her as a racist. Even though it was a purely party line vote. Democrats know she will run again; this censure is designed to sully her reputation."

This vote would only take place in the Senate. The House of Delegates had no power to censure a non-member, and Parrish was not a member of the House.

While the story of Parrish's comment had died down a few weeks earlier, the media brought it back specifically to meet the needs of Democrats. As soon as the "For the People Criminal Justice Reform" bills passed, Senate Democrats said that they planned to bring up the anti-Parrish resolution vote.

Republicans cried foul, saying her remark was so benign that most Virginians had forgotten all about it, but the next day the story of Parrish's remarks were back on the pages of the *Press Democrat* and *the Richmond Daily Dispatch*. MNN returned to the story, running panel discussions on the impact of "Parrish's racist remark." To remind their viewers, who of course didn't remember the incident, for much of the day the network ran with the crawl, "Virginia State Senator Tells Woman of Color to Go Back to Where She Came From."

Willow Bush asked a pundit, "Do you think that with this resolution censuring State Senator Parrish, that white politicians, and white people in general, will stop telling people of color to go back to where they come from, whenever they get uppity?"

The pundit responded in the affirmative, that this resolution "could help stop such hateful rhetoric in the future, and therefore it was necessary to pass it."

After a couple of days of debate and with only two days to go before the official end of the special session, the senate gathered for a vote. MNN took a live feed from the floor of the State Senate; Willow Bush teased it throughout the hour. "You are looking at a live shot from the floor of the Virginia State Senate in Richmond. We expect a vote soon on a resolution condemning State Senator Angela Parrish for making a racist remark."

On the show with her were Bob Sharp and Steve Cohen. As the dean of the Virginia press corps, it made some sense to have Cohen on as a guest. As far as Sharp, well, he claimed to be a former Republican from Virginia, and most importantly, he would give MNN's narrative.

But first, Willow Bush had some breaking news. "I want to start with some breaking news. A member of the Norwegian Parliament, Jens Goering has nominated Governor Ronnie Norton for a Nobel Peace Prize for getting this criminal justice reform package passed. Steve, your comments?"

Cohen, smiling, responded, "What a day for Governor Norton, and what a day for Virginia. I think this package of six bills is historic, and for Norton it guarantees that he will be judged by history as a transformational governor, no doubt. As far as a Nobel prize possibly goes, remember, right now it is just a nomination."

Willow chimed in, "Yes, true."

Cohen went on, "But clearly it will be deserved. And I thought of something. As you know, I am a huge Barack Obama fan, but he got a Nobel prize for nothing specific. Governor Norton has really accomplished something here. Understand, I love Obama, so no disrespect, but Norton truly has an accomplishment, something which promotes peace. Who can disagree, a fair criminal justice system promotes peace. As they say, know justice, know peace."

Willow Bush concurred, "And what a contrast to what is happening now in the Virginia State Senate chamber right now, where a member, Angela Parrish, is going to be censured for her racist remarks."

With the live shot from the floor of the State Senate in the corner of the screen, Willow went to Sharp. "Bob, as a now former Virginia Republican, but a person who spent years working for Republican candidates in the state, how does it make you feel, that the most prominent Republican in the state is about to be officially sanctioned for making racist comments?"

Sharp rambled, "Look, I am a Reagan conservative. Sadly, the Republican party left me, but as a Virginian I think it is sad that in this day and age we still have racist things being said by legislators, but as painful and embarrassing as it may be, Senate Democrats are right on this one. We can't allow political leaders

Elections Have Consequences

to say racist things and not hold them accountable. Parrish told a woman of color to leave the country. That is racist, and we must collectively condemn that. So, Parrish represents a departure from Ronald Reagan's positive, inclusive conservatism, for a dark exclusive anti-immigrant Republican party. So, I was happy when Parrish lost, but the Virginia GOP is still attached to her. It is still her party and I don't know when it will change."

Cohen then interjected, "Willow, can I say something here?"

"Yes, Steve, please do."

Cohen pointed out, "Parrish made her own bed, not just with that ugly comment, but also for the fact that she was given an opportunity to make a last minute apology on the Senate floor and refused. I have been told by a high level source that the Democrat Senate Majority leader offered Parrish floor time to speak, if she was willing to apologize. Parrish said she would take the time, but as far as offering an apology she replied to the Majority Leader by raising her hand and making a circle with her fingers" (Cohen demonstrated) "and said that there was zero chance she'd apologize."

Cohen in disbelief said, "If she had just issued a half-hearted, or even insincere apology, there would be no censure vote today, but she is so pig-headed and stubborn that she can't even do that."

Willow and Sharp nodded in agreement, but before she could go to Cohen, something unexpected happened.

On the live feed she could see that there appeared to be some commotion on the floor. Nearly half the senators got up off their chairs and started walking out. Willow didn't know what was going on; it took several seconds for a producer to tell her, through her ear piece, that Republican State Senators were walking out of the Chamber.

Elections Have Consequences

Cohen could see it on the monitor. He muttered, "Oh God!"

Willow cut off the vacuous Sharp and went to Cohen. In an excited voice, she asked, "Steve, what is going on?"

"Republicans are going to deny Democrats a quorum. With them walking out, Democrats can't call the vote."

Willow responded, "Wow, what an underhanded trick!"

Cohen, realizing that he was on MNN, went into the proper virtue signaling mode. "This is disgraceful, to realize you are going to lose, and rather than go down honorably, you walk away. I can't ever remember a minority in the state legislature, in any state, walking off the job because they didn't get their way. This is an embarrassment to our state."

Sharp delivered his final thought. "Ronald Reagan never would have approved of such a thing. Walking away because you are going to lose. Really immature."

Willow went back to Cohen. "Quickly, Steve, I only have about 10 seconds. Is the Virginia Republican Party now officially dead?"

"Yes, I think at least as far as the eye can see, but I do think Virginians want a two party state. Who knows what the other party will be." Cohen joked, "Maybe the Green Party will become the opposition."

***

Meanwhile, back at the governor's office a party was being held to officially celebrate the successful special session. But in between partying, Brand, Jackson, Beaman and the new Secretary of Public Safety, Patti Phillips, were watching the proceedings taking place in the State Senate

Mark Thompson had resigned due to differences he had with the governor regarding decisions made in dealing with the riots.

Elections Have Consequences

The media didn't spend too much time talking about those differences, and Norton appointed Patti Phillips, a former sheriff of Henrico County, to replace him.

"Well, it's obvious what they're doing; they're leaving to deny a quorum and block the vote. The session only lasts two more days so they'll try to run out the clock," Jackson said.

Norton asked, "Is there anything we can do?"

"Well, through Patti you can order the State Police to arrest them and bring them back to vote, otherwise the special session will expire."

Brand favored the idea of arresting them, but Norton said, "No, let them go. At least we can say we drove the Republicans out of Richmond."

They all laughed. Beaman added, "That will help with the base."

No doubt Norton was in a generous mood. He had a great legislative victory, a Nobel Prize nomination, and state Republicans were literally on the run.

This beautiful fall day would be the pinnacle of Ronnie Norton's career, but unbeknownst to him at the time something else happened that day, which he'd learn about later. It seems that a guy who joined Beaman's team of stalkers had developed pangs of regret. Brad Gray, who had followed Angela to the Manassas Battlefield and spied on her with binoculars, a man who knew all about Beaman's black ops funded in part with taxpayers' money, decided to tell Federal authorities all he knew.

Gray had a two and half hour conversation with some men with the FBI at the J.Edgar Hoover Building in downtown DC. The Bureau decided to open an investigation into Norton and his

Elections Have Consequences

relationship with Beaman, and they made the decision not to tip Norton off. But that was a scandal for another day. For now, the media had a new hero, a social justice warrior governor, and Norton had a new nickname. He was no longer "Huggy Bear," but now "America's Governor."

Norton went back to the party on the first floor of the Governor's Mansion, in the room where Stonewall Jackson's body lay in state after he was killed at Chancellorsville, and where Norton had held his bizarre press conference the day after the Huggy Bear scandal broke. As drinks were being served and celebratory hors d'oeuvres were being passed around, Norton became philosophical. "They say being governor can change a man. And I think it's true, so I will admit, my views have slightly altered since the day I was inaugurated governor." The crowd of about 20 staffers laughed. Many of those staffers had worked for him for years and remembered him as the moderate State Senator from Fairfax.

"Now, I may not be the most educated man, but I do read books." The crowd cheered. "Reverend Brand was nice enough to give me a reading list when I got elected, and in my free time I've been reading from the list. In fact, I keep a copy of it in my suit pocket. However, I fear I may not be reading as fast as Reverend Brand would like." Ann smiled and the crowd laughed.

"Last night I finished a book by Dr. Eleanor Hubbard on the transgender movement. I must say that she is one of the most brilliant writers and thinkers I have ever encountered. And I am totally convinced that gender fluidity is a fact; it is settled science." The crowd approvingly cheered.

"Believing that there are only two genders, and that they are permanent, can't be backed up by science. We all have a duty to abandon such old, unscientific nonsense. We must accept facts, the sooner the better. We must get rid of hateful campaigns like, "protect girls sports;" we can't be protected from reality, from progress, from the future." The crowd applauded.

He went on to make his point on embracing progress: "Earlier this year Lurleen Bennett became the first trans Miss Virginia. She will now be going on to Atlantic City to compete for the Miss America crown. And you know something? She will win. She has to win, because she represents the future and progress. The judges know they must embrace progress. Just like we all must embrace progress. Indeed, we all have a duty and a responsibility to accept social change, not resist it. We can't live in the past."

Norton was very prescient. Later that fall, in Atlantic City, Lurleen Bennett was the first transsexual to be crowned Miss America. Watched by an estimated 70 million people, Lurleen walked down the aisle. With the traditional bouquet of roses and wearing the Miss America sash, she waved to the crowd as a recording of Bert Parks singing "there she is, Miss America" played in the background.

"Under my administration, we paved the way to getting rid of 3,000 racist statues. One of the last statues will come down a week before my term ends." The crowd cheered. "Those monuments are more than just racist symbols; they are also symbols of an old, backward Virginia, a Virginia stuck in the past. While getting rid of them won't guarantee that we end racism and usher in a new era of tolerance, justice and inclusion, it is, however, a powerful first step. And in the words of that great Chinese proverb, even a journey of a thousand miles begins with a single step."

Elections Have Consequences

Norton concluded his talk. "On a personal level, I believe what really matters in life is that you treat others the way you'd like to be treated. That you do what is right, not just what is popular, that you have the courage of your convictions. I remember the words my mother taught me:

Dare to be a Daniel,
Dare to walk alone,
Dare to have a purpose firm,
Dare to make it known.

"As governor I have tried to leave our great Commonwealth better than it was when I took office, and I think I have achieved that."

His son Mark chimed in, "Dad, I think the people of Virginia truly deserve to have you as governor."

Norton took his son's remark as a compliment and responded, "Thanks, son, you may be right. As I've always said, elections have consequences."

# # #

About The Author

David Shephard is a native (and very proud) Virginian. Raised in Fairfax County, David graduated from George Mason University and majored in Government and Politics. He spent decades in politics, campaign consulting, raising money and lobbying. He is also a longtime conservative blogger writing for numerous blogs, including his own, "The Virginia Gentleman," blog.

David lives with his wife and two cats in Manassas.

Made in the USA
Middletown, DE
12 April 2023